MURDER

AT

WHALEHEAD

I want to see the sea roar on the eastern shore.

Joe C. Ellis

Corolla, NC

Joe C. Ellis

BOOKS

Upper Ohio Valley Boo[
71299 Skyview Drive
Martins Ferry, OH 439

D1024343

Upper Ohio Valley Books
Joe C. Ellis
71299 Skyview Drive
Martins Ferry, OH 43935
Phone: 1-740-633-0423
Email: joecellis@comcast.net
www.joecellis.com

ISBN : 978-0-9796655-0-9
Printed in the U.S.A.
First printing, May 2007

PUBLISHER'S NOTE

Although this novel, *Murder at Whalehead*, is set in an actual place, the resort village of Corolla, NC, on the Outer Banks, it is a work of fiction. The characters, names, and plot are the products of the author's imagination. Any resemblance of these characters to real people is entirely coincidental. Many of the places mentioned in the novel—the Whalehead Club, the Currituck Lighthouse, the Black Pelican restaurant, etc. are wonderful places to visit on the Outer Banks. However their involvement in the plot of the story is purely fictional. It is the author's hope that this novel generates great interest in this wonderful region of the U.S.A., and as a result many people will plan a vacation here and experience the beauty of this setting firsthand.

CATALOGING INFORMATION
Ellis, Joe C., 1956-
Murder at Whalehead by Joe C. Ellis
ISBN 978-0-9796655-0-9
1.   Outer Banks—Fiction. 2. Corolla, NC—Fiction
3.Mystery—Fiction 4. Suspense—Fiction 5. Inspirational—Fiction.
6. Martins Ferry, OH--Fiction

Attention Filmmakers, Editors, and Publishers:
If you are interested in Film/Television Rights, Foreign Rights, or American Publishing Rights to *Murder at Whalehead*, please contact:

Michele Rubin
Writers House
21 West 26th St.
New York, NY 10010

Acknowledgments

The author would like to thank the following people for their help.

Donna Swanson and Denise Nash for their great critiques of the entire novel. Gretchen Snodgrass for her excellent line edit of the manuscript. Terry, Tony, Karla, and Steve at Novel Alchemy for their comments and catches of the first few chapters of the rewrite. Michele Rubin of Writers House for her hard work and great quote. Nancy Haddock, an upcoming author at Berkley Books, for her encouragement and another great quote.

My family: Judy, my wife, who rarely complains about my endless hours in front of a computer screen. My kids, Rebekah, Sarah, and Joseph, with whom we have shared many vacations on the Outer Banks and hope to share many more. Double thanks to Rebekah for doing a final read-through and making several catches everyone else missed. Finally, to all those readers who read my first novel, *The Healing Place*, and kept insisting that I write another one.

A Note to Readers

If you enjoy *Murder at Whalehead*, please email all of your friends and tell them about it. Also, I would like to hear from you. Email me with any comments or questions at joecellis@comcast.net and visit my website at www.joecellis.com.

In my hometown of Martins Ferry, Ohio, I will be offering signed copies of this novel to help raise money for various worthy causes. If you have a worthy cause and would be interested in the use of *Murder at Whalehead* as a fundraising tool, please email me or visit my website for more information.

For those of you interested in reading my first novel, *The Healing Place*, the first edition has sold out. However I plan to publish a second edition in the fall of 2007. Email me, and I will notify you when the second edition of *The Healing Place* becomes available.

Sincerely,

Joe C. Ellis

Chapter One

Laura Redinger drew in a deep breath and let it out haltingly, trying not to cry. She listened—silence, except for the wash of water around the piers supporting the old boathouse. Her arms ached, but yanking the chains as hard as she could didn't budge the U-bolts that kept her spread-eagled against the wooden plank wall. The cuffs on her ankles had dug into her skin, bloodying her feet.

"Somebody help me!" she yelled. No answer. A single light bulb dangled from a wire slung from the middle rafter, casting deep and distorted shadows from the objects around the room—the slats of crab cages, lengths of thick rope, floaters and netting hanging from the cavernous ceiling, the spokes of her wheels and handlebars against the opposite wall.

Why did he bring me here? He must be a psycho. "Oh God please, somebody help me," she whimpered. She took another breath and screamed. Her throat hurt from yelling. *He wants to kill me. I know it. I could see it in his eyes. But where'd he go?* Concentrating, she slowed her breathing and listened. Footsteps. Coming up the walkway from shore. "Help me! Somebody help me! Who's out there?"

The door creaked on its hinges.

She stared into the dark opening. "Whoever you are, please get me out of here."

* * *

Earlier that day Laura Redinger pedaled her blue mountain bike north along Route 12 into a strong headwind. The salty breeze winnowed her long auburn hair. She should have ponytailed it with a scrunchy, but that would have been too confining. Today, June second, she was truly free. Today she turned twenty-one.

A red Camaro zoomed by, and a longhaired teenage boy stuck his head out the passenger-side window and yelled, "Hey, sweet mama!"

She eyed him, smiled, but didn't wave. Too young. She was an adult now. If she wanted, she could stop in Grouper's Grill at the Timbuktu Plaza and chug down a Bud Lite without having to worry about a fake I.D. But she would rather keep riding. Biking toned her body for bikini season. With the miles the pounds dropped off. Today's excursion would be a new record. Her destination—the Currituck Lighthouse, a twenty-mile trek from her apartment in Kitty Hawk.

The Camaro slowed almost to a stop, and as she caught up, the pimply-faced kid shouted, "You're really hot! What's your name?"

"That's for me to know . . ." She picked up the pace as if to race the car. " . . . and you to never find out."

The car pulled even again. "You look like the Tomb Raider girl. What's her name?—Angelina Jolie."

"Thanks," she said, laughing. She glanced down at her body, quad muscles tensing as she pumped the pedals. Her low-cut tank top exposed generous cleavage. *Not as thin as I wanna be, but getting there for sure.* A wonderful sense of power washed over her—the power to turn a guy's head, the primal ability to allure. Sailing along on the bike, being young, attractive, and free felt amazing.

The kid pounded the side of the door and thumbed toward the back seat. "We've got a couple boogie boards in the back. Wanna ride some waves with us?"

She shook her head, conscious of how her hair bunched and flowed with the motion. "I'm too old for you. Go find some high school babes to hit on."

"Awww. Don't play hard."

A loud horn blew from behind. Laura glanced over her shoulder to see a fat guy driving an old pickup truck and losing his patience. The horn blared again, and the Camaro sped away, the boy laughing and waving. She smiled as she slowed down to catch her breath. *Good riddance. High school boys—they can be so juvenile.*

Around the next turn and beyond a large dune crowned with sea oats, Laura spotted the Corolla water tower, a giant aqua mushroom. Only a mile to go. Perhaps she'd stop at the quaint bookstore in the old village to see if they had any signed copies of her favorite book—David Payne's *Early from the Dance.* Now that was a great novel. Five times she'd read it, every summer since she'd turned sixteen. Romance and tragedy, it was the kind of story that made her ache for love and dream of a special man who could turn her world inside out.

Five minutes later she passed the miniature golf course and Corolla Sports Center. Cars lined the parking lot, and vacationers sauntered in and out of the glass doors that fronted the massive barn-shaped building. June delivered the tourists who rented the expensive vacation homes that had sprouted everywhere. So much had changed in the last ten years on the northern shores.

Peddling through an "S" curve, she spotted the redbrick lighthouse—it hadn't changed for over a hundred years. Not the tallest but definitely the most exquisite one on the Outer Banks, it towered above live oaks and willows. Even the loblolly pines seemed dwarfed in its presence.

She made a quick left turn onto the road that led to the base of the lighthouse. Glancing toward the Currituck Sound, she caught sight of the Whalehead Club, an old hunting club beautifully restored by the county's historical society. The large yellow building gleamed in the sun, its steep copper roof reflecting shades of gold with hints of patina muting the glow. Near the bridge that crossed to the man-made island on which the structure loomed, a small crowd gathered around a medium-built, tanned man who sat on a picnic table, holding up a deck of cards. *What in the world is he doing? Some kind of magic act?* He wore an orange t-shirt with cutoff sleeves and baggy denim shorts.

A sheriff's car pulled off the road into the grass, and a muscular deputy stepped out. She recognized the lawman—Kenny Queen, a guy she'd dated in high school. Queen was buff back then—a kid with a great body, but now he looked like a real man.

As she drew closer she turned her attention to the tawny-skinned guy. He shuffled the cards with machine precision and then shot the deck from one hand to the other with a rapid zip. A tattoo of a crouching devil leered from his bare shoulder, his arm muscles lean but defined. He had large brown eyes, close-cropped black hair and the beginnings of a mustache and goatee. Was he black? She couldn't tell.

Laura stopped next to the deputy and leaned on one leg. "Hey, Queen. Long time no see." She noticed her reflection in his mirrored shades and raked an unruly tress of hair with her fingers.

He smiled and nudged his black ball cap slightly upwards. "What's up, Redinger? It's been a year or two." He repositioned the cap and crossed his arms, his biceps threatening to burst his sleeves.

She pitched her voice low, "Who's the guy with the cards?"

"Calls himself Jack Blaze. Works as a guide at the Whalehead Club."

"A friend of yours?"

Queen grunted and shook his head sideways.

"Do it again!" a nappy-headed blond boy pleaded. "Let me pick the card this time." The kid held his hand out, but the man clasped the deck between his palms, and when he separated his hands and fluttered his fingers, the deck disappeared. Gasps escaped around the circle of observers.

Blaze spread his hands and said, "Sorry, kid. I've got places to go, and the cards left town." His accent sounded northern like the New York girls in her sorority. His gaze met Laura's, those dark eyes piercing through her. "But if this young lady here has a quarter . . . ," he raised his hand toward her, " . . .I'll perform one more feat before I leave."

"Me?" Laura touched her breastbone. His stare both jarred and thrilled her. "I-I might have a quarter." She felt her face flush as she dug into her pocket and pulled out a few coins—several pennies, a nickel, and a quarter. "Yes. Here's one."

The crowd separated as Blaze slid off the picnic table and stepped toward her. He whisked the coin from her palm and spun slowly, holding it out for all to see. After completing the circle he bared his teeth like a vampire ready to strike, placed the quarter between his incisors and bit down, snapping the coin away. He pursed his lips and raised his hand, revealing the quarter with a large chunk removed from Washington's head. His nostrils flared and eyebrows knotted.

Several people stepped back and the blond kid reached for his mother's hand. Murmurs rippled around the circle. "He bit the quarter in half," someone whispered.

Blaze raised the damaged coin to within two inches of his pursed lips. His cheeks filled with air, and he blew a hard puff, his hand jolting. The quarter appeared whole again.

"How'd you do that?" Laura blurted.

His eyes widened as he flipped the coin into the air. "Magic."

She caught it, examined it closely, and then met his stare. His gaze triggered uneasiness within her—attraction and fear. When he finally smiled, the attraction gained a solid foothold. She'd never met a man like him before. "Could you do another trick?" she asked.

"Sorry. I don't do tricks." He walked through the bystanders toward Route 12 in the direction of the Corolla Light Resort shops. Everyone watched him depart. After about twenty-five yards he stopped and about-faced. "I call them feats." With a smile and salute he turned and headed toward the shops.

"Now he's an unusual man," Laura said to Deputy Queen.

"Umm-hmm." Queen placed his hands on his hips and inhaled, expanding his massive chest. "Doesn't hang around long when I show up."

"Maybe he doesn't like you."

"Yeah, but why? What's he hiding? Walks all over town on his days off performing tricks. Regular Whodinny. Been tryin' to keep my eye on him, though. Kinda creepy, isn't he?"

"I think he's kinda cute."

Queen shook his head. "You've always had an odd taste in guys."

"That's true." She jabbed him in the ribs with her elbow. "I went to the senior prom with you." She launched the bike forward, lifted her feet onto the pedals, took off toward the Whalehead Club, made a U-turn, and headed in the direction of the shops. Smiling, she passed Queen.

"Very funny, Redinger."

She glanced over her shoulder and waved. "See you around, Queen."

"If you're lucky!"

Kenny Queen was an all right guy but not her type. In high school he had a one-track mind—sports. That's all he'd talk about whenever they went out. Jack Blaze was intriguing. It might be interesting to get to know him.

"Hey, Redinger! Hold up a second!"

Laura hit the hand brakes and spread her legs to catch herself when the bike stopped. She twisted to peer back at Queen. In his uniform, a slate gray shirt with a black stripe on the sleeves, his badge pinned to his chest, knee-length gray shorts, and black holster and pistol, he looked suddenly striking.

"I'd be careful 'bout chasing after Whodinny. He's an oddball."

She winked. "Thanks for the advice, but I can take care of myself."

Laura couldn't find Jack Blaze at the resort shops. He'd disappeared. She chuckled to herself. Vanished like the Great Houdini. Oh well, maybe she'd run into him in the village somewhere. After grabbing a chicken sandwich at the Wild Horse Café, she hopped on her bike and pedaled to the lighthouse. She intended climbing to the top to celebrate her birthday at the highest place in Currituck County, but today forty or fifty tourists waited in line to mount the spiral staircase to the observation deck. She'd stop back later. Instead she decided to pedal the two blocks to the Island Bookstore to check on that signed David Payne novel.

With the sun in her face and the ocean breeze at her back, she coasted along the gravel road through the historic village, passing the one-room schoolhouse and old church. She loved spending her summers at home on the Outer Banks. Throughout the school year she attended Penn State on a cheerleading scholarship. By the end of next semester she hoped to complete her degree in elementary education. State College, Pennsylvania was okay but wasn't home. Someday she hoped to teach at one of the local grade schools.

She swerved into the bookstore parking lot, hopped off the bike, inserted the front tire into the bike rack, and skipped up the few steps into the store. Within three minutes she found the novel with a sticker on the cover indicating an autographed copy. She opened it to the title page and saw the signature just above the author's printed name. What a great day. At the checkout she had the exact amount of change—no need to break her last twenty. Everything was going her way. She felt sure she'd meet up with Jack Blaze again before she headed home.

In the parking lot she slipped the book into the storage bag under the seat. It fit perfectly. When she reached for the handlebars to tug the bike out of the rack, she noticed the flat front tire. *Oh Crap. What am I going to do now?* She panned the area, seeing several small specialty stores—beachwear shop, gift shop, fruit and vegetable stand—but didn't notice anyone who looked mechanical. She recalled the nearest gas station was about a half mile farther up the main road. It wouldn't take long to push the bike there. Maybe she'd run into someone along the way who could help.

Five minutes later as she pushed her bike along Route 12, a little black Pontiac slowed to a stop. The tinted driver's side window lowered halfway, and a man's voice asked, "Need a lift?"

She peered into the interior, but it was too dark to identify him. "I've got a flat tire," she said as she shaded the sun with her hand and squinted. *This might be a mistake. Oh well, I can at least get a closer look.* She leaned her bike against a light post and walked across the road toward the car.

Chapter Two

"*Somebody help me!*"

Byron Butler waded through knee-deep water towards the voice. She sounded desperate. A brackish smell assaulted his nostrils. He glanced over his shoulder into the blackness. Two red eyes appeared and vanished. Prickles crawled up his back and crossed his scalp. Something crept in the shadows, watching him.

Her muffled screams shifted his attention to a large rectangular silhouette above the water. He reached and touched a wooden wall—some kind of boathouse? He could hear her crying and pleading for someone to save her. Where's the door? He moved along the edge until he came to a corner. Slivers of light sliced through cracks. In the glow he saw a doorknob above him. He stretched, reaching between two rails, but couldn't grasp it. How do I get to it?

The moonlight limned a walkway above the water. Byron climbed onto it. He peered at the shore, saw the red eyes, and hesitated, sensing the presence of evil.

"Get me out of here, please!" she yelled.

He rushed to the door, pulled it open, and saw the girl chained to the back wall. She resembled his daughter, Chrissy, tall and lean with long blonde hair streaked with highlights. But she wasn't his daughter. Her face looked so familiar, a thin nose and deep-blue eyes. She wore only panties and a bra.

"Hurry," she said. "If he comes back he'll kill us."

She glanced over his shoulder and her expression froze into a carving of terror. Byron spun to see the red eyes. The black form of a man raised a knife.

Byron sucked in a quick breath and sat up, his heart thudding into his throat. He blinked to adjust to the darkness of the bedroom. Placing his palms on his forehead, he tried to remember the girl—early twenties, thin, blonde hair, her face contorted by fear. *Was it at a lake? Some kind of boathouse?* For the fifth time in the last month the nightmare had jolted him awake.

The first time was four weeks ago after Dr. David Godfrey had removed his appendix. That night in the hospital Byron blamed the dream on painkillers, but now he had no explanation. He felt physically recovered from the operation and had even started running again. The appendicitis attack had given him a break from the stress of ministry. The Scotch Ridge Church's Board of Elders recommended he put in fewer hours until fall. But the emotional turmoil hadn't eased. At night, the dreams recurred, lucid and puzzling—the young woman screaming for help and . . . the other dream—the strange man with the coin.

Byron propped himself on his elbow and peered over his wife's shoulder to see the alarm clock—5:15 A.M. Later that day his family and the Mulligans would be packed and ready to head to the Outer Banks. It'd been a long time since he'd been to the ocean. *Maybe there I can find some answers.* Byron lay back down. He knew he needed more sleep for the exhausting drive.

* * *

"Yeah, Byron," Elijah Mulligan said as he stretched the rubber cord and clipped the metal hook to the bike rack. "There's no doubt in my mind. God still gives certain people prophetic dreams and visions, just like in Bible days."

Byron set the suitcase on the ground next to his white Caravan. He gripped the frame of one of the three bikes suspended on the back of Elijah's blue Suburban and shook it to make sure all were tightly secured. "I'm not nearly as conservative as you in my theology. Visions are for Pentecostals and Bible-thumping Baptists, not for Presbyterian pastors like me."

Elijah combed his fingers through his long salt and pepper beard. His smile was barely visible beneath his thick mustache. "You see, the Lord's trying to move you further to the right." The large man pointed to the east. "And the right is in that direction—the Atlantic. God knows you need some surf, sand, and seafood. Maybe you'll end up walking on water. Or at least body surfing."

"Body surfing, maybe. Walking on water is out of my league. That's why I don't get these dreams. I'm not ready to go off the deep end when it comes to faith."

The wind tousled the scraggly hair that rimmed Elijah's bald head. "You're not going nuts. Remember Ezekiel's vision. The Lord transported him to a valley full of bones and told him to command them to live again. When Ezekiel obeyed—shake, rattle and roll—the bones reconnected, muscles and flesh formed, and skin covered their bodies." His eyes widened, brown irises floating in pools of white. "Before him rose up an army of the dead."

"Right. That'd be a new one for me—raising the dead."

Byron didn't need supernatural phenomena to confirm his faith. He took a more practical approach. To him, the sunrise was miraculous. Seeing a robin on the branch of an oak tree spoke of the existence of a divine creator. Nothing moved him spiritually more than a long run on an October day down a country road resplendent with the colors of autumn leaves. His faith had developed over the years because of inner spiritual hunger rather than unexplained wonders—no signs, no visitations by angels, no strange images of Jesus appearing in the wood grain of the church's front door.

He liked it that way. Those preachers who practiced sensational exhibitions in their services disgusted him. Enticing nonbelievers with so-called miracles or scaring them with end-times bombast held no place in his ministry. He wanted his congregation to see God's hand in the beauty of freshly fallen snow or hear God's voice in a newborn baby's cry. He didn't need dreams or visions.

"You okay with the boys riding in your car?" Byron asked.

"No problem," Elijah said. "It'll be fun. I've got plenty of stories to keep them entertained."

Byron glanced into the side yard. Matt, Mark, and Chrissy were tossing a football.

"Kids!" Byron called. "Get over here."

Chrissy threw a bullet just beyond Mark's outstretched arms as Matt leapt to knock it down. The ball bounced and wobbled to a stop under the maple tree. "Great try, Marky! You almost caught it!" Chrissy yelled. She pivoted and looked at her father.

"Tell your mother we're ready to go, will ya, Stilts?"

"Sure, Dad. I'll get her." She ran to the back door, her long strides covering the distance quickly.

"Mark and Matt!" Elijah hollered. "Get over here. I need to tell you something."

Mark retrieved the ball, and together they jogged over and gazed up at Elijah. Byron wondered what the big man wanted to say to his sons.

Elijah put his massive hands on their shoulders. "Now listen. We're heading into Martins Ferry to pick up my nephew, Dugan. It's a total surprise. He has no idea we're taking him on vacation with us. You boys are how old? Twelve?"

The twins nodded, their newly buzzed heads just beginning to sprout brown hair.

"Dugan's only ten. He's been through a lot this past year—his ma and pa breaking up and all. Try to be patient with him. I know it's not easy. I've lost it a few times when he starts telling his tales. He tends to . . . how should I put this? He tends to fib a lot. You know what I mean? He's got quite an imagination. You've gotta take what he says with a grain of beach sand." Elijah stood back and put his hands on his hips.

"No problem," Matt said.

Mark shrugged. "Okay."

"Dugan'll be fine," Byron said. "These boys get along well with just about anybody. Your nephew'll fit right in."

The kitchen door opened. Lila Butler and Annie Mulligan stepped onto the deck carrying grocery bags.

"You boys help Chrissy tote the coolers," Lila shouted. "Then we'll be ready to take off."

Chrissy peeked out the doorway. "Get in here and help, you goobers. I want to go to the ocean."

* * *

Dugan Walton swallowed to get rid of the knot that rose from his stomach into his throat. The tight feeling in his neck always bothered him when he studied a crime scene. Swallowing didn't help. The knot returned as he leaned to examine the corpse. Blood soaked the victim's t-shirt. Her arms were striped with deep cuts. *Must have tried to fight off her attacker.* His attention moved to the girl's head. Through tangled hair, she stared at him, that blank stare of death. He looked away, breathing in deeply and letting it out slowly. With renewed courage he studied her face and noticed the slice lines across her forehead and cheeks. *The killer used her skin like an etch-a-sketch.* Dugan's stomach quivered. He glanced around the library. Several people stood at the counter, waiting to check out books. A white-haired old man sat at a computer station, surfing the internet.

"What ya lookin' at, Doogie?"

Dugan turned in the direction of the familiar voice.

Chucky Longbone placed his hands near the book and leaned over the table. "That's gross!" The ten year old had light brown skin and shoulder-length black hair.

"Shhhhhhhhh!" the librarian warned from across the room.

"Is she dead?" Chucky whispered.

"Course she's dead."

"That's not real, is it?"

"Course it's real. Looky here." Dugan closed the book and showed him the title: CASE CLOSED: STUDIES IN FORENSIC INVESTIGATION. He flipped back to the crime scene. "This was the work of the Boone County Slasher. He carved pictures on his victim's faces."

Chucky pointed to the girl's cheek. "That looks like a star."

"It's a pentagram. Check out the forehead. See those numbers?"

"Sixes. One, two, three of them," Chucky said

"Most serial killers leave clues. A good investigator always checks for that kind of thing. You can tell by those pictures that the *Slasher* worshiped the devil." Dugan closed the book and patted the top. "That's what I want to be."

"A serial killer?"

"No, Tonto, you knucklehead. A detective. A homicide investigator. That's why I study these cases. It's in my blood." Dugan motioned Chucky to sit down. He whispered, "My father's in the FBI. That's why he had to leave home. He's on a big case."

Chucky's eyes narrowed. "I thought your daddy was a used car salesman in Bridgeport. My grandpa bought a car off him two weeks ago."

"Quiet, Chucky." Dugan tensed his brow, his nose wrinkling. "That's his cover—a used car salesman. The Feds give him the top murder cases in the Ohio Valley. Sometimes he calls me for advice. That's why I'm always studying."

"You telling me the truth?"

Dugan gripped Chucky's arm. "Course I am. This is all top secret. You can't tell a soul. You promise?"

Chucky nodded, his eyes dark and serious. "I promise." He glanced over Dugan's shoulder. "Uh oh. Here comes a couple dirtballs."

Dugan twisted in his seat and saw two boys wearing baggy denim shorts and black t-shirts shuffling toward them. The taller one had shaggy brown hair, and the shorter one was chubby and walked with his hands in his pockets.

"Well, look who's here," the fat one said. "The Karate Kid and his retarded sidekick, Tonto Longbone." He pulled his hand out of his pocket and popped a jawbreaker in his mouth.

"More like Stupid and Stupider," the tall one said.

"Stupid is what stupid says," Dugan fired back.

"Is that what your mommy always told you, Forest?" Leonard Scales, the tall one, asked.

"What's this?" Tyler Maxwell said, the jawbreaker protruding like a giant boil from his cheek. He picked up the book.

"Give it back," Dugan said.

"Hold on a minute, Karate Kid. I just want to take a peek." He opened the book, and his tall buddy peered over his shoulder. "Whooweee. I haven't seen this much blood since Randy Bell fought Magoo Fry on the playground last week."

"Dugan's studyin' to be a government agent like his daddy," Chucky said.

"A government agent?" Leonard asked.

Laughter exploded from Tyler and Leonard as the large book slipped from Tyler's hand and clunked on the table. The librarian, a plump woman with horn-rimmed glasses, marched over and demanded they be quiet or she'd throw them out. Then she saw the book.

"Who took this book from the adult section?" she asked, eyes peering over her glasses.

All three boys pointed at Dugan. He lowered his head and stared at his hands.

She picked the book up. "I could suspend your library card for this. You know you're not allowed in the adult section. Am I right?"

Dugan nodded. "Yes, Ma'am." His cheeks felt like they were on fire.

The librarian stuck her finger in front of the boys' faces. "This is your last warning. Keep quiet or I'll throw *all* of you out."

"We'll be quiet," Tyler said.

She turned and waddled away like a duck with the book tucked under her wing.

Leonard and Tyler slid into the chairs across from Dugan and Chucky.

"Way to go, knuckleheads," Dugan said.

"So your old man's a government agent, huh?" Leonard asked.

Tyler rolled the jawbreaker around in his mouth and jutted it back into the pouch of his cheek. "I believe that like I believe you've got a black belt in karate."

"I do, whether you believe it or not."

"Shoot. You couldn't even whip Mary Lou Preston," Tyler said.

"That's right," Leonard said. "She challenged you to a fight last summer at the park, and you walked away like a yellowbelly."

"It wouldn't a been a fair fight with my knowledge of martial arts. Besides, I don't fight girls. It's against the code."

"What code?" Leonard asked.

"The Karate Honor Code. I've sworn only to use my skills in self-defense and never against women." Dugan sat back and crossed his thin arms. He had red hair that curled just over the rims of his large ears. A pattern of orange-brown freckles spattered his face like a speckled egg.

"You're a frickin' lethal weapon. Do you have to register your body with the police department?" Tyler asked as red drool trickled from the corner of his mouth.

Leonard giggled. "I wouldn't call him a lethal weapon. More like a lethal wimp."

Dugan balled his hands into fists and tapped them on the table. A wave of anger brought the knot back into his throat, making it hard to swallow. He wanted to jump across the table with both fists flying, clobbering their knuckleheads. As the scene whirled in his mind, he grabbed the edge of the table and took a deep breath.

"You all right, Doogie?" Chucky asked.

Dugan heard the words, but they seemed distant, as if someone on the other side of the room spoke them.

Chucky grabbed his elbow. "Doogie?"

He blinked.

Leonard and Tyler leaned forward.

"He's in a trance, kinda like the Hulk," Leonard said.

Tyler giggled. "Better watch what ya say. He'll snap you like a Popsicle stick."

"I'm gonna have to hire Mary Lou Preston to be my bodyguard," Leonard said. "She'll kick his butt for me."

Tyler tried to smother a laugh, but it burst out like a spooked pheasant, and all heads around the library turned.

Dugan slammed his fists on the table and stood, knocking his chair backward. It jolted a rack of paperbacks that timbered, dumping the books helter-skelter across the floor.

"I ain't scared a nobody!" Dugan shouted. "I'll fight you right now. You, Mary Lou Preston and every danged person in this library. Bring it on!"

In the terrible silence that followed, Dugan regretted every word. From two tables away, a middle-aged man with a thick brown mustache lowered his newspaper and glared at him. A large high school boy, Martins Ferry High School's star running back, stepped from between two rows of books, placed his hands on his hips and jutted his chin. Standing amidst the scattered paperbacks, an old lady held a romance novel with a bare-chested hero embracing a black-haired beauty on the cover. She lowered the book, dropped it onto the pile and raised her hand to her mouth.

Dugan blinked, gulped, and tried to smile, but the expression on the librarian's face froze the attempt in mid-effort. She stomped to the table and thrust out her hand.

"Give me your card!" she demanded.

Not the card. Not the card. Please, not the card. The library was Dugan's refuge—the place he felt at home when home wasn't so great. In here he could wander through the aisles, pull down a Hardy Boys novel and become lost in a world of words. In the library fathers were legends and young boys, heroes. Here he felt like somebody important.

Dugan reached into his pocket and felt the plastic card. "H-H-H-How long? A week? Two weeks?"

Her eyes narrowed and her face tightened as if something had sucked all liquid from her head. He pulled the card out of his pocket, and she snatched it from his hand.

"Three months," she said.

"Three months?" Dugan gasped. He felt sick. "That's the entire summer."

"That's right. You're banned from here for three months. I don't want to see you set one foot inside that door." She pointed to the entrance. "Maybe now you'll think twice before causing trouble on my watch." She turned and faced the boys. "I want all of you out of here, now."

They looked at one another.

"Now!" she barked.

The boys jumped to their feet and stumbled into each other as they hurried to the exit. Dugan followed, but hesitated to glance at the rows of books before leaving.

As the library door closed behind them, the boys stopped and glared at each other.

Tyler shrugged. "That's the third time I've been kicked out of the library this year."

"Your mama'll be real proud of you," Dugan muttered.

"Like heck," Tyler said. "She'll kill me if she finds out."

"Maybe I'll tell her," Dugan said.

"Maybe I'll smash your face."

"Maybe you won't have to," Leonard said. "Look who's comin'."

Rounding the corner of Hanover and Fifth Streets, a pony-tailed girl wearing bib overall shorts and a pink t-shirt strode toward them. With muscular legs, she bounced rather than walked. As she neared the boys, she slowed, and her mouth puckered with disgust as if she had taken too big a bite out of a lemon.

In unison, Tyler and Leonard said, "What's up, Mary Lou?"

"Out of my way, losers. Got no time to waste talkin' to fifth grade flunkies," she said as she shoved Leonard into Tyler.

"Wait a minute, Mary Lou. I've got to warn you," Tyler said.

"Warn me 'bout what?" She paused, her fingers touching the door handle.

"The Karate Kid just got us booted. The librarian's steamed. Madder than a bucket-load of rattlesnakes."

"So what?" she said. "You Sesame Street rejects probably deserved it. I don't come to the library to play games. When're you clowns gonna realize this ain't the Big Top?" She turned, her ponytail swishing across her shoulders, and pulled the door open.

"That's not all," Tyler said.

Mary Lou paused a half step into the library.

"Lethal Wimp here told everybody in there he could kick your butt."

She turned, her eyes on fire. "That better not be true."

"It's true," Leonard Scales said. "He shouted it so everyone in the place could hear. That's why we got kicked out."

"No way. Tell me you didn't say that, Doogie Walton, so I don't have to hurt you."

With wide eyes, Dugan swiveled his head.

She turned and grabbed Chucky by the collar. "Tonto, you never tell a lie. Did Bubblegum Brain say that or not?"

Chucky trembled and looked from Dugan to Mary Lou. Slowly he nodded.

Dugan thought he saw steam coming out of her nose like a mad bull on Looney Tunes. He wanted to fall on his knees and pray for mercy, but he knew it was too late.

Chapter Three

"That does it," Mary Lou said. She shoved Dugan, and he backpedaled into an old green Volkswagen. Stunned and blinking, he watched the green-eyed wildcat close in. He knew he had to fight or be pulverized. His hands swooped slow circles between him and Mary Lou as if the motion created an invisible wall. Then they snapped, hatchet-like, into a defensive position, the right in front of the left. The howl he released began deep in his lungs and leapt from his mouth like a demon dog from hell: "Yeeeearrowwll!" He hoped the dramatics would put a scare into her.

It didn't work. Mary Lou took one step forward and pounded him in the stomach with a short left. He bent over, wind knocked out of him. She followed with a right uppercut that caught Dugan squarely on the left eye. His head flew back faster than it had jerked forward. He stumbled backward onto the hood of the Volkswagen, rolled off and landed on his knees and elbows in the street. Burying his face in his hands for protection, he heaved, struggling to get air back into his lungs. When he finally managed to inhale, a sob escaped followed by a flood of tears and more sobbing. Fortunately, Mary Lou didn't kick his noggin. For that, he felt grateful. When he opened his eyes and peeked through his fingers, he saw her standing above him, hands on her hips, shaking her head.

"What a loser," she said. "Don't ever tell anyone you can whip me again. You hear me, Doogie Walton?"

Dugan pushed himself up onto his knees, swallowed his sniffles, wiped his eyes with the back of his hand and bobbed his head. She about-faced, her ponytail swooshing behind her, flung open the library door and entered.

"You're pitiful," Lenny said. "An embarrassment to all middle school boys in Belmont County."

"What happened to your lethal fists?" Tyler asked. "You always brag about your black belt. Nothing but a big lie. Come on, Lenny, let's blow this book stand. Doogie Breath here is stinkin' it up." Tyler and Leonard walked away, Tyler digging deep into his pocket for another jawbreaker.

"You all right, Doogie? Your eye's all puffy and red," Chucky said. He reached down, grabbed Dugan by the elbow and pulled him to his feet.

Dugan wiped his hand across his nose, smearing snot and tears. "I'm fine," he said. "I had to do it that way, Chucky. The Code, you know. I pretended to fight. It's against the Karate Code to hit a girl."

"I know, Doogie. I know."

Chucky walked Dugan home. They didn't say much along the way, but Dugan felt glad Chucky didn't mind being seen with him.

*　*　*

The first thing his mother said when Dugan entered the kitchen was: "Dugan Walton, where have you been? I told you to be home by noon." When she noticed his swollen eye, she gasped, "What happened to you?" She rushed to him and cupped his cheeks with her hands. Peering over her shoulder, Dugan glimpsed Uncle Elijah, Aunt Annie, and the Butler family.

Despite the pain from his left eye Dugan smiled and shouted, "Uncle Elijah and Aunt Annie! What 're you doing here?"

"You all right, boy?" Elijah asked.

"Let me see that eye," Annie said. Aunt Annie was his mother's sister and worked as a nurse at Wheeling Medical Park. She had a gentle way with animals and kids. With long, brown hair and big blue eyes, she was awful pretty, even for a woman a few years older than his mom.

Dugan's mother leaned back, allowing her sister to inspect the damage.

"You're gonna have quite a shiner," Aunt Annie said.

"It hurts, but I'm fine," Dugan said.

"Tell us what happened," Uncle Elijah said.

Dugan broke out of his mother's grasp and slipped by Aunt Annie to the middle of the kitchen. He glanced from face to face and noticed all five of the Butlers staring at him, waiting for an explanation. "It was three against one, Uncle Elijah. But I put up a heck of a fight, and I guarantee you this: I was the only one left standing. They all took off."

Elijah arched his back, hands on his hips. "Three against one? Come on now, Dugan."

"Honest Injun. You can ask Chucky Longbone."

"Don't lie, Dugan," his mother said.

"I ain't lyin', Ma. They all skedaddled."

"We need some ice for his eye," Aunt Annie said.

"Did you hurt anybody?" Elijah asked.

"You should have seen me, Uncle Elijah. Knowin' I had to defend myself, I took my karate stance." Dugan repeated the hand motions and snapped into position. "Yeeeearrowwll! 'Bout scared them to death. Before I knew it, they were gone."

"Quit lying!" his mother shouted. "You didn't scare anybody. You're standing here with a black eye and tear steaks down your face. Tell the truth."

Dugan blinked his good eye. His mouth tightened, and he fought the urge to bawl. "I . . .I . . . am telling the truth. Honest, Ma."

"I don't believe you, Dugan," his mother said.

Dugan hung his head, and the tears streamed down his face.

Elijah reached and picked him up. The large man had no problem holding him in the crook of his right arm. Dugan didn't know what to think. Looking into the round, bearded face and expecting a lecture, he blinked a couple times, spilling more tears.

"Now, now, Dugan. Get a hold of yourself."

Aunt Annie approached with some ice cubes wrapped in a washcloth. "Here. Hold this on your peeper."

Dugan clasped the wet bundle to his eye. It felt cold but good.

Elijah said, "May I ask you something?"

Dugan sniffled and smeared tears across his cheek with his free hand. After a shaky breath he said, "Okay, Uncle Elijah."

"Do you have any plans for next week?"

Dugan shrugged. *I won't be hangin' out at the library.* "I don't know. I'm probably grounded," he said.

How would you like to go on vacation with us?"

"Huh?"

"You heard me."

"Really?" Dugan thought he might be kidding. Rarely did anyone want to spend time with him. "With all of you? Are we going together?"

The twins nodded, and Chrissy said, "Sure, Cap'n. We'll have lots of fun."

Uncle Elijah lifted him higher, almost to the ceiling. "We're going to the ocean—the Outer Banks."

"The ocean! I've never been to the ocean!" Dugan lost his grip on the washcloth and the ice cubes tumbled onto the linoleum. Mark and Matt scrambled to pick them up.

Uncle Elijah lowered Dugan to the floor.

"I packed your suitcases already," his mom said. "They're in your bedroom."

"Go get 'em, boy," Uncle Elijah said. "It's time to head to the beach."

* * *

About three in the afternoon, the two vehicles strained up one of Maryland's many mountains along Interstate 68. Byron's eyes drifted from watching the back of Elijah's Suburban to the undulating forest that rippled from the top of the mountain into the valley and rose again as it faded into the atmospheric blur. Nearing the top of Sideling Hill, Byron caught a glimpse of the slice of mountain exposed by the construction of the interstate. A towering wall of shale and sandstone loomed above, massive and imposing.

"Hey Stilts, look at that," Byron said. "Can you imagine how old those rocks are? Millions, I bet. Hundreds of millions of years old."

"Awesome," Chrissy said. "It's like we're looking back into time." Eighteen years old, Chrissy had her mother's striking green eyes and her father's confident smile.

"Bet ya could find all kinds of fossils on the face of those rocks," Byron said.

"I don't like traveling through these mountains," Lila said. "The uphills put a strain on the motor, the downhills are too steep, and the curves too sharp."

"I think it's beautiful," Chrissy said.

"Me too," Byron said.

"You two coconuts fell out of the same tree. I'll be glad when we hit the coast." Lila skimmed her hand forward. "Flat and straight,"

Byron chuckled to himself. Lila was right. Chrissy and he shared the same temperament, the same adventurous spirit. Competitive and obsessive, they gave one hundred percent whether running a 5K footrace or playing a silly game of charades.

But they could butt heads like mountain goats. Two months earlier they collided on whether or not high school seniors should be allowed to go on an un-chaperoned trip to Myrtle Beach. Most of Chrissy's friends' parents granted permission, but Byron wouldn't stand for it. During a heated argument, Chrissy insisted her father didn't trust her. Lila had to stop the ruckus and smooth things over. She always played the role of peacekeeper, preserving the close link between father and daughter.

"Will there be young adults my age down here?" Chrissy asked as they descended the mountain.

"Young adults?" Byron grinned. "You mean kids, don't ya?"

"No, Dad. I mean young adults. I'm eighteen now. Voting age. Eligible for the military."

"Of course," Lila said. "Why wouldn't there be young people your age there?"

"Because Jennifer Thomas told me the Outer Banks caters to families like Disneyland. Her folks go every year, and she hates it—tons of little kids all over the place."

"There'll be plenty of young adults, believe me," Byron said.

"Sure, Dad, I'll have to hang out with junior high boys all day."

Byron swallowed, trying to remain cool. "Nothing wrong with spending time with your brothers."

"I want to meet people my own age. Maybe go out on a date,"

Byron gripped the wheel harder. His shoulders tensed. "A date? This is a family vacation, not some MTV road trip."

"Please, you two. We've never been to the Outer Banks before. We don't know what to expect," Lila said.

"It'll probably be boring," Chrissy said.

"It's those doggone MTV reality shows. Everything's got to be hip and hedonistic anymore for kids to like it," Byron said.

"Please you two. Let's just drop it. No sense in arguing about things we don't know yet," Lila stated calmly.

Byron felt his face flush and tensed his brow. "I can't help it. I'm disgusted with these shows where young people get drunk, expose themselves to each other and then hop into bed. It makes me sick. These networks show anything to make a buck. It's as simple as that."

From the back seat, Chrissy leaned forward and spoke loudly in her father's ear. "I hope you don't think I'm one of those kind of kids. I just want to hang out with people my own age."

"I didn't say you were one of those kind of kids, now did I? I'm just stating fact: the moral standards of this country have totally collapsed. It can't be denied. But believe me, there are consequences to the behaviors these shows promote. I hope you know that."

"Don't worry. I'm not hopping in and out of the sack with the football team. I'm probably the last virgin at Martins Ferry High School."

"You should be proud of that, honey," Lila said.

"That's right," Byron said. "Never follow the crowd. The Bible says, 'The road to destruction is wide, and like sheep, many young people go often astray.'"

Chrissy snorted. "You made that verse up."

"It's in there somewhere."

"Can I ask you a serious question, Dad?"

"Shoot."

"I want an honest answer."

"Just ask the question."

"Were you a virgin when you married Mom?"

Silence descended like a thick curtain dousing a window's light.

Byron cleared his throat. *How in heaven in do I answer this one honestly?*

Lila turned and glared at Chrissy. "I was a virgin when your father married me, young lady."

"I didn't ask if you were. You've informed me of that fact often. I want to know if Dad was a virgin."

Byron coughed and gulped. "No," Byron said.

"Were you promiscuous?"

"Chrissy!" Lila gasped.

"You think I'm a hypocrite, don't you?" Byron asked. "You think I didn't practice what I preach to you."

"No. I just asked a question. But now that you mentioned it, did you practice what you preach?"

Byron knew the answer to that question was a resounding, "No," but he kept his mouth shut. The last thing he wanted to share with his daughter was the details of his teenage sexual exploration.

"Look," Lila said. "Elijah's turning into that rest stop. Good. I need a bathroom break."

"Yes," Byron said. "I think we all need a break."

* * *

At seven o'clock in the evening, driving south along North Carolina State Route 158, Elijah slapped his knee and breathed rapidly to shake off the sleepiness that pressed upon him. Occasionally, as the drowsiness drew his eyelids down, he would jerk his head up, eyes wide again, heart thumping.

"Pull over and let me drive," Annie said.

"No. I'm fine. I can make it."

"You're gonna kill us all."

"Don't be ridiculous. I'm wide awake now."

The road was flat and straight with intermittent small towns offering typical fast food cuisine, gas stations on every other corner, bait shops and roadside markets. To Elijah, this was the longest stage of the journey, especially when you entered Currituck County. Their destination could be seen eastward across the Currituck Sound, but no bridge spanned the water to the Outer Banks for another twenty miles until you got to Kitty Hawk.

"Uncle Elijah," Dugan whined. "How much farther?" He sat sandwiched between the twins in the back seat.

"Not far now. Twenty miles south, then one mile east across the bridge, then we backtrack twenty miles north. Less than an hour."

"I can't wait to get there," Dugan said. "The first thing I'm gonna do when we get to the beach is rent a surf board and ride the waves."

"A surfboard?" Matt said. "You're crazy." The twins resembled their father, Byron, and were difficult to tell apart, except that Matt had a moon-like sliver of a scar across his right cheek. When he was ten, he and his brother collided in the outfield in an attempt to catch the same fly ball. Mark lost a tooth, and Matt needed seven stitches just below his eye. In temperament they were more like Lila, their mother—cautious, honest and very disciplined.

"Have you ever surfed before?" Mark asked.

"Oh yeah," Dugan said. "I'm an expert. I've got lots of trophies at home. I hope they have some big waves at this beach."

"Wait a minute, Dugan," Elijah said, glancing in the rearview mirror. "You told us you've never been to the ocean. How can you be an expert surfer if you've never been to the ocean?"

He paused and glanced into the rearview mirror to see his uncle eyeing him. "Well . . . uh . . . Easy! I'm talkin' about street surfin' on my skateboard. I'm the best skateboarder in Martins Ferry. I know all the tricks. Wave surfin' can't be much different."

Elijah shook his head. "Right," he said, disgust boiling over within him like unattended soup. "Dugan, you need to learn to tell the truth."

"You kill me," Matt said. "Always tellin' stories like you're some kinda big deal."

"Yeah," Mark said. "Like earlier today when you told us you whipped three guys at once with Kung Fu. That's a load of baloney."

"Whadayamean? It's true," Dugan pleaded. "I got a black eye out of it, but those kids took off. I was the last man standing. I wish Chucky Longbone was here. He'd tell ya."

"Right," Mark said.

"Riiiiight," Matt echoed.

"And I'm a good skateboarder too. Maybe not the best in Martins Ferry but one of the best. You'll see. You'll see when we get to the beach."

"That's enough. That's enough, Dugan. No more stories," Elijah ordered, his volume quelling the boys' bickering.

With a cautious glance, Annie reached over and patted Elijah's knee. "Easy, big fellow," she said, smiling.

Elijah inhaled deeply and slowly released his breath. He peered into the rearview mirror and noticed the boys eying him. With his deep voice he said, "It's my turn to tell a story."

"Is it a true story, Uncle Elijah?" Dugan asked.

"Well, as far as I know. One of the old timers at the Whalehead Club told me this tale."

"The Whalehead Club?" Mark asked.

"Ye-s-s-s-s, an old hunting club," Elijah said and laughed, a spooky, spine-jiggling staccato of laughter.

"This is a ghost story, ain't it, Uncle Elijah?"

"That's right, Dugan," Elijah said.

"Good. I love scary stories."

"Then be quiet and pay attention," Mark said.

"They call the Outer Banks the Graveyard of the Atlantic." Elijah took a quick peek into the mirror and saw the three boys leaning forward, listening intently. "Do you know why?" They shook their heads. "Because of the Diamond Shoals—the shifting underwater sandbars. More than two thousand ships have sunk just off the shores in the last four hundred years. Most of the ghosts people claim to see on the Outer Banks were shipwreck victims washed up on the beach. But they don't realize they're dead. Usually at twilight you can catch a glimpse of one or two wandering along the dunes or through the marshes.

"The most infamous ghost, though . . ." Elijah made a low gurgling sound in his throat, coughed, and swallowed, "you definitely don't want to run into—Albert Douglas Mason, the Carolina Strangler."

"Why'd they call him the Carolina Strangler?" Dugan asked.

"He was a murderer. Killed for the pure pleasure it gave him. Used his alligator belt as a noose." Elijah shook his head. "Would slip it around his victim's neck and pull until it cut off the airway."

"Elijah, please," Annie said. "You're gonna give these boys nightmares."

"No he won't," Mark said. "We like these kinds of stories."

"Albert choked eight woman on the back streets of Charleston back in the 1890's. The law chased him up north and arrested him in Baltimore. Sent him back down by schooner to Charleston to be tried for murder.

"The ship caught on a sandbar near Whalehead Beach in a fierce nor'easter and sunk. Albert tried to swim to shore but didn't make it. His body washed up the next day. It was about this time of year—early summer. That's when the Carolina Strangler walks the dunes and marshes of the Outer Banks. If you see a man coming toward you wearing a drenched prison suit and carrying a belt, you know it's the ghost of the Carolina Strangler."

"But a ghost can't kill you, can it, Uncle Elijah?" Dugan asked.

"Well, you wouldn't think so, would you? But the Carolina Strangler's not your average ghost. Back in June of 1935 the lighthouse keeper's daughter was about to walk home from the Whalehead Club where she worked as a part-time servant. The dishwasher warned her some villagers had spotted the ghost of Albert Mason crossing the marsh near the lighthouse. He offered to walk her home, but she refused his company. Said she didn't believe in ghosts."

Elijah made that low gurgling sound again and gulped. "The sun had set, and a fog had moved in. From the kitchen window the dishwasher watched the young girl cross the bridge and walk down the road toward the keeper's house. She disappeared into the fog. That night when he was finishing up the last pot, there came a pounding on the door. It was the girl's father, the lighthouse keeper. Asked where his daughter was."

Elijah glanced in the rearview mirror. The boys' eyes were wide, mouths open.

"Did they find her?" Matt asked.

Elijah nodded. "Terrible thing to happen to a person that young. The search party hunted all night. Didn't find her till the next morning when a thirsty volunteer dropped a bucket into the cistern. There she was at the bottom. Drowned. When they pulled her body out, they discovered bruises around her neck in the pattern of alligator skin."

"Who told you that story, Uncle Elijah?" Dugan asked.

"A few years ago a ninety-year-old man told me."

"How'd he know it was true?"

"He was the dishwasher at the Whalehead Club."

Chapter Four

Dugan leaned over Mark and gazed out the car window. "Those houses are huge! Do movie stars own them?"

"Some do," Elijah said. "I heard Tom Cruise owns a house along here somewhere."

"How come they're on big posts?" Dugan asked.

"Most of these homes have been built in the last ten years. The posts make it possible to withstand hurricane-force winds. Instead of a block foundation, those posts give a little and keep the main part of the house ten feet off the ground."

"Look at that one," Dugan said. It was a three-story tan structure with white trim and a brown roof. Large decks wrapped around the upper two floors, with five gables jutting here and there across the front, large triangular windows filling each gable. Beyond that house, four other homes sat atop the dunes, fading into the distance—one light blue, one bright yellow, and two in shades of gray. To Dugan they looked like mansions.

"Will our beach house look like those houses?" Mark asked.

"Yeah, but not quite as big. Ours has four bedrooms and three and a half bathrooms," Elijah said.

"Three and a half bathrooms!" Dugan exclaimed. "I've never been in a house with three and a half bathrooms."

"And a hot tub," Annie said.

"Cool!" Matt said. "The kind that shoots bubbles out like on T.V."

Turning and looking at the boys, Annie smiled. "Just like on the commercials."

"I can't wait to get there," Dugan said. "This is gonna be my best vacation ever. How much farther, Uncle Elijah?"

" 'Bout ten minutes."

* * *

As the cars approached the house, Byron arched his back and lifted his rear from the seat. "My butt went numb an hour ago," he complained.

"My stars and garters! Look at that house," Lila said.

He couldn't wait to get out and stretch his legs. The driveway widened and split, allowing cars to park under each side of the house. Clad with weathered sea green wood siding and white trim, the structure loomed three stories with decks stretching the length of the front on the second and third levels. A large window—a semicircle—filled the gable high above them. Through the window they could see the cathedral ceiling. Between the driveways, wide wooden steps led to the main entry on the second floor.

Everyone exited the vehicles, gathered at the foot of the steps and gazed upward.

"I wasn't expecting this," Byron said.

"It's beautiful," Chrissy said.

"I told you we'd be living in luxury for the next week," Elijah said. "This ain't a one-room cabin in the woods with an outhouse."

After grabbing suitcases, they ascended the steps. Dugan dropped his bags on the deck while Elijah fumbled with the digital key-card lock system. To Dugan's left hung a large, green hammock and beyond that, perched on the railing, a gray squirrel tilted its head as it chewed on an acorn.

"Check it out," Dugan said. "A crazy squirrel."

Everyone looked and laughed. The squirrel jumped from the rail, scurried beneath the hammock and appeared at their feet, standing on its hind legs.

Lila stepped back and gasped. "Will he bite?"

"Golly, no," Byron laughed. "Can't you see? He's begging, trying to mooch some food."

"Let's call him Moochy," Matt said.

The door swung open. "Voila," Elijah said. "These key cards actually work."

"Don't you boys let that squirrel in this house, you hear?" Lila said.

"Yes, Mom," the twins said.

"Sorry, Moochy," Dugan said.

Together they walked through the second floor dropping suitcases into the appointed bedrooms. Annie and Lila assigned Chrissy the smallest bedroom and the boys the larger one with the double bunks. Byron and Lila took the master bedroom on that floor. It had its own bathroom with a whirlpool tub.

Oak steps led to the third floor, a spacious area with vaulted ceilings, oak paneling and a stone fireplace. Light poured in from all sides through large windows. A sliding glass door opened onto an expansive deck lined with recliners, chairs and a gas grill. Loblolly pines extended their branches over the deck and had littered pinecones across the wooden boards. At the bottom of the door, his tiny hands pressed against the glass, sat Moochy the Squirrel. The boys laughed, rushed over and tapped on the glass.

"This must be the great room," Byron said.

"I've never seen anything like this," Lila said. "It truly is great. And look at the kitchen."

The kitchen, adorned with honey oak cabinets and an assortment of pans hanging from hooks above the sink, branched off from the great room with only a counter dividing the space. A large dining table surrounded by ten chairs occupied the end of the great room, and the door to the second master bedroom was located on the opposite side.

"Here's our bedroom," Elijah said as he swung the door open, revealing a huge four-poster bed. "Fit for a king, eh?"

Byron walked over and glanced in. "Elijah, I must hand it to you. This place is amazing,"

"I told you, good buddy, this vacation was divinely ordained," Elijah said.

"Uncle Elijah, Uncle Elijah." Dugan pestered.

Elijah's eyebrows knotted. "What is it Dugan?"

"Can we ride our bikes?"

Elijah eyed Byron and shrugged.

"I guess so," Byron said. "Just don't go very far."

"How do you get to the Whalehead Club?" Dugan asked.

"The Whalehead Club?" Byron said.

"An old hunting club built in the 1920's," Elijah explained. "Now it's a tourist attraction. We'll check it out later this week. It's a neat place—cork floors, Tiffany lights, old paintings—it's worth seeing."

"Sounds great. Why do you boys want to ride over there?" Byron asked.

"To see the ghost of the Carolina Strangler," Dugan said.

Mark and Matt laughed.

"Albert Douglas Mason." Elijah grinned. "I told them the story about a ghost who walks through the marshes and over the dunes this time of year."

"I see," Byron said. "How far is the place?"

"Not far," Elijah said. "Just a few blocks down the main road and to the left."

"Okay boys," Byron said. "You can check it out, but stay on the sidewalk and watch crossing the streets. Be back here in an hour, before it gets dark."

* * *

As Dugan pedaled down the sidewalk, the first thing he noticed was the redbrick lighthouse. The three boys slowed to a stop, straddled their bikes, and stared at the tower. The black cone top above the glass stood out against the blue sky. A steady breeze whipped through Dugan's red hair and fluttered his t-shirt.

"Awesome," Mark said. "It must be two hundred feet high."

"Got to be," Matt said. "So the ships can see it at night."

"How far's the ocean from here?" Dugan asked.

"Must be a few hundred yards that way," Matt said, pointing to the right side of the lighthouse. "See the sand dunes? The ocean's on the other side."

"Wow!" Dugan couldn't remember ever having this feeling before. Everything seemed strange and wonderful as if he had landed in Oz. He breathed deeply, and the salty air tingled his nose. Raising his hands, he shouted, "Yes!" and smiled at Matt and Mark.

The twins smiled back, whooped and hollered.

Maybe Mark and Matt were starting to like him. Wouldn't that be neat? A new world had opened before him with a red tower, beautiful homes, dunes, waves and ghosts. He hadn't felt this happy for a long time. Maybe life wasn't so bad after all.

"Look," Mark said. He pointed in the opposite direction, toward the Currituck Sound. Through the trees, the boys saw the large yellow building perched on the edge of the water, the sun flashing off its steep golden roof.

"The Whalehead Club!" Matt shouted.

"Let's go," Dugan commanded as he shoved forward, glided, lifted his feet and pedaled toward the access road just ahead.

The lane, newly paved and lined with small trees, curved through a wide, well-tended lawn to a bridge that crossed a small channel of water. When they reached the sign and information booth, they glided to a stop.

Matt read it aloud: "THE WHALEHEAD CLUB—Guided Tours daily—10: 00 A.M. to 5:00 P.M."

Mark glanced at his watch. "It's quarter after eight. Maybe we're not supposed to be on the property this late in the day."

"So what. No one's around," Dugan said. "You guys chicken?"

"No," they said at once.

"Let's go then." Dugan pushed forward and pedaled more tentatively as he crossed the bridge, Mark and Matt weaving behind.

They slowed to a stop in the parking lot in front of the Whalehead Club. The building consisted of three sections—a larger section in the middle with two matching ends. From their viewpoint, the most imposing part of the structure was the roof. It rose steeply to the ridge. The setting sun reflected off the shiny surface, and five large chimneys were evenly spaced along the top. In some places, a greenish coating had formed over the copper surface. Across the lower portion of the roof, nine yellow dormers divided up the space. Extending from each end were porches with thick posts supporting a flat roof.

"Don't look that scary to me," Dugan said.

"Nah," Mark said. "It's not run down at all like a haunted mansion."

"Practically new lookin'," Matt said.

Mark pointed to the roof. "I wonder what's splattered all around that center chimney? It looks like someone spilled a bucket of paint."

"I think it's . . . it's . . . bird crap," Dugan said.

"That'd be some humongous bird," Mark said.

Dugan pointed. "Look at what's comin' out of the chimney."

"Sticks," Matt said. "Big sticks."

"A bird couldn't lift limbs that size, could it?" Mark asked.

"Sure," Dugan said. "An eagle could. That's an eagle's nest on top of that chimney."

The twins looked at Dugan, then back to the chimney.

Mark gripped his handlebars. "I'd love to see the bird that built that nest."

"Me too," Matt said.

From behind, a raspy voice said, "You boys, there! What're you doing here?"

With his back and neck prickling, Dugan slowly turned to see a thin old man leaning on a cane. He was bald on top with white hair on the sides that lashed across his face in the steady wind. Wearing a loose black jacket and baggy pants, he wavered before them like a ghost, cane slightly shaking.

"Just lookin'," Mark said.

He took a step toward them. "Lookin' for what? Trouble?"

"No," Dugan said. "We're lookin' for the ghost of the Carolina Strangler."

The old man smiled, teeth yellow and gapped. Leaning on the cane, he said, "You won't find Albert Douglas Mason here. He walks the marshes." He turned, raising his cane, and pointed across a small pond toward the woods. "Yonder you'll find him."

"Thanks," Matt said. "We'll be goin' now."

The old man nodded, and as the boys pedaled away, he said, "Don't linger there after dark. You might get lost and fall into a quagmire."

The boys picked up speed, crossed the bridge and followed the road to where it narrowed by the woods. Here the asphalt stopped and a rutted gravel lane continued. Trees and high weeds overhung the lane with intermittent dirt paths veering off each side. After advancing several hundred yards, the boys slowed to a stop to investigate their surroundings. Dugan peered down one path. In the twilight, it looked like a tunnel, the trees and weeds forming the walls and ceiling.

"That guy back there was creepy," Mark said.

"At first, I thought he might be a ghost," Matt said.

"I bet he was the dishwasher Uncle Elijah told us about—the one that worked in the kitchen," Dugan said.

"What're we gonna do now?" Mark asked

"I've got a great idea," Dugan said. "Let's play bike catchers on these paths."

"Bike catchers?" Matt asked.

"Yeah," Dugan said. "It's just like regular tag 'cept ya ride your bikes."

"Not it," Mark said.

"Not it," Dugan repeated.

Matt slapped his leg. "Shoot. Guess I'm it."

"Close your eyes and count to twenty," Dugan ordered.

As Matt began counting, "One-thousand-one," Dugan shoved off and hightailed it down the road. After forty yards he made a skidding left turn onto a narrow, sandy path. The softer surface made progress more difficult, and occasional muddy spots challenged his steering skills. Ahead, he saw another path veering off to the left.

As he slowed to make the turn, he heard rambling noises in the weeds. His heart jumped, and he swerved around the turn, almost losing his balance. *Must be some kind of animal. Maybe a deer.* Up ahead he saw a wide puddle so he pedaled hard, sat and lifted his feet. The tires splashed through the water, and Dugan let out a "YeeeeeeeeHaaaaaaaa!" He coasted with a wide smile breaking across his face like a wave on the seashore. Turning onto another path, he thought about all the hours he'd spent at the Martins Ferry Library reading stories about the Hardy Boys and looking through detective books. *Now . . . Now I'm having my own adventure. And it's real. It's really real.*

He slowed to a stop and listened. A large fly buzzed around his ear, so he swatted at it several times. Two mosquitoes alighted on his forearm. *This place is full of bugs.* He slapped them, lifted his hand and saw blood smears. *Can't see far through these weeds. Wonder where Mark and Matt are?* Gazing down the path, he noticed the color had drained from everything, as if the sun had stole them when it disappeared below the horizon. In the half-light the trees and bushes quivered eerily in the steady breeze. Peering through the weeds, thirty yards ahead, he detected movement—something large.

"Mark, is that you?" he called.

The weeds shifted and rustled, the sound of feet tramping indecisively, changing directions. Whatever was out there was huge. Dugan blinked and imagined Albert Mason with his alligator belt. The rustling grew louder. Dugan sprang forward, pushing the bike and lifting his feet to the pedals. Energy rushed through his body as he pumped his legs, sprocket and chain churning the back tire through the sand. He sailed through another puddle, over a slight hump, and around a curve. Leaves and branches from the overhanging trees slapped his face, but he charged forward, picking up speed.

Twenty yards ahead, the path split. Dugan veered to the right but failed to notice the fallen branch across the path. The front tire hit the branch, and he somersaulted over the handlebars into the weeds, rolling several times. He lay face down, the tall weeds swallowing him.

As his breathing slowed, the first thing he noticed was an awful smell and a buzzing sound. To make sure nothing was broken, he moved his arms and legs and rolled onto his side. Sticking out of the weeds three inches away from his nose, the bottom of a bare foot startled him. Mud had dried on the ball and heel, but the ankle looked pale, almost gray. A fly alighted on the big toe and fidgeted. Up close the insect looked like a monster. Rising slowly, Dugan's eyes followed the leg to the torso of a girl wearing just under panties and a bra. Her head slanted to her shoulder. She glared at him with dull, wide eyes, mouth open as if she died mid-scream. A fly crawled out a nostril and joined the swarm above her face. Her neck was black and blue, and one arm looked out of whack, a broken bone threatening to break through the skin. Long brown hair, matted and tangled, trailed off into the weeds, a few strands crossing her face.

Despite the shock of the terrible scene, Dugan couldn't look away. He noticed her forehead—someone had taken a knife and carved a symbol, similar to the girl in the book at the Martins Ferry Library. *The Boone County Slasher? No. He's in jail. Could it be the Carolina Strangler?* Dugan's stomach cramped. He gagged and vomited.

When he caught his breath, he looked up to see the girl's blank stare. He took a step backward. Deep in the weeds, rustling noises exploded. *The killer's coming after me.* Backing out quickly, his foot caught on a root, tumbling him onto his rear. He turned over, scrambled to his feet, and rushed out of the weeds. Grabbing the bike's handlebars and lifting it to the road, he charged down the path and jumped onto the seat like a cowboy mounting a running horse.

Trying to remember the twists and turns, he made his best guesses. His stomach knotted and his heart pounded, but his legs kept pumping the pedals. Finally, the path emerged onto the dirt lane. Up ahead he could see Mark and Matt straddling their bikes in the middle of the road. As he neared, he shouted: "The Carolina Strangler! He's coming! Get out of here!" He sailed between them.

Darkness had rapidly descended, making it difficult to see large stones in the road. The front tire bumped over a baseball-sized one, almost tipping him over. At the end of the tunnel of overhanging trees, he could see the light of the opening where the asphalt road and the grounds of the Whalehead Club began. With all his strength, he pedaled toward the light.

Chapter Five

When he reached the asphalt road, he didn't slow down. Dugan had never been so afraid in his life. He had no doubt the murderer had made the rustling noises in the weeds. *Now he's after me. I found the crime scene—all the evidence the experts need to identify the victim and charge the killer.*

Dugan's lungs burned and leg muscles throbbed, but he wouldn't slow down until he reached the vacation house and Uncle Elijah. Then they could call the cops. Then he, Dugan James Walton, would show them all—he'd lead them to the body and help nab the killer.

To his great surprise, the first person Dugan saw as he neared the house was a policeman, a tall, broad-shouldered man with blue eyes and dark brown hair. He stood at the bottom of the steps talking to Chrissy. Dugan skidded to a stop in front of them.

"You look like you just saw a ghost, Cap'n." Chrissy said.

"I found a dead girl!" Dugan huffed, trying to catch his breath. "And the killer's after *me*."

"What're you talking about?" Chrissy asked.

"The Carolina Strangler is at it again. He chased me through the marsh but I was too fast for him. But this time it's not a ghost."

Chrissy tilted her head. "Huh?"

The policeman put his hands on his hips. The cop looked like Superman, his muscles rippling under his blue short sleeve shirt.

"He's talking about Albert Mason, the Carolina Strangler," the policeman said. "Did you see his ghost walking the marshes?"

Dugan nodded. "Man, am I glad you're here."

"Dugan, this is Deputy Queen," Chrissy said. "He patrols this area for the Sheriff's Department."

The deputy stuck out his hand to shake Dugan's, and as Dugan grasped it, he could sense the man's strength.

"How can I help you, Dugan?"

Just then, Matt and Mark pulled up on their bikes.

"Listen," Dugan said. "We were out on those paths playin' bike catchers. When I stopped to rest, I heard someone in the weeds. He was big, stumblin' around like a drunk man. It was hard to see through the bushes, but I heard him comin' after me with his alligator belt."

Laughter burst from Mark and Matt.

"I'm not kiddin', guys. I found a dead girl out in the marsh. She had bruises around her neck."

"You're nuts," Mark said. "It was only a ghost story, Dugan. The Carolina Strangler can't kill anyone. He's been dead a long time."

"Maybe so . . . but . . . but . . . I found a body." Dugan looked up at Deputy Queen. "Someone killed that girl and now he's after me."

Laughter exploded from Mark and Matt as they slapped each other on the back. Deputy Queen said, "Are you sure it was a person, Dugan? It might have been a dead animal."

"'Course it was a person. I know a person when I see a person."

The twins laughed again, and Deputy Queen shrugged, and his mouth twisted into a half-smile.

"You kill me, Dugan," Mark said. "Always tellin' stories. Don't you understand? Nobody believes a word you say."

"What's going on?" a voice thundered from above.

Everyone looked up to see Elijah standing at the top of the steps.

"I swear it's true," Dugan said.

"What's true?" Elijah asked.

Matt said, "Dugan claims the Carolina Strangler was chasin' him with his alligator belt. Then he found a dead girl that the Strangler killed out in the woods."

Elijah's lips tightened, and he shook his head. Dugan noticed his Uncle's face turning red like one of those oversized professional wrestlers—the hillbilly one—about to shout at the crowd.

Elijah held up his finger. "Dugan, what did I tell you about speaking the truth?"

"But, Uncle Elijah . . ."

"Quiet!" he commanded. "You don't have to make up stories so people will like you."

"I'm not makin' up stories."

"Shooshhh, boy. Quit talking and listen. You let your imagination run away from you, and it gets you into trouble." Elijah pointed to his temple. "You need to understand the difference between what you imagine and what's real. If you don't, people will never believe you."

Dugan's eyes watered and his throat tightened. He wanted to scream that he wasn't a liar. That a killer was on the loose. That a young girl was dead. That any one of them could be the next victim. But he couldn't. The lump in his throat had expanded to the size of an apple, and water had pooled in his eyes, threatening to break over the lids. Instead he gathered every ounce of willpower just to keep from crying like a baby.

Deputy Queen reached out and touched his shoulder. "Dugan, there's a lot of wildlife in these woods along the sound. You probably saw a dead deer—one that got hit by a car and wandered into the woods to die. And the noises you heard in the weeds—probably a horse. The northern shore of the Outer Banks is a wildlife preserve. Lots of wild horses roam through the woods and marshes."

Dugan's lower lip trembled. He looked at Deputy Queen and shook his head.

Queen knelt. "Now listen," he said more sternly. "Did you ever hear about the boy who cried *wolf?*"

Dugan nodded.

"Our department takes any report of a dead body very seriously. But if someone has cried *wolf* in the past, we won't waste our time investigating. There're more important jobs to do. Do you understand?"

A tear broke over the rim of his eyelid and trickled down his cheek. Dugan wiped it with the back of his hand. He blinked several times. Knowing he was about to bawl, he pulled away from the officer and charged up the steps. Elijah tried to reach out and stop him, but Dugan slipped under his grasp and darted into the house.

He ran into his bedroom, slammed the door behind him, leapt onto the bed and buried his head in the pillow. The release of the first sob ruptured the dam of tears, his lungs heaving. He reached over, grabbed the edge of the quilt, and wrapped it around his body. Turning and twisting, he twirled the covers and sheets around him like a cocoon and sunk into its darkness, leaving only a small hole at the top to breathe.

In the warmth, his cries slowed as he gathered his thoughts. *Things ain't any different here. Nothing has changed. No one likes me. Nobody believes a word I say.* He grasped his shoulders in a self-embrace and remembered Deputy Queen's touch and his words: *Did you ever hear about the boy who cried 'wolf?'* Dugan sniffled and swallowed. He took a deep breath and released it. *The boy who cried 'wolf.'*

Lifting his chin, he looked for the light of the opening of the blankets. *That's who everyone thinks I am: The boy who cried 'wolf.' Why do I* make things up? Why? I can't help it. Ever since Dad left I've been making up stories. Why did he leave? What did I do to him? Why doesn't he love me? He felt the lump forming again in his throat, but he swallowed it. No more. No more stories. I don't care if people like me or not. I can't be anybody but myself.

With his feet he pushed the twisted end of the blankets, sliding his body upward, toward the opening. But I did see the dead girl. I know I did. That's the truth. His head popped out of the hole, and he squinted against the light and took a deep breath of fresh air. Staring out the sliding glass door that opened onto a small side deck, he saw the gray squirrel on the rail.

"Moochy!"

The squirrel leapt to the deck and pressed its nose to the glass.

Dugan squirmed out of the blankets and grabbed his suitcase. He unsnapped it and pulled out a bag of Cheetos. Sliding the door open, he knelt, but the squirrel backed away. He ripped off the top of the Cheetos bag, and shook a couple into his hand. The squirrel leaned forward, nostrils expanding. Dugan extended his hand, and the squirrel inched closer. When the squirrel got to within reaching distance, it grabbed a Cheeto and scrambled across the deck to the top of the railing.

"You don't like me much either, do you, Moochy?" Dugan popped the remaining corn twist into his mouth. He looked across the yard at the vacation homes lining the street. In the faint light, he saw a boy and his father returning from the beach. The boy carried a body board, and the dad rested his hand on his son's bare shoulder.

"That was a blast, Dad. Those waves were awesome this evening. Are we gonna do it again tomorrow?" the boy said.

"Sure, Jimmy. Sure," the father said. "We'll hit the beach every day this week."

The father and son climbed the steps to their house and entered. Dugan felt like crying again, but then he sensed something small pressing on his knee. When he looked down, he saw Moochy, the critter's small paws barely touching him. Quickly Dugan scooped out another Cheeto and gave it to the squirrel. This time Moochy didn't flee. It sat next to Dugan and munched on the treat. After it gobbled the last bite, the squirrel reached out and touched Dugan's knee again. Dugan smiled and handed Moochy another corn twist.

* * *

"What a wonderful place," Lila said.

Byron squeezed her hand as they crossed the street. "Can you believe these houses?"

For the last twenty minutes they had been exploring the neighborhood, marveling at the elegant homes along the way. As they turned the corner they saw Chrisy and a policeman talking.

"Why's your daughter talking to a cop?" Byron asked.

"My daughter? I thought she was your daughter."

Byron grunted then said, "Either the boys already got into trouble or Chrissy already found a date."

"Trouble, I don't want. A date, I can handle," Lila said.

From thirty yards away, Chrissy and the policeman waved.

"He's a good-looking young fellow," Byron said as he waved back.

"Well built."

"Figured you'd notice that. Oh well, a cop is much better than a beach bum."

"Behave yourself," Lila said as she let go of his hand and elbowed his ribs. "Don't scare him off in the first two minutes."

"Mom, Dad, this is Deputy Queen," Chrissy said.

Queen stepped forward and extended his hand. "Call me Kenny."

"Good to meet you, Kenny," Byron said. Queen was about his height, six-feet-one or two inches tall. When they shook hands, Byron liked his strong grip and noticed his muscular arm. "You must pump some iron."

"Try to keep in shape," Queen said. "Not much happens in Corolla, but I want to be ready just in case." Queen nodded at Lila. "Nice to meet you, Ma'am."

Lila smiled and shook his hand.

"Was my daughter disturbing the peace?" Byron asked.

Queen laughed.

"Yeah, Dad," Chrissy said. "I tried to round up all the college kids in the neighborhood for a wild party, but I couldn't find any."

"I've got 'em all locked up in jail," Queen said. "All three of them."

"This is my kind of town," Byron said.

"Actually, I was just making my rounds. I saw Chrissy sitting on the steps so I stopped to say hi."

"Keep an eye on her," Byron said. "She can stir up some trouble."

Chrissy put her hands on her hips. "Me? What about Dugan?"

"What about Dugan?" Lila asked.

"He just came through here announcing a killer's on the loose."

Deputy Queen shook his head. "That boy's got some imagination."

"A killer?" Byron asked.

"Yeah," Chrissy said. "He told us a murderer was chasing him with an alligator belt."

"That's not all," Queen added. "According to Dugan, there's a body of a girl lying out there in the marsh somewhere."

Byron straightened, the image of the woman from his dream flashing in his mind. "A body?"

Queen smiled and nodded.

Byron looked up at the front door. Although Dugan's tendency to tell tales cast doubt on his credibility, Byron couldn't help wondering about the possibility. *A dead girl? Just a boy's runaway imagination? I've got to talk to Dugan. Find out whether or not . . .*

"Dad. Dad!" Chrissy's voice snapped Byron out of his thoughts.

When he looked at her, he noticed Deputy Queen's hand extended to him.

"It was nice meeting you, Mr. Butler," Queen said.

Byron shook his hand. "Likewise. It's good to know this area is secure."

"Hate to take off so soon, but I've got some more rounds to make. If there're any problems in the neighborhood this week, just call the sheriff's office. I'm at your disposal."

"We appreciate that, Kenny," Byron said. "But this place seems quite peaceful. I don't anticipate any trouble."

"We like to keep it that way," Queen said. "Chrissy, I'll see you bright and early tomorrow morning."

Chrissy smiled. "Hope you can keep up."

"Don't worry. I'm in pretty good shape." The officer waved and walked away.

"Nice young man," Byron said.

"Pretty good looking, huh?" Lila asked.

"He's okay," Chrissy said. "We'll see how tough he is. Tomorrow morning I'm taking him on a six-mile run along the beach. If he can keep up, I might let him take me to dinner."

"You're all heart," Byron said.

"I try to keep high standards, Dad. You know how it is."

* * *

Byron entered the house and went straight to Dugan's room. He knocked and listened.

"Who is it?" Dugan asked.

"Byron. Can I come in?"

"I guess."

Byron opened the door and noticed the rims of the boy's eyes were red, and remnant channels of tears lined his face. Dugan sat on his bed, the covers twirled in a heap at his feet and an empty *Cheetos* bag lying beside him.

"Are you all right, Dugan?"

He took a deep breath. "I'm okay."

"Chrissy told me about . . . you know . . . about the body."

Dugan looked up. "Do you think I'm a liar too?"

"No son, not at all. That's why I came to talk to you." Byron moved the covers and sat on the end of the bed. He reached over, gripped Dugan's ankle and smiled. "Tell me what happened."

"Mr. Butler, I know I make up stories sometimes, but I swear I saw that dead girl. It was terrible. Someone strangled her and dumped her in the marsh."

"How do you know she'd been strangled?"

Dugan raised his hands to his throat. "She had black and blue marks on her neck and her mouth was wide open like she was trying to breathe but couldn't. I'm positive she was dead. The smell was terrible and flies buzzed all around her. I'll never forget her face."

"Was she blonde?"

"No," Dugan said. "She had long brown hair. It was all tangled."

Byron knew the boy had seen something, but it wasn't the blonde girl from his dream. "It's dark now, but tomorrow morning, first thing, you can lead me to the body."

"Really?"

"I believe you saw something out there, Dugan. You wouldn't be afraid to return to the scene of the crime, would you?"

"No sir. I'm not afraid. I want to be an investigator just like my father."

"Like your father?" Byron asked.

Dugan lowered his eyes and shook his head. "I'm sorry. There I go making up stories again. My dad ain't a detective. He's just a used car salesman in Bridgeport. I hardly ever see him anymore."

Byron patted Dugan's knee. "I know how you feel."

Dugan glanced up.

"I never saw my dad when I was a kid either," Byron said.

"Why not?"

"He didn't want to claim that I was his son. Kids made fun of me all the time and called me nasty names."

"Why'd they do that?"

"Not having a father made me different. So I tried to prove that I was just as good as anyone else. In grade school I got into a lot of fights."

Dugan nodded. "Kids pick on me all the time."

"Hang in there, buddy. Just because your dad's not there for you doesn't mean you're not as good as the next kid. In fact, tough circumstances can help you become a stronger person. In high school I became a distance runner. I set a goal to become the best runner in the state."

"Did you?"

"Yes I did. In 1982 I won the state high school cross country championship. Those kids who used to make fun of me came up and congratulated me."

"I want to be an FBI agent one day," Dugan said.

"Make it a goal. If you believe in yourself and work hard, one day I'll be calling you Agent Walton."

Dugan smiled. "Even if I become famous, you can still call me Dugan."

"Tomorrow morning, you and I will become partners on your first investigation." Byron stuck out his hand. Dugan grasped it and shook vigorously.

Chapter Six

Byron crawled into the king size bed, exhausted. Facing him, Lila slept peacefully. The packing, long drive, unpacking and exploration of new surroundings had worn them out. When his head hit the pillow, he expected to drift off quickly into slumber land. The bed felt comfortable and spacious—too big, really. Compared to their bed at home, this one seemed immense. Byron was used to his wife's nearness at night. She loved the security and warmth of his body next to hers. The space between them made him feel isolated.

As he lay staring at the ceiling, he thought about the first night in the hospital. Dr. Godfrey had removed his appendix about four in the afternoon. He tried to fall asleep early that evening, but the painkillers had worn off and his gut felt like it was splitting open every time he moved. Finally he pressed the button to summon the nurse. When she entered the room, he informed her he needed something for the discomfort and something to help him sleep. Within three minutes she returned and injected the anti-pain potion directly into his I.V. Within seconds Byron felt the effects of the medicine. His vision twirled, and his muscles tingled. The tension in his back and stomach eased and then fully slackened. He turned into Jell-O. He glanced at the door and saw the nurse exit into the glow of the hallway. The room gently spun, and he closed his eyes. The anxiety faded along with the agony in his abdomen. His head sunk into the pillow, and within a minute or two he fell asleep.

About midnight the urge to urinate awakened him. *Just a few more minutes. Don't want to get up yet.* He tried to relax and ignore the pressure on his bladder, but it was too intense. When he opened his eyes the hospital room seemed foggy. *It's cold in here.* He looked through the blur to the mirror above the sink and noticed an odd glow in the reflection. When he sat up, he felt no pain. He unplugged the I.V. monitor and towed it toward the bathroom. Before entering, he inspected the mirror. The light falling in from the half-open door sent deep shadows across his face. His premature gray hair and white mustache made him look older than his forty-six years. Because he had left his glasses on the over-bed table, he had to lean closer to see his pale complexion and bags under his eyes. He noticed how gaunt his face had become from running seven miles a day. *Is this what happens to you when you get old? My hair's gray, my cheeks are hollow, I'm gaining wrinkles and losing body parts.*

When he leaned back from the mirror, his features transformed. His hair became darker and face fuller. *What in heaven's name? Must be the lighting. That's not me.* He squinted, and the tanned stranger in the mirror became clearer—a young man with intense eyes. Byron's heartbeat accelerated, arms and legs tingling. *I must be dreaming.*

The man reached through the mirror and picked up a coin sitting on the counter

He raised it to his mouth and placed it between his teeth. Byron squinted to clear his vision. The stranger bit the coin and snapped it away from his mouth. He handed it through the surface of the mirror to Byron. A large chunk had been bitten from the coin. The stranger held out his hand and said, "Give it back."

Trembling, Byron handed him the coin. The man held it near his mouth and blew a quick burst of foggy breath. The mist dissipated, and the coin was whole again. He dropped it onto the reflected counter, and it rolled through the surface of the mirror and settled near the sink.

Byron backed away and the man disappeared. *I'm dreaming. I'm dreaming. Wake up. Open your eyes.* His eyelids felt as if they had been glued shut. He breathed rapidly, his pulse racing.

He opened his eyes and blinked. *No fog. I'm in my bed.* Looking around the room, he inspected the dark corners and glanced at the mirror. Now he really had to get to the bathroom quickly. As he sat up, the pain stabbed deeply into his stomach. He struggled to his feet and unplugged the I.V. monitor from the outlet. Rushing to the bathroom, he remembered the face of the stranger in the mirror. As he passed the sink, he stopped and stared at his reflection. His gray hair was disheveled, and a light coating of silver whiskers covered his jowls. He rubbed his cheeks and chin, feeling the stubble. *Just a dream. I'm the only one in the mirror.* He turned to enter the bathroom. But as his shadow moved past the counter, a glint caught his eye. At the edge of the sink lay a quarter.

* * *

The memory of the strange dream caused adrenaline to surge through him. Sweat trickled down his ribcage. He shook off the odd sensation and rolled over. His shifting disturbed Lila, so she turned to face the wall. He scooted closer, sliding into the curve of her back, draping his arm across her side and belly. She murmured indistinguishable words and placed her hand over his. Feeling the rise and fall of her breathing and the warmth of her body, his thoughts settled, and he soon fell asleep.

* * *

When he awakened, he looked at the digital alarm clock on the nightstand: 5:00 A.M. Although the room was dark, he saw his surroundings with clarity, surprised to be so lucid, so edgy at such an early hour. Knowing he couldn't fall back asleep, he slipped out of bed and walked to the window. Night still shrouded the world outside, but from the east, pale light crept skyward.

Byron climbed to the third floor and entered the kitchen. Guessing the sun would not rise for another hour, he made a pot of coffee and opened a box of glazed doughnuts. With a doughnut balanced on the rim of his cup, he managed to slide the glass door open and step onto the deck. From there, leaning on the rail, he could see the horizon, the Atlantic Ocean, a dark grayish-green met by the charcoal-gray sky giving way to dawn. Byron sipped the coffee, and its warmth coated his insides. The slight breeze against his face and the expanse of ocean and sky divided by a horizontal line, a line drawn by God, calmed his nerves. He stood, looking at the horizon, eating his doughnut and drinking coffee. *I'm here—at the edge of this continent, looking at heaven and earth. Is this where I'm supposed to be, God? Why here?*

Behind him, he heard the glass door sliding.

"Good morning," Dugan said, rubbing his eyes.

"I thought I'd have to wake you up."

Dugan walked to the rail and gazed at the horizon. "No sir. I didn't sleep too good. Kept having dreams 'bout that dead girl. I kept seeing her face in my mind."

"Did that frighten you?"

"A little. But something else bothered me too. It's not right—her laying out there in those weeds all night. I feel terrible 'bout it."

"Why does that make you feel so bad?"

"Cause I'm the one who knows she's there. It's my fault nobody believes me. If I hadn't told so many lies, Deputy Queen would have followed me to the body. Instead he told me about the boy who cried *wolf.*"

Byron reached out and cupped Dugan's shoulder. "Don't feel bad about that. You've gone through some tough times lately. Let me get you a big bowl of Cocoa Puffs and a glass of orange juice. By the time you finish your breakfast, the sun will be peeking over the horizon. Then you and I will look for that body."

Dugan looked up at Byron and smiled, and Byron rubbed the top of his head.

*   *   *

They walked briskly in the gray dawn. When they passed the Whalehead Club, Byron stopped and eyed the expansive lawn and small lake fed by an inlet from the sound. An eerie sense of déjà vu swept over him. Thin fog rose from the grass and water, combining with the weak light to produce a wavering effect of the building's appearance. A chill rose from his stomach, into his chest, needling out through the hairs on his head. *My imagination—it's worse than a kid's. I must have seen that building in a photograph somewhere.* When he turned away, he saw Dugan ten steps ahead of him.

"It's this way," Dugan said, pointing to where the asphalt road split the woods.

Byron noted the lay of the land. He saw the overhanging trees where the gravel lane began, the dark tunnel into the marsh. As they walked on, he couldn't help glancing over his shoulder at the Whalehead Club.

Through the maze of paths, Byron followed the boy. The sun had risen, and looking up, Byron saw flecks of blue through the leaves and branches. Birds tweeted and chirped around them, a discordant commencement of sound.

Rounding the next turn, Dugan stopped and pointed. "It's right ahead, deep in the weeds. Can you smell it?"

Byron whiffed the air, recoiling at the odor of death.

Dugan's body became rigid. "Pastor Butler, I don't want to go any farther."

"That's okay, Dugan. I'll go look. Right ahead of us?"

He pointed again. "Yeah. Can you see all the flies buzzin' above the weeds? Right there."

Byron advanced cautiously. As he entered the weeds, the smell intensified, nauseating him. The flies swirled in a frenzied cloud ten feet beyond.

Chapter Seven

"Did you make him look?" Elijah asked. He sat at the head of the table at the far end of the great room. Facing each other, Lila and Byron sat next to him.

"Yes," Byron said. "He had to see it for himself."

"Hmmmph," Elijah scooped up a forkful of scrambled eggs. "Best thing to do. He needs to confront reality. Until he learns what's real and what's not, no one will trust him."

Byron shook his head. "I'll never forget the shock on his face when he saw the dead deer. His mouth dropped open, and his eyes . . . his eyes filled with confusion. I honestly think he expected to see a girl's body. He looked like a kid who just got hit in the face with the cold water of life. I tried to encourage him, but he didn't say a word all the way home."

"He's an odd kid," Elijah said.

Annie lowered a large plate stacked with pancakes onto the table. "He's not an odd kid. When life deals you a rotten hand, you either fold or play it out. Dugan's trying to play it out the best he knows how. He's not a quitter. At least, not yet anyway."

Elijah plunged his fork into the top four flapjacks, lifted and dumped them onto his plate. "Yeah, but no matter how bad the cards might be, I don't consider lying a proper strategy."

"Can't you understand?" Annie said. "It's his defense mechanism. When a father rejects his own son, it can shatter a kid's self-image. Makes him feel like a nobody. He wants to feel loved and respected—he wants to be somebody."

Byron nodded and noticed Lila glancing at him.

"Would anyone like a refill on coffee?" Lila asked as she scooted her chair out.

Elijah and Byron raised their cups.

"The boy needs discipline," Elijah muttered.

Byron shook his head. "I don't know. I tend to agree with Annie. All kids need discipline, but at this point in his life, Dugan needs support and encouragement to hang in there."

Elijah shrugged as he flooded his pancakes with syrup. "Maybe. But discipline couldn't hurt."

Lila approached the table with the carafe of coffee, and as she filled the men's cups, she said, "I told the twins not to accuse Dugan of lying again. They need to learn some compassion in situations like this."

"They were wrong to accuse him of lying," Byron said. "I won't stand for that. They should never call someone a liar unless they have proof. I'll have a talk with Mark and Matt."

"But he was lying," Elijah said.

"Who's to say? The twins didn't know that for sure. It's possible Dugan really believed he saw a body. At first I thought it was a dead girl until I got closer. The weeds made it difficult to see clearly."

"I guess I should give Dugan the benefit of the doubt," Elijah said.

"Shhhhsssh." Annie whispered, "Someone's coming up the steps."

The four adults turned to see Chrissy, clad in a Nike tank top and pink running shorts, spring to the top of the stairs. Her ponytail bobbed as she wiped her forehead with the back of her hand. Sweat flowed profusely from every pour of her body.

"What?" she asked. "Did I interrupt something? Must have been talking about me." She put her hands on her hips.

"No dear, not you," Lila said.

"I asked Dugan to lead me to the dead body this morning," Byron said.

"Did you find it?"

"Yes."

Leaning forward, Chrissy planted her hands on her knees, eyes wide. "Really?"

Byron nodded. "We found a dead deer."

"Poor Dugan," Chrissy sighed. "Wait till Mark and Matt find out. They won't show any mercy."

"They better," Byron said. "Or they'll suffer the wrath of their father."

Chrissy straightened. "Don't worry. Dugan's my little buddy. I won't let 'em pick on him."

"By the way," Lila said. "Did Deputy Queen pass your test?"

"Yeah," Byron chirped. "Did you show him any mercy on that six mile run?"

Chrissy smiled. "Didn't have to. He's in better shape than me. We ran three miles up the beach and back. He barely broke a sweat."

"Does that mean he qualifies for as a potential dinner date?" Byron asked.

Chrissy raised her eyebrows. "It certainly improves his chances. Besides that, he's got a nice tush."

"Chrissy," Lila gasped.

"Come on, Mom. You know he's good looking."

"That's true, but that doesn't compel me to comment on a man's rear end in mixed company."

"What else do you know about this fellow besides the fact that he's got a nice butt?" Byron asked.

"Well . . . for one thing, he was a state champion wrestler." Chrissy said.

Byron raised his eyebrows. "Very impressive."

"And the Sheriff's Department named him Officer of the Month in May. He seems pretty intelligent."

Annie winked at Lila and said, "A body and a mind."

"Of course, I'm not impressed with just looks and brains," Chrissy said.

Byron laughed. "Of course." He eyed Chissy, thinking how much she's matured in the last year. No longer Daddy's little girl.

Lila reached and grasped Byron's wrist. "You're looking for someone with depth of soul, like your father."

Chrissy walked over and hugged Byron around the neck. "That's right, Mom. Just like dear ol' Dad."

"Hey," Byron said. "You're getting sweat all over me."

Elijah looked up from his empty plate. "Any more pancakes?"

*   *   *

That afternoon the July sun blazed the neighborhood, baking the asphalt roads and shimmering the sea grasses that sprouted in generous patches across the dunes. The two families walked a couple hundred yards to the beach, lugging folding chairs, beach bags and a large yellow umbrella. The boys carried body boards they had found in the storage room of the vacation house. Cutting through a gap between two sand hills, they crossed the wide stretch of almond sand to where the terrain angled gently to the waves. Here, Byron and Elijah planted the umbrella, the women spread blankets, and the boys charged into the surf.

"Don't go out too far! You hear me?" Lila yelled.

"Relax, Hon," Byron said. "Elijah and I will get out there with them."

Elijah removed his denim fisherman's hat and rubbed his bald head. A grin spread the thick tufts of his salt and pepper beard. "Aarrr, matey. Last one in is a lowlife land lubber!" he said as he sprung toward the waves.

With a head start, Elijah beat Byron to the water, high-stepping the first wave and plowing headfirst into the next. The boys laughed, and Byron turned just as the wave slapped his back, jolting him forward. Twenty-five feet beyond the churning water, Elijah surfaced like a white whale and stood waist-deep, squirting water out his mouth.

"Shiver me timbers, me boys!" he shouted as he grasped his elbows. "'Tis a col' sea on such a hot day!" He turned to see a large wave mounting, ready to break. With perfect timing, he leapt, planting his chest on the crown with his arms spread. The wave lifted the big man, bearing him to shore.

To Byron, Elijah looked like Poseidon, triumphantly riding the crest. He almost expected to see dolphins skimming the water at his sides. But then as Elijah closed in on them, the wave broke violently against the shore, plummeting and tumbling him into the sand. When he turned over and sat up, another wave crashed on top of him. The boys whooped with laughter.

"You okay?" Byron asked.

Elijah managed to stand and steady himself. A string of seaweed draped across his face and down his shoulder. He stripped it away and flung it into the surf. His eyes grew large as he hitched up his bathing suit. "Me thinks me shorts is full of sand. Oh well, me mateys, thus is the hazards of body surfing!"

Then he charged back into the sea and dove into the next wave. The boys and Byron followed, Matt, Mark and Dugan tugging their body boards behind them.

For thirty minutes Byron and Elijah frolicked in the waves with the kids. Byron hadn't felt such pure joy for years. It didn't take long for the boys to master the art of body board surfing. Again and again they cruised into shore on the Styrofoam wedges, sometimes crashing with the waves onto the beach, but always struggling to their feet for another round.

Finally Byron and Elijah trudged through the surf and across the sand to where the ladies relaxed on the blankets. Lila sat on a short-legged beach chair under the umbrella, reading a romance novel. White sun block coated her nose. Soaking up rays, Annie and Chrissy lay on their stomachs on a large blue-and-white striped quilt. The men flicked water droplets off their arms and legs onto the women.

"That's cold! Quit it!" Annie commanded as Chrissy giggled.

"Hey Stilts," Byron said. "Which direction did you and Deputy Queen run this morning?"

Chrissy, wearing a white bikini turned over and sat up. She leaned forward and pointed to her left. "That way."

Byron hesitated, thinking his daughter should be wearing something more modest. But he shook off his urge to reprimand and asked, "How's the terrain in that direction?"

"Beautiful. 'Bout a mile from here, the wildlife preserve begins. Just dunes, beach and ocean. No roads and very few people. Kenny said if you have a four-wheel-drive vehicle, you can drive clear to Virginia along the beach."

"Sounds good. Think I'm gonna go for a run."

"You'll love it. Guess what we found about two miles from here?"

"An old pirate ship?"

"No. A dead sea turtle. It smelled, but it was huge."

"That's my goal then: to the dead sea turtle and back."

"Go for it, Dad."

Lila lowered her book and peered over her sunglasses. "You better be careful, Byron. You know you just got out of the hospital four weeks ago."

"Don't worry. Doctor Godfrey said I could exercise just as long as I don't overdo it."

"Four miles on a hot day is overdoing it."

Byron bent and touched his toes. "Four miles is nothing. In high school I could run fifteen miles a day."

"You're not in high school any more."

* * *

Byron tied up his Sauconys and headed north. Because the tide was receding, he had plenty of firm wet sand to provide a stable running surface. For the first mile he had to keep his eye out for kids and beachcombers, weaving in and out to avoid collision. As he neared the wildlife preserve, the crowd thinned, allowing him solitude to more acutely sense his surroundings. The sun blazed down, but he loved the feeling of exertion in the heat, breathing hard, sweating. The steady breeze helped to cool him, filling his nostrils with the bite of salty air and sea life. The steady rhythm of waves created natural music, a soothing melody accompanied by random cries of gulls. Byron watched the communion of sea and sand before him—the way the water rushed up the slope after the waves collapsed against the shore. He strove to run along the edge where the sea foam settled after the water drained into the sand. Occasionally, he misjudged and splashed through shallows of back-rushing tide.

Looking ahead, he noticed large posts rising from the water, extending across the beach and over the dunes. Several thick cables drooped from post to post creating an unusual fence. As he neared, he figured he would have to climb through one of the bigger gaps in the cables, but then he saw a vertical opening to the left, just big enough for a man to angle through. *This must be the beginning of the wildlife preserve.* He emerged from the tightly positioned poles, scanned the beach on the other side of the posts, and saw no one. He estimated his view of the coastline to be more than two miles and the vastness excited him. Through the soft sand, he cut back to the shoreline and picked up his pace. *One more mile before I turn back.*

The sense of adventure overwhelmed him, and he felt adrenaline rejuvenating his muscles. Looking east to the flat line of sky and sea, he thought about the Creator and creation. *I'm the first man. I'm Adam exploring a new paradise. I'm free. For a precious few minutes, no worries to bind me, no responsibilities to find me. I'm romping along the seashore on the edge of Eden.* Fifty yards out to sea, flashes of reflected sunlight caught his eye. He slowed his pace and looked. A school of dolphins, in perfect synchronization, leapt out of the choppy water, gracefully arcing, plunging and leaping again.

"I name you dolphins!" he shouted. "You will be the Oracles of the Sea—the Prophets of the Ocean!"

As he increased his gait, he noticed the dolphins keeping pace, their parallel path sparkling with flashes of sunlight against wet-slick bodies.

"Come along, my friends, for I am a prophet too. The Lord has given me dark dreams. We will journey together!" he yelled.

With every step his exhilaration increased. A flock of black pelicans approached from the north, gently gliding in single file barely above the ocean's surface.

"Aha!" he shouted. "I call you pelicans! You will be the Fishers of the Sea!"

With a tilt of beak and wings, the leader rose gently, and the six followers kept formation as if tethered by an invisible line. The first pelican dipped, almost touching the water's surface, and the line of birds slanted and leveled. As they passed, the wonder of it all awed Byron—the endless horizon, the fish and fowl, the water lapping at his feet. Suddenly he felt one with all creation, a sense of connectedness to the Eternal. Running faster, not feeling his feet touch the ground, he seemed to float just above the up-rushing water and sand. He kept this pace for two-hundred yards, but then his legs grew heavy and slowed as his breathing accelerated. Looking up, he saw a black lump in the middle of the beach one hundred yards away. *The dead sea turtle.*

To get to the turtle, he had to cross the dry sand. It hampered his progress, clinging to his shoes like hands grasping at his feet. When Byron reached the carcass, he leaned on his knees, heaving to catch his breath. The smell sickened him, so he pinched his nose, half-covering his mouth. The flies had consumed the fins, head and tail, leaving a three-foot black-green shell. They flew in and out of the six apertures, infesting the insides with maggots.

Byron backed away. He looked into the cloudless sky, sweat pouring down his face, stinging his eyes. *This run has been too wonderful to spoil with the sight of this.* With his fingers, he wiped his eyes and squeegeed his forehead. Staring into the blue emptiness, Byron suddenly felt alone and vulnerable. He turned away from the turtle and stumbled through the soft sand. Once he found good footing, he ran, slowly at first, but increasing the speed slightly every few hundred yards. The energy and exuberance he possessed during the first half of the run had left him. Now, to maintain pace, he called on his will and his ability to battle pain.

As he approached the cable-strung posts, he looked to the top of the dunes and saw something amazing: three wild horses, a black stallion and two mares, one brown and one white, scampered down the steep side, kicking up sand and tossing their heads. Byron stopped immediately and watched. *Must be the Spanish Mustangs I read about—the descendants of shipwrecked survivors that swam to shore four hundred years ago. Incredible.* Eighty yards in front of him, they crossed the beach, the black stallion leading the way. When they reached the surf, they galloped along the waterline toward him, slowing now and then to splash and play in the shallows where a sandbar stifled the waves and formed a small lake.

Byron's whole body tingled. The horses had approached to within thirty yards and didn't seem to notice him. The black stallion stepped out of the water and walked directly toward him, stopping five feet away. Byron stood perfectly still. The horse snorted and waved his head toward the dunes. Still standing in the foot-deep water, the two mares looked up. The stallion waved its head again, as if it were commanding Byron to look in that direction. When he looked, he saw the top of the Currituck Lighthouse about three-quarters of a mile away, barely visible above the beach houses that lined the tops of the dunes.

The stallion snorted, whinnied, and rose up on its hind legs. Byron backed away, tripped over a piece of driftwood, and fell on his rump. Quickly, he turned over and jumped to his feet. The horse, now standing on all fours, waved its head again. Byron cautiously circled around the animal, turned slowly, and began to jog toward the posts. When he glanced over his shoulder, he saw the black shape walking toward him. He picked up his pace, but now he could hear the cupping of the horse's hoofs against the firm sand as it broke into a trot. Instantly, Byron's jog turned into an all-out sprint. He saw the small opening in the cable-post fence about forty yards away. The sound of the horse's hooves bore down on him. He cut across the soft sand, and the horse caught him, its nose bumping his shoulder. But with the posts looming, the stallion cut away, and Byron slipped through the narrow gap.

On the other side of the fence, Byron stood rubbing his shoulder, breathing hard. The stallion faced him, glaring through the cables, and waved its head again toward the lighthouse.

"What?" Byron said. "What do you want from me?"

The horse snorted, turned, and walked away.

For the last mile of his run, Byron couldn't keep from staring at the beacon of the lighthouse and wondering, *Lord, what are you trying to tell me?*

Chapter Eight

Byron spent the rest of the day at the vacation house in a contemplative mood. Several times Lila became annoyed because she had to repeat simple questions to him. He couldn't focus on the interactions around him. Instead, his mind stewed with images of a black stallion, the terror-stricken face of the girl in his dream, a dead deer in the marsh where a body should have been, and the beacon of the Currituck Lighthouse. After dinner he decided to take a walk through the neighborhood to the resort shops.

The shops, like the vacation homes, stood on large posts, their weathered siding stained gray. Wooden ornamentation garnished the apexes of the gables, and white trim bordered the windows. Instead of sidewalks, shoppers crossed planked walkways that wrapped around, intersected, and connected each shop. On the directory sign in the parking lot, Byron counted three clothing stores, two restaurants, two gift shops, a bakery and a rental store offering bicycles, videos, kayaks, fishing equipment and surfboards. Craving chocolate, he traversed the network of walkways to the shops in the rear and found the bakery.

A robust man with curly black hair and a bushy mustache stood behind the glass case, arms spread, hands flat on the top of the counter. The delightful smell of baked goods lifted Byron's head as he inhaled deeply.

The man raised his hands in a sweeping gesture. "What can I do for you theeze fine evening?" he asked with a Greek accent.

Byron scanned the shelves of pies, breads and sweets. He saw baklava and some strange spinach pastry but zeroed in on the doughnut section. "That's exactly what I want," he said as he pointed. "A dozen chocolate covered doughnuts."

"Theeze are on a good special," the man said. "Half price. Can't beat that."

"Not stale, are they?"

He held up his hands and shook his head. "No, no, no no." His jowls flapped like a bloodhound's. "Day old. That ees all."

"I'll take 'em."

The baker dipped his head. "You will not regret." He snatched a bag and square of wax paper to extract the doughnuts from the tray. "May I ask where you leeve?"

"What?"

"Leeve. Where from?"

"Where I live? Oh yes. I'm from Ohio."

"Ohio? Eets a boring place. I've been to Dayton. All flat and no ocean. You like to feesh?"

"Fish? Fishing's okay."

"I love to feesh." He set the box on the counter and extended his hands. "Caught a three foot shark off shore yeesterday. Lot's of leettle sharks in these waters."

"Really?"

His eyes widened as he picked up the box and wax paper again. "Oh yes."

While Byron waited, the Greek baker aligned the doughnuts in the box and talked about his latest 'feeshing' adventure. Byron glanced around the shop and saw a display rack holding a stack of newspapers. He grabbed the top one. The headline startled him: NAGS HEAD WOMAN FOUND DEAD.

"Add this to my total," he said, holding up the paper.

"Certainly, sir," the Greek said as he punched numbers into the cash register.

With the box of doughnuts tucked under his arm, Byron exited the store but stopped at the closest rail to lean and read the article. Two sentences in, he knew the story offered no clues to the puzzle that lingered in his mind. Relatives visiting from Tennessee had found a sixty-five-year-old woman dead on the kitchen floor of her beach home at Nags Head. She had lain there for a week, apparently succumbing to a massive heart attack. Making a surprise visit, her youngest sister's family spied her through the kitchen window and managed to disengage the lock on the back door. Officials still awaited the autopsy report but noted that a history of heart disease and no signs of forced entry ruled out foul play. *This doesn't help. Lord, you've got to give me some clue. Something to guide me. I need to know what's going on.*

Byron popped open the box of doughnuts, and choosing one with ample chocolate icing, he lifted it with thumb and forefinger. The pleasure of the taste rippled through him, easing the anxiety that had strained his body and spirit. Before he reached the end of the maze of walkways, he had gobbled the pastry.

Once he cleared the shadows of the resort shops, he looked over his shoulder. The Currituck Lighthouse loomed above the trees. He turned and raised his left hand to his temple, shielding the sun, which hovered above the far shore of the sound. *Tomorrow I will climb to the top of that lighthouse. There must be something up there the Lord wants me to see.* With that intention declared and another doughnut in hand, he ambled away, sensing the tension slowly drain out of him with every bite.

By the time Byron climbed the front steps of the vacation home he had consumed four doughnuts. He saw Elijah slumped in the hammock suspended between two posts of the second floor deck, slowly swinging.

"Here," Byron said, plopping the box on top of Elijah's stomach. "Take these before my arteries clog up and my heart explodes."

Elijah grasped the box and tilted it to see the contents through the cellophane window. "Mmmmmm. Chocolate covered doughnuts. How many did you eat?"

"Too many."

"I can see the headlines now: PRESBYTERIAN MINISTER DIES OF DOUGHNUT OVERDOSE."

"Yeah. Another one of those religious scandals—done in by my fleshly lusts. Speaking of headlines, you can have this too." Byron tossed the newspaper, and it landed on Elijah's chest.

"Thanks, Byron," Elijah said. "I can use this to cover my eyes while I catch forty winks."

Byron leaned against the post. "Elijah, didn't you tell me that lighthouse down the road is open to the public?"

"Sure. For six bucks they'll let you climb clear to the top."

Byron nodded and stared at his feet. "First thing tomorrow, I'd like to head over there."

"Sounds good to me. Wonderful view from up there. Bring the families along?"

"Not necessarily. If they want to go, that's fine, but if they don't, I want to go anyway."

Elijah clasped his hands behind his head and rose up slightly. "Why?"

Byron walked to the door and opened it. "Something I need to see from up there. That's all." He turned to enter the house.

"Hey, good buddy, wait a minute."

He paused, holding the door open. "What?"

"The kids want us to take them on a late night beach walk. I told them I'd check with you first."

Byron patted his stomach. "After all those calories, a beach walk sounds like the perfect prescription."

"We'll wait till it gets good and dark, and the ghost crabs come out." Elijah said, chuckling.

"Just what we need," Byron said. "More ghosts."

* * *

About ten o'clock that evening, Dugan reminded Elijah and Byron about the beach walk. Byron instructed him to round up everyone and wait on the front deck. When the two men stepped out the door, a gaggle of kids greeted them. Byron shined his flashlight across their faces, half of them unfamiliar.

"Howdy," a toe-headed boy with wire-rimmed glasses said. His smile widened, revealing a gap between his top two front teeth.

"Do I know you?" Byron asked.

"These are our new friends," Dugan said. "Jimmy Washburn and his sister, Janey. They're from next door. Aunt Annie and Jimmy's mom went for a walk together today. Their folks said it was okay to go with us."

Janey, six inches taller than Jimmy, had copper hair and big golden eyes, like an owl.

"I'm Leroy Tubbs," another boy said. "I'm from across the street. My daddy said I could go too." Chubby, with a shaved head, he reminded Byron of the *Nancy* comic strip character, Sluggo.

"Okay," Byron said. "That makes six kids, two old guys and one ..."

"Goofy teenager?" Elijah suggested.

"Young adult," Chrissy corrected.

Byron slapped his daughter on the back. "That's just what I was going to say, Stilts."

"Right, Dad."

"I'm surprised you want to go with us. Figured Deputy Queen would be stopping by again," Byron said as he elbowed Elijah.

In comedic falsetto, Elijah blurted, "Oh, Deputy Queen, you're so strong and handsome. Can I squeeze your bicep?"

Laughter erupted from the six children.

Chrissy slugged Elijah's shoulder. "Very funny. Just remember. It's dark out tonight, and you never know what a goofy teenager will do."

"Ooooooh! I'm scared." Elijah trembled his hands and wobbled his head. "Shakin' in my shoes."

"Come on, Dad," Mark said. "Let's go! I want to see what the beach looks like at night!"

The kids echoed shouts of agreement.

"Everybody gather 'round me," Byron said. "You kids got to promise to stay right with me and Elijah. We don't want to lose anybody tonight. You got it?" He shined the flashlight around the circle of nodding faces. "Okay. Let's go."

Elijah and Byron followed that morning's route to the beach, walking a block south and two blocks east to the gap between two sand hills. In a star-spattered sky, the moon hung over the horizon, waxing as if swollen on the right side. It cast a silvery sheen on the sea grass and sand, highlighting the crests of the waves. The night was hot and humid, but the breeze blew steadily, giving some relief. Walking across the sand, they scanned the beach as best they could in the moonlight and saw no one. The children giggled and jabbered, poking and pinching each other in attempts to heighten the jitters.

Halfway across the beach, Elijah took the flashlight from Byron, stuck it under his chin and twirled around, confronting the children. The light caught his protruding features and cast eerie shadows across his cheeks and forehead. He widened his eyes, and the kids gasped with fright.

"Are ye skeered, youngins?" Elijah asked in a rough tone.

Dugan laughed and the others joined in. "You don't scare me, Uncle Elijah."

"Me neither," Mark and Matt chimed in.

"You look like a pirate," Leroy said. "A real pirate."

Elijah lowered the light and pointed it at the children. "Aye, me mateys. Leroy speaks truly. I be a descendant of the great pirate, Blackbeard, who roamed these coasts hundreds of years ago."

"Blackbeard?" Janey said, her golden eyes shining in the flashlight's glow.

"That's right, me lady. The one and only. Are ye skeered now?"

"No way. You don't scare me," she said.

"Okay, then. If none of ye be skeered, we'll approach the beach, but I must warn ye. There'll be plenty of ghost crabs out tonight." He pointed the light at their feet. "I hope ye all be wearin' shoes, or else the ghost crabs will pinch off one of ye toes."

"There's no such thing as ghost crabs, is there, Uncle Elijah?" Dugan asked.

"Wait and see, me matey. Wait and see."

When they reached the firm wet sand, Elijah cast the light along the shore. Before them lay a multitude of white circular objects.

"Look at all them shells," Dugan said.

"They can't be shells," Mark said. "I just saw one move."

Janey screamed. "They're crabs! One just crawled over my foot."

A hoard of crabs scrambled in their direction. The kids jumped back, yelling and screaming.

Elijah laughed, a raucous sound that bellowed from deep within his chest. He shined the light on the children, who had huddled together, holding onto each other. "You sure you kids want to continue this beach walk? I think you're all scaredy cats. Maybe we better turn back before it's too late."

Janey stepped forward. "I ain't scared. These little ol' crabs can't hurt ya."

"Watch out!" Elijah hollered. "There's one right by your foot."

Everyone watched a large ghost crab crawl up to Janey's sandal and stop.

"Run, Janey!" Jimmy yelled. "It'll pinch your toe off!"

She stood, hands on her hips, not moving. "Naw it won't. If you don't bother the crab, it won't bother you."

"'Atta gal," Chrissy said. "We gotta show these guys who's got more nerve. Give me a high five." She stepped toward Janey and raised her hand. Janey reached up and slapped it, and the crab scrambled away.

"Fellows," Byron said. "Looks like the girls want to keep going. Do you?"

"Course we do, Dad," Matt said. "We can't let no girls make us look like sissies."

"All right, then. Make sure you stick with Elijah and me. We'll lead the way."

As the two men walked along the shoreline, the kids kept pace, picking up shells and dallying at the edge of the tide. To the children, the abundance of ghost crabs became tolerable as they took turns leaping and skipping around and over them. Occasionally, a wave rushed up the incline farther than expected and soaked their feet. Whoops of laughter followed as they stomped through the backwashing water.

As they walked, Byron confessed to Elijah that his afternoon run had perplexed him. He had become obsessed with the lighthouse because of the black stallion. Byron always believed you communicated with God through prayer—pouring out your heart and then quietly listening, This kind of spiritual communication made sense to him. For God to speak to a man through an animal seemed mythical. He always mistrusted sensational stories from fanatical believers. Many times throughout his ministry Byron heard people testify about fantastic experiences of how God intervened to deliver them from difficult circumstances. He considered most of their stories exaggerations—a sign of spiritual immaturity. Byron strove to represent his faith intelligently and practically.

"Don't be so fast to condemn those who hear from God differently than you," Elijah said. "The Lord doesn't limit himself to speaking to people through Bible reading and prayer."

"I understand that," Byron said. "God speaks to me through a sunrise or the beauty of new-fallen snow as well as through the inspired word. But would he send a horse to focus my attention on that lighthouse? Don't get me wrong. A horse is a beautiful animal. Its form speaks to me of God's creative power. But does it have the intelligence to receive a message from God and deliver it to me? Wouldn't you consider that a little preposterous?"

"Not at all. God can definitely speak to us through animals. Don't you remember the story of Balaam and the ass? Balaam failed to see the angels that surrounded him, but the donkey could. Balaam beat the animal again and again because it wouldn't budge. Finally the ass spoke and said: 'Balaam? Are you blind? Can't you see all these angels?' That's when God opened his eyes."

"I don't interpret that story literally," Byron said. "If God could make animals talk, why didn't that horse say, 'Hey you idiot. Look at the doggone lighthouse!' Instead it just waved his head in that direction."

"But you knew. You sensed it inside—God's Spirit directed you to look at the lighthouse."

Byron considered Elijah's words and nodded. "I must admit. The sensation of God speaking to me was overwhelming."

Elijah spread his hands. "Then what difference does it make whether or not you could hear the horse speak out loud?"

"None, I guess."

"God has spoken to me through animals," Elijah said.

"Really?"

"Remember when Chrissy disappeared about six years ago, and I found her in the woods?"

"I'll never forget that."

"A robin directed me to her. I asked God for a sign, and he sent a bird to show me the way. I'm not kidding. I followed a robin and found your daughter. No doubt about it. A man can learn a lot from God's creatures."

Suddenly Elijah straightened and arched his back. In the flashlight's glow, his eyes grew wide with panic.

"Are you all right?" Byron asked.

"Arrrrrghhh!" he gasped. "I feel something strange on my back." He began prancing around in the sand, shaking his body. "WhaaWhaaaWhaaaWhaaat's goin' on?" he hollered.

The children circled him, giggling at his funny steps and gyrations. He looked like a pro running back doing a touchdown dance.

As he pirouetted, hopped, and skipped through the tide, he reached his hand down the back of his shirt and bellowed like a bull elephant. "AiiiAiiiAiiAaaaiiiiiii! Hellllp me! Helllp me! HeeelllllllPPPP ME!"

The kids laughed louder and Byron shouted, "What's wrong?"

He stopped, but his body still wobbled and wiggled. In the light, his face was as white as the moon. "There's something crawling all over my back," he yelped.

The kids quit laughing as Byron rushed forward and grabbed the back of his shirt. He pulled the shirttail out and up and shined the light on Elijah's back. There, claw clenched and dangling at the end of the shirttail, hung a small ghost crab.

From fifteen feet away, Chrissy burst into uproarious laughter.

Elijah shook the little crab off the end of his shirt and looked up. "Chrissy Marie Butler! Wait till I get my hands on you. I'm gonna throw you in that ocean for slippin' that critter down my shirt."

"Who's skeered of little ghost crabs now?" Chrissy called back, then took off running along the beach.

Elijah sprinted forty yards before oxygen debt slowed him down to a jog. He stopped and leaned on his knees, heaving. Between breaths he yelled: "You're lucky . . . you've got long legs . . . .and good lungs . . . You . . .You. . . goofy teenager!"

After regrouping and walking another quarter mile, Byron announced it was time to turn back. The kids booed and pleaded to go further. Acting as mediator, Elijah offered an alternative: If the kids agreed to quit complaining and head home, he would tell a good pirate story when they got there. The proposition almost worked, but the children wanted to sit around a beach fire and hear the tale. Because they lacked the necessities to build a fire, Chrissy suggested walking to one of the many gazebos along the dunes, sitting in a circle on the wooden floor and pretending the flashlight was a fire. With the status gained by one-upping Elijah, Chrissy easily influenced the children, and they headed for the nearest gazebo.

Wooden steps with weathered railings climbed the steep sand hill to a short walkway suspended by piers above the dunes. The walkway cut through the middle of the gazebo and traversed another fifty yards or so across the sandy landscape to a parking lot offering beach access to that neighborhood's vacationers. The troop of night explorers ascended the steps, crossed the walkway and circled the gazebo. Once seated, they focused on Elijah who took the flashlight and balanced it on end in the middle of the floor. The light cast jagged shadows through the framework onto the plywood ceiling. The wind whispered through the sea grass, and the distant lapping of waves offered a haunting rhythm, ideal for the telling of ghost stories.

Elijah reached up and grasped his beard, pulling and twisting it around his forefinger until it formed a curl and sprung free. Taking a deep breath, he said, "Aye, me mateys, this tale was tol' me by me grandpappy, who was tol' the tale by his grandpappy, who was tol' the tale by his grandpappy whose very grandpappy was the notorious Edward Teach himself, otherwise known as the bloodthirsty pirate, Blackbeard." Finishing the sentence out of breath, Elijah glanced around the circle and noticed the children, eyes riveted upon him.

Waving his hand across the top of his head, Elijah said, "He was a big man with a broad black hat, white skull and cross bones emblazoned 'cross the middle. Course his beard was long, curly and black against his blood-red overcoat. He carried two pistols and three daggers slung from a leather strap that crossed his chest and a long, sharp sword he handled with extraordinary skill. The bravest captain on the high seas would go weak in the knees when he spotted the skull and cross bones waving atop the mast of Blackbeard's ship, the *Queen Anne's Revenge*."

"Is this a true story, Uncle Elijah?" Dugan cut in.

"Of course 'tis, boy. Don't interrupt me. Now where I be? Ah yes, Back in those days piracy ran rampant. The small towns and villages that dotted the Carolina coast huddled in the shadow of fear cast by these murderous fiends. Local sailors who manned fishing and trading vessels faced constant threat of attack.

"Of all the pirates that stalked these treacherous waters, by far, Blackbeard was the most dreaded. Any captain with courage enough to rally his crew to battle, faced the fight of his life. The *Queen Anne's Revenge* would fire off her many cannons and, through the smoke, close in on the unlucky vessel. To snag and couple the ships, the pirates tossed grapplin' hooks, quickly wrappin' and securin' the rope. Just before boardin', Blackbeard would tie long red-ribbon fuses to his hair and beard and light them. They sputtered and smoked, giving diabolic aspect to his features. The frightened sailors swore he looked like Lucifer himself. Many fainted or gave up on the spot. Those who didn't met a violent and bloody fate.

"As his reputation grew, few challenged Blackbeard. Most would run like cowards or just give up without a fight. The pirate grew rich and built mansions on Ocracoke Island just south of here and in the town of Bath on the mainland.

"But the people of North Carolina grew weary of his devilish ways and called upon Governor Spotswood of Virginia to do something. A fearless man by the name of Lieutenant Robert Maynard vowed to the Governor he would capture or kill the troublesome scallywag. On a cold day in November, Maynard spotted the skull and cross bones flying high above the *Queen Anne's Revenge* in an Ocracoke inlet.

"Maynard gave the order to attack, and his cannons exploded. A terrific battle unfolded as musketry and cannon fire ripped the air and tattered the sails of both ships. Lacking experience sailing the Ocracoke waters, Maynard hung his ship on one of the many sandbars. Blackbeard, observin' their misfortune, closed in for the kill. Once the pirates tethered the ships together, Blackbeard lit his red-ribbon fuses and led the charge. Hand to hand, the sailors and pirates fought with fierce determination. In the midst of the battle, Blackbeard and Maynard faced off, each wielding deadly swords. With his size and strength advantage, Blackbeard managed to disarm the Lieutenant, slicing his hand and flinging his sword to the deck. With a devilish gleam in his eye, Blackbeard prepared to run Maynard through. From behind, a young sailor suddenly swung his cutlass with all his might. Blackbeard felt the sharp blade slice through his neck. When he turned to look, his head fell off.

"They say Blackbeard continued to fight for another ten minutes, too stubborn to die, but I don't know for sure if that be true. When he did finally keel over, the pirates lost heart and surrendered. Lieutenant Maynard strung 'em up on the spot, hangin' 'em from the cross masts. Then he took Blackbeard's head and fastened it to the bowsprit. They threw his body overboard, and some say it circled the ship three times before it washed into shore.

'That night as Maynard's ship headed north along the Outer Banks, a storm hit, rocking the boat with tremendous waves. The head of Blackbeard slipped off the bowsprit and fell into the sea. Arrgggh, me mateys, they say Blackbeard's ghost still trudges these beaches, lookin' for his lost head to wash up on shore.

Elijah paused, scanned the faces of his listeners, slowly turned and looked out to sea. Following his lead, the kids gazed at the star-studded horizon, their ears attuned to the eternal chorus of crashing waves and rushing water.

They listened, not speaking for more than a minute. Then Dugan said, "Did you hear that?"

"I heard it," Leroy said, eyes bugged with fear. "Someone's singing. It sounds like a pirate."

"Shhhhh! Janey said. "Listen."

Then Byron heard it—a man with a whiskey-rough voice singing:

Fifteen men on a dead man's chest,
Yo ho ho and a bottle of rum.
Drink and the devil be done for the rest,
Yo ho ho and a bottle of rum.

The children stood, bodies tensed.

"Relax now," Byron said, extending his hand, fingers spread. "No need to get worked up."

The voice grew louder as the singer approached the steps.

Fifteen men of a whole ship's list,

Yo ho ho and a bottle of rum.
Dead and be damned and the rest gone whist,
Yo ho ho and a bottle of rum.

Dugan gulped, his knees visibly shaking. Leroy took a step back. The sound of wood creaking from the weight of a large man combined with the murderous strain.

The skipper lay with his nob in gore,
The scullion's axe his cheek had shore,
And the scullion he was stabbed times four,
Yo ho ho and a bottle of rum.

Byron tried to reach out and clasp Mark's pant leg, but he and the other children had slowly backed out of range. The voice grew louder, harsher.

Twas a cutlass swipe or an ounce of lead,
Or a yawning hole in a battered head,
And the scupper's glut with a yawning red,
Yo ho ho and a bottle of rum.

When the silhouette, rimmed by the moon's glow, rose above the top step, it appeared headless, carrying a sword in one hand and a round object in the other.

"It's Blackbeard!" Leroy yelled. The six children sprinted down the long walkway toward the parking lot.

Chapter Nine

Surprised, the man rose up, lifting his head above hunched shoulders. He planted his cane, leaned and said, "What's all this commotion?"

Elijah grabbed the flashlight and shined it on him. He was tall and wide, wearing black sweat pants and a dark t-shirt. In the crook of his arm he held a soccer ball.

"Turn that cursed light off," he said, blinking. His close-cropped hair was as silver as the moon, and a multitude of wrinkles scored his tanned face.

"Who are you?" Elijah demanded.

"The King of England! Who the heck are you?"

Elijah lowered the light.

"Sorry. You startled us," Byron said.

"Startled you? I 'bout lost my ticker. What's going on here?"

Byron took the flashlight and shined it on himself. "I'm Byron. This is my daughter, Chrissy, and this is Elijah," he said, redirecting the light.

"I'm Howard Hicks," he said, lifting the soccer ball. "My granddaughter left this on the beach today. I told her I'd do my best to find it. Got lucky. Found it right on the edge of the tide."

"It's nice to meet you, but we can't talk," Byron said. "The six kids with us just took off running. They thought you were Blackbeard."

"Blackbeard!" He tossed the soccer ball a few feet into the air and caught it. "They probably thought this was my head."

Elijah, Byron, and Chrissy ran down the walkway and into the parking lot. Byron called for Mark and Matt, and Elijah yelled for Dugan. Listening, they heard nothing and decided to walk a block west and try again. They called out but heard no response.

"Which way do you think they went?" Byron asked.

Elijah shrugged. "If they lost their sense of direction and turned north, they'll pass through several neighborhoods until they reach the wildlife preserve about half mile from here. Hopefully, they turned south, back toward our neighborhood."

"Did you hear that?" Chrissy asked.

Byron tilted his head.

Chrissy pointed. "That direction. It sounded like Mark."

"Mark!" Byron hollered.

"Over here," came the faint reply.

Elijah headed south. "This way."

Two blocks down they found Mark and Janey. Mark's eyes were wide, and Janey was gripping his hand. When Byron shined the light on them, Mark looked down at their linked hands, smiled, and let go.

"Where is everyone?" Byron asked.

"They scattered," Mark said. "Who was that back there? Blackbeard's ghost?"

"Course not," Elijah said. "Just a man taking a walk."

"I think Matt, Leroy, and Jimmy kept running that way," Mark said, pointing in the direction he and Janey had been heading.

"How 'bout Dugan?" Chrissy asked.

"Don't know," Mark said. "Dugan's pretty fast. He took off runnin' like his pants were on fire."

They walked three blocks south, yelling as they progressed. Below a streetlight they stopped and listened. A block away, three kids appeared under another streetlight. Byron hollered and got their attention. The boys ran to them.

"Is everyone all right?" Matt asked. "What happened to the man with the sword?"

"What sword?" Elijah said. "He was carrying a cane."

"A cane?" Leroy said.

"Yeah. A cane and a soccer ball."

"Did you guys see Dugan?" Chrissy asked.

"No," Matt said. "I think he went in the other direction."

"Oh no," Elijah said. "Lord help us if he headed north. He's probably a half mile away by now."

* * *

Dugan stood in the darkness, listening to himself breathe. He tried to recover from the all-out sprint as quietly as possible. The killer had seen him in the marsh that day—he was sure of it. The man with the sword wasn't Blackbeard, and he wasn't after the other five kids. At the end of the parking lot everyone had turned left, so Dugan cut right. *Good.*

They'll be safe. As his breathing slowed, the anxiety that twisted his insides increased. *I just hope he doesn't find me. Got to make my way back to the beach house by some roundabout route.*

Looking skyward, he could see the stars twinkling between the branches and needles of tall pines that stood between him and a massive house. The lights were out except for the glimmer from a small third floor window. Sweat trickled down his forehead as he pressed his back against the shadowed side of a storage barn. *Now Uncle Elijah has got to believe me. When he saw the weapon, surely he believed me. Oh no . . . Uncle Elijah! I hope the killer didn't harm him or Byron . . . or Chrissy.* He edged to the corner of the shed and peeked down the road in the direction of the parking lot. Under a streetlight fifty yards away he saw the silhouette of a man carrying a sword. Then he heard the song—the yo ho ho song about the blood and the rum and the dead men. His heart thumped, as if someone was rapping on his chest. *I can't hide here. He might see me. He's tracking me.* A prickling sensation, like invisible needles, covered his body. He couldn't stand still. His legs churned as he turned the corner of the storage barn and fled down the street.

Behind him he heard the man yell, "Stop, boy! Stop! Don't run! I'm not Blackbeard."

A surge of energy jolted through him like an Olympic sprinter breaking a world record. After two blocks his leg muscles grew heavy. He slowed and cut through a yard. A clattering noise erupted to his right as a black shadow leapt toward him. Outlined by moonlight, a Doberman halted in midair and fell violently, jerked to the ground by his chain. The dog scrambled to its feet, yapping inches from his ankles. Dugan backpedaled, turned and stumbled over a lawn chair. It collapsed like a trap over his knees. The barking intensified. A back door opened, and a man stepped out onto the deck with a flashlight. Dugan raised his hand to his face as the light stung his eyes.

"Get out of here, you juvenile delinquent!" The man yelled. "Try to vandalize my property, will you? I'll turn my dog loose on you!"

Dugan staggered to his feet, sprinted to the front of the house and crossed the main road. Headlights flashed on him, and the sound of tires squealing sent him reeling to the right to avoid a skidding car. Behind him he could hear a car door open and a man yelling. The car door slammed shut. As he sprinted down the sidewalk, Dugan glanced over his shoulder and glimpsed the man charging toward him. He cut into the shadows down a sandy path. *Everyone's out to get me.*

As he ran down the path, branches from overhanging trees slapped his face. He swatted his hands in front of him to block the whacks. The path opened onto a gravel road. He stopped and leaned on his knees. Through a space in the overhanging trees the moon beamed down upon him. He turned and faced the path. From the black tunnel he heard footsteps and the whipping of branches.

"Stay there! Don't move!" someone shouted from the darkness.

Dugan sprinted down the moonlight-splattered road and veered to the right onto another path. Even in the darkness the paths seemed familiar. After several turns, he stopped and crouched to listen and catch his breath. Hearing nothing, he stood and walked as silently as possible through the blackness. A spider web wrapped around his face like a veil. He brushed it away, blinking. *I think I've been here before. These are the paths where we played bike catchers.* His toe caught on a root, and he fell, his hands skidding on the sandy ground. He struggled to his feet, brushed himself off and walked on.

For fifteen minutes he wandered through the maze of paths, occasionally stopping to listen for footsteps. Hearing nothing, he believed he had lost the man who trailed him.

He hadn't felt this lonely since last summer when his father took him on a camping trip to the New River Gorge National Park. His parents had recently divorced, his mother receiving full custody. At first his father made regular appearances. One Friday in July he showed up with a new tent in the trunk of his Toyota. After the three-hour drive to the park grounds, they turned onto a dirt road into the wilderness and found an isolated spot along the river to pitch the tent. His dad told him to start setting up camp while he went for some refreshments. They had passed through a small town ten miles back, and Dugan had noticed a few stores, a gas station, and a beer joint with a sign above the door: RIVERSIDE BAR. At the four-way stop his father had glanced at the sign, while waiting for a pickup truck to pass through the intersection. He looked at it again, this time a few seconds longer, before pulling away.

Dugan knew that second look wasn't a good thing. One of his father's bad habits was drinking. You could be sure two others would follow like fawns crossing the road after their mama—smoking and gambling. He told his dad they didn't need refreshments. The river water looked crystal clear. But his father insisted that drinking river water would be risky. Besides, it wouldn't even take half an hour to get there and back.

After his father left, Dugan opened the tent box and read the instructions. Step by step he did his best putting it together, driving the pegs, setting the poles. The whole time, replays of his parents' late-night arguments echoed in his brain: *You're drunk again. Shut up! And you probably blew all the money we've got at the poker table. Leave me alone, woman. Leave you alone? How am I supposed to pay the bills? I work hard for my money. Can't a man have a little bit of fun? You make me sick. Get off my back.* Many nights Dugan had lain in bed, eyes wide open, listening to their accusations and curses.

After erecting the tent, he decided to explore the riverbank and find some wood for a fire. That kept his mind off his dad's whereabouts for a while. Plenty of dry branches and sticks had lodged between the large rocks along the shoreline. Dugan hauled an armful of wood back to the camp and returned to the river's edge to skip flat stones across the water. He admired the beauty of the scene—the tall pines and birches along the opposite shore and the brown outcrops of rocks on the steep green ridges. A hawk dove from the top of a pine, snagged a fish off the surface of the water and carried it to a large rock in the middle of the river. As he watched the bird eat its prey, he noticed the sun had set, draining blue from the sky. He figured his dad had been gone almost two hours.

Returning to the campsite to start a fire, he hunted for matches in the few boxes of equipment his dad brought along. No luck. Not even a flashlight. He emptied the tackle box, looking in every little plastic compartment. Rubbing two sticks together like a boy scout didn't work either. The effort only raised a blister on the web of skin between his thumb and forefinger.

When night fell, he sat in the blackness of the tent listening to crickets and owls and every little noise that rustled in the woods. He tried to curl up in his sleeping bag and pretend he was home in bed, but fear and loneliness twisted his insides like tag team wrestlers torturing the underdog. When he couldn't stand it any longer he bawled for ten minutes. Crying didn't help; he still felt lonely and scared.

After several hours he imagined his father's car had swerved off the narrow dirt road and plunged over the embankment. In his mind he could see his dad draped over the steering wheel, bleeding from gashes on his forehead.

Gathering his courage, he crawled out of the tent. A sliver of moon and a multitude of stars highlighted the edges of the rocks, plants and trees. He managed to climb the hillside to the road and walked for what seemed like more than a mile through the darkness. All along the way he yelled, "Dad!" When he became hoarse, he decided to turn around. The walk back to the campsite in the silence was painfully lonely. He didn't sleep that night.

At dawn he set off again. After walking several hundred yards down the road, he saw a green truck coming his way. He held up his hands to stop the driver, a park ranger. He had to wait four hours for his mother to arrive at the ranger station.

"Where's Dad?" was his first question.

She shook her head and said they'd talk about it later. He slept all the way home. That evening after a good supper, his mother informed him his father had spent the night in jail. He had drunk too much and gotten into a fight at the bar after losing all his money in a card game.

After that incident, his father rarely showed up on weekends. When he did, his mother never allowed Dugan to go anywhere with him. On one of those rare Saturday afternoons when his father visited, they had sat on the back porch while his mother cooked dinner. Dugan asked him what really happened that night. His father hinted that he had a government job no one knew about. He couldn't give Dugan details. That night some serious action came his way and he had to take care of business. The story about getting arrested was a cover his superior officers invented to prevent his secret assignment from being discovered. He instructed Dugan not to tell anyone. Dugan just nodded. But the nod wasn't enough to stop the doubts from filling his mind. *Would his father outright lie to him?* Deep inside he knew the answer to that question.

The fear and loneliness of his midnight walk along the New River Gorge returned like a bad rash as he wondered along the paths through the marsh. Then he smelled death and knew he neared the spot where he had found the girl. He remembered her face, the blank stare that wouldn't release him. His heartbeat quickened, and he wanted to run. Instead, he closed his eyes and calmed himself. *The dead can't hurt me. I got to worry about the living.* He looked in the direction of the weeds where Byron had found the deer. A strange sensation flowed over him, almost like the spirit of the girl calling to him. He didn't hear any words, just the feeling that justice needed to be served. Dugan shrugged his shoulders and wondered if he imagined it.

Down the path he heard an owl hoot. He turned and looked. It cried again. Something inside told him to walk in the direction of the owl. As he neared, he saw the bird perched on a branch exposed by the moonlight. Its large golden eyes reminded him of Janey's eyes. She was a pretty girl. He liked her the instant he saw her. She and Jimmy had been tossing a Frisbee in the next-door yard when he introduced himself. She seemed to like him until Mark and Matt showed up. Then she couldn't take her eyes off Mark. *That's the way it always goes. I'm used to it. Girls don't like me much.*

"I don't understand girls. Do you, Mr. Owl?" he said. The owl pivoted on the branch and flew farther down the path. "Guess you don't have much to say on that subject."

The owl hooted again, and Dugan followed. Every time he neared the bird, it flew to another tree. Tracking the owl, he wove through the paths until he reached the Currituck Sound. The water lapped gently against the shoreline, reflecting the moon in shimmering dabs of light. He approached the owl to see if it would fly again. It blinked at him as it perched on the branch. Dugan moved closer, to within five feet. The owl turned its head almost completely around and back again.

What is this place? Does it have something to do with the girl? The owl rotated its head again. He inspected his surroundings. Although the path had led him to the water, it abruptly turned and re-entered the woods. Posts rose from the water where a dock had long ago secured boats, the side timbers and planks missing. He stood beneath four tall pines. The owl had alighted on a branch of the tree nearest the water. Dugan slowly turned and noted the details of the scene. The moonlight on the tree trunk revealed a large heart someone had carved. Stepping closer he reached out and traced the letters inside the heart—K.Q. and L. R., but the L.R. had an 'X' gouged over it. He wanted to remember everything, just in case he had to return there.

The owl hooted. Dugan turned to see the black shape of a man twenty feet away on the path.

"Don't move," the man said.

With an explosion of wing beats, the owl thrust into the sky, screeching.

Dugan darted onto the path and into the woods, but he heard the man's footsteps pounding behind him, closing in. He tried to turn left onto another path but lost his balance and tumbled into the weeds. When he turned over, the black shape towered over him.

Chapter Ten

They searched the Corolla neighborhoods for half an hour looking for Dugan. Finding no sign of him, Byron and Elijah decided to head back and call the police. They figured they could hunt again after walking the children safely home. Dropping off Leroy, Jimmy and Janey, they crossed the driveway and climbed the steps to their vacation home. Byron prayed that Dugan would be waiting inside with Lila and Annie.

They quickly checked the bedrooms on the second floor, but to no avail. Byron glanced at Elijah and shook his head, wondering if his friend shared his unsettling notion: *If Dugan isn't upstairs, this could be a long night.*

They mounted the steps to the third floor and saw Annie and Lila sitting at the table sipping from mugs. Byron glanced around the room.

"That was a long walk," Annie said. "We thought you got lost."

Lila stood. "What's wrong?"

"Did Dugan come back here?" Elijah asked.

"No," Annie said. "He's not with you?"

Byron shook his head.

The color drained from Lila's face. "Don't tell me you lost him. How could you lose him?"

"It's my fault," Elijah said.

"It's not your fault," Byron said.

"I told a story about Blackbeard the pirate, and the kids thought they saw Blackbeard's ghost. They took off running. We managed to round them up except for Dugan."

"You and your stories," Annie said. "If he's lost, we need to call the police right now."

Lila motioned toward the kitchen. "The emergency numbers are next to the phone."

Annie's face tensed, lines forming on her brow, her crows feet deepening. "If we don't find that boy soon, I'll have to call my sister. She'll be hysterical."

Byron picked up the phone and dialed the County Sheriff's Office. He gave them Dugan's description and the approximate location of his disappearance.

Hanging up the phone, Byron said, "The dispatcher told me an officer would be by to take a full report as soon as possible."

"We're heading back out to look again," Elijah said.

"We're coming with you," Annie said.

"Someone needs to stay here and wait for the officer," Byron said.

A series of chimes resounded through the great room. They looked at one another, not sure where the sound emanated.

"That's gotta be the doorbell," Chrissy said.

Everyone rushed down to the entry hall and saw Deputy Queen in uniform through the small window of the front door.

"That was fast," Byron said. "I just called less than two minutes ago."

Chrissy yanked the door open. Beside Deputy Queen stood Dugan.

"You looking for this little guy?" Queen asked.

Everyone's mouths dropped open, and Annie hugged her nephew and planted a big kiss on his cheek.

"Where'd you find him?" Elijah asked.

"Deep in the marsh."

"How'd you know we'd lost him?" Byron asked.

"I didn't. I was patrolling the neighborhoods when a kid flew across the street in front of me. Almost hit him. When I stepped out of the squad car, a man yelled from his porch that some delinquent had just vandalized his property, so I took off after him. Took me twenty minutes to track him down on those paths through the marsh. When I finally caught him, to my surprise it was Dugan."

"I'm sorry, Uncle Elijah," Dugan interrupted. "I thought the killer was after me. And I didn't mean to break that guy's lawn chair. Somehow I tripped over it when I cut through his yard. His dog 'bout bit my leg off."

Elijah cupped his hands under Dugan's arms and lifted him to the ceiling. "I'm just glad to see ya, boy. Just glad to see ya!" He lowered him and kissed his forehead, then gently returned him to the ground.

A smile slowly broke across Dugan's face. "You mean I'm not in trouble?"

"All of us ran like crazy, Dugan," Mark said. "You just ran faster than anybody else, and we lost you."

"Besides," Annie said. "It's your uncle's fault. He shouldn't be telling you kids those kinds of stories."

Elijah lowered his head and raked his fingers through his beard.

"Nobody's to blame," Byron said. "But I can tell you this." He placed his hand on Queen's shoulder. "I'm thankful for this young man."

"Three cheers for Deputy Queen," Chrissy said.

Elijah slapped Queen on the back. "I second that. Hip, hip hooray!"

They all joined in: "Hip, hip hooray! Hip, hip hooray!"

Queen grinned and said, "No need to thank me. Just doing my job. Believe it or not, they pay me for doing stuff like this. That's why I love being in law enforcement."

"Kenny," Byron said. "Tomorrow evening we're having a big cookout about seven o'clock. How about joining us?"

"Love to, but I'm on duty." He raised his hand and rubbed his chin. "What I could do though is stop over during my break for a little while."

"I'll have a big hamburger with all the trimmings waiting for you," Elijah said.

"With onions and tomatoes?" Queen asked.

"Swiss cheese and pickles too, if you want."

Queen extended his hand, and Elijah gripped it. "You've convinced me. Can't pass up a home-grilled hamburger."

After the families thanked Deputy Queen again, he informed them he had to get back to headquarters and file a report. Chrissy insisted on walking him to his vehicle.

The three boys crowded at the window and giggled.

"Oh, Deputy Queen, what big eyes you have," Mark squealed.

"Oh, Deputy Queen, what a cute nose you have," Matt giggled.

"Oh, Deputy Queen, what a nice butt you have," Dugan snickered, and all three laughed like hyenas.

"That's enough fellows," Byron said. "Either get upstairs or into your room."

Still laughing, they charged into their bedroom and shut the door.

Once Annie and Elijah climbed the stairs, Byron put his arm around Lila and said, "We need more good guys like Deputy Queen in this world."

"You and Deputy Queen have something in common," Lila said.

"Really? What's that?"

She reached behind him and patted his rear end. "You both have nice rear ends."

"I think you've got good taste in men," Byron said.

* * *

On Tuesday morning, Elijah, Byron, Chrissy and the boys drove to the resort shops to check out the two-man kayaks. At the beach on Monday, the kids had seen several people challenging the waves in what looked like plastic canoes. The boys thought it would be a blast. Most people struggled just to get into the slim boats in the roaring tumult of the shallows. Those who managed to seat themselves would paddle for several yards until a wave broke over them, tipping the kayak and dumping the occupants into the sea. All of them wore life jackets and quickly bobbed to the top. None of the kayakers were able to break through to the calmer waters beyond the breakers. Mark and Matt claimed they had the coordination and smarts to accomplish the feat. Dugan immediately declared that he and Chrissy would beat them to it.

A young man, probably in his late twenties, lifted a bright blue kayak from the rack in front of the store. He wore black-framed sunglasses and had blond streaks through his sandy hair. The boat looked to be about twelve feet long, but he had no problem carrying it across the parking lot to Elijah's Suburban.

"How much does it weigh?" Byron asked.

"'Bout sixty pounds," the man said. He wore a yellow t-shirt with *Ocean Atlantic Rentals* arced in blue across the front over a beach scene with chairs and umbrellas. He lowered the kayak to the ground. Two yellow bowl-shaped seats were mounted inside, and two paddles lay tucked beside the seats. In front of each seat was an orange life jacket. "Do you want another blue one?"

"No. We want red," Dugan said.

As the man returned to the rack, Byron and Elijah heaved the kayak to the roof of the Suburban. After securing both kayaks to the top of the vehicle with elastic cords, they pulled out their wallets.

The man extracted a receipt book and pen from his back pocket. "That'll be ninety bucks each plus tax. Comes to $96.50 a piece. They're yours the rest of the week. Due back Saturday morning."

"Fun don't come cheap, do it?" Elijah mumbled.

"Any helpful hints?" Chrissy asked the young man.

The man peered over his sunglasses and smiled. "Sure. Take it to the sound side first to get used to it. Once you learn to navigate the thing properly, then try the ocean. Not many beginners can handle it in the ocean."

"We'll do fine," Chrissy said.

Elijah drove to Heritage Park near the Whalehead Club where they could access one of the many docks along the sound. After the men unstrapped the kayaks, the kids hoisted them onto their shoulders and toted them along the shoreline toward the nearest walkway that extended out into the sound. Several pink-flowering crape myrtles cast shadows across their paths, and scruffy grass grew in sandy patches. They carried the kayaks up steps and across a long wooden walkway. At the end steps descended into the sound's shallow water.

After they lowered the boat into the water, Chrissy held it steady while Dugan climbed in. Then he grabbed the steps' railing to secure the kayak as Chrissy stepped in. Mark and Matt repeated the procedure. Within minutes, both kayaks were skimming across the sound, the double oars dipping and stroking the water with reasonable rhythm.

A seagull, one eye normal and one a solid light blue, landed on the dock rail, squawking and looking for handouts. "It's Sinbad the Seagull," Elijah chuckled. "Sinbad want a cracker?" Elijah pulled a package of peanut butter crackers out of his pocket, unwrapped them and broke off a chunk. Carefully he extended the morsel to the one-eyed seagull. The bird gobbled the treat and cried for more.

Byron heard Lila calling his name. He glanced to the shoreline and spotted her and Annie taking their morning stroll. He waved and motioned them to come onto the walkway. "Is that your new best friend?" Annie called.

Elijah grinned. "Animals just adore me."

"Yeah, they mistake you for Grizzly Adams," Annie said.

The women walked to the end of the pier, and Lila shaded her eyes. "Are those kids safe out there?"

"Sure they're safe. They don't even need those life jackets. It's only three feet deep," Byron said.

"I hope so," Lila said.

"Later on they'll try the kayaks out in the ocean," Byron said.

Lila frowned and wrinkled her forehead. "I don't think that's a good idea."

Byron felt a prick of irritation at his wife's words. She constantly worried and too often overprotected the kids. "Hon, you've got to lighten up. It's perfectly safe. Let these kids have some fun."

She crossed her arms and focused on the children. More than fifty yards away now, both crews paddled furiously, racing toward a tree stump.

"Go Dugan and Chrissy!" Annie shouted.

Matt and Mark opened a slight lead. When they crossed in front of the stump they raised their paddles into the air and shouted, "We're the champs! We're the champs!"

"Rematch! Rematch!" Dugan yelled.

"Good job, kids!" Lila hollered. "Everyone's a winner!"

"Would you ladies like to climb to the top of the Currituck Lighthouse with us this morning?" Byron asked.

Lila turned and tilted her head. "You know I'm afraid of heights."

Annie glanced in the direction of the redbrick spire. "I've been up there twice in the last few years. I'll pass. Lila and I can take the kids to the beach."

"You'll miss a great view from up there," Elijah said, offering the bird another chunk of cracker.

"No thanks," Lila said. "I get queasy standing on the third floor deck of our rental house."

"We'll come down to the beach as soon as we're done," Byron said.

"Take your time," Annie said. "We can handle things."

"Owwww!" Elijah shouted. He shook his hand and jumped up and down. "You son of a b-b-b-b-bird brain! That one-eyed seagull just bit me!"

"Give him a break," Annie said. "With one eye, the poor thing lacks depth perception."

The bird screeched for more crackers, and everyone laughed.

* * *

Later that morning Elijah and Byron walked to the lighthouse. The redbrick tower, capped with an ornate iron parapet and a huge glass-encased light, rose majestically above the live oaks, willows, and loblolly pines. A line of about thirty people waited in front of the small workhouse, which served as the entrance to the spire. Two brick-trimmed windows on the front provided natural light for the climbers one-third and two-thirds of the way to the top. Looking up, Byron could see six people hugging the rail and gazing toward North Carolina.

"If I could go back in time and live life again, I'd return to this sand spit of an island in 1900 and become the Keeper of the Light," Elijah said wistfully.

"The Keeper of the Light? Why?" Byron asked.

Elijah shrugged. "To me, that would be as noble an occupation as any."

"What do they do?"

"You mean 'what *did* they do?' Nowadays it's all automated. But back then, the light keeper had a lot of responsibility."

Byron squinted up at the light. "Don't think it could have been too hard. Every evening you show up, flip a switch and the big beam comes on."

"Wrong, O ye helpless pawn of modern technology."

"Enlighten me, then," Byron chuckled.

The line advanced to the workhouse steps, and Elijah pointed to the door. "To start with, that little room housed the drums of kerosene. How do you think you got the kerosene to the holding tank on top?"

"Elevator?"

"Very funny. Try 214 steps. Then you would have to pump air into the oil to create enough pressure to feed the mantle on top. After you climbed to the lantern room and waited for the kerosene to soak the mantle, you'd light it with a candle."

A man wearing black-framed glasses with thick lenses collected their six dollars and handed each a brochure. Inside the workhouse on a round oak table sat a vase of yellow day lilies, fragrantly scenting the air. Old photographs and drawings of local scenes hung on the walls. A wooden shelf displayed an array of antique bottles and jugs.

"I don't get it," Byron said. "How can a wick provide a strong enough light to be seen by sailors ten miles out to sea?"

Elijah gripped Byron's arm and turned him to a large plaque on the wall. "That's how. It's called a Fresnel Lens."

Byron took a minute to read the educational poster. Above the information in quotes were the bold words, *To Illuminate the Dark Space*. A black and white portrait of Augustin Fresnel filled a large oval beside the paragraphs. Byron read how the inventor used tiers of prisms curved around a single light source to refract and reflect the light into a concentrated beam. The Currituck lantern possessed a First Order Lens—the largest one made.

"After lighting the mantle the keeper cranked the clockwork mechanism which turned the light on a wheeled track." Elijah pointed into the next room where the spiral staircase began. "Every two and a half hours he had to climb these steps to re-crank the mechanism. Add to that cleaning the lenses, maintaining the property, refueling the tanks and feeding your family—believe you me, it was much more than flipping a switch. The Keeper of the Light worked hard."

With the okay of the attendant, a thin, elderly man wearing wire-rimmed glasses, Elijah and Byron entered the base of the tower and began the climb. The iron spiral staircase, painted forest green and anchored to the brick, rose to a platform about twenty feet above them. Looking upward at the narrowing pattern, Byron observed the ascent consisted of a series of steps and platforms. Upon reaching the fifth platform, Byron heard Elijah huffing. They paused in the light of a tall window.

"Climb these steps every two and a half hours to crank the clock mechanism, huh?" Byron asked.

Elijah leaned on the curved brick wall and looked out on the bright day. "Yeah. Can you imagine that? Not a job for a lazy man. Good for the heart, too. But that's not why I would have wanted the job."

"What's the appeal for you?"

"That plaque at the bottom says it all: *To Illuminate the Dark Space.* That's quite a purpose in life."

Byron nodded. "I guess the good Lord wants us all to be lights."

"That's right. 'You are the light of the world. A city on a hill cannot be hidden. Neither do people light a lamp stand and put it under a bowl.' Matthew 5:14."

"I see," Byron said. "As the Keeper of the Light you would fulfill a great purpose both literally and spiritually."

"A light in a dark space saves lives. Over the last 125 years, do you realize how many ships avoided disaster because of a faithful light keeper?"

"Hundreds?"

"Thousands. The shoals off these shores are unmerciful. Those who fail to see the light are doomed to destruction. It's the old story of light verses darkness. Good and evil. Are you taking notes, preacher?"

Byron pointed to his temple. "Got it all right here. Let me ask you something, Elijah. Do you believe Satan is an actual person or just a symbol of the embodiment of evil? In seminary I had professors who believed man personalized evil. You know, gave evil a face—we created Lucifer in our own image to make evil more understandable."

"You should know better, good buddy. I believe the Bible. Satan *is* a real being, the essence of evil, yes, but a real personality. His goal is destruction and death."

"I don't know. It's just hard for me to imagine a real live Prince of Darkness. You know how liberal seminaries corrupt us Presbyterian ministers. But then something happened that has made me wonder."

"What happened?"

"It's the dream I keep having: I'm standing in knee-deep water. When I look into shore I see these red eyes and sense a horribly evil presence. A girl cries for help, and I enter this room where she's tied up. The red eyes follow me into the room." Byron took a deep breath. "It's frightening. I wake up trembling."

Elijah put his hand on Byron's shoulder. "God has given you a glimpse of the enemy."

"But I'm not sure what it all means."

"Hard to say." Elijah rubbed his beard and pointed to the steps. "Let's climb."

At the seventh platform the stairs twisted into what looked like a double helix as they extended higher into the narrowing tube. From there, one more platform and one more set of stairs would lead to the parapet. Byron could feel the weariness growing in his leg muscles after climbing the final set of stairs. When he stepped out of the door onto the platform, the wind rushed against him, knocking him off balance. Elijah reached out and steadied him as they moved to the rail.

"The wind is unchecked up here. It'll knock you off your feet if you aren't prepared."

Byron's eyes widened as he stared out to sea. "What a beautiful view," he said. "The ocean, the dunes, the houses, the trees. Everything! I didn't realize how high up we would be."

"Gives you a new perspective on the world, doesn't it?" Elijah asked.

"A bird's eye view." Byron turned and squinted up at the glass-enclosed lantern. "To Illuminate the Dark Space. Maybe that's why I'm here."

"What do you mean?"

He grasped Elijah by the shoulders. "I want to look at the other side."

Elijah shrugged, turned and led him around the platform.

Facing the Currituck Sound, Byron could see the keeper's house, and about a quarter mile away, the Whalehead Club. "This is it," he said.

"This is what?"

"What I was supposed to see. Remember when I told you about the stallion?"

"Oh yeah. You said the horse kept waving his head toward the lighthouse. Made you want to find out what was up here."

"It's like déjà vu—the Whalehead Club, the trees, the road, the keeper's house and the people below. I feel like I've seen this all before. It's weird."

"I get that feeling sometimes," Elijah said. "Like finding a missing puzzle piece on the floor. I pick it up and finally get to complete the puzzle."

"Yes. This is the missing piece. For some reason, I'm supposed to be right here. It fits. I can't explain why. It's something I'm feeling inside."

Elijah nodded.

A large shadow passed over them, and Byron ducked. He looked at the ground and saw the shadow drift across the grass, sidewalks and road.

"What was that?" When he looked up, he saw a huge bird gliding on the wind toward the Whalehead Club.

"A sea eagle," Elijah said. "A big old osprey."

"Incredible! Look at that wingspan—six or seven feet!"

"She's nested on that chimney for several years now. The Whalehead Preservation Society considers her their mascot."

Byron gripped the rail, leaned and watched it soar. "Quite a regal bird."

"Yessir. A friend of mine, an old man who worked at the club back in the 30's, swears the osprey protects the place from evil."

"From evil?" Their eyes met, and Byron wondered if Elijah felt the same chill down his back.

Elijah nodded. "From evil."

The osprey lifted its wings, extended its talons, and alighted on the chimney nest.

Chapter Eleven

By the time she and Dugan lugged the kayak three hundred yards to the beach, Chrissy's arms felt like lead. Annie and Lila toted the umbrella and blankets and, as they crossed the sand, looked for an ideal spot. Finding an opening among the colorful camps of sun worshipers, they dropped their burdens. Mark and Matt were already slipping into their life jackets.

"You wait for your sister before you go traipsing into those waves with that canoe," Lila ordered.

"But Mom," Mark complained. "She's Dugan's partner."

"I don't care. Don't go into that ocean without her nearby. Remember: safety in numbers. Now help me plant this umbrellas in the sand."

"Aw, Mom," Matt said as he stooped and grabbed the base of the pole.

"Hey, Stilts!" Mark hollered. "Hurry up. We want to try these kayaks out."

Chrissy rubbed her forearms. "Hold your horses, Mark. Let me get some blood flowing in my muscles again."

Dugan pointed down the beach. "What's goin' on over there?"

A group of about twenty people had gathered around a dark-haired man. He stood in the middle, talking and gesturing. Everyone seemed mesmerized. Chrissy thought he looked Puerto Rican or Mexican. "Let's check it out," she said.

As they neared, Chrissy studied his face. His eyes were large and dark brown, eyelids slightly drooping, creating a mysterious quality. He had close-cropped hair, somewhat nappy. Thick eyebrows, a thin mustache, and goatee added to his mystique. Standing shirtless and wearing blue knee-length trunks, he looked strong but not overly muscled like Kenny Queen. On his shoulder the blue-violet image of a devil had been tattooed; the figure squatted with its laughing face thrust upward, flames leaping around its tail, hooves, and horns.

"Do that again! Do that again," a pony-tailed blond girl insisted. About four feet tall and wearing a florescent pink bathing suit, she stood holding a playing card in her hand, the ace of spades.

"I need a new volunteer," the man said, and he scanned the faces of the crowd. Hands shot up all around, but his dark eyes locked onto Chrissy's. "You."

"Me?" she said, pointing to herself. When she stepped forward and everyone looked at her, she felt self-conscious. She glanced down at her body, her slim long legs and tanned torso contrasting with her white bikini.

"Think of a card," he said as he shuffled the deck.

Chrissy gazed into his eyes. "Okay . . .uh . . . queen of spades."

He stopped shuffling and spread the cards fan-like, face down between his thumbs and fingers. "Pick one. Any one."

Chrissy's fingers hovered above the deck, stopped two-thirds of the way and selected a card. When she looked at it, her eyes bugged out— queen of spades. "How'd you do that?" she asked as she showed the crowd.

A strange smile broke across his face. "Think of another."

Chrissy looked at the ground and then at the faces of the bystanders. "Jack of . . . jack of hearts."

He held out the deck. This time her hand vacillated across the cards until it steadied over the next to last card on the left. She quickly pulled it out and looked—jack of hearts. Her mouth dropped open as she lifted the card for all to see. The crowd applauded.

The beach magician held up his hand to stop the applause. "That's not all," he said as he shuffled the deck again. He turned back to Chrissy. "As I flip through these cards, I want you to say stop. When you do, insert the first card back into the deck wherever I stop."

Chrissy nodded.

Slowly his thumb brushed across the edges of the cards as they flipped one by one.

"Stop!" Chrissy yelled.

He lifted the remaining cards, and she inserted her card approximately halfway into the deck.

"Now the other one," he said as he repeated the process.

This time she allowed most of the cards to flip by before saying 'stop.' She inserted the card.

Holding his hand palm up, he set the deck on it for all to see. He eyed Chrissy. "Your two cards are somewhere in the middle of this deck, correct?"

"Yes. That's right," she said.

"I want you to take your finger and tap the top card."

Chrissy stepped forward and carried out his instruction. The man stiffened as if her touch through the cards somehow shocked him. The crowd laughed nervously.

"Did you feel that?" he asked.

"I . . . I . . . felt something," she said.

"Take the first two cards off the top of the deck."

Carefully she picked the first two cards up and turned them over—the queen of spades and the jack of hearts. Everyone gasped and applauded.

Chrissy stared into the mystic depth of his eyes. "How did you do that?"

"Magic," he said. Then he turned to the crowd and thanked them. Many called for another trick, but he assured them he would return tomorrow. They applauded again then filtered away. Dugan, Matt and Mark headed back to the kayaks. The magician turned to Chrissy and said, "Nice working with you, Miss . . .?"

"B-Butler," Chrissy stammered. "Chrissy Butler. And you are?"

"Jack Blaze." He held out his hand and shook hers gently. "I'd love to hang out with you, but I'm due at the Whalehead Club in ten minutes."

"Oh." Chrissy smiled. "You must be a professional entertainer—an illusionist."

Jack laughed and shook his head. "One of these days I will be. That's why I walk the beaches and practice my craft. For now, though, I'm a tour guide at the Whalehead Club."

"Stilts!" Mark yelled from behind. "Come on. We want to try out these kayaks!"

Chrissy turned around. "I'll be there in three minutes. Now go away!"

"Stilts?" Jack asked.

"That's what my dad and kid brothers call me."

He looked at her legs and smiled. "I can see why."

Chrissy felt her face flush. "Anyway, we spent the morning racing those things on the sound. Now comes the big challenge—my twin brothers verses Dugan and me—who will be the first to paddle their kayak beyond the breakers to the calmer waters? Big competition."

"Are your brothers always this competitive?"

Chrissy pulled back a tress of blond hair the wind had fluttered across her eyes. "Are you kidding? They love to win—especially if they're competing against me. This morning they won six out of six kayak races. I don't like to lose, but my little buddy, Dugan, takes it harder than I do."

"There's a secret, you know."

"A secret? What do you mean?"

"To getting through the waves. Tell your partner to come here."

Chrissy turned and looked in the direction of the boys. Dugan was funneling into his life jacket. "Hey Cap'n! Come here!" He looked up and trotted over.

"Hi," Dugan said.

The magician extended his hand. "I'm Jack."

Dugan shook it vigorously and said, "Nice to meet ya. I saw the trick with the two cards. That was way cool."

"Thanks, Dugan."

Chrissy put her hand on Dugan's shoulder. "Jack wants to tell us the best way to conquer the waves."

Jack kneeled in the sand. "Join me down here."

After Chrissy and Dugan crouched, Jack smoothed out the grains in front of him.

"Listen. If you watch the waves carefully, you'll notice they approach shore in sets at various angles." With his finger he drew a line representing the shore. "One set of waves may come in at this angle." His finger traced five rows at a slight angle. "The next set may come in from a different direction." To the right of the first set of lines he drew five more. "Now look. In between this set of waves and the other set is your window of opportunity. You have to be patient and watch how the waves are breaking. When you see two sets coming in at different angles, aim in between. You may catch a few of the smaller breakers on the end of the waves, but hang in there and keep paddling. If you do that, you'll split the seam—go right in between."

He stood and extended his hands to Chrissy and Dugan and pulled them to their feet.

"Makes sense," Dugan said. "Let's do it."

"Sorry I can't stay to witness this battle of Titans, but like I said, I'm late for work."

"Thanks for the advice," Chrissy said. "Hey! I just remembered. This evening my family is having a cookout. My father loves card tricks. Could you stop by, have a bite to eat and perform that trick for my dad?"

"Love to. Where're you staying?"

Chrissy explained the location of their vacation house. Familiar with the neighborhood, Jack assured her he could find the place. He waved and jogged toward the gap in the sand hills. As Chrissy walked back to the family's beach plot, she kept thinking of Jack's eyes, those dark brown eyes and long lashes with lids slightly darker than his tawny skin. She inhaled deeply and sensed an exhilaration building in her chest, threatening to erupt. Knowing the boys anxiously waited to drag the kayaks into the waves, she felt happy to have an outlet for the energy that mounted within her.

"Let's go!" she yelled, grabbing her life jacket and strapping it on.

Leroy, Jimmy, and Janey had arrived. Mark stood next to Janey, pointing out to sea and explaining the goal of the competition.

"Your strap is loose on your life jacket, Mark" Janey said. She reached out and tugged the white belt between the double-ringed clasps. Looking at Dugan, she said, "Do you need help with yours, Dugan?"

Because of his wiriness, Dugan's jacket hung limply on him. "Mine's fine," he said. "I need room to breathe."

"May the best team win," Janey said.

"Don't worry. We will," Mark laughed.

"Be careful!" Lila warned from under the shade of the umbrella.

Mark and Matt picked up their kayak and charged into the surf.

"Hurry up, Stilts!" Dugan hollered. "They're gettin' a head start.

"Don't panic, Cap'n," Chrissy said. "Remember what Jack said."

They lifted the boat, carried it to the edge of the water, and studied the waves. Mark and Matt had already climbed into their kayak and furiously paddled in the direction of a mounting wall of water. The wave lifted the front of the boat like a toy and crashed on top of them. The twins tumbled in the shallows as their blue boat rolled into shore with the wave. It skidded onto the sand in front of Dugan and Chrissy. Both paddles followed closely behind.

Mark and Matt plodded through the backwash and grabbed the kayak and paddles. Matt looked up and hollered, "What're you waitin' for? High tide?"

"Let's take it a little deeper this time before we get in it!" Mark instructed over the roar of the surf.

Chrissy grasped Dugan's elbow. "Over that way," she said, pointing to the right. "There's the seam. That set of waves breaks to the right and this sets breaks to the left." They picked up the red kayak and jogged down the shore. After wading fifteen yards into the water, they held the boat securely in front of them, timing the waves.

The twins had taken their kayak thirty yards out, the water not-quite chest high. Matt steadied the kayak as Mark tried to jump into the boat. After three tries a big wave collapsed on them and whisked away the kayak. Again they had to chase it into shore.

Dugan and Chrissy braced themselves as they held the kayak on the surface of the rising and falling water. Both shivered. They adjusted their position by moving to the left and then right as they watched the waves. A large wave broke to their left and unfurled toward them. Chrissy hollered, "Now!" As the tail of the wave spilled into them, they lifted the boat.

Once the water settled, Chrissy held the kayak as Dugan climbed into the front. With her long legs, she stepped into the back, almost tipping it, but they quickly regained their balance. Each grabbed a paddle and stroked the water with efficient rhythm. The boat cut across the undulating gray-green surface at surprising speed.

"Head for the seam!" Chrissy yelled. The intensity of their paddling increased as waves broke on each side of them, threatening to tip them. Forty yards away Chrissy could see the calmer water. Between here and there the tails of waves on both sides curled, about to break over them.

"Hold on!" Chrissy shouted. "Here they come!"

They lifted their paddles as the first one hit. It jolted and soaked them but failed to capsize the kayak. The second one sent them shooting to the left, rising and dipping. Chrissy felt like she was riding a dolphin. With the two waves behind them, they dug the paddles hard into the water on the left to re-steer the boat to the east. Once turned in the right direction, they stroked like Olympic oarsman going for the gold. The kayak jostled over the rough water, but the smaller waves couldn't topple them. The farther out they rowed, the calmer the sea became. Finally, they coasted far beyond the breakers. They turned the kayak and looked to shore.

Chrissy spotted Janey jumping up and down with her arms in the air. "Look there, Cap'n. Janey's cheering for you."

With both hands Dugan held up his paddle. Janey waved her arms to signify her congratulations.

Chrissy extended her hand. "Great job, Cap'n. We finally beat those goobers."

Dugan lowered the paddle and shook her hand. "I knew we could do it."

Chrissy watched Matt and Mark drag their kayak onto the beach. Janey, Jimmy and Leroy pointed out to sea, showing the twins the location of the champs. Chrissy and Dugan pumped their fists in the air, grinning. The twins shielded their eyes from the sun to focus on the victors, as if they were saluting them.

"Now that we're out here, what'll we do?" Chrissy asked.

Dugan shrugged. It seemed so quiet on the calmer waters. They didn't have to yell over the roar of the waves. "Ain't this cool," he said.

"Just think, Cap'n. We're the only ones with this view. Must be hundreds of people along the shore, but we're the only ones looking in. Everyone else is looking out. Quite a perspective, huh?"

Dugan nodded. He looked to shore, then out to sea. "Kinda strange out here, ain't it? Miles and miles of ocean. Makes me feel small."

"The ocean tends to do that to people. Dad says it puts him in his place. Reminds him how big God is."

Dugan pointed. "What's that?"

Further out to sea she saw the object floating on the water. "I don't know," Chrissy said. "Some kind of animal or fish, maybe."

"Can we check it out?"

Chrissy glanced at the shore. "Mom's got to be going crazy by now, seeing that we're this far out. Probably having a conniption fit." She turned and looked at the object. "Oh well, it's only another fifty yards. Let's do it and then get back as quickly as possible before Mom explodes."

What seemed like fifty yards was more like a hundred. As they approached, the dark shape readjusted its form, wings shifting and beak lifting to reveal a black pelican. It squawked and tried to fly, but the effort failed, and feathers scattered, blown by the wind.

"It's injured. Look at all the blood," Dugan said.

"Poor thing got tangled in fishing line and hooks."

"Let's try to get it into the boat," Dugan said. "Maybe we can save it."

* * *

On shore, Lila Butler paced like a nervous border collie unable to gather its herd. The kids and women had stood together and watched the red kayak diminish as its occupants paddled out to sea. With every distancing yard, Lila's nerves tightened and threatened to snap. Annie tried to assure her Chrissy and Dugan were safe, but the intensity of Lila's anxiety negated any comforting words.

"What's gotten into them?" Lila asked. "Why are they going out so far?" She clasped her hands over the top of her head and slid them down her cheeks, leaving red marks on her face.

"Man, they're out there!" Mark proclaimed. "I can hardly see 'em."

"Shhhhh," Annie warned. "Your mother doesn't need your commentary."

"Maybe they're caught in a riptide," Matt said. "And it's carrying them out to sea."

Biting her fingernails, Janey lowered her hand. "Don't say things like that, Matt."

"But it could happen," Matt said.

Annie grabbed Lila by the upper arm and turned her toward shore. "Look. Over there. The lifeguard is watching them with binoculars."

Lila ran to the guard chair. The young man, tanned, tall and lean, stood on top of the ten-foot platform, gazing through field glasses.

"Do you see the children?"

The guard lowered the binoculars and looked down. "Those your kids in the kayak?"

"One of them."

"They're not supposed to be out that far."

"Tell me something I don't know," Lila said impatiently. "What're they doing out there?"

He peered through the binoculars again. "They found something on the water. Can't tell what it is."

Lila exhaled, lowered her head, and squeezed her eyes shut. After taking a deep breath, she looked at the guard again.

"I'll have to yell at them when they get back to shore," he said still peering through the glasses.

"Please do! You have my full endorsement."

The guard lowered the binoculars, rubbed his eyes and quickly raised them again. He leaned forward and his mouth dropped open. "Someone call for Quint and the *Orca*!"

"What'd you say?" Lila asked.

The binoculars slipped from his hands and clunked on the platform as he fumbled for his whistle. He stuck it in his mouth and blew a long, loud blast. "Out of the water! Clear the water!" he shouted. Seizing a red flag from its holder on the platform, he waved it violently as he trumpeted short bursts from the whistle. He stopped and looked down the shoreline to make sure the other guards had caught his signal. They too waved flags and blew whistles. "Clear the water!" he shouted again. Then he descended, his feet quickly stepping down the cross supports of the chair.

*   *   *

Dugan and Chrissy maneuvered with their paddles to align the boat within arms' length of the fluttering pelican. Dugan was leaning over, reaching for the pelican when Chrissy finally saw it. With every propulsion of the shark's tail, the dorsal fin lunged closer.

"Dugan!" she screamed.

He pulled the bird from the ocean just as the shark's head thrust upward, water spilling over the blunt nose and small black eyes. The wide jaws clamped onto the end of the Pelican's wing, plucking its feathers. The bird screeched as the shark's body, gray and slick, slashed against the kayak, then plunked with a large splash into the water. The boat rocked and swirled sideways. Dugan almost toppled into the ocean but somehow managed to hold on to the pelican.

Grabbing an oar, Chrissy shouted, "Put that bird down and help me row!"

Dugan plopped the pelican between them and grabbed the paddle. To turn the kayak toward shore, Chrissy stabbed the oar into the water several times, and the boat swung around. In the panicked moments as they struggled to generate forward movement, the oars slapped the water haphazardly, creating little advancement and lots of splashing. That's when the dorsal fin rose again and cut through the surface, passing parallel to the kayak. Dugan's paddle missed the fin by inches. He saw the tail slice by and realized the fish was as longer than the boat—more than twelve feet.

"Get in rhythm!" Chrissy yelled as she paddled and counted: "One—two, one—two, one—two." Dugan caught on and the kayak accelerated.

The shark cut to the right, its fin like a gray sail fifteen feet in front of them. Chrissy watched it circle back toward the boat and then submerge. Her arms felt shaky, and hollow fear caused a sudden bout of nausea. But the boat skimmed steadily over the choppy surface. Looking into shore, she could see the empty shallows and the crowd standing at the edge of the water, their faces white with horror. In the middle stood her mother, hands clutched in prayer.

Thirty yards away the breakers began. But the fin appeared again, this time charging straight toward the middle of the boat. As it neared, the shark turned parallel and raised its head to bite the edge of the kayak. That's when Dugan lifted his paddle and whacked its wide snout. The tail whipped violently, throwing a curtain of water over them. Its head broke the surface again, but Dugan, holding his oar like an axe, chopped directly onto the shark's little eye. The great fish thrashed beside them, stirring the water like a bubbling cauldron.

"Paddle!" Chrissy screamed. This time their oars dipped simultaneously and fluently. Within seconds a large wave lifted and thrust them forward, the kayak skimming with great velocity ahead of the curl. As the boat charged up the slope of the bank and skidded onto the sand, the crowd closed in and cheered. Dugan stood and lifted the pelican. The lifeguard reached down and pulled Chrissy to her feet. Fighting back tears, she staggered to her mother's side, and they embraced.

Leroy grabbed a large blue beach towel and shook the sand off of it. Running up to Dugan he draped it around his shoulders and proclaimed: "All hail, King Dugan!"

The spectators applauded and divided as Dugan, clutching the bloody bird, walked toward his Aunt Annie. She extended her hands, and he carefully transferred the weakened creature into her arms.

"He's hurt, Aunt Annie, really bad," he said.

"We'll fix him good as new," Annie said.

When Dugan turned, he saw Janey step toward him. "I'm so proud of you." She spread her arms, hugged him, and kissed his cheek.

Dugan looked like he was about to faint when Mark cut in front of him and said, "Hey, Doogie, we want a rematch."

That snapped Dugan out of it. "Anytime," he said. "Anytime."

Lila stepped in between them. "Those kayaks are going back to the rental store right now! Do you hear me? Right now!"

"Aw, Mom. I was just kidding," Mark said.

Chapter Twelve

Dugan turned the small key on the padlock, unhooked the lock, and lifted the clasp on a wooden box shaped like a treasure chest.

"Thanks, Uncle Elijah," he said. "This tooth is going in my pirate's chest!" He held a large shark's tooth between thumb and finger, examining it. "This came from a humungous shark. Probably a great white."

"Might be, Dugan," Elijah said. "I got it at the gift shop next to the bakery. Thought I'd get you something to remember your battle with that nasty shark. I should've been there to see that."

"The life guard said it was a female bull shark. He could tell by the color and wide nose."

Elijah scratched his beard. "How'd he know it was a female?"

"He said females are much bigger than males, and that one was huge. Last year a bull shark killed a man off Cape Hatteras. Bit his foot right off and took a big chunk out of his back. That's what the life guard said, anyway." Dugan opened the box and carefully placed the tooth inside.

"What do you got in there?" Elijah asked.

"All kinds of neat stuff. Mostly cool shells I found along the beach, but looky here." He reached into the corner of the box and pulled out a white object, flat and round.

"Well I'll be! A sand dollar, and a big one at that." Elijah took the sand dollar and examined it. "It's perfect. No cracks or chips. Did you know mermaids use these in the soda machines at the bottom of the ocean?"

Dugan laughed. "Soda machines. That's funny, Uncle Elijah."

He handed it back to Dugan and looked in the box. "What's that green thing?"

"That's sea glass. It looks like a jewel, doesn't it?"

"Very impressive. Where'd you find it?"

"Janey gave it to me. She found it on the beach today. Her mother told her sea glass comes from wrecked ships—bottles and stuff. The water and sand grind and polish it real smooth. "

"Janey? She's as pretty as a mermaid, ain't she?"

Dugan shrugged.

"I thought she was Mark's girl," Elijah said.

Dugan closed the box and snapped the lock. "She was until that shark came along."

"I guess almost getting eaten alive has its benefits." Elijah reached out and patted Dugan's head. "Do me a favor, would ya, boy?"

"Sure, Uncle Elijah."

"Try not to get lost or eaten the rest of the vacation."

Dugan smiled. "Don't worry. I don't plan on it."

"Look there," Elijah said, pointing to the sliding glass door. "Moochy's back, beggin' for lunch."

Dugan glanced out and saw the squirrel. "Can we feed him?"

"Sure." He patted his shirt pocket. "I've got some cheese crackers in my pocket."

The big man and wiry boy passed through the sliding glass door onto the deck. There they tossed crackers to Moochy and recounted stories of danger and daring and near-disaster.

* * *

When Byron returned from the lighthouse, Lila wouldn't speak to him. She wanted time alone in their bedroom to recover from the trauma of the day. Standing outside the door, he listened to her cry and decided it best not to force reconciliation until he fully understood what had happened. After hearing the story from Mark and Matt, Byron wrestled with his responsibility in the episode. He remembered his words to his wife: *Honey, you've got to lighten up. It's perfectly safe. Let these kids have some fun*—words he'd regularly repeated throughout these childrearing days. Lila had always been overprotective. He didn't want his children growing up reserved and fearful. Whenever Lila agonized over circumstances and possibilities, Byron played the devil's advocate and encouraged activities that developed courage. He wanted his kids to be strong and bold.

Of course he would never promote an activity that would put his children in harm's way. *Today's incident should never have occurred. What got into Chrissy? Sometimes she goes too far. Is that my fault? She's an intelligent girl.*

She should've known better. Makes me wonder about her judgment. Then again, maybe kids paddling kayaks in the ocean wasn't such a good idea. I should've told them not to go in until I got there. But what could I've done? Once Chrissy and Dugan paddled beyond the breakers my hands would have been tied. Chrissy, Chrissy. What were you thinking?

Later that afternoon he walked down the hall and knocked on Chrissy's door.

"Who is it?"

"Your father."

"Come in."

She sat on her bed wearing jeans shorts and an Outer Banks t-shirt with dolphins leaping over waves. One of her mother's romance novels rested on her lap.

"Hi, Dad," she said, her eyes large and melancholy.

"Are you all right?"

"I'm fine. Still a little jittery, but I'll get over it."

"Your mother's not taking it too well."

She hung her head. "I know. Mom always gets pretty emotional over things. Hope she's not too mad at me."

"She's thankful you're alive. I'm the one she's mad at." He pointed to her chest. "I should have bought you a shirt with a shark on it."

"I'll stick with dolphins, thank you very much."

Bryon sat on the bed and grasped her ankle. "Chrissy, you know sometimes you push things a little too far. You make unwise decisions."

"I know we shouldn't have paddled out that far, Dad, but at the time it didn't seem so far. When we got there and found the wounded pelican, we just had to try to save it. I didn't know that stupid shark wanted Pelican planks for lunch."

"I think his choice of a main course changed once he saw you and Dugan in that kayak."

"That's true."

"Listen. I'm not mad at you. I just want to emphasize that you need to think clearly and make wise decisions in these kinds of circumstances. There're always consequences to bad decisions. The good Lord was gracious today. But you can't count on God to suspend the natural laws of life whenever you mess up."

"I know that, Dad. But what were the chances we'd meet up with a shark—one in a thousand at least. And you always encourage us to help those in need. Do you mean to tell me you would have left that injured pelican out there to die?"

"That's not my point."

"But would you?"

"I just want you to learn to make more responsible decisions."

Chrissy took a deep breath and tightened her lips.

Byron patted her shin. "Let's just put this behind us and face the future a little wiser. Shoot, this evening at the cookout, your mother'll be over it and everyone'll be fine. We'll joke about that old shark that Dugan thumped on the noggin. When Kenny gets here, you can tell him all about it."

"That reminds me," Chrissy said. "I invited someone else to the cookout."

"Really? Who?"

"His name's Jack Blaze."

"Another guy? But you already invited Kenny Queen."

"I didn't invite Kenny. You did."

"Oh, yeah. I guess you're right. Well, who's this Jack Blaze?"

"I met him on the beach today. He does card tricks. You'll like him. Without Jack's advice, we would've never made it past the breakers."

"He told you how to get through the waves?"

"Yeah, and it worked liked a charm."

"Hmmmph." Byron stood and walked to the door. "What did he have to say after you met up with the shark beyond the waves?"

"He didn't stick around to see that. He had to go somewhere."

"I see," Byron said as he left the room. *Sent them out into the deep but didn't stick around to see what would happen.*

He decided to walk to the bakery and pick up some pastries and a newspaper. There and back, even after eating three chocolate-covered doughnuts, he couldn't shake a negative impression of someone he hadn't even met yet, someone by the name of Jack Blaze.

* * *

In the great room that evening, Byron stretched out on the recliner reading the newspaper. Chrissy sat on a stool next to him as Lila braided her hair.

When the chimes sounded, Byron said, "That's some fancy doorbell."

"Could you get that, Daddy? It's probably Jack," Chrissy said.

"Of course," Byron said, collapsing the recliner's leg support and dropping the paper. "I need to size this young fellow up before I let him near my daughter. See if he passes the old Butler standards of excellence."

"Please, Dad. We're not planning on getting hitched. He's just a friend," Chrissy pleaded.

Lila raised a threatening finger. "Be nice."

Be nice, Byron thought as he descended the stairs. *I'll be nice, all right.*

The first thing Byron noticed when he opened the door was the young man's skin tone—he wasn't white. He appeared to be the same shade as the children of an interracial couple who recently joined the Scotch Ridge Church. With a white mother and black father, the kids' skin was somewhere between a light brown and olive.

Byron extended his hand. "You must be Jack?" The man's handshake was soft and slippery.

"I'm guessing you're Chrissy's father? Nice to meet you."

Byron nodded. "I'm Byron Butler." He didn't like the sound of Jack's voice. It reminded him of a doped-up rock star. And his eyelids were too dark and droopy.

Because the man wore an orange tank top, the large tattoo of the devil on his shoulder immediately caught Byron's attention. That was even more disturbing. *What's this guy into? The occult?* "That's some tattoo."

Jack grinned. "It's a part of me."

The grin, almost a smirk, triggered Byron's memory. "Have we met before?"

"Maybe. It's a small world."

Byron analyzed his face, but he couldn't quite account for the strange sensation of déjà vu. "Follow me. Everyone's upstairs." At the bottom of the steps, Byron stopped and said, "Chrissy tells me you taught her and Dugan the secret of how to paddle a kayak beyond the breakers."

"Secrets are my specialty."

"Did you know she and Dugan ran into a large shark out there?"

He nodded.

"Chrissy told me you left. How'd you find out?"

"I'm a guide at the Whalehead Club. Big news gets around. A kid in one of my tour groups mentioned it."

"Weren't you concerned?"

Jack rubbed his goatee. "Sure. But by then the incident was over. Fate's a funny thing, Mr. Butler. Some people think life is random, but I don't think so. Sometimes we have to battle sharks."

As Byron noted the man's dispassionate demeanor, he thought, *Yes, sometimes we have to battle sharks.* "Do me a favor, would you, Jack?"

He lifted his chin.

"For now on, keep your secrets to yourself."

The young man grinned, and for a moment Byron thought he resembled a shark.

When Byron led Jack into the great room, Dugan ran up and said, "Hey, Jack, wanna see my shark's tooth?"

Jack gave Dugan the thumbs up sign. "What'd you do? Knock that tooth out with your oar?"

Dugan laughed. "Gosh, no. Uncle Elijah gave it to me. Come over here." He tugged him to the counter where he kept his locked pirate's chest, inserted the key and opened the padlock. After extracting the tooth, he gave it to Jack, who held it up to the light and examined it. Mark, Matt and Chrissy gathered around, and Dugan narrated a detailed account of the fight with the shark. Chrissy interjected occasional particulars from her perspective, and the twins offered glimpses of the scene from the spectators' view.

Jack handed back the tooth, and Dugan placed it in the box.

"Quite a few interesting items in there," Jack commented.

"I'm keeping these things to show my mom and all my friends back home. I've got shells, sea glass, a sand dollar, a starfish and now, a shark's tooth—all of it from the ocean. You could never find this cool stuff in Ohio." He closed the lid and snapped the padlock.

"You're quite the man, Dugan," Jack said. "There's something else of great value in that box you didn't mention."

"Really? Something worth money? What is it, Jack?"

"Memories."

Byron noticed Chrissy's expression when Blaze said that word. She seemed enchanted by this odd stranger. Although his words were few, she hung on each one and constantly studied his face like an artist preparing to draw a portrait. Byron had never seen his daughter react this way toward a guy before. It annoyed him, chaffed that tender place in a father's heart that guarded the best interests of a daughter.

Chrissy took Jack by the elbow and ushered him into the kitchen to introduce him to Annie and Lila. After courteous greetings, he informed them he hailed from New York City but ventured to the Outer Banks for summer employment and an opportunity to hone his illusionist skills by performing for beach crowds. The ladies warmly welcomed him and insisted he demonstrate his magical powers after dinner. Chrissy led him onto the deck to meet Elijah. Through the glass, Byron could see Elijah and Blaze shake hands, then Elijah talking and gesticulating with the spatula as the flames licked the ground beef.

When they re-entered the great room, Lila recruited Chrissy to help in the kitchen. Jack talked to the boys and meandered around the room admiring the décor of the vacation home.

Soon the sliding glass door opened and Elijah stepped in, holding a tray stacked with steaming burgers. "Hope everybody's hungry," he announced. "Hamburgies are ready!"

The families gathered around the long table, and Lila asked Byron to say the blessing.

Byron hesitated. "Maybe our guest would like to offer a blessing for us this evening?"

Everyone looked at Jack.

With his eyelids slightly closed, he glanced around the table, nodded and extended his hands, one to Chrissy and one to Dugan. Following his gesture, the others linked hands. Slowly he bowed his head, and everyone bowed.

"This food is the gift of the whole universe," he began, quietly but clearly. "Each morsel is a sacrifice of life. May the energy in this food give us the strength for the journey of life. Along that path may each accomplish his purpose in life and be illuminated by the light that shines from within. We are grateful for this food. Amen."

"Amen," Elijah said as everyone released hands. "I must say, Jack, that was an interesting prayer."

"Thank you," he said.

"Just one minor complaint," Byron said.

Lifting his chin, Jack gazed at Byron.

"I can't recall you mentioning God," Byron said.

Jack smiled, that half-smirk of a smile. "Maybe you weren't listening with your heart."

Before the uncomfortable silence could saturate the atmosphere, Annie said, "Let's eat. There's a lot of good food here. Dugan, scoop out some of that potato salad and pass the bowl. Elijah, get those hamburgers moving around the table. There's plenty of iced tea and soda." With Annie's encouragement, casseroles, salads, pastas and rolls crossed and circled the table. Plates filled to overflowing, and conversations sprang up and blossomed. Before long, everyone seemed to have forgotten the prayer—everyone, that is, except for Byron.

"Hey, Jack," Elijah said, lifting the large plate of burgers from the middle of the table. "You didn't get one of my specialties. Best burger you'll taste in these parts." He extended the plate across the table.

"No thank you," Jack said as he waved his hand. "I'm a vegetarian."

Elijah raised his eyebrows, his mouth gaping momentarily. "A vegetarian? You don't eat meat?"

Jack nodded.

Annie quickly said, "Not everyone clogs their arteries with saturated fats, Elijah."

Elijah sat the plate down. "Hmmmph." He picked up his hamburger and chomped an extra large bite.

After filling up on the variety of foods, everyone scooted back from the table, satisfied and smiling. Annie and Lila went into the kitchen and returned with apple pie and slices of watermelon.

"Hope everyone saved room for dessert," Lila said.

"I'll have to loosen my belt buckle, but that's no problem," Elijah said.

The ladies served the pie and watermelon, and the diners scooted back to the table and dug in again. The boys ate a slice of pie and two slices of watermelon each.

When the conversation slowed, the boys began to pound the table and chant, "We want a card trick. We want a card trick. We want a card trick."

"Yes, Jack," Lila said. "Chrissy told me you amazed her at the beach today. I'm anxious to see your magic."

Blaze reached into his back pocket and pulled out a deck of new cards. "I would like to perform this feat in honor of the hero of the day, my man, Dugan. Could someone unwrap the cards for me and examine them to make sure it's a normal deck?"

Byron volunteered. He tore off the plastic wrapping, carefully scrutinized the box, pulled the cards out and flipped through them. "Seems pretty generic," he said.

"Would you kindly shuffle them for us?"

With unusual intensity, Byron shuffled the deck, constantly looking at the faces of the cards as they riffed through his hands. Finally, he extended them to Blaze.

Jack spread the cards in his hands and tilted them facedown toward Dugan. "Pick any card and show it to everyone."

Pulling a ten of clubs from the deck, Dugan held the card for all to see.

Blaze formed the deck into a neat pile and set it on the table in front of Dugan. "Now, cut the deck and insert the card wherever you would like."

Dugan cut the cards deeply and placed the ten of clubs toward the bottom. Then he put the remaining cards on top.

"Watch carefully," Blaze said as he rubbed his hands together over of the deck. He picked up the cards and placed them on his palm. "Dugan, I want you to take your finger and thump the top card, and do it with the same determination you thumped that shark with on the head today."

Dugan smiled, reached out and with a flick of his wrist, rapped the top of the deck with his finger.

Jack placed the deck on the table and spread his hands. "Friends, do not underestimate the power of determination, especially in a young man like Dugan. His whack on that shark's head sent the beast swimming back to the depths of the sea. And just now, that same determination raised the ten of clubs from the bottom to the top of the deck. Dugan, please take the top card and show everyone."

Anxiously, Dugan snatched the top card and turned it over—the three of hearts. The wrong card released sighs of disappointment around the table. Dugan's shoulders slumped, and Byron shook his head. Blaze appeared confused.

"Maybe it's the next card," Dugan said. He reached out and turned the next one over—five of diamonds. Quickly he flipped through six more, but none was the ten of clubs. "I'm sorry, Jack. I must have lost my determination."

"You have nothing to be sorry about, Dugan," Byron said. "It's not your fault. Am I right, Jack?"

The magician seemed stupefied. He glanced around the table, eyes confused. Feeling embarrassed for him, everyone avoided his gaze except for Byron. With a shaky voice, he said, "Dugan, would you please look through that deck and find the ten of clubs for me?"

"It's probably still near the bottom," Byron said.

Dugan turned over the deck and spread the cards. "It's not here," he exclaimed.

Byron separated them more thoroughly; making sure two weren't stuck together.

"I'm sorry," Jack said. "I have underestimated Dugan's metaphysical powers."

"What do you mean?" Byron asked.

"Dugan, is there a special place in this room where you keep things that are important to you?" Jack asked.

"My pirate's chest! But it can't be in there 'cause it's locked, and I'm the only one with a key." He reached in his pocket and pulled out the small golden key.

Mark jumped out of his seat, hurried to the counter and snatched the wooden box. He ran back and placed it in the middle of the table. "Open it, Dugan. Open it!"

Hands trembling, Dugan inserted the key, popped open the lock and flipped the lid. The ten of clubs rested in the corner next to the sand dollar.

Everyone gasped.

Dugan's eyes widened. "Did I do that?"

"Never underestimate one's power of determination," Jack said.

Byron sat dumbfounded. Something strange had happened right before his eyes and he could not fathom how it had been pulled off. He glanced at Chrissy and noticed she was enthralled, mouth open, eyes intent on the illusionist. Smiling his sickening smile, Blaze met Chrissy's gaze. Byron wanted to reach out and shake her—break the spell.

"That was awesome!" Matt shouted. "Do another one!"

"Please. Please. We want to see more," Chrissy said

Elijah leaned back in his chair and rubbed his beard. His expression darkened as if he wanted to interrupt this mystical demonstration and send the magician on his way. Byron noticed Elijah's consternation and tried to make eye contact, but he couldn't get his attention.

"Enough of the card tricks," Blaze said. "Does anyone have a quarter?"

"I have one down in my bedroom," Dugan announced.

"My purse is out in the kitchen," Annie said.

"Never mind," Byron said. "I have one." Byron reached into his pocket. As he handed Blaze the quarter, that odd sense of reliving a moment returned.

Blaze took the coin and began to rub it between his thumb and finger. "I have learned to change the molecular structure of metal simply by rubbing its surface. The heat generated by friction weakens the metal's composition." The motion of his thumb and finger accelerated, machine-like. He stopped and his eyes widened. As he raised the coin to his mouth, he bared his teeth like a vampire. He bit down on the edge and snapped it away. Quickly he lifted the quarter to the center of the circle of faces. Everyone focused and saw a chunk of metal had been bitten out of the top of the coin. Blaze slowly drew the quarter back to within an inch of his mouth. He pursed his lips, and with the jerk of his head and a quick burst of air, the quarter became whole again.

"Oh my great grandmother's grave!" Annie gasped. She took a deep breath. "That gave me chills."

"That's impossible," Lila said. "How'd you do that?"

Blaze handed the quarter back to Byron. As he examined the coin, he remembered exactly where he had seen Jack Blaze before.

Chapter Thirteen

Byron managed to pull Elijah aside and lead him through the sliding door onto the deck. Remembering the strange dream of the man in the mirror reinforced Byron's suspicions—if the dream foreshadowed danger, then Blaze posed a threat. Byron trusted Elijah's judgment when it came to people. He had a knack of seeing below the surface to character and motives. Closing the door behind them, Byron joined Elijah at the railing where they gazed at the horizon, the early evening sky fading to blue-gray above the Atlantic.

"What do you think of Mr. Magic?" Byron asked.

Elijah glanced over his shoulder and then at Byron. "I have a hard time trusting a man who specializes in deception, but maybe that's just me."

"How'd he do it? I can't figure it out."

"I've seen guys perform great card tricks before but nothing like that. And the quarter. He bit a piece out of it right in plain view. It's too unnatural."

"How 'bout that prayer?" Byron asked. "Where'd he come up with that mumbo jumbo?"

"It sounded Buddhist—food being the gift of the universe and the light that shines from within—very New Age."

"Did you notice how he used the power of suggestion?" Byron asked. "He talked about metaphysical capabilities and altering molecular structure. He wants us to think he's superhuman. I think he's got the boys believing he's some kind of miracle man, and Chrissy can't take her eyes off him."

"Reminds me of something a conman would do."

"A conman?"

"You know—try to impress you, gain your trust and then rip you off."

"This might sound crazy, but I've seen this guy before."

Elijah faced Byron. "Where?"

"In a dream I had one night at the hospital."

"Are you serious?"

"I swear his face appeared in the mirror of my hospital room. One of the strangest experiences I've ever had."

Elijah rubbed his hairy chin. "That's weird. Sometimes God warns believers through dreams. In a dream God told Joseph to take Mary and Jesus and escape Bethlehem before Herod's soldiers slaughtered the innocents."

Byron nodded. "I keep thinking about a scripture I read this morning during my devotional time—2 Corinthians 11:14."

Elijah tilted his head. "Can't quite recall that one, good buddy."

"For Satan himself masquerades as an angel of light."

"Whew." Elijah leaned on the railing. "Just felt the confirmation of the Spirit."

"Look." Byron pointed below. "Kenny just pulled up in the police cruiser. Maybe he knows something about Blaze."

Elijah waved and shouted: "Hey big fellow! I'm ready to put a half pound o' ground round on the grill for you!"

Kenny slammed the car door, smiled and tipped his ball cap. "What're you waitin' for, Elijah? I'm hungrier than a grizzly on the first day of spring! Remember. You promised to put on all the trimmings."

"Hope you cops get along with the fire department around here!" Elijah yelled.

"Why's that?"

" 'Cause I've got some hot peppers that'll start a three-alarm blaze in your mouth!"

"I can take it! Pile 'em on, big man!"

"I'll send Chrissy down to let you in, Kenny," Byron said. "Elijah and I want to talk to you about something important."

"Sure thing. Be right up."

Elijah plopped a large ground beef patty on the grill as Byron turned and entered the great room. Sitting on the floor in front of the television, Blaze dealt cards to Chrissy and the boys. The sounds of pots clanging and water splashing emanated from the kitchen where the women scrubbed the supper dishes.

"Hope you're not playing for money," Byron said. "Mr. Blaze might be a card shark."

Chrissy flashed him a dirty look. "We're playing *Hearts*, Dad. You wanna play?"

"No thanks. Hate to interrupt, but Kenny just arrived. Could you go down and let him in?"

"I'll be back in a minute," Chrissy said as she laid her cards on the floor. She sprang to her feet and hurried down the steps.

"Do you know Kenny Queen, Jack?" Byron asked.

"Yes, I know Queen. He makes regular security checks at the Whalehead Club where I work."

Byron thought he noticed a slight irritation in Blaze's voice. "Nice young man, Deputy Queen."

"I don't know him that well. We talk occasionally, but we don't hang out."

"Trust me," Byron said. "He's a nice guy."

Blaze shrugged.

When Chrissy and Kenny arrived at the top of the steps, everyone greeted the young officer. Annie and Lila rushed out of the kitchen, and Annie hugged him, saying, "How's the young man who found my lost nephew?"

Kenny smiled. "Doin' fine. Just finished my rounds. Couldn't pass up your invitation. Looking forward to tasting one of Elijah's famous hamburgers."

"You won't be disappointed," Annie said.

Dugan had already charged over to his pirate's chest, opened the lock and extracted the shark tooth. He squeezed in between Mark and Matt and thrust it in front of Queen's face.

"Looky here, Deputy Kenny! A real shark's tooth from a great white."

He inspected the tooth. "Ain't that somethin'?" He tapped its tip against his muscled forearm. "Wouldn't want to be on the receiving end of that shark's hello—*Glad to meet ya, soon to eat ya!*"

The twins laughed and slapped Dugan on the back.

"I almost got ate today!" Dugan exclaimed.

"That's what I heard. Word gets round these parts fast." Queen mussed Dugan's hair. "I'm glad you and Chrissy showed that ol' boy who's boss."

Standing outside the group, Blaze commented, "Sharks don't care who's boss."

"'Scuse me?" Kenny said, and everyone looked at Blaze.

"They're not that intelligent—just prehistoric killing machines ruled by their cravings."

Queen's smile widened as he gripped the handle of his nightstick. "With a good thump on the head you can show anyone who's boss. Right, Dugan?"

Dugan nodded.

Byron tried to stifle a smile but couldn't.

Annie stepped forward. "Kenny, do you know Jack?"

"Sure, I know Blaze," he said. "We've talked a few times at the Whalehead Club when I'm making my rounds."

"The Whalehead Club?" Lila asked.

"Yeah, that's right," Kenny said.

Lila stepped next to Byron and grasped his hand. "Oh, Byron, I want to take a tour of the Whalehead Club tomorrow. It's such an odd looking building compared to these beach houses. I think it would be fascinating."

"I'm up for that if everyone else is," Byron said.

"You might get ol' Blaze here to be your tour guide," Kenny said. "Wouldn't that be a treat?"

"I'd be happy to guide you, Mrs. Butler," Jack said. "And you're right—It's a great old building, an unusual Art Nouveau design."

Kenny raised his eyebrows and pursed his lips. "Art Nouveau?" he chimed with a bad French accent, his hand limply dangling from his wrist.

Everyone laughed except for Jack.

Annie reached up and patted Kenny's cheek. "Now quit that," she said. "Using that goofy accent when Jack's trying to educate us about local architecture."

"No offense taken," Blaze said. "I realize Queen's knowledge of artistic style is limited."

Queen's forehead wrinkled as he pulled out his nightstick. "I think I need to show this ol' boy who's boss." Then he laughed, reached out, and tried to tap Blaze on the shoulder with it.

Blaze jumped back, almost lost his balance but caught himself. His face reddened.

"Take it easy now, Blaze. Just rattlin' your cage a little."

Blaze's eyes narrowed as he stepped out of Queen's reach. "I'm sure you've rattled a lot of cages along the way."

Queen quickly slid the nightstick back into the loop on his belt. "Didn't mean to scare ya. Just havin' a little bit of fun. Tell us more about the Whalehead Club."

"Yes, Jack, please," Lila said nervously. "Tell us more about the Whalehead club. When was it built?"

Before he could answer, the glass door slid open as Elijah peeked in and said, "Hey, Deputy Queen, I thought you were hungrier than a grizzly bear?"

"You got that right," Queen said.

"Well, get out here and bring a big bun with you. Your burger's 'bout done."

Annie led Kenny into the kitchen and supplied him with a plateful of potato salad, slaw, baked beans and a bun. After leading him onto the deck, Byron closed the sliding door. Glancing into the great room, Byron saw Lila and Chrissy intently listening to Blaze as he pointed and gestured. Byron figured he was giving a preview of tomorrow's tour. *Please Lord, anybody but him,* Byron prayed. *I'll take an old biddy who chokes us with her halitosis before I'd tour that place with him.*

"That smells like heaven," Kenny said. "Lay that juicy hunk o' beef right on this bun."

Elijah lifted the burger. The grease dribbled off, and flames leapt up, making Elijah flinch.

"Don't drop it on the floor, big man," Queen said. "I haven't eaten for three hours. I'm famished."

"Young guys," Elijah said. "Eat all they want and never gain a pound. Wait a minute now, fellow." Elijah took tongs and lifted a banana pepper off the grill. "You sure you want this? It's hotter than the asphalt on the devil's playground."

"The hotter the better," Queen said.

Elijah draped the pepper across the burger, and Queen took a big bite. His eyes bulged, and he blew short puffs. Grabbing a glass of iced tea from the table next to the grill, he gulped it, liquid streaming down the sides of his face and neck.

Elijah laughed uproariously, doubling over. "Told you it was hot!"

"Wheeweee! My eyes are watering."

"After you get a hold of yourself, we need to ask you a question," Byron said.

Queen pounded his chest several times and swallowed. "I think I'm all right. Fire away."

"What do you know about Jack Blaze?" Elijah asked.

Queen glanced through the glass pane, eyes fixing on Blaze. "I call him Whodinny. Always doing magic tricks for the tourists—on the beach, at the Whalehead Club, at the resort playground."

"You have to admit, he's pretty good," Byron said.

"He's all right," Queen said. "Give me a chance and I could figure out any trick he does. Course, I'd have to watch real close to catch it. He's a strange bird, though, ain't he? Puts on an act like he's really some kind of Merlin. People walk away believing he has mysterious powers. Guess that's how he gets his jollies."

"Do you think he's dangerous?" Byron asked.

Queen laughed. "Blaze? He seems harmless. You never know for sure though 'til you check somebody's background."

"And he's got that devil tattoo," Elijah added.

Nodding, Queen said, "That's true. I know he's from New York City. That tattoo might be some gang-related symbol."

"Gang related? I don't like the sound of that," Byron said.

Kenny rubbed his chin. "Tell you what. I'll ask around. Maybe somebody knows something about him. If I could get hold of his driver's license, I could run a check on him."

Byron pictured Queen poking Blaze's license number into a police computer. Would that be going too far? No. Not where his daughter is concerned. He stared at the horizon and wondered if he was becoming paranoid. Had these dreams and visions pushed him beyond the fine line of reason? He decided caution was acceptable, but for now there was no need to pry into Blaze's private life. "That's a possibility, Kenny. But only if necessary. Keep your ears open. Maybe someone knows something about him."

"Sure thing, Byron. I'll ask a few people, but I'll keep it friendly, unofficial."

"Thanks."

As Kenny ate the hamburger and gulped iced tea, Byron told him about the trick with the missing card and Dugan's pirate's chest. Then Elijah described the eerie episode with the quarter. Somewhat embarrassed, Elijah confessed he thought Blaze just might possess some kind of occult power.

"No way," Kenny said. "He's as human as the rest of us. He must have used a prop for the quarter trick. Presto-chango-bingo-bango. It's all done with sleight of hand. A good illusionist can switch objects faster than the untrained eye can see."

"I don't see how," Elijah said. "He bit a chunk out of that quarter in plain view."

"A good prop makes the magician look good," Kenny said. "Cards are a different story, especially if he's using a regular deck. To figure out the card trick, I'd have to watch him."

Elijah stuck his hand out. "Betcha can't figure it out."

Kenny set down his glass of tea. "What?"

"I'll bet you lunch at the Wild Horse Café tomorrow if you can tell me how he does that card trick."

"Okay, big man," Kenny said, shaking his hand. "I could stand a good lunch, and tomorrow's my day off. Follow me. It's time to bust Whodinny's bubble."

Kenny led them into the great room. The women and boys had gathered around Jack, watching him perform an elaborate shuffle—cards shooting like a streaming ribbon from one hand to the other.

"Hey, Blaze," Kenny said.

Everyone turned and looked at Queen.

"Elijah and Byron tell me you amazed them with some fancy card trick."

Blaze sent a spate of cards shooting from one hand to the other, swiveled the deck with his fingers and smiled. "Some refer to what I do as tricks. I like to call it *Magic*."

Queen raised his eyebrows. "Riiiight. *Magic*," he said. "Anyway, Elijah here will buy me lunch at the Wild Horse Café if I can figure out how you do it. You up for the challenge?"

"Usually I don't perform under these circumstances. Magic is an art, not a competition. But for a man of your intelligence, Queen, I will accept your challenge."

"You don't mind me revealing your secrets in front of these admiring fans?"

"I'm not worried," Blaze said.

Kenny smiled and winked at Chrissy. "All right then. Pick your best trick. I'm ready."

Blaze shuffled the cards furiously, machine-like, his hands becoming a blur. Stopping, he spread a fan of cards in front of Kenny's face. "Look at the cards. Don't touch any. Mentally pick one out and think about it."

"Ooooooohhhh, goody," Kenny said as his eyes scanned the cards. "The powers of mental telepathy. You will attempt to read my mind."

"Some minds are easy to read," Blaze said.

Queen peered over the cards into Blaze's dark eyes. "I might surprise you, Blaze."

"I doubt that."

"Okay, I got the mental picture of the card. Now what?"

"Write it down on a piece of paper and give it to Chrissy for safe-keeping."

Lila retrieved a pen and slip of paper from the counter in the kitchen and gave it to him. Kenny walked to the dining table, jotted the name of the card and quickly folded the paper. Holding it up, he said, "Okay, Chrissy. Come and get it."

Chrissy walked to the table and reached for the paper. When she tried to pull it from Queen's fingers, he wouldn't let go. She smiled, yanked it out of his hand and slid it into the pocket of her shorts.

"Just seeing how strong you are," Kenny said.

Chrissy gently elbowed his ribs. "You'd be surprised how strong I am."

Kenny smiled and elbowed her arm.

Blaze walked to the table, and everyone gathered around. Handing the deck to Kenny, he said, "I'll let you do the honors. Spread the cards out facedown."

With a circular hand motion, Kenny spread the cards near the edge of the table.

"To make this feat even more difficult, I need a large piece a paper," Blaze said.

"I've got something you could use," Lila said. She hurried into the kitchen and returned with a local tourist map. "Will this do?"

"Perfect," Blaze said. "Could you please place it over the cards?"

Lila gently positioned the map, completely covering the cards.

Blaze pointed to Queen's belt. "Is that knife standard issue?"

Kenny reached for the white handle of a hunting knife slung in a leather sheath from his belt. "Not hardly. My father gave this to me after I won the state wrestling title."

"May I use it?" Blaze asked.

Queen shrugged and unsnapped the loop. "Handle it with care. It has great sentimental value. My father passed away a year ago last June." He pulled the knife from the sheath, delicately grasped the top of the blade between his fingers and handed it to Blaze.

Seeing Blaze's hand tighten on the hilt tensed Byron's body, nervous energy charging through his muscles.

Baring his teeth, Blaze scowled at Queen and yanked the knife above his head. Queen's hands flew up and he stepped back, losing his balance. Before Byron could react, Blaze turned and stabbed the knife through the map into the table. When he let go, the handle quivered. With help from Elijah, Kenny kept from tumbling backwards.

Queen erupted. "Why the heck ya do that?" His face reddened and his eyes flamed.

"Take it easy, Queen," Blaze said with an exaggerated southern accent. "Didn't mean to scare ya. Just rattlin' your cage a little."

Byron's heart thumped. He took a deep breath and tried to relax. He sensed Queen's restrained animosity, as if the cop called upon every ounce of self-control to keep from wringing Blaze's neck. When Queen stepped forward, Byron prepared to jump between them, but Queen reached for his knife instead of Blaze's throat. He hesitated, hand hovering above the knife handle as he focused where the blade entered the map. His distraction drew everyone's attention to the blade's point— the tip had pierced the map in the center of a drawing of the Whalehead Club. With a quick jerk, he removed the blade from the table, but the map stuck to the end of the knife, sagged and fluttered as Queen tried to shake it off. Finally he turned the blade over. As the corners of the map fell away, everyone saw the card stuck to the tip.

Chrissy reached out and carefully extracted it from the point. When she turned over the jack of hearts, Queen's eyes widened. Reaching into her pocket, she pulled out the folded paper and unwrapped it. Everyone's mouths dropped open when they saw the writing—Jack of Hearts.

"You did it!" Chrissy blurted. She looked at Jack, eyes filled with amazement. "That's the card!"

She handed it to Kenny, and he examined both sides. His eyes filled with confusion. "That's impossible," he said. Flicking his wrist, Queen spun the card at Blaze. Like a rattlesnake striking, Blaze's hand snatched it from the air.

"I'm wounded, Queen," he said as he extended the card flat in his hand. "You don't want to keep this for a souvenir?"

"No thanks," Queen said.

Chrissy stepped forward. "Can I have it?"

Blaze rubbed the whole in the middle of the card. "This Jack's heart is pierced, but it's all yours." Blaze lifted the card with the tips of his fingers and offered it to Chrissy. "Now, if everyone will excuse me, I must be on my way. The food was delicious and the company, for the most part, enjoyable."

"I'll walk you to the door," Chrissy said.

"That would be very kind of you." He nodded to the women. "Ladies, thank you for your hospitality." Then he glanced at Byron and Elijah. "Gentlemen, nice meeting you."

Everyone seemed speechless until Lila stammered, "Th-Thank y-you for the . . . entertainment, Jack."

"Always a pleasure," he responded.

After Chrissy and Jack had descended the stairs, the women returned to the kitchen and the men moved into the middle of the great room.

Elijah asked, "Okay, Kenny, how'd he do it?"

Queen shook his head. "I'm still chompin' on it. Not sure yet."

"See what I mean? Spooky, huh?" Elijah slapped Kenny on the back. "You owe me lunch."

Queen smiled. "I haven't given up yet, big man."

"Do you still think he's harmless?" Byron asked.

"I'm not sure of that either. Better keep your eye on him."

After the men discussed several possible explanations for the card trick, but finding none satisfactory, Kenny looked at his watch. Rising, he said, "Fellows, I've got to get back to work."

"Do me a favor, would ya, Kenny?" Byron asked.

"Sure thing."

"Check and see why my daughter's taking so long to say goodbye to Merlin."

Queen chuckled and gripped his nightstick. "Want me to thump him once while I'm at it?"

* * *

"Aren't you afraid of Kenny Queen? He's a lot bigger than you," Chrissy said. They stood at the end of the driveway, looking at the violet-black sky spangled by innumerable stars.

"Never fear those who can hurt the body. Fear only the one who has the power to destroy the soul," Jack said.

"And according to Jack Blaze, who might that be?" She pointed to the devil tattoo on his arm. "Him?"

"He's only a shadow from my past—something I've left behind, but I still carry the image as a reminder. Your father wouldn't believe it, but I'm a spiritual man."

"You still haven't answered my question. Who has the power to destroy the soul?"

"A Jew would say Jehovah; a Muslim, Allah; and a Christian, God Almighty."

"You've covered the three major religions, but you still haven't answered my question."

Jack reached out and touched her cheek. "Do you feel the steady breeze from the ocean?"

Chrissy lifted her head and sensed the wind against her face, tossing her hair. "What's that got to do with it?"

"You can't see the wind, but you can feel it. Words can't label something so deeply felt."

Chrissy put her hands on her hips. "You are a strange man, Jack Blaze. Should I be afraid of you?"

He drew nearer. "Can you read my mind?" he asked.

In his eyes Chrissy saw the reflection of a thousand stars. She wondered if he wanted to kiss her and hoped that he did.

From behind them, Queen's voice interrupted, "Hey, Chrissy!"

They turned and Chrissy said, "Hi, Kenny."

"Your father wondered what happened to you. Still out here with Whodinny, I see."

"We're just enjoying the breeze," Chrissy said. She didn't know whether to feel resentful over Queen's interference or relieved.

"Before I hit the streets again, I wanted to ask you something," Kenny said.

Chrissy turned away from Jack and faced Kenny. "What's up?"

"Do you like lobster?"

"Love lobster."

"Great. How would you like to go to the Black Pelican tomorrow evening? Serves the best lobster on the Outer Banks. Then we could play some miniature golf or whatever you like."

"Sounds wonderful, Kenny, but I already have a date for tomorrow night." She turned and looked at Jack.

"I see." He lowered his head and kicked at a stone. Looking up, he said, "You move pretty fast, don't ya, Blaze?"

"Fast enough," Jack said.

Queen smiled. "Just remember. I enforce the speed limits around here." He tipped his hat to Chrissy. "Maybe some other time."

"Maybe," Chrissy said.

After Queen climbed in the cruiser, he slammed the door, gunned the engine and roared down the street.

"Don't go away mad," Jack said. "Just go away."

Chrissy laughed.

"How did you know I wanted to take you out tomorrow night?" Jack asked.

"You're not the only one who can read minds."

"Really. Okay, read my mind again. What time will I pick you up?"

"Hmmmmmmm." Chrissy tilted her head. "That's easy. 'Bout seven."

Jack nodded. "I think you've got the gift." He looked beyond her to the house. "You better get back inside before your dad calls the cops on me."

"Too late for that. Deputy Queen's already on the case."

Chapter Fourteen

The morning sun shone through an octagonal window, brightening the bedroom floor with a skewed polygon of light. Byron entered the bathroom and fished his electric razor from the assortment of toiletries scattered atop the double sink. While Lila padded on makeup, he clicked on the shaver and buzzed off the gray shadow on his jaws and chin. His sun-reddened complexion of the last two days had started to tan.

"You know Jack Blaze is not white," Byron said.

"Obviously." Lila rubbed the bisque shade on her cheek.

"I figure his mother's white and his father's black."

Lila paused and eyed Byron. "Now how would you know that?"

"Law of Averages. In most interracial marriages the woman's white and the man's black."

"Sometimes I wonder about you, Byron Butler."

Byron doused his hand with *Old Spice* aftershave. "Whadaya mean? I'm just stating a fact." He patted the stinging liquid on his cheeks.

"But it sounds racist. Does it bother you that our daughter is attracted to a man who may be half black?"

"You know I'm not prejudiced. I have lots of black friends."

"But none of them is interested in your daughter."

"That's irrelevant. Besides, how do we know Chrissy likes this Jack Blaze? I think she has a crush on Kenny Queen."

"No way," Lila said. "Are you blind? She's mesmerized by Jack. Queen's like all the guys she dated in high school. Jack's different—mysterious."

Byron squirted a dollop of toothpaste onto his toothbrush. "Sounds like you like the guy."

She picked up her eyeliner pencil and leaned toward the mirror. "I like him. Sometimes he startles me. When he raised the knife during the card trick, I almost screamed. I know he does it for effect, but the drama seems too much sometimes."

"Too much? I thought he was gonna plunge the thing into Kenny's chest."

"Don't be ridiculous. He was putting on a show. Kenny overreacted."

"I think he did it to even the score. When Kenny tapped him with his nightstick he almost fell over. Seemed like a conditioned response—like it wasn't the first time a cop tried to hit him with a nightstick."

Lila blinked and examined her lashes. "What are you saying?"

"I wonder about his background—Where is he from? What has he done in his life? Why is he here?—that sort of thing."

"Ask him the next time you see him," Lila said.

"He doesn't give straight answers." As Byron flossed his teeth, he thought about the possibility of Chrissy falling in love with Blaze. Images of children, black, white, mixed, appeared in his mind, running and playing in the backyard of the parsonage. "It's the children of a mixed couple who suffer most."

"What?" Lila asked, pausing to glare at Byron.

"It's difficult for them. Race becomes an identity issue. Am I white? Am I black? Who am I?"

"Why are you even worried about that? Byron, there comes a time when you have to trust your daughter's judgment. She's a smart girl. When it comes to her future spouse, she will make the right decision. Besides, it doesn't come down to whether someone is white or black, but whether it's God's will they be together. Am I right or wrong?"

Byron dropped the piece of floss in the trashcan next to the sink. Although he didn't want to admit it, he knew she was right. "Hurry up. I think everyone's ready."

* * *

When they arrived at the Whalehead Club, a greeter collected their fees, gave them yellow stickers imprinted with the letter 'F', and instructed them to walk around to the back where someone would organize them into a tour group. Byron admired the building as they circled it–the perfect symmetry, the repetition of dormers and columns and chimneys. The steep copper roof, butter yellow walls, and white trim gleamed in the sunshine, giving the structure a cheerful appearance. The restoration of the building had been accomplished immaculately.

Everything was clean, sharp, neat—even the lawn grew thick and green, manicured like the fairway of a championship golf course.

Arriving on the backside, they watched a large man dressed in a white linen suit talking to a dozen or so people gathered on the porch. He had gray hair, medium length and neatly parted. His voice, low and resonant, carried across the lawn to where they waited. He told the group he grew up in Corolla and worked at the Whalehead Club as a teenager in the 50's when Ray T. Adams owned the place and entertained government dignitaries. With grave intonations he mentioned Adams died unexpectedly inside the house on December 31, " . . . the last day of the year 1957," as he put it. His words and manner impressed Byron. *This guy's the Real McCoy, a longtime native. He knows what he's talking about. Lord, let this man be our guide.* Then Jack Blaze stepped out of the back door and waved at them.

"Hi, Jack!" Chrissy exclaimed, waving back.

He walked to them, smiling.

Byron wished he could wipe the annoying smirk from Blaze's face. He turned away and watched the man in the white suit lead his group into the house. *Just my luck. We're stuck with Mr. Magic. Lord, give me strength.*

"Good morning," Jack said. "What a beautiful day to tour the Club."

"Isn't it wonderful?" Chrissy asked. "There's not a cloud in the sky."

The boys, who had been watching a family of mallards cross the lawn, turned and greeted Jack. Annie and Lila complimented his outfit, a yellow polo shirt and khaki shorts. Pinned to his shirt, a brown nametag identified him as a tour guide.

"I must say, you ladies look quite stunning."

This comment led the women into a discussion about their apparel and recent clothing purchases at the local shopping center. Jack recommended a few stores with exotic styles and unusual items he thought they might enjoy checking out.

Elijah leaned closer to Byron, pitching his voice low. "Wonder what kind of tricks he has up his sleeve today?"

Watching Blaze talk to the women, Byron noticed he gravitated to females and children and barely recognized the presence of adult males. "This one's called wrapping unsuspecting admirers around your finger," Byron whispered.

Elijah grunted and nodded.

A tall blond girl crossed the porch, emerging from the shadow onto the lawn. She shaded her eyes with her hand and called out, "Tour group F, could you please gather around me!"

Byron looked at the sticker on his breast pocket. He slapped Elijah on the back. "We're F. The Lord must have heard my prayer." Stepping closer to the women and Blaze, he said, "Hey gang, our tour guide is waiting by the porch. We better get going."

"Aren't you our guide, Jack?" Annie asked.

"No," he said. "I'm leading group G. Just wanted to say hi and see how everyone's doing."

"Too bad," Lila said. "It was nice talking to you again."

As the families gathered around the blonde, Byron glanced over his shoulder and noticed Chrissy lingered behind, talking to Blaze. A few stragglers arrived as the guide shouted again for her group to assemble around her. Byron tried to be patient, but Chrissy's lack of consideration irked him. With his hands on his hips, he faced her and Jack, hoping they would see him, but they continued their conversation, oblivious to his posturing. *What's gotten into her? Can't she see we're ready to get started?* He heard the tour guide announce she was taking a head count. Frustration tightened his chest, increasing the rate of his breathing. Finally, he could not subdue his irritation. "Chrissy!" he yelled. "Come on! You're holding us up."

Chrissy touched Jack's shoulder, smiled, and said something to him. Byron guessed she complained about her father's impatience. As she approached, Byron observed Blaze, whose eyes seemed to follow her every step.

"Take it easy, Dad. I was only twenty yards away," she said.

Byron felt his face flush. He wanted to lecture her on the practice of common courtesy and the importance of setting aside one's own agenda for the good of the group. But then he wondered if his indignation was justified. Was he obsessing over trivialities? He didn't want to become an over-possessive father bent on controlling his daughter's every move. His discomposure tangled his tongue, keeping him from responding to Chrissy's retort.

Blaze shifted his eyes to him, grinned, and nodded. At that moment Byron sensed his dislike for Blaze festering into enmity. Knowing a preacher of Christ's gospel could not indulge such a sentiment, Byron turned away and tried to exorcise his feelings and Blaze's face from his mind. But the more he tried, the more Jack's creepy expression intruded on his inner vision.

Relief from his turmoil came suddenly when he looked more closely at the blonde tour guide. As she finished counting heads, she smiled, and Byron knew he had seen her somewhere before. Tall and thin like Chrissy, she wore a white blazer over a blue knit top and white slacks. Her hair, straight and streaked with highlights, fell to the middle of her back. With cheerful blue eyes and a wide white smile, she reminded Byron of someone who might work in commercials. *Maybe that's where I've seen her before,* he thought. *On a toothpaste commercial.*

She cleared her throat and said, "My name is Adrienne Lawrence. Welcome to the Whalehead Club. Together we will explore one of the most unusual buildings ever constructed on the Outer Banks. The Whalehead Club is a unique slice of American history built in the Roaring Twenties, a decade of bathtub gin, the first transatlantic flight, the Model T, and silent movies." Adrienne pushed her hair behind her ears and continued. "After World War I, businesses prospered and America swelled with hope. In 1922, buoyed with optimism and enthusiasm, a Philadelphia businessman and his wife, a French Canadian socialite, built this *Mansion by the Sea.* Currituck County and the Whalehead Preservation Society have embarked on a labor of love to make possible the full restoration of this building. Because of their efforts, today you and I have the privilege of stepping back in time as we enter these doors."

The tone of her voice struck chords of memory in Byron's mind. So many images and impressions had revisited him over the last few days that he hesitated to speculate with any confidence about their meaning. His trust-in-reason approach to life had been shaken by strange dreams and visions. Or were they all figments of his imagination? *That's it. I've seen her in my dreams.* His heartbeat quickened and breathing accelerated. *She's the girl chained to the wall in the boathouse.* He tried to relax and listen.

She made a sweeping motion toward the porch with her arm. "The original owners of the house, Edward Collings Knight and his wife, Marie Louise LeBel Knight, decided to emphasize an unusual style in the design of the house. It's called Art Nouveau—a decorative style that became popular in Europe and the United States in the late 1800's and early 1900's."

She pointed to the entrance. "Observing the railings and the door decorations, you will notice curving lines and detailed patterns, both telltale features of this highly organic style. Above, on the frieze, you will see a kissing swan motif. Louis Comfort Tiffany, the American stained-glass artist, and Gustav Klimt, the Austrian painter, were two of Art Nouveau's most famous practitioners. Inside the house you will discover many of Tiffany's incredible creations. Follow me, please." She stepped onto the porch and opened the walnut door.

Once inside, she gathered everyone at the bottom of a wide staircase near the entrance. "Edward Knight was a successful executive with the Pennsylvania Railroad and heir to a sugar fortune. In the late 1800's, he became a member of the Lighthouse Club, a prestigious hunting club located approximately where this structure sits today. He had recently married his second wife, Marie Louise, who loved waterfowl hunting. Because the hunting club did not allow women members, Edward decided to buy the entire property—a four-mile tract of land along the Outer Banks from ocean to sound."

Elijah elbowed Byron. "If you can't join 'em, buy it out from under 'em," he said for all to hear.

Several tourists chuckled, and Byron smiled on the surface but inside he felt flustered. Was she the girl in his dream? Now he wasn't so sure. But why did she look so familiar.

Adrienne Lawrence cleared her throat and waited for everyone to quiet. "The construction of the house began in 1922 and continued through 1925 at the cost of $384,000. You must remember that the twenties was a decade of opulence and excessive spending before the onslaught of the Great Depression. At today's prices, it would cost more than four million dollars to build such a palatial home. And that doesn't include the cost of the property."

Murmurs and wows echoed among the group, and Dugan turned to the twins and said, "Four million dollars! I wish I had four million dollars."

"Me too," Mark and Matt piped.

Adrienne motioned to her left. "Now, if you will follow me to the southeast wing of the house, we will look at the kitchen and dining area."

The first thing Byron noticed when he entered the kitchen were the Pepto-Bismol pink-tile walls. The color seemed to coat the back of his retinas. A large stainless steel preparation table took up most of the space in the middle. Adrienne explained that the facility could be leased for weddings and special events throughout the year, the kitchen staff providing for catering needs. Directing everyone's attention to the back wall, she pointed out a single white tile amidst the ocean of pink. This oddity, she interpreted to be the Knights' view of nature's uniqueness—every plant, every snowflake, every human being has individual qualities that sets it apart from all others.

In the dining room, Lila and Annie gushed over the water lily lighting fixtures and custom-carved chairs and table with curved trim and repetitions of the kissing swan motif and water lily buds. Adrienne commented that the lights were custom creations from the Tiffany Studios made by applying green glass over two layers of white glass.

"Edward and Marie Louise were artistically-minded people," Adrienne said. "During the construction, Edward would issue specific instructions to the craftsmen about his design ideas for certain rooms in the house. When Marie Louise arrived, she would demand they tear everything down and start over according to her vision for the room. It's no wonder it took three years to complete the work. Although the couple butted heads often over artistic preferences, all research indicates they had a solid marriage."

Elijah raised his hand.

"Do you have a question, sir?" Adrienne asked.

"Yes, ma'am," he said. "A friend of mine, who worked here as a boy back in the thirties, told me the Knights had a weird relationship, kind of a flip-flop one. Is that true?"

Adrienne averted her eyes. When she looked up, her face blushed slightly. "Well, . . . yes. Their relationship may have been perceived as . . . unorthodox. Marie Louise was a strong woman who loved to hunt. She would walk the property, shooting snakes and muskrat and waterfowl. Feeling more comfortable in a flannel shirt and riding pants, she liked roughing it with the guys. I guess you could say she had a lot of masculine qualities. Edward, on the other hand, was very fastidious. He was a meticulous record keeper, creating a detailed log of every person who stayed at the house. During the nine years they resided here, the Knights welcomed over one hundred guests, some staying for months at a time. Edward made sure all things were in order and everyone was happy. Unlike Marie Louise, he enjoyed the domestic responsibilities."

"Does that mean she wore the pants in the family and he wore the apron?" Elijah asked.

Everyone laughed and Adrienne nodded. "Many people would agree with your assessment. Now, let's move to the other end of the first floor and look at the great room."

Two banks of windows on opposite walls flooded the large room with natural light. A magnificent Steinway grand piano, dark brown and highly polished, graced the northwest corner. The propped-open top revealed myriad wires and felted hammers. On the wall across from the entrance stood a ten-foot mirror with an elaborate mahogany frame. Intricately carved water lily buds and leaves repeated their pattern through the wood. Glancing around the room, Byron imagined the excessiveness and frivolity of parties long past, guests imbibing bootlegged gin, cigarette and cigar smoke blurring the scene and clouding the ceiling. The room had corduroy walls and an odd cork-tile floor. To Byron the floor felt spongy. *Seems like I'm walking on a cloud.* He imagined men, wearing three-piece suits, waltzing with women in sleek, sleeveless dresses that swished just above their ankles—like a scene out of *The Great Gatsby.*

To his right he spotted a portrait of a person he assumed to be Edward Collings Knight. The man's bald head glowed in contrast to the umber background. Dressed dapperly in a black suit and tie, he gazed with whimsical eyes, his droll mouth framed by an exquisite curled mustache and well-trimmed beard. On his lapel, a red rose contrasted with the inky tones of his suit. On the other lapel he wore a red ribbon with a silver medal dangling from it. Byron wondered what Knight had been thinking while posing for the portrait. *Could he have ever imagined one day his house would be one of the Outer Banks' major tourist attractions? And here he is, looking out from the frame of his picture with that odd expression, watching us.*

With a huge grin, Elijah raised his hand again, and the tourists turned and noticed him.

Adrienne asked, "Since you are quite the inquisitive one, could you please tell me your name?"

"Certainly, young lady. My name is Elijah Mulligan and my question is this: Is it true what I heard about these cork floors?"

She shook her head. "Mr. Mulligan, I'm almost afraid to ask, but what did you hear about these cork floors?"

"I was told that Mrs. Knight loved her whiskey. To keep her from breaking bones when she overindulged, Mr. Knight had cork floors installed in many of the rooms throughout the house. She'd fall down and bounce right back to her feet."

Chuckles and murmurs rippled around the room.

"Mr. Mulligan," she said, pausing and taking a breath. "My advice to you would be not to believe everything you hear. I can tell you this about the Knights. They were well loved in this community. They often opened their home to the Corolla residents for ballroom dances, and every Christmas they provided a tree for the church and bought presents for every man, woman, and child around these parts—more than one hundred people. They also offered employment to many of the villagers, hiring cooks, servants, maintenance workers, and hunting guides. The townspeople of that day would have been unanimous in recognizing the positive contribution the Knights made to Corolla. Does that answer your question, Mr. Mulligan?"

Elijah shrugged. "Not exactly, but that's okay. I'm sure you guides have been instructed to be careful about how you answer some of these more delicate questions. I understand."

Adrienne shook her head. "I'm not sure you do, but if there are no other questions, we will move back down the hall to the stairway and explore the second floor living quarters."

As the tourists filed into the hall, Byron hung back and drifted to the middle of the room. He glanced at the portrait of Knight one more time and then faced the tall mirror on the opposite wall. To the right of his shoulder in the reflection, two red spots appeared like glowing eyes. The presence of evil washed over him—the same sensation that had enveloped him in his recurring dreams. Byron whirled around to face the eyes. Edward Collings Knight gazed at him from the picture frame, Knight's odd smile sending needles of fear through his body. But then Byron noticed the red rose and red ribbon in the portrait. He took a deep breath and slowly exhaled. *I think I'm starting to lose it.*

Adrienne Lawrence led the group up the stairs and through a series of guest rooms on the second floor. Pastel colors—blues, yellows, lavenders, mauves, limes—brightened the walls, each room a different hue. Numerous doors led from one room to another, creating an interconnecting maze of suites. At the end of the hall they gathered in front of the remaining two doors. Adrienne explained that the Knights, as typical of the wealthy in those days, preferred separate bedrooms. Entering the door on her left, she said, "This was Edward's room."

The dozen tourists spread out in the spacious room. Light streaming in from a dormer window cast an odd sheen on the furnishings—a wide mahogany dresser, an expansive desk with a padded chair with roller wheels, a nightstand with a Tiffany lamp, and a king-sized, four-post bed covered with a blue and white quilt.

Dugan reached out and grabbed Elijah's hand. "I wonder if she knows anything about the murder of the lighthouse keeper's daughter?" he asked.

Everyone turned and looked. Elijah put his forefinger to his lips and shushed him.

"I beg your pardon?" Adrienne asked. "What murder?"

"The lighthouse keeper's daughter," Dugan said. "The ghost of the Carolina Ripper chased her from here to the lighthouse. He caught her, choked her to death with his alligator belt, and then tossed her body down the well."

Elijah tightened his lips, his shoulders tensing.

"That's some story," Adrienne said. "Are you sure it's all true?"

"Of course it's true. My Uncle Elijah told me that story, and he never lies. Right, Uncle Elijah?" Dugan turned and stared at his uncle.

"W-Well . . . uh . .uh . ." Elijah stammered. "I was told that story by an old timer who has lived in this village all his life. I admit, I may have embellished it a bit, but . . . "

Adrienne smiled. "Embellished it? Hmmmm. I see." She faced Dugan. "Well, young fellow, I've heard the story of the Carolina Strangler walking the marshes, and I've heard the story of the light keeper's daughter who drowned in the cistern, but I've never heard the two stories put together. That must be the part you embellished, huh, Mr. Mulligan?"

Elijah's face reddened as he glanced at the tourists' amused expressions. For the first time during the tour he kept his mouth shut when everyone expected a snappy answer.

Finally, Dugan asked, "You didn't lie, did you, Uncle Elijah? You didn't put those two stories together just to make a better ghost story?"

"We'll talk about this later, boy," Elijah mumbled. "Now pay attention to the tour guide."

Miss Lawrence led the group to the to the third floor where they inspected the servants' quarters. They paused in the middle of the hallway where she stated: "The Whalehead Club was the first structure on the Outer Banks to have an elevator and an outdoor swimming pool. Although the swimming pool was filled in many years ago, the elevator still works. In the Knights' day, it had been used to move luggage and furniture to the second and third floors."

As Byron listened, he noticed a small door several feet off the ground and about four feet tall with a padlock on it. A yellow sign with black letters posted on the middle of the door warned: NO ACCESS. For some reason the sign kept drawing his attention. He stared at the letters, the black lines blaring against the yellow background. Adrienne Lawrence's words faded as if she were drifting away, disappearing into darkness. He tried to picture the girl from his dream and match their faces. Should he tell her she may be in danger? She would think he was crazy.

"Sir!"

Byron turned and saw everyone had vanished. For a few a moments he felt disoriented

"Sir! Are you coming?" Adrienne called from the dark end of the hall. "We're taking the servants' steps back down to the kitchen."

"Yes, I'm coming."

She waited while he walked to her.

"I'm sorry," he said. "I was fascinated by that small door in the middle of the hallway."

"You don't want to return to the ground floor through that door," she said.

"Why not?"

"That's the roof access. It leads to a hatch near the middle of the ridge. Back in the day, a maintenance man would climb up there to clean the chimneys. Believe me, one slip on that roof, and you're in for a long drop to the ground."

"I see," Byron said.

She turned to go down the steps.

"Miss Lawrence, I need to tell you something."

She paused and faced Byron.

"My name is Byron Butler. I'm a Presbyterian minister from Ohio."

"A Presbyterian minister?" she asked.

"Yes. I feel like I know you from somewhere, like I've seen your face before."

Her eyes brightened. "My father's a Presbyterian minister in Kutztown, Pennsylvania. His name is Wilson . . . Wilson Lawrence."

"Of course!" Byron exclaimed. *She looks exactly like her father. No wonder I have this odd feeling.* "Wilson and I attended the Pittsburgh Theological Seminary together back in the eighties."

"That's incredible. You know my father. Small world."

"We had several classes together—Greek and Hebrew, I believe. He was in one of my study groups that met regularly."

"I'll mention your name next time I talk to him . . . Byron . . . Byron . . ."

"Butler. Byron Butler. Back then I had fewer wrinkles and black hair."

She smiled. "I'm sure he'll remember."

"Pardon me for asking, but why are you working here?"

"This fall I start medical school at Penn State. My family vacations here almost every June. I thought this would be a great summer job before the long grind begins."

"Isn't that something?" Byron commented. "My daughter, Chrissy, wants to be a doctor."

"Some day I'd like to become a medical missionary in Uganda . . . Lord willing." She turned and looked down the narrow stairwell. "We'd better get moving. They'll think we got lost."

Descending the steps, Byron felt some relief from the foreboding anxiety that had gripped him when he first had seen Adrienne. *Wilson Lawrence. We sat next to each other in class. No wonder her face seemed so familiar. I've got to control these anxiety bouts . . . before I go nuts.*

The tour ended on the front lawn. Adrienne Lawrence talked about the Whalehead Preservation Society's newest project—working with the Wildlife Commission to establish the Currituck Wildlife Museum in the basement of the Whalehead Club. She encouraged the tourists to stop in the Whalehead gift shop and asked if there were any more questions.

Pointing to the steep copper roof, a heavyset man with a thin mustache asked, "Why does the Preservation Society allow that osprey to nest on the chimney? The bird droppings create a huge mess up there—an eyesore."

"That's Grace," Adrienne said. "We named her after a school teacher who served this community for many years in the thirties and forties. The locals say the teacher was one of the first people to ever try to clean up birds after getting covered with bilge oil. Miss Grace was a protector of defenseless creatures. Since our organization treasures those same values, we thought it appropriate to call the bird Grace. She's a symbol of protection and preservation of life. We don't mind the bird droppings. That osprey watches over the Whalehead Club."

"Hmmmph," the man grunted.

As the crowd dispersed, Byron watched Grace. She perched at the edge of the chimney and peered down, her white crown aglow in the sunshine. She spread her gray wings and thrust forward, powerfully flapping. As Byron watched, Grace's shadow passed over him.

Chapter Fifteen

Byron and Elijah walked along the beach for two miles. Each carried a plastic grocery bag half-filled with shells. The late-afternoon sun blazed relentlessly, but the steady breeze from the ocean helped to cool their perspiring bodies.

"Must be ninety-five degrees." Byron glanced at his shoulders and arms. Even through sunglasses they appeared red. "Lila covered me with sun-block. I hope it does the job."

Elijah stopped and examined Byron's back. "You look like a lobster." Elijah took off his denim fisherman's hat and wiped his brow with his forearm. He tugged it tightly onto his dome. "That's why I wore this t-shirt. Can't stand to get sunburned."

"I'd rather look like a lobster than a redneck," Byron said.

"I do my shopping at Wal-Mart, kiss my own wife on New Year's Eve, and enjoy sautéed squirrel meat. Does that qualify me as a redneck?"

"Do you have any cousins named Bubba?"

Elijah laughed, startling a nearby sandpiper into flight. "Yeah. Three of 'em."

Byron nodded. "I think you qualify."

They had embarked on their shell-hunting expedition two hours before low tide, and now the receding waters deposited a variety of specimens along the shore—mostly clam, scallop and cockleshells, but an occasional moon shell or auger tumbled in the backwash.

"There's the dead sea turtle I told you about," Byron said, pointing to the middle of the beach.

"I can smell it," Elijah said.

They ambled over to the carcass and examined it.

"Wonder why death has such a terrible odor?" Elijah asked.

Byron leaned on his knees, studying the carcass. "Decomposition. Compounds break down into elements. Just a natural process."

"Yeah, but in *God's* blueprint of creation, why do dead things smell so badly? There's got to be a reason." Elijah straightened and stepped back from the turtle.

Byron rubbed his chin. "Well . . . The stench serves as a warning. Diseases can be caught from dead things. Centuries ago they burned the bodies of plague victims to control the spread disease. I remember reading somewhere about a strange outbreak of plague in the early 1900's that occurred among two specific groups of people—librarians and avid readers of romance novels."

"Romance readers and librarians? What caused it?"

"The paper manufacturer used mummy wrappings in the production process. A printing company purchased the paper to make romance novels. Apparently the wrappings came from Egyptians who had died of the plague. The librarians and readers who fingered the pages became infected."

"I'll stick with Tom Clancy novels and the Bible," Elijah snorted.

"Let's go," Byron said. "I'm tired of smelling this dead turtle."

As they walked northward on the firm, wet sand, the stench of decay lingered in Byron's soul. Looking for shells lost precedence as he mulled over his intense disdain of Jack Blaze. The odor of the turtle and talk of death refueled the angst that had burned so fiercely within him in Blaze's presence at the Whalehead Club and the day before at the cookout. As the tide lapped the shore, Elijah scrambled to scoop up shells, but Byron focused on inner scenes—Blaze biting a chunk out of a quarter, violently raising a knife, and gazing longingly at his daughter. The images swirled, faded in and out. He remembered Chrissy touching Jack's shoulder, and Lila defending his antics as overzealous theatrics.

Then his wife's words confronted him again: *Does it bother you that our daughter is attracted to someone who may be half black?* Byron didn't like the insinuation of the question. He always had considered himself an open-minded humanitarian. In principle, he believed God created all men equal. Throughout his life he had formed relationships with upstanding black men and women. What bothered him over the last few years was the subculture of young black people who popularized obscene rap music, gang affiliation, sexual immorality, drugs, crime, and violence. Whenever he saw a group of black teens gathered around a car blasting ghetto music, he couldn't help feeling uneasy. The negative images of hip-hop stars draped in golden chains with scantily dressed 'hos' hanging on their arms had saturated the media, and Byron couldn't stand it.

As he ruminated, the possibility that prejudice had gained a foothold in his life bothered him. *Maybe it's me. Am I seeing Jack Blaze through biased lenses? His smile irks me. It's so contemptuous of authority. But the women and kids don't notice it. I don't mind if Chrissy begins a friendship . . . or a . . . relationship with a good black man, but I will not stand to see her enchanted by some hood who bedazzles people with magic. But is he a hood? What do I really know?* Then the image of the devil tattoo materialized in his mind's eye—the leaping flames and thrown-back, scoffing head. *Was that tattoo a visible sign of something evil deep inside?*

Byron felt something slimy wrap around his ankle. Stopping in the shallow water that rushed back toward the sea, he stared at his feet. When the backwash cleared, he saw a string of disc-shaped beads slung around the top of his water shoe. He reached down and peeled the clinging strand from his foot and examined it.

"Hey, Byron!" Elijah called from twenty yards up the beach. "What'd you find?"

"Don't know." He held up the dripping strand.

"That's a mermaid's necklace," Elijah said.

"Mermaid's necklace?"

"Whelk eggs."

Byron shook the viscid thing from his fingers and rubbed his hands on his trunks. Handling some sea creature's sticky eggs did not appeal to him. "What's a whelk?"

"A scavenger and a carnivore." Elijah held up his plastic bag. "See all these measly shells?"

"Yeah."

"I'd trade ten times this many to find a good whelk shell."

Byron caught up with Elijah. "Did you say a carnivore?"

"Yeah. It's actually a sea snail with a huge shell. I found one out here two summers ago. It's on my mantle at home. A whelk will attach itself to a crab or lobster, bore a hole through its shell with its rasp tongue and then suck the life out of it."

"To a lobster?"

"That's right, buddy." He patted Byron's red back. "A whelk can kill a lobster."

They walked another half mile to where strange stumps protruded from the shallows and sand like menacing black figures emerging from the sea.

"Hundreds of years ago this used to be a cedar forest," Elijah said.

"How could a cedar forest grow in the midst of tidal waters?" Byron asked.

"These are shifting sands, good buddy." Elijah pointed out to sea. "Eight hundred years ago the shoreline was out there somewhere. This was dry land. Huge cedars sunk their roots here. As time passed, the tides and storms redistributed the sands. These stumps are ancient."

A large wave crashed in front of them and swirled around the roots of the tree trunks. When the water receded, Elijah walked down the slope and into the water amidst several of the stumps. His eyes widened, and he plunged his hand into the surf.

"Jackpot!" Elijah yelled. From the water he pulled a huge tan shell with swirling brown stripes just as another wave broke over his calves.

"Is that a conch?" Byron asked.

"No. It's a big whelk. And look. The bugger's still in it." He sloshed through the water to Byron and turned the conical shell over. Poking his finger into the opening, he said, "It withdrew into the shell for protection. See. That's its tail."

Byron saw the posterior of the slimy creature. He imagined the gargantuan snail crawling along the bottom of the ocean, attacking lobsters. "How are you going to get it out of there?"

"Oh, I'll get it out. We'll put a big pot of water on the stove when we get home. I'll boil it till it falls out. We can fry it up and eat it if you want."

"I think I'll pass on that one, Bubba," Byron said.

Elijah laughed and shouted, "Yeeehaww! Got me a big whelk shell! Let's head home."

*　*　*

On the way back, Elijah lost interest in shell hunting. Byron figured the whelk more than gratified his beachcomber's cravings. As they approached the cabled posts that separated the public beach from the wildlife preserve, Byron remembered how the black stallion chased him to the opening. His strange hospital dreams and vacation experiences had become a simmering stew in his mind. *What did it all mean?* Whenever he gazed into the cauldron, faces appeared and disassembled like reflections in a pond broken up by a dropped pebble.

Weaving through the opening in the posts, Byron said, "I'm worried about my daughter. I think Jack Blaze has put a spell on her. What do you think?"

"She's got the moon-eyes for him all right."

"He's a strange one."

"Sure has some strange powers," Elijah said as they angled to the shoreline.

"He's good at what he does."

"I would say he's evil at what he does."

Byron stopped and faced Elijah. "Really? Evil?"

"Well . . ." Elijah reconsidered. "Maybe that's too strong a word. I don't want to judge a man before I have all the facts, but when I'm around him, I sense something unnatural. In the Old Testament, pagan magicians accomplished miraculous feats by conjuring occult powers. Remember Pharaoh's sorcerers? Using their secret arts, they turned their staffs into serpents."

"Yes, but did they perform the feat by calling on some diabolical power or through secret arts? Blaze may know secrets to some incredible tricks, but I doubt if he is in league with the devil."

"I know what I see," Elijah responded. "He reads minds, bites chunks out of metal, and somehow transfers cards through mid-air into locked boxes. There's no reasonable explanation. I truly believe some people tap into the dark side of the spiritual realm. That's why God forbade sorcery and witchcraft. In the Old Testament witches and sorcerers were executed."

Byron chuckled. "Maybe we ought to find an extra big pot and boil Blaze in oil."

Elijah held the whelk up and shook it. "Very funny, Byron. But I'm serious. Keep your eye on Jack Blaze. I wouldn't be surprised if he did something totally out of this world. Something beyond card tricks and mind reading. Mark my words."

Elijah's estimation of Blaze's abilities seemed overblown to Byron. Blaze may not have supernatural powers, but could he be possessed by the supernatural? Byron remembered watching crime documentaries on serial killers who claimed the practice of yielding to demonic entities led them to commit heinous acts. Their victims trusted them, believed they were nice guys.

Byron slipped deeper into his thoughts. *In the dark woods of a remembered dream red eyes glowed. A silhouette wielding a knife paced down a walkway and entered a boathouse. A girl screamed, yanking at the chains that fastened her to the wall. Byron stood between the killer and the girl, but he still couldn't see the killer's face. Only red eyes.*

"You all right, Byron?"

Elijah's words jolted Byron out of his vision. He looked up and saw the Currituck Lighthouse above beach houses to his right. "I'm okay, I guess."

"You haven't said anything for more than five minutes."

"I don't know what I'm going to do about Chrissy and Blaze."

"There's a simple solution. Tell Chrissy Blaze is off limits. You don't like him or trust him."

"She's eighteen years old, Elijah. I don't think that's going to work. It'll turn into *Romeo and Juliet*. The more I forbid her to see him, the more she'll want to be with him."

"Sometimes you have to put your foot down, Byron. Besides, we're leaving in three days. She'll get over it."

Byron took a deep breath and kicked at a cockleshell. It tumbled down the slope and into the surf. "Maybe you're right. I'll have a serious talk with her when we get back."

* * *

As they approached the vacation house, Byron saw Lila on the second floor deck, waving. He waved back but then realized she wasn't looking at him. He saw a small black Pontiac pull out of the driveway and caught a glimpse of blonde hair through the window. Lila's gaze followed the car. For a few seconds the notion that Jack Blaze had just driven off with Chrissy in the front seat sent a wave of terror through him. Then he remembered Chrissy mentioning a possible dinner date with Kenny Queen. He recalled her entering the great room and reporting that Kenny had passed her fitness test—the six-mile run along the beach. *And at the cookout, didn't Kenny tell us today was his day off?*

Lila saw them and yelled, "Find any good shells?"

Elijah held up his plastic bag and whelk shell. "Hit the jackpot!" he shouted.

"Where's Chrissy?" Byron asked.

"On a date," Lila replied.

"With Kenny Queen?"

"No. With Jack Blaze. They just left."

Byron's heart dropped into his stomach. "What? You *are* kidding, right?"

Lila looked confused. "Whadaya mean, am I kidding?"

"Where'd they go?" Byron asked.

"Some seafood restaurant. I'm not sure which one."

Stopping and looking up at his wife, Byron squawked, "Why didn't anyone ask me about this? You know how I feel about Jack Blaze."

She spread her hands, palms up. "I guess Chrissy felt she didn't need your approval. She's gone on lots of dates without asking you first."

"With high school boys. Blaze is not a boy."

"Byron, your daughter is eighteen years old. Jack's probably twenty or twenty-one. They're going out for a nice meal and a round of miniature golf. This isn't a crisis."

"You know I don't trust him," Byron fumed. He turned to Elijah. "Do you believe this?"

"Calm down, Byron. Nothing has happened yet," Elijah said.

Yet, Byron thought. *Yet*. The image of Blaze's black car driving by replayed in his mind. "I just can't let this happen. I've got to do something."

"What're you gonna do?" Elijah asked.

"We'll follow them. Keep our eye on them."

"No, you will not!" Lila commanded. "This is ridiculous, Byron."

"We don't know anything about him, Lila! Nothing!" Byron shouted.

"Be quiet. The whole neighborhood will hear you," she said.

Byron looked around but didn't see anyone paying attention. "I want to know a man's background before my daughter climbs into a car with him."

"He's a talented magician, not some bum off the street," Lila said. "The Whalehead Club hired him to be a tour guide. I'm sure they don't hire just anybody. He puts on his magic act for everyone in the community."

"That's what worries me. He puts on an act." Byron shook his head. "If I could just find out more about him."

A sheriff's car pulled along the curb near the driveway, and the window slowly lowered. Wearing mirrored sunglasses and smiling, Kenny Queen nodded and waved. "What's up, fellows?"

"Hey, Deputy Queen!" Elijah hollered. "Thought this was your day off."

"It was," Queen said. "Had big plans, but they fell through. Got a call this morning from another officer, Dirk Windsor. His wife's in labor. He had to rush her to the hospital. I told him I'd cover for him. What else do I have to do?"

"You're a bighearted man," Byron said.

"It's nothin'. Dirk would do the same for me—," Kenny chuckled. "That's if I ever get married and have a kid."

Byron and Elijah walked over and leaned on the car.

Looking over his shoulder, Byron saw Lila watching from the deck. Very quietly, he asked, "Kenny, remember the other night when I told you I'd like to know more about Jack Blaze's background?"

"Sure. I haven't found much out yet. He came down from New York City for the summer to work at the Whalehead Club. 'Bout all I know." Queen pulled off his sunglasses and smiled. "But I could find out more."

"Could you?" Elijah asked.

Queen nodded.

Byron said, "Without my permission, Chrissy just left with Blaze."

"You know where they went?" Kenny asked.

"Some seafood restaurant. That's all we know," Byron said.

"Bet I could make an educated guess," Kenny said. "At the cookout the other night I asked Chrissy to go to the *Black Pelican* with me. Best seafood restaurant around. She told me she already had a date with Blaze."

"Sorry about that, Kenny. My daughter doesn't always make the best choices."

"Don't worry about it. Tell you what. Give me about an hour or two. I'll try to keep my eye on 'em. Card tricks aren't my specialty, but I can still work some magic."

"Magic?" Elijah asked.

"Sure. Within two hours I'll come back here and tell you anything you want to know about the boy, including the location of every mole and scar on his body."

Byron lowered his eyes. "I hate the thought of invading someone's personal files, but my daughter's involved now, and I'm worried."

"Don't worry. I'll watch out for Chrissy."

"You don't know how much I appreciate this, Kenny."

"That's what I'm here for: *to serve and protect*. I'll stop back later on and let you know what's going on."

"Thanks," Byron said.

"Hey, big man," Kenny said. "What're you going to do with that whelk?"

Elijah turned it over, exposing the slimy tail of the snail. "We're gonna boil the shell out of him. By the time I'm done, we'll know the location of every mole and scar on his slimy body."

Kenny slid his sunglasses on and gave the 'thumbs up' sign. "We better get to work then," he said, and pulled away.

Chapter Sixteen

Chrissy and Jack sat at a corner table near the window at the *Black Pelican*. The smell of baked bread and seafood flavored the air as the buzz of patrons' conversations and laughter rose and fell like the waves against the shore fifty yards beyond their window.

"Elijah thinks you have occult powers," Chrissy said. "I overheard him telling Annie." She picked up her glass of Pepsi and sipped the straw. When she put it down, she grinned, feeling somewhat foolish for reporting Elijah's overreaction.

Jack raised his chin, his dark eyes meeting her gaze. "What do you think?"

Chrissy studied his face. His mustache and goatee grew somewhat sparsely, typical of a man in his early twenties. Thick but short, his black hair appeared half-combed, half-mussed, as if the strands defied attempts to direct or control. More than any feature, his eyes attracted her. They were deep brown, with heavy lashes, secretive and seducing.

"I think you are . . . mysterious," she said. "You're like a riddle that very few people can figure out. And you like it that way, don't you?"

"Very few people enter my real world. Most see what I want them to see."

Chrissy sat back. She wore a sleeveless cotton top, salmon with white trim and V-notch collar. A delicate gold chain and cross sparkled against her tanned neckline. "Are you afraid to allow people into your real world?"

Jack smiled. "No. It's by design."

"Jack Blaze, the mysterious stranger—the man with mystical powers." She leaned forward, elbows on the table. "Is that the image you're going for?"

He nodded. "To most people I'm an uncertainty, someone to be wary of. I'm surprised your father allowed you to go out with me."

The guilt Chrissy had been suppressing resurfaced. She had not sought her father's permission because she knew he would have refused it. *I'm not a kid anymore. Some girls get married at my age. Dad's gotta learn he can't control everything I do.* She picked up her spoon and tapped it against her glass, but the distraction didn't ease the discomfort. To change the subject she said, "This is an unusual restaurant." She pointed across the room. "Why is there a huge rowboat hanging from the ceiling?"

Jack shifted in his chair and looked. "That's a rescue boat. For many years this building served as the Kitty Hawk Lifesaving Station. Orville and Wilbur Wright hung out with the crewmen here."

"The Kitty Hawk Lifesaving Station? Seems like that's what they should have named the restaurant. Why do they call it the *Black Pelican?*"

"To the locals the black pelican was an omen of impending disaster. When Nor'easters blew in, the bird would appear and swoop down on the men watching the storm. They noticed the pelican's appearance always coincided with a shipwreck. As time passed, the lifesaving crew kept their eye out for the bird. Whenever they saw it, they knew disaster would strike and prepared for a rescue."

Chrissy remembered the black pelican she and Dugan had rescued. The image of the bull shark thrusting out of the water, rocking their kayak sent a chill through her. Although her muscles tensed, she forced herself to relax and not let on how the experience affected her. She wondered if they would have paddled out to it had she known the legend of the bird.

"How do you know all this historical stuff?" she asked. Jack held up the paper placemat. "I'm a fast reader."

Chrissy could see the restaurant had summarized its history and pelican legend with words and pictures on the mat. "You are quite the observer, aren't you?"

"In the business of illusion, I have to be."

The waitress, a middle-aged redhead, approached and inquired if they were ready to order. Chrissy wanted the grilled tuna with a garden salad and red potatoes.

"Give me the penne pasta with veggies and cream sauce. And smother it with Parmesan cheese. I'll take a side salad too with French dressing," Jack said.

She nodded and scribbled their orders. As she reached to collect their menus, she knocked over the pepper grinder. Flustered, she quickly righted the shaker and apologized.

Very gently, Jack said, "Don't worry. Everything'll be all right."

As she straightened, the woman hesitated and looked at him, touched by his words. "Thank you," she said and walked to the salad station.

"Do you know her?" Chrissy asked.

Jack rubbed his chin. "No, but I could tell you all about her," he said. "Her name is Marcia. She's a single mom with a teenager at home—probably a daughter who's having relationship problems with her boyfriend. She struggles to make ends meet. To complicate things, the daughter is facing a lot of peer pressure—sex, drugs, alcohol—that sort of thing. But Marcia's a strong woman. I think they'll make it through."

Chrissy shook her head. "I don't believe all that. How can you know those kinds of details about a person you've only seen for a minute or two?"

Jack placed his elbows on the table, palms and fingers pressed together. Peering to the side of his hands, he said, "I know her name is Marcia because it's on her nametag. She looked to be about thirty-eight or forty, but she wasn't wearing a wedding ring. At her age, chances are she's divorced with custody of at least one child. That's why she's working as a waitress—to try to make ends meet. If she gave birth in her early twenties, the kid would be in her teens now. I could tell by the stress in her face, especially around her eyes, that she hasn't been sleeping well. Yet the woman is still attractive. I would assume her daughter inherited her mother's looks. That means lots of boys are interested. Besides, the daughter is probably seeking a father figure in a relationship with an older boy. High school relationships are usually stormy experiences. Add to that the normal pressures of teenage experimentation, and you have a home environment with tension and high drama."

Chrissy sat back. When she had looked at the waitress, her only thought was to order the meal and hope for good food and service. Jack's analysis made sense. "Okay, you've impressed me with your observations. But it's still just a guessing game. How do you know she's a strong woman?"

"Being a waitress is a difficult job. You're on your feet all the time, and despite your life's circumstances, you have to maintain a pleasant rapport with customers if you expect to be tipped well. Without inner strength you won't last. Marcia's nametag was faded and worn. She's been doing this a long time. She's a tough woman."

"You sure know the life of a waitress."

"My mother was a waitress."

Jack's incisive conclusions elevated Chrissy's fascination with him. She wondered what he thought of her and her family. "You mentioned your surprise that my father would allow me to go out with you. Of course, you're right. I didn't even tell him about this date. Why do you think he'd have a hard time trusting you?"

"That's easy," Jack said. He leaned back in his chair and placed his hands behind his head. "Your family is from a small town in Ohio, probably a blue collar town or a farming community. That culture has conditioned your father to hope for a certain type of future son-in-law. His ideal is more along the lines of Kenny Queen—athletic, well-built, aggressive, enthusiastic, successful at what he does—simply put: the All-American boy. I, on the other hand, come from the tough streets of New York City—a totally different culture."

"You don't talk like a street kid."

"Not any more. Reading a book a week over the last four years has improved my vocabulary. I'm an evolving person, but I doubt if your dad sees that. He notices my penchant for magic and the distant nature of my personality. It's easy to understand his distrust of me. But the most significant factor in his attitude is the fact that I'm black."

"You're black? I didn't know that."

"Yes. My mother was white, but my father was black. In this society, that makes me black. Does that bother you?"

"No. Of course not." Chrissy felt her face flush. She knew Jack sensed her embarrassment and was probably analyzing her reaction. "I thought you were Puerto Rican or Mexican. I guess I didn't think that much about it."

"But your father does. My being both a young black man and a mystical person disturbs him. It's obvious in the way he interacts with me. Your mother is more tolerant. She even likes me. Most kids and women do."

"Why's that?"

"My father left us when I was three years old. Not long after that, the cops arrested him in a drug raid. He died two years later in a violent altercation in prison. I never really knew the man. I grew up without any male guidance. Without a dad, I never learned to get along with male authority figures. My mom looked out for me. She stood up for me and believed in me. Whenever I'm around fathers or principals or cops, I feel uncomfortable, like a fish out of water. I don't mean to rub certain men the wrong way. It's just who I am. It's too bad, though, that your father doesn't like me."

"Why's that?"

"I sense he's troubled about something."

Chrissy smiled and said, "Yeah. He's troubled about his daughter spending time with you."

Jack shook his head. "It's more than just his dislike of me. There's something deeper. The funny thing is, I believe in fate. I sense a strange connection with your father. There's a reason he and I are here on the Outer Banks."

"Hopefully not to punch each other out."

Before Jack could comment, the waitress arrived with salads and bread. She lowered the food, being careful not to knock anything over. "Can I get anyone a refill?" she asked.

"No thank you," Chrissy said. "But would you mind if I ask a personal question?"

For a few seconds a puzzled look clouded the waitress's face. "I guess not. What do you want to know?"

"Do you have a teenage daughter?"

She rolled her eyes and the tension in her expression faded. "You must know Marty. Oh that girl. She drives me crazy."

"Is she still dating the same guy?" Chrissy asked.

"Do you mean George? I could kill him. He didn't bring her home last night till after midnight. I grounded her for two weeks. I swear I'll ring both of their necks if they keep this up. I'll tell Marty I ran into you. What's your name?"

"Chrissy."

The waitress smiled and nodded. "You two enjoy your salads. I'll be back with your food in a few minutes."

Leaning back, Jack held his hands out, palms up. He picked up his fork, stabbed an olive, and held it near his chin. "Didn't realize you knew Marcia's daughter, Marty," he said before eating the olive.

Chrissy grinned sheepishly. "Now I feel guilty. She thinks I'm a friend of the family. I should have kept my mouth shut, but I just had to know."

"You never lied to her. She made incorrect assumptions and then, feeling more at ease with you, revealed a few harmless facts about her daughter."

Chrissy raised her finger. "But I allowed her to believe her assumptions. I never offered the truth."

Jack nodded. "Most people tend to believe their assumptions without investigating other possibilities. Magic tricks rely on that principle. If I can keep my audience focused on their own perception of reality, the impact of the trick can be executed with greater ease. Everything I do and say narrows their focus. When an illusionist controls the focus of an audience, then *shazzam*—he can work the magic."

"That's how you did the trick with the quarter, isn't it?" Chrissy asked.

Jack smiled. "Maybe."

"You rubbed the coin and talked about the molecular structure of the metal. With your skills you easily made the switch with a trick quarter you had hidden in your palm. But you already had planted the idea—you controlled our focus."

"I think I've told you too many of my secrets already. I'm hungry. Let's eat."

Chrissy laughed. She picked up her fork, stabbed an olive and held it up. "What's the matter, Jack Blaze? Getting tougher to control my focus?"

After enjoying their meals, Jack suggested they head back to Corolla for that round of miniature golf. Chrissy bragged she could teach him a thing or two when it came to handling a putter but promised to keep her eye on him in case he had any tricks up his sleeve. Jack confessed his skills as a golfer left much to be desired—he and his homeboys from his inner-city neighborhood rarely hung out at the country club. Despite his lack of skill, he believed he could rise to the competition by exercising the strength of his mental game.

Before Chrissy left the table, she reached into her shorts pocket and pulled out a five-dollar bill. Feeling guilty about her conversation with the waitress, she slipped the money between the bills Jack had left for the tip.

* * *

Jack drove a black Pontiac Sunfire. Sliding into the front seat, Chrissy saw the statuette of the Virgin Mary stuck to the top of the dashboard. She had noticed it on the drive to the restaurant but didn't mention it. To begin a date with a conversation about religion seemed too forward. Now that they had opened up to each other over dinner, she felt comfortable exploring more sensitive topics. Her curiosity about the statue intensified, but she waited until he pulled onto the highway before she mentioned it.

"Jack, are you Catholic?"

He glanced in her direction and smiled. "'Fraid not."

"Why do you have a statue of the Virgin Mary on your dashboard?"

"My mother was a devout Catholic. That was one of her last gifts to me."

"Did your mother pass away?"

"Yes. She died of esophageal cancer about a year ago."

Chrissy noticed his voice slightly changed its inflection. Sensing his effort to control his emotions, she sat quietly for more than a minute. Finally she said, "You must have loved her very much."

Jack nodded and swallowed, and she watched his Adam's apple rise and fall. "I'm rather . . . eclectic in my religious beliefs," he said.

"Eclectic?"

"I believe there's truth in all religions. I've read the Bible, the Koran, the four Vedas of Hinduism. I've studied eastern philosophy and Confucianism. One must be open minded to grasp the deeper spiritual truths that unite all faiths."

"You'll probably think I'm some kind of Jesus freak."

"Why? Because your father's a minister?"

"No. Because I want to become a Christian missionary. Hopefully a medical missionary to some country in Africa. I want to help people physically and spiritually."

Jack nodded, a hesitant bobbing of his head. "That's really quite noble of you. Much more noble than my aspirations."

She turned in her seat and focused on his profile. "Why? What do you want to do with your life?"

"I want to be a street entertainer. An illusionist. Not one of these guys with big props and special effects on some stage in Las Vegas. My magic will be basic—cards, coins, rope—whatever is on hand and easy to carry with me. I'm going to travel the world and perform for ordinary people on the street. To me, the spontaneous reaction of random spectators is the greatest reward."

"But you'll starve. Nobody'll pay you for performing tricks on the street."

"Money's not that important to me. However, there're ways to make this lifestyle self-supporting—special appearances, videotapes, books, stunts, speaking engagements. If I'm good enough, money will not be a problem. Besides, I've learned to live ascetically. The challenge is to raise my art to that level where people notice and word spreads."

"Is that why you're so dramatic whenever you perform? Do you want people to actually believe you have supernatural powers? I noticed the faces of the people at that beach. They were totally amazed. Do you want people to think you're some kind of guru or messiah?"

"I don't claim to be a guru or messiah. I allow people to believe what they want to believe. To me it's a performance. For those who watch, they must decide if I'm an angel or a demon."

Chrissy shook her head. "You *are* a horse of a different color, Jack Blaze. I've never met anyone like you."

"I'll take that as a compliment.".

The thirty-minute drive up Highway 12 to Corolla flew by as they discussed religion, music, sports, movies, and even pets. They both loved cats. Jack had found a stray white kitten when he arrived at Corolla in late May. He kept it in his apartment and claimed it could do tricks like a dog—roll over, beg, and walk on its hind feet. Chrissy raved about her beautiful Manx named Baby. Because it didn't have a tail, the neighbors thought it was a small bobcat when they first saw it.

As they entered Corolla, Jack looked in his rear view mirror and saw flashing lights. He glanced at his speedometer. When Chrissy heard the siren, she turned and looked out the back window.

"Were you speeding?" she asked.

"I don't think so. Forty miles an hour," he said as he pulled off to the side of the road.

The police cruiser angled in front of them, its blue and red lights flashing in their eyes. Although the sun had set, there was sufficient light to identify the officer as he stepped out of the vehicle.

"It's Kenny!" Chrissy exclaimed.

Jack rolled down his window.

Queen strode toward them, exhibiting the impassive demeanor of a state trooper. When he leaned and looked in the window, his frigid countenance melted into a smile. "Surprise. Surprise. It's Whodinny and Miss Chrissy Butler. Returning from a tasty meal at the *Black Pelican*, I presume."

"Very perceptive, Queen. Thanks for recommending the place," Jack said.

Kenny's smile disappeared as his lips stiffened. "Deputy Queen, if you will, please? I am on duty, and there's such a thing as respect for the law."

"Kenny," Chrissy chimed in, "I thought this was your day off."

His smile returned. "Duty called. My buddy's wife went into labor, so I volunteered to cover his shift."

"That's very commendable of you," she said.

He shrugged. "Not really. We look out for each other. May I say you look quite lovely this evening?"

Chrissy leaned forward. "Yes, you may. Thank you very much."

Queen stood and glared at Blaze. "Where're you headed in such a hurry?"

Jack pointed. "Down the road another mile to the miniature golf course."

"Do you know how fast you were traveling?"

"Forty miles an hour."

Queen's jaw shifted as he stifled a smile. "That's what I clocked you at. But the speed limit's thirty-five. There's a sign around that last turn."

"I didn't notice it," Jack said.

"Too bad. I'll have to see your license."

Jack unbuckled his seatbelt, reached into his back pocket and pulled out his wallet. Quickly, he withdrew his driver's license and held it in front of him, making Queen reach into the car for it.

Queen snapped it away and studied it. "I'll be back in a minute." He marched to the cruiser, slid into the front seat, and slammed the door.

"Did you see a sign around that last turn?" Jack asked.

"I don't remember," Chrissy said. "There might have been. Do you think he'll give you a ticket? I always heard five miles an hour over the speed limit was a safe cushion."

Jack crossed his arms. "Apparently not around here."

Sensing hostility in his voice, she sat quietly, staring out the window for several minutes. Finally she said, "What's taking him so long?"

"He's trying to make me sweat," Jack answered.

"Why? What did you do to him?"

Jack turned and smiled, easing the tension. "May I say you look quite lovely this evening," he said, mocking Queen's southern accent.

Chrissy laughed. "Do you think he's jealous?"

"Of course. He's very competitive, and right now, you're sitting next to me and not him."

"There you go again with those accurate observations," Chrissy said.

The cruiser door popped open. "Here he comes."

Queen marched back to the Sunfire, handed Jack the driver's license and leaned on the roof. "I'm gonna let you off with a warning this time, Mr. Whodinny." He lowered his head and looked at Chrissy. "If it wasn't for that lovely lady there, I probably wouldn't be so . . . magnanimous."

"That's a big word for you, Queen," Jack said.

"Watch it now, fellow. I could very easily write out a $120 ticket."

"That won't be necessary, Kenny," Chrissy said. When Kenny looked at her she smiled and batted her eyes. "I'll make him behave the rest of the evening."

Kenny smiled and nodded. "I'm sure you will." He stood and raised his index finger, then tilted it toward Blaze. "But I'm gonna keep my eye on you too."

As Queen walked away, Jack said, "I think you just saved me one hundred and twenty dollars."

*   *   *

When the doorbell rang, Byron rushed down the steps to answer it. Seeing Kenny Queen, he stepped outside onto the second floor deck and shut the door behind him. Byron tried to calm himself. Worrying about his daughter's safety for the last two hours had tightened his nerves like the skin of a snare drum, but he didn't want to appear frenzied.

He took a deep breath. "Did you find them?"

Kenny nodded. "For now, everything's cool. They're at the miniature golf course 'bout a half mile down the road. But I better keep my eye on them."

Elijah opened the door and stepped onto the deck. "I thought that might've been you, Kenny," he said.

"You must've found something out," Byron said.

"Sure did. The boys's got a rap sheet longer than Rip Van Winkle's beard."

"I knew it. I just knew it," Byron fretted as he paced across the deck and back

"What kind of trouble has he been in?" Elijah asked.

Kenny pulled a notebook from his back pocket. "Mostly gang related crimes—car theft, disorderly conduct, possession of marijuana, public intoxication, aggravated assault, unlawful use of a weapon . . ."

"Unlawful use of a weapon?" Byron repeated.

"He's been in a few turf wars."

Byron spread his hands. "Why isn't he in jail?"

Kenny looked up. "He did serve some time as a juvenile, but he's been clean for three years."

"He hasn't been in trouble for three years?" Elijah asked.

Kenny shook his head. "That might only mean he's a lot smarter now. Knows how *not* to get caught."

"Or," Elijah interjected, "maybe he straightened up."

"I wouldn't count on it," Kenny said.

"No." Byron said. "That guy doesn't get the benefit of my doubt."

"What do you want me to do?" Kenny asked.

"What can you do?" Byron asked.

"Well . . . If things stay quiet tonight in the resort neighborhoods, I'll keep my eye on them. They go anywhere besides home, I'll follow. If they don't show up here in an hour, you know I'm on his rear end. And by the way, Elijah, that's exactly where a two-inch scar is located."

"Huh?" Elijah reacted.

"His left buttock."

The flicker of comprehension entered Elijah's eyes. "I get it." He slapped Kenny on the shoulder. "You did work some magic, big boy. We're proud of ya."

Kenny grinned. "You could say I boiled the shell out of the snail."

Chapter Seventeen

The evening with Jack served to make him even more intriguing and attractive to Chrissy. They were playful, yet competitive as they putted their way around the course. But with every hole they played, one question nagged her. Whenever Jack bent to retrieve his ball from the hole, his t-shirt sleeve rose up on his shoulder, exposing the devil tattoo. By the time they reached the ninth hole, she had mounted a four-stroke lead, and her curiosity matched her advantage. After placing the ball on the tee at the tenth hole, she faced Jack and blurted out, "Why do you have that grotesque devil on your shoulder?"

Jack lifted his sleeve and looked at the blue image. "It's a part of who I am," he said nonchalantly.

The answer unnerved her, but she tried not to show it. *What does that mean? Is Satanism a part of his religious exploration too?* She lined up the putt and tapped the ball. It veered quickly left and dropped into a water hazard six feet away. After she extracted it from the water, an odd urge overcame her to shake it toward Jack, and a few drops sprinkled him. His left eye and cheek twitched as a droplet trickled down his face.

Her boldness returned. "What do you mean, 'a part of who you are?'"

Holding the putter delicately, he leaned over the ball, studying the line of his shot. He stroked, sending the ball down the middle of the carpet between the two hazards. It dropped into the center of the hole.

He straightened, wiped his hand across his cheek and looked at his fingers, rubbing them to spread the moisture. "Have you ever heard of the *Demon Posse?*"

Amazed by the shot, Chrissy had to collect her thoughts to answer the question. *The Demon Posse? What's he talking about? Maybe it's a cult or some kind of strange sect he has studied.* Without a clear connection to the reference, she shrugged and shook her head. "No idea what that could be."

"A New York street gang. I was a member." He walked past her and extracted his ball from the hole. The blue devil flashed again and disappeared under the sleeve.

Chrissy placed her ball next to the hazard. By the time she three-putted, the score was tied.

"You belonged to a street gang?" she asked as they waited for the foursome in front of them to finish the next hole.

He raised his putter, slid the head into the crook of his arm, and held the shaft like a Tommy gun. "I don't like talking about my gangsta' days," he said with an accent like that short guy in the old crime flicks her dad loved to watch.

"Everyone in the Demon Posse had the same tattoo?"

He nodded. "I'm not proud of it, but I won't hide it. I believe a person is the sum of his past. You would be quite shocked if I totaled up the things I've done."

Quite shocked? Who is this guy? Maybe my father's suspicions are on the money. Chrissy watched Jack place his ball on the ground. He struck it, this time not so straight. It rolled to a stop ten feet from the hole. His miscue heightened her competitive instinct. "I may be from a Podunk town in eastern Ohio, but I'm not so easily shocked." She lowered her ball onto the tee. "Tell me what you've done, if you don't mind doing the math." She stroked the ball, and it rimmed the cup, stopping three inches from the hole.

"For one . . . " He paused and putted. The ball rolled four feet by. " . . . I stayed drunk or high about half of my teenage years."

"Sounds like a lot of the kids at my high school."

"For two, I stole cars." This time he putted too hard and his ball jumped over the hole. "Three—assault with a deadly weapon—I stabbed a couple guys in fights over drug territory."

Tapping her ball into the hole, Chrissy said, "You demonstrated your skill with a knife quite impressively last night during the card trick." Although her words exposed a veneer of bravado, inside apprehension grew.

"Playing with knives got me ten months in the Spofford Juvenile Corrections Facility and two years probation." Reaching out with the putter, he nonchalantly tapped the ball into the hole.

Chrissy pulled out the scorecard and pencil. "I got a two."

Jack grinned. "Give me a three."

"Yeah, right. You must have skipped your math classes at reform school. I counted four strokes."

"Just wanted to see if you were paying attention," Jack said as he walked to the next hole.

"Have you broken your ties with the Demon Posse?" she asked when she caught up.

"Except for this." He lifted his shirtsleeve to expose the tattoo, then lowered it. "Remembering my days in the Posse helps me to understand three things: who I was, who I am, and who I can be."

"Why is it so important to be reminded of those days when you were a . . . a . . ."

"Thug?"

"Yes, a thug."

"Ancient Chinese philosophers believed that opposites maintained the balance of life—man and woman, day and night, summer and winter, heaven and earth, good and evil. The one embraces the other. Within each are seeds of the other. Those seeds harbor the potential for change."

"I think you lost me. Do you mean that within evil there is good? I've always believed that evil and good were separate things."

Jack dropped his golf ball onto the cement walk next to the tee. It bounced, and he caught it and held it up. "Within the person who practices evil are seeds of good. Within the person who practices good are seeds of evil."

"I guess I believe that . . . sort of," Chrissy said. "We are free to choose good or evil. Is that what you mean?"

"Do you like popcorn?"

The question seemed irrelevant. *Maybe he's hungry.* "Yeah, I like popcorn. Do you?"

He held up the ball again. "Think of a popcorn seed. How does it taste?"

"I would never eat the seed. It's too hard."

He squeezed the ball. "Exactly. It's hard and tasteless. If you tried to chew it you could crack a tooth. But within that seed is the potential for incredible change. In the right environment—hot oil—that seed could become a puffy snack." He slid his hand up his arm under the sleeve and rubbed the tattoo. "This is the hard seed I once was. But within me was the potential for change. I just needed the right environment."

The analogy made sense, and she tried to find more familiar comparisons in her own spiritual background. *Was it like being born again? Is he talking about the power of God to totally transform a life?* "What made you change?" she asked.

Jack pointed to the hole. "We've fallen behind. Let's play the hole and then we'll talk."

It took three holes to catch up with the players in front of them. As they waited at the fifteenth tee, Chrissy asked the questions again: "What made you change?"

"During my incarceration at Spofford, my mother contracted cancer. Knowing her time on earth would soon end, she visited me every day. She always wanted to pray with me before she left. At first I protested, but as the disease progressed, her love and sadness broke through my hard shell. I began to look forward to those prayers. She ended with the same words every time: 'Holy Virgin, please ask your Son to save my Jack's soul. Show him the way.' She believed God had a special plan for me."

"Do you believe that?"

"Yes."

"How do you know?"

"When I was a boy I loved magic. My mother and I would go for walks, and I would insist on turning down 25th Street so I could check out the magic stores. We never had much money, but she always set aside some of her tips to buy me a simple prop or a deck of cards. I read every book in the library on the subject and practiced for hours so I could entertain her friends.

"One day when I was walking home from school, I saw Old Mrs. Lowman sitting on her steps. She never smiled. Her husband had died a long time ago, and her children had moved away. I asked her if she wanted to see a card trick. She just looked at me with dull eyes. I performed the trick, and she began to laugh. I'd never heard her laugh before. As soon as I entered the front door that day, I told my mother I wanted to be a showman.

"My mother always believed in me, even when I got in trouble. After I joined a gang in high school like everyone else on the block, Mom would lecture me every night, saying God gave me a gift. But I shut her out."

Chrissy noticed the change in Jack's voice whenever he talked about his mother. It became meek, edged with emotion. His eyes stared blankly beyond her when he described his downward spiral into gang life and his mother's faithfulness and unconditional love through it all. Although they played through several holes, Chrissy lost her competitive focus because she became enrapt in Jack's story. By the time they reached the eighteenth hole, she realized she had forgotten to mark down the scores.

"So your mother's prayers changed you?" Chrissy asked as Jack placed the ball on the tee.

"Her prayers started me on a journey into a new environment where those seeds of good took root and transformed me."

Chrissy nodded. Her apprehension had faded as the details of Jack's history unfolded. "This is the last hole," she announced. "Since you began your story, I forgot to mark the scores. I'm not sure who's winning."

"Let's say we're tied. Whoever wins this hole is the Corolla Miniature Golf All-time Champion. Agreed?"

"Give it your best shot."

He stroked the ball, and it rolled over two humps, faded to the right and died three feet from the hole.

Chrissy placed her ball on the tee. "So tell me. When did the change take place? What made you plant those seeds of good?"

"When I finally got out of Spofford, Mom was in the hospital battling the final stages of the disease. She begged me not to return to my old ways. I promised her I would fulfill my purpose in this world. That's when she gave me the statuette of the Virgin Mary. She said one last prayer and then passed on. After she died life became very lonely. Loneliness drives some people crazy, but I didn't mind. I never returned to the Demon Posse. Spent most of my time in the library reading about history's great mystifiers and illusionists—Robert-Houdin, Max Malini, Alexander Herrmann, Harry Houdini. My studies led to the feats of Indian fakirs and eastern philosophy. To fulfill my potential as an illusionist, I believed I had to increase the depth of my spiritual knowledge, so I studied the religions of the world. Everything I do derives from the core of my spiritual being. I want my work to reflect not just mental skill and physical dexterity, but also spiritual power."

Jack's religious explorations reminded Chrissy of eating at a smorgasbord. He examined the wide variety of food but selected those that suited his tastes. Although she lacked his worldly knowledge, she felt secure in her faith. *What does he think about Jesus?* She wondered. *Does he regard Christ at the same level as Confucius, Muhammad and Gandhi—a great spiritual teacher?*

She stepped up to the ball and focused on her shot. Carefully she swung the putter, rapping the ball solidly. It curled over the two humps and headed to the right, smacking Jack's ball and knocking it into the hole. Chrissy's ball ricocheted off the sideboard, and stopped six inches from the hole.

"I win." Jack said.

"Don't tell me. You used your spiritual powers to control my ball."

He shook his head. "No. Sometimes we need people to send us in the right direction."

Chrissy smiled. "Can I ask you a deeply religious question since you seem to have all the answers?"

"Of course."

"In your opinion, who is Jesus of Nazareth?"

Jack paused, as if shuffling his thoughts to find the right words. "Well, Jesus was either the Son of God, or . . . " He reached down and pulled his ball from the hole, then stood, clutching it in front of her. " . . . or he was the greatest illusionist who ever lived." His fingers unfolded and the ball was gone.

Chrissy's mouth dropped open.

Jack said, "Either way, I admire him greatly."

Chrissy tapped her ball into the hole. "That's the weirdest thing I've ever heard anyone say about Jesus."

"I must admit," Jack said. "I haven't come to a final conclusion about Jesus. When I study his life and ministry, I am intrigued. I like the idea that he worked wonders by drawing strength from the core of his spiritual being. I remember reading a gospel account where a sick woman touched him, and he experienced a sudden release of spiritual power. In that sense, I want to learn from his example."

Chrissy had never been vocal about her faith. Being the preacher's daughter intensified the pressure to conduct her life with uttermost piety. Of course, for that same reason, most preachers' kids she knew were holy terrors. Although she rebelled against her parents' rigid rules occasionally (she even got drunk at a party once), most of the time she set a good example. As she looked at Jack, Chrissy sensed a hunger for truth within him. His ideas seemed muddled like stew made from leftovers—bits and pieces tossed in from every religion and philosophy he studied. His goals were ambitious and somewhat egocentric, but something about him intensely attracted her. *Would God approve of falling for someone who believes so differently from me?*

She knelt to retrieve the ball from the hole. Her hand sunk deeper into the hole past her wrist. Finally, she realized the ball had dropped into some collection bin beneath the ground. Her eyes widened. "So that's how you did the disappearing ball trick!"

Jack laughed boisterously.

She suddenly realized this was the first time she'd ever heard him laugh.

Standing, she pushed him.

He back-stepped, tripped over the sideboard and fell on his rump in the grass, dropping his putter.

Chrissy gasped, put her hand over her mouth and tried to smother her own laughter, but it exploded like a bronco out of the gates, bucking its rider.

Jack looked up with a wide grin.

Embarrassed, Chrissy leaned and extended her hand. Before she could steady herself to pull him up, he tugged hard. She lost her balance and fell into his arms, rolling side by side on the grass. Their laughter stopped when their eyes met. Those deep brown eyes mystified her. Before she could rationally consider the next move, he drew her closer and she kissed him. Although their lips pressed for only a second or two, she felt a wonderful surge throughout her body. She wondered if he felt it too.

*   *   *

On the way home, Chrissy noticed Jack glancing into the rearview mirror. He seemed distracted, occupied with his thoughts.

"What's wrong, Jack?"

"I believe Deputy Queen is tailing us. Don't turn around. I don't want him to know we know."

Chrissy wondered if her father had something to do with this. *Dad doesn't trust me.* Waves of indignation flowed over her. She imagined confronting him, insisting he apologize for treating her like a child who needed a chaperone. Then she remembered her decision to conceal her date with Jack from him. A mixture of guilt and fury streamed into her brain, burbling into confusion. She looked at Jack. An intense urge to reach out and touch his cheek overwhelmed her, but the hooves of the devil appeared from below his sleeve when he turned the steering wheel. A cold chill embraced her like a sudden gust of north wind on a hot day.

"Do you want me to lose him?" Jack asked. "With Queen, that wouldn't be too hard."

The flames of attraction and anger leapt again. "Yes. Lose him."

Jack turned right down the first side street, then left and right again, weaving through a resort neighborhood. Halfway down a road lined with immense houses, Jack pulled into an empty driveway and drove under a large deck between the beams. He proceeded to the end of the cement slab in the dark shadows of the deck as twilight faded into night.

After he jolted the shift into park, he turned off the lights and engine.

"Who lives here?" Chrissy asked.

"I have no idea."

"No idea?"

"It's a rental house. Probably empty for the week."

Chrissy nodded as a car whooshed by behind them.

"That was Queen," Jack said. He started the engine, backed out and headed in the opposite direction. "I think we lost him already."

"Where to now?" Chrissy asked.

"I've got an idea. A place he'll never find us."

Jack turned back onto Route 12 and drove past the Whalehead Club entrance. Then he made a left turn onto a dirt road. After several intersections and turns, he pulled onto the grass next to the Currituck Sound. A series of tall pines towered above them. Before Jack turned off his headlights, Chrissy noticed someone had carved a heart and initials in the trunk of the tree directly in front of them. The bottom letters had been X-ed out. *The remnants of a broken heart*, Chrissy thought. *I hope mine's not next.*

Jack shifted in his seat and put his hand on Chrissy's headrest. "What feat would you like me to perform now?" he asked.

"Talk," Chrissy said. "Just talk."

* * *

Byron sat on the front steps in the dark as Kenny pulled the sheriff's car into the driveway.

After he stepped out and slammed the door, he raised his hands in frustration and said, "I lost them."

"You lost them?" Byron groaned. "How'd that happen?"

"I don't know. They were fifty yards in front of me. Blaze made a couple turns on some back streets then vanished. Poof. Gone! I've been driving these neighborhoods for the last twenty minutes, but I can't find them anywhere. They've disappeared."

Elijah opened the front door, strode across the deck and down the steps to where they stood. "What's up, boys?"

Kenny waved, but Byron, eyes laden with worry, didn't respond.

"Did he try to shake you on purpose?" Byron asked.

"I don't know. I think so. He must have noticed me in his rearview mirror."

"That's not good," Elijah said. "Do you think Blaze is up to something?"

"There's no doubt about it," Byron said. "He had no reason to cruise these neighborhoods unless he thought he was being followed. I think he wants to get Chrissy alone somewhere."

"Maybe they just wanted to check out these beautiful vacation homes. Some of these streets could compete with the Hamptons," Elijah reasoned.

"I don't know," Kenny said. "I could accept that possibility if they didn't disappear so fast on me."

"What do we do now?" Byron asked.

For several minutes the men discussed options. Kenny suggested alerting his fellow officers to keep an eye out—nothing official at this point, just precautionary. Elijah wanted to give the young couple the benefit of the doubt and wait another half hour before they made any moves. With a harried expression, Byron insisted on splitting up, getting into their vehicles, and scouring the neighborhoods from here to the wildlife preserve.

As they debated, the black Sunfire pulled into the driveway. Chrissy stepped out and said, "Hey, everybody! Jack has something incredible he wants to show us!"

As the couple walked up to them, Jack said, "Good evening, gentlemen. Deputy Queen, what a pleasant surprise."

The three men grunted and nodded.

"Everybody upstairs," Chrissy ordered. "Jack agreed to debut an incredible feat just for our family. He tells me this could be the very thing that makes his career as a street magician."

Chrissy and Jack trotted up the steps as the three men glanced at each other, eyes wary. "Here we go again," Elijah mumbled. "Mumbo jumbo presto chango."

"You coming up?" Byron asked Kenny.

"No," Kenny said. "I've had enough of his act for one night."

*　*　*

In the great room, Jack gathered everyone near the fireplace and made them crowd together. Dugan squeezed between Mark and Matt, using his elbows to open a gap where he could get a better view in front.

"Quit pushing," Matt said, as he rubbed Dugan's red head with his knuckles.

"Boys, settle!" Lila commanded. "Jack's trying to get us organized so he can do his trick."

"It's not a trick, Mrs. Butler," Jack corrected. "I like to call it a feat."

Lila smiled. "Very well, Jack. An amazing feat."

Because they were taller, Jack positioned Elijah and Byron in the back row with their wives and Chrissy in front of them. Byron felt like they were being posed by a rude photographer for a family portrait.

"I've never tried this in front of people," Jack said. "The last time I did it before a mirror in my apartment, I became extremely dizzy and sick. It takes a lot out of me. I need all of you to stay grouped together right there in case I fall backwards. Hopefully you'll catch me."

Dugan and the twins raised their hands like they were spotting someone on the tumbling mat during gym class. "Like this, Jack?" Dugan asked.

"That's good, boys," Jack said. "Keep your hands up just like that."

Jack faced the opposite direction. Glancing over his shoulder, he positioned himself about six feet in front of them. He took a deep breath and closed his eyes. Slowly raising his arms like an eagle on an updraft, he exhaled, drew in a deep breath and held it. He rose off the ground, his feet hovering four inches above the wooden floor. He floated for several seconds as gasps and shrieks erupted from the spectators. When he descended, he collapsed forward, grasping his stomach.

Chrissy shrieked, "Jack! Are you all right?"

"Jack floated!" Mark hollered. "I saw it! He came off the ground at least a foot!"

Lila and Annie rushed to kneel beside him. "Are you okay?" Annie asked

Visibly shaken, Jack nodded, blinking his eyes and recovering his breath.

"I've never seen anything like that," Lila marveled.

Dugan stood speechless, eyes wide and mouth open.

Elijah leaned and whispered into Byron's ear: "He tapped into the power of darkness. There's no other way he could do that. It's not possible."

Byron stared at the strange man who trembled on his hands and knees with the women attending him. Elijah's words echoed in his ears— *the power of darkness . . . the power of darkness.*

Chapter Eighteen

Byron kept his mouth shut the rest of the evening. When Blaze had brought Chrissy home reasonably early from their date, Byron felt foolish for fearing the worst and jumping to false conclusions. For a short while he wondered if Blaze had left his crime days far behind. Then the levitation performance stunned him. He could think of no reasonable explanation. Elijah's claim that Blaze somehow performed the feat by calling on some occult power troubled him deeply. *I don't believe that's possible, is it? It can't be.* That night, he couldn't sleep. Tossing and turning, adjusting the covers, he drove Lila crazy.

"What is wrong with you?" she asked.

"Jack Blaze—he's what's wrong with me."

"What're you talking about?"

"Tomorrow I'm going to lecture Chrissy about dating strange men without checking their background. Then I'm going to insist she no longer see Blaze."

"Checking their background? Chrissy informed me he was the perfect gentleman this evening. He brought her home before 9:30 and then put on that amazing demonstration for us. Don't you think that was incredible? I've never seen anyone do anything like that."

"He's strange, Lila. I have no idea how he levitated. Maybe it has something to with that devil on his shoulder."

"Don't be ridiculous, Byron. You're talking crazy."

Byron sat up and leaned over his wife. "Oh yeah. I'm talking crazy, huh? Let me tell you this about Mr. Wonderful. He has a criminal record."

"A criminal record? How do you know that?"

Byron sat back against the headboard. "I had Kenny Queen check him out."

"You what?"

"You heard me. I didn't trust Blaze. Kenny pulled him over for speeding and ran a check on his driver's license. The guy's a hood—public intoxication, stealing cars, possession of marijuana, assault with a deadly weapon—all gang-related activities. He spent time in a correctional facility."

Lila sat up. "Correctional facility? Do you mean jail? Recently?"

"Well . . . Three or four years ago."

"Three or four years ago? He had to be sixteen or seventeen then."

"So. Do you want your daughter dating a man with a criminal record?"

Lila took a deep breath and exhaled. "I guess not. But he's such a great illusionist. How could he still be involved in crime and yet be so committed to perfecting his magic act?"

"Lila, that's what illusionists do. They create illusions—make you believe something that's not true. He has you and Annie bewitched."

Lila shook her head. "Byron, am I bewitched or are you bewildered? Sometimes people change. How about your best friend, Elijah Mulligan? He served two years in prison for manslaughter, and he's sleeping in this very house with us."

"Please," Byron said. "When Elijah was nineteen years old he killed a man in a fist fight. That was about forty years ago. We know the Lord changed Elijah's life. Jack Blaze, we don't know."

"Go ahead and lecture Chrissy if you want. I can tell you right now though, you better prepare for a battle. Chrissy is strong-willed, and guess who she gets that from?"

Byron slid back under the covers and stared at the ceiling. The spectacle of going head to head with his daughter nettled him. "I know. I know. She gets it from me."

"That's right," Lila said. "I should know. I've had to live in the same house for 18 years with two hardheads. Lord, help me."

The last thing Byron remembered before finally falling asleep was the red digital numbers on the alarm clock—4:45 A.M. When he opened his eyes he saw 9:12 and noticed the pattern of light slicing through the slats in the blind. He turned over to face an empty bed. *Lila's up already. Probably fixing breakfast. But I'm not hungry.*

He sat up, swung his legs across the mattress and planted his feet on the floor. His head felt heavy, so he closed his eyes and allowed it to hang. With blood rushing to his brain, he had to stiffen his legs and arms to keep from toppling over. Raising his head slowly, he tried to breath deeply, but a quivering knot in his chest interrupted his inhale. Byron hated this agitated feeling. When he opened his eyes, he saw his Bible on the dresser. Time alone with God always countered these kinds of mental bogs. Lately he had neglected his morning prayers and Scripture readings. The spiritual malnutrition had become apparent.

He stood, picked up his Bible, and walked to the glass door. The morning sun, muted by a thin layer of clouds, lit the deck with soft light. After sliding the door open, he stepped onto the wooden planks and breathed the sea air. Immediately he sensed a weight lift from him as if God had been waiting outside to infuse him with new life and strength. He sat down on a cushioned redwood deck chair, the Bible resting on his lap.

Closing his eyes, he prayed. The words trickled slowly at first, but then burst like a dam as torrents of concerns and confessions poured forth. His supplication lacked organization. From Chrissy's involvement with Blaze, to his own strange dreams and visions, to admitting his weaknesses and fears, and back to Chrissy, the words flowed tumultuously. When his soul finally emptied, he stood, leaned on the rail with one hand, Bible in the other and gazed at the sky. The weather had been clear and hot all week, but now white clouds drifted steadily eastward with few blue openings. He sensed his spiritual life had become like those clouds, airy and variable, blown by winds over which he had little control. *Help me, Lord. Plant my feet back on solid ground. Speak to me about the confusion that has shaken my life.*

By habit, Byron's Bible readings followed the common lectionary. Instead of sticking with the charted selections, he decided to open it randomly and hope for a Spirit-led passage. The pages separated and fell open to Daniel chapter ten. *I should have guessed. A book filled with dreams, visions, and revelations.* He sat down and looked at the heading of the chapter: *Daniel's Vision of a Man.*

The words of the first few verses seized Byron's attention. Daniel had been in a distressed state for several weeks, eating and drinking little, struggling to understand a vision he had received from the Lord. In front of him a strange man appeared, frightening in appearance. Although the others with Daniel did not see the man, they were overcome by terror and fled. Feeling helpless and drained of strength, Daniel faced him. The man touched Daniel, making him tremble. Then the man told him to carefully consider his words because he had been sent to explain the vision, which concerned an event yet to happen. Daniel confessed that anguish had overcome him because of the vision God had given him. The man touched Daniel again and told him not to be afraid. As the man interpreted the vision, Daniel gained strength.

Upon finishing the chapter, Byron closed the Bible. He wondered if God was speaking to him. *What are you saying, Lord? Am I so desperate that I'm grasping for answers by reading my circumstances into this passage of scripture, or are you really trying to tell me something?* Daniel's quandary over a disturbing vision seemed an incredible parallel to Byron's life. Naturally he thought the strange man who appeared only to Daniel was Blaze. As he read on, though, he realized the man had been sent from God to help solve the riddle of the vision. Blaze didn't fit that description. *Will someone else appear to help me understand? Someone from whom I could draw strength?*

As if in a trance, Byron ruminated for several minutes over the words of scripture, plugging various combinations of scenarios and people into the slots offered by the account. Nothing seemed to fit. He felt no closer to understanding his part in this convoluted scenario than when he rolled out of bed twenty minutes ago. Deciding he must read the next chapter, he thumbed through the pages to find the Book of Daniel again but stopped when he heard footsteps.

"Good morning, Daddy."

He looked up and saw Chrissy. She wore a white tank top and purple Nike running shorts. "Where are you going?"

She stood with her hand on the rail, the sunlight through the clouds blurring the edges of her form. "For a run," she said, "down the beach."

"By yourself?"

"Yes. Why?"

"Chrissy, we need to talk."

She sat down in the matching chair on the other side of a small redwood table. "I agree. We do need to talk."

Byron glanced at his hands clutching the Bible. He placed it on the table between them. Looking squarely into her eyes, he said, "I don't want you to see Jack Blaze anymore."

"Why not?"

"I don't like him."

"But I do."

"He's not who you think he is."

Chrissy sat back, eyebrows tensing. "Did you ask Kenny Queen to keep his eye on us last night?"

"Yes. But my instincts proved accurate. Jack Blaze is a hood. Kenny discovered Blaze has a criminal record longer than a Tolstoy novel."

Chrissy stood and put her hands on her hips. "I know all about Jack Blaze."

"Did you know he served time in a correctional facility?"

"He told me everything—smoking pot, abusing alcohol, stealing cars, knife fights—You can't tell me anything I don't already know."

For a few seconds Byron remained speechless, caught off guard by Blaze's openness with his daughter. But then the obvious question loosened his tongue: "Why do you want to be with a man who has led that kind of life?"

"Let me ask you a question," Chrissy responded. "Are you the same person you were at seventeen years old?"

Byron glanced down at his crossed feet. Remembering those promiscuous days sent uncomfortable twinges through him, making his leg muscles tighten and toes squirm. "No. I'm not the same person."

"If anyone should understand Jack Blaze, you should, Daddy."

Byron looked up. "Why me?"

"Because he grew up without a father too. That must be why he said he felt a connection with you."

"A connection with me? I offer my sympathies to him for growing up without a father, but I didn't join a gang or steal cars or stab people with knives."

Her shoulders slumped as she rolled her eyes. "You grew up in Martins Ferry—a little steel community on the Ohio River. Jack grew up in the middle of New York City. There's a big difference, you know."

"And that difference is one reason I don't want you to see him anymore. Growing up in those kinds of negative surroundings can damage a person psychologically. I believe he has issues and problems from the past lodged so deeply that you can't recognize them or even begin to understand."

"Do you think I'm a child?" she snapped. "Have you no confidence in my judgment? I'm not blind to Jack's character. I know his background is far from perfect, but he's working harder than any young man I know to make something of his life. He gives tours all day long at the Whalehead Club, then he spends six to eight hours perfecting his illusions."

"That's the other reason," Byron snarled. "Those illusions. Elijah thinks he draws power from sources of spiritual darkness to accomplish those feats, and I'm beginning to wonder."

Chrissy clasped her cheeks. "Now I've heard everything! Since when did you start leaning toward Elijah's fundamentalist ways?" She held out her hands, fingers curled. "Next thing you know we'll be handling rattlesnakes right before we collect the offering at Scotch Ridge Church."

"Very funny, Miss Prissy Presbyterian. If you know it all, then tell me: how did he bite that quarter in half or float four inches off the ground? Surely he revealed his secrets to you."

"A good illusionist never reveals his secrets, but I'm not naïve enough to believe he has supernatural powers. The quarter had to be some kind of prop."

Byron crossed his arms. "What about the levitation?"

"Don't you remember how he gathered us together almost like he was posing us for a picture?"

"So what."

"It just seemed odd he made sure we were all in one small space, as if he wanted to control the angle at which we observed him. Then he turned slightly to barely block the front of his right foot. He's good at it. Knowing exactly what we could see, he must have risen up on the ball of his right foot creating the illusion."

Byron closed his eyes and tried to remember if Blaze had turned his back to them at a slight angle, but the image of Blaze's heels rising off the ground had shocked him so much he couldn't recall. "Well . . .well . . . maybe you're right, but why did he act so exhausted and sick afterwards. He collapsed right in front of us."

"Jack does everything dramatically. He's like a method actor. To produce the most effective illusions, he believes the performance must come from deep within his soul. He's very spiritual. You and he are more alike than you realize. Jack's just somewhat misguided."

Byron raised his finger. "There! You summed it up perfectly with one word: *misguided.* I do not want my daughter spending time with someone who's heading in the wrong direction. The path he's on could very well lead to destruction."

Chrissy leaned on the rail and glared at her father. The way her lips tightened and eyes narrowed made her look ten years older. "And I thought Jack was melodramatic." She shook her head. "I'm sorry, Daddy, but you're way off this time. You've always told me to follow God's will and not knuckle under to people who try to pressure me into doing the wrong thing. I've always taken that advice seriously. God has brought Jack Blaze into our lives for a reason. Maybe we can help him. I don't know, but I intend to spend more time with him."

Byron felt his face burn. "Listen carefully, young lady. I'm still your father, and you still live under my roof. This young man is trouble. He's . . . he's . . . evil. I forbid you to see him."

Chrissy's nostrils flared. "Is that really why, Daddy? Because he's evil? Or is it because he's black?"

Byron shook his head. Words jumbled in his mind and lodged at his mouth like a mob trying to escape a burning building.

"I'm leaving," Chrissy seethed. She stomped across the deck, disappeared around the corner, and thundered down the front steps.

Byron jumped up and leaned on the rail. Words finally erupted: "Get back here! Chrissy! Do you hear me?"

By then she had already broken into a quick stride, her blonde hair tossing as her form diminished down the street.

He pounded his fists on the railing. *Doggone it, that girl is strong willed.* When he hung his head and closed his eyes, darkness descended. In the isolation of his thoughts he felt desperate. Chrissy's words pummeled him, jolted the broad-minded exterior he had always displayed. Not wanting to discuss the confrontation with Lila, he decided to slip on his sandals and walk to the resort shops. He could think of only two things that could ease his misery: exercise and chocolate-covered doughnuts. Before leaving, he glanced in the bathroom mirror. His hair was disheveled and his t-shirt wrinkled, but he didn't care. *That's what I look like on the inside too. No sense trying to fool anybody.*

* * *

When he entered the bakery, the large Greek baker exclaimed, "Eets my friend from Ohio! Back for more chocolate covered doughnuts? Just feenished a new batch. Very fresh."

Byron nodded. "I'll take a dozen."

The baker leaned on the counter, his eyes filling with concern. "You look a leetle . . . what's the word? . . . frazzled. Too much Agiorgitiko last night?"

"What?"

"You know." He tilted his head, held an imaginary bottle and gulped. "Greek red wine. Seemilar to Merlot."

Byron managed a smile. "No. I'm not hung over. Just a little dazed."

"These doughnuts will do the trick," the baker said as he snagged a box.

"Couldn't hurt."

"Whenever I'm a leetle dazed, I go feeshing. Clears the cobwebs."

Byron wished the resolution of his confusion was as easy as tossing a line into the waves. The mixture of visions and fears churned incoherently in his mind. Nothing seemed certain.

"I'm afraid fishing wouldn't help me," Byron finally responded.

The Greek tucked the last doughnut into the box, closed the lid and placed it on the counter. "Forgive me for asking. I do not want to be insensitive, but you seem very upset. Is eet because you know the meesing girl?"

Byron needed a few seconds to grasp the strongly accented words. "Did you say, 'missing girl?'"

"Indeed." He pointed to the newspaper rack. "Her picture's on the front page."

Glancing to his right, he saw the stark headlines: KITY HAWK WOMAN REPORTED MISSING. Beneath the black words the smile of a young brunette in the color photograph beamed from the page. The image staggered Byron. As he stepped toward the rack the strength drained from his leg muscles. He lifted the newspaper and stared at the image. She was beautiful. Her chestnut hair flowed in large curls around her face and over her shoulders. With deep umber eyes, thick lashes and brows, she reminded Byron of the girls on the front of Chrissy's fashion magazines.

Byron folded the newspaper and stuck it under his arm. "I'll take a paper too," he said. After he dug his wallet from his back pocket and paid the baker, he grabbed the box of doughnuts and hurried to the door.

On the way out he heard the Greek say, "So sorry about the meesing girl."

Byron navigated the maze of suspended walkways that connected the shops and sat down on a bench in front of Ocean Atlantic Rentals. He plopped the box of doughnuts beside him, unfolded the paper, and read quickly.

> Police seek public assistance in determining the whereabouts of 21-year-old Laura Redinger. The Kitty Hawk resident was reported missing by her parents on Tuesday evening after she failed to return phone calls for several days. Her parents, who reside in

Manteo, told authorities their daughter always checked in with them by phone on Sunday evenings. On Monday, after calling the Holiday Inn where Redinger worked as a receptionist, her parents discovered she had been absent from her job for two days. The hotel management told police they tried to contact her by phone and even sent an employee to her apartment, but to no avail.

"We have concerns for her safety," Chief Randall Davis stated. "She may have taken off on a whim, but it's highly unlikely. According to everyone we've talked to, the young woman was a dependable girl."

Harley Austin, a fellow employee, noted Redinger was the type who stayed out of trouble. "She was a cheerleader and homecoming queen in high school," Austin said. "A real popular kid with a good head on her shoulders. Doesn't make sense that she would take off without telling anyone."

Chief Davis said he intends to intensify the search and follow all available leads. "We are making an appeal to any witnesses in the Currituck and Dare County vicinity. If you have any information, please contact the Kitty Hawk Police Department.

Byron lowered the paper and wondered if she was the girl in his dream. *Or was she already dead?* He remembered following Dugan through the marsh. *Was she the one Dugan found in the weeds?* He wanted to rush back and show Dugan the picture. *Maybe that's not such a good idea. We found a deer in the weeds. I saw it with my own eyes. Besides, the girl in my dream was blond, like Chrissy, not brunette. Is this just another ingredient to throw into the pot?*

Walking back to the vacation house, he considered all the coincidences. There were too many. If this girl was still alive, he wanted to help find her. But how? Blaze's sneering face appeared in his mind. Byron imagined the girl tied up in a back bedroom of Blaze's apartment. He scolded himself for concocting such a scene without any kind of evidence. All the things that bothered Byron —his visions, Blaze's devil tattoo and supernatural feats, and the dead deer in the marsh—offered no justification to point his finger at Blaze. *The police would think I'm crazy. They'd probably arrest me.*

Yet he knew the possibility of Blaze being a suspect wasn't out of the question. He wondered how Blaze would react if he saw the picture of the girl. Byron wanted to show him the picture and watch his eyes. Maybe then he could pick up a vibe, a sense of guilt, or at least a flash of recognition. He would study Blaze's every move, every nuance of expression. If Blaze appeared ill at ease after seeing the girl's photo, then it wouldn't hurt to do some investigating. Maybe he could find a clue, any scrap of evidence he could present to the police.

I wonder where Blaze lives? Byron imagined breaking into Blaze's house and hearing muffled screams. He pictured himself opening the bedroom closet door and finding the brown-haired girl, tied and gagged. He reproved himself again. *No,* he thought. *Don't demonize a man just because you don't like him. But I wouldn't mind knowing where Blaze lives just in case more suspicions arise after he sees the photograph. Where can I get his address? Of course! The Whalehead Club.*

Byron sprang from the bench and oriented himself. The Whalehead Club was directly west of the resort shops. He scooped up the box of doughnuts, crossed the walkway, and descended the steps. The distance to the Whalehead Club was less then six hundred yards, and Byron covered it briskly.

Arriving, he saw a line of vacationers forming near the front porch. He approached one of the attendants, an elderly woman with silver hair and bright red lipstick.

"I'm sorry," she said, "You'll have to get in line if you want to take a tour."

Byron raised his hand and smiled. "We took the tour yesterday. It was fascinating. Our guide did such a wonderful job, we wanted to send him a thank you card."

"How nice," she said. "What was his name?"

"Jack Blaze. I was hoping you could give me his address."

"Oh . . . well . . . I don't know." She glanced around the grounds. "I haven't seen Jack today. Must be his day off. Guess it wouldn't hurt to give you his address. Give me a minute. I'll have to look through the employee records in the office."

"Thank you so much. I truly appreciate it."

After the woman entered the front door, Byron looked heavenward. *Forgive me for lying, Lord, but I'm desperate. You're the one who got this thing started. I'm just trying to figure how to work out my end of the deal.*

She returned and handed Byron a slip of paper. "He's probably home working on his magic act. That's all the boy thinks about."

"Thank you so much," he said. "You don't know how much this means to me."

As Byron walked away, he glanced at the address: 212 Barracuda Street, Corolla, NC. He repeated it to himself several times, folded it, and stuck it in his pocket.

Walking back to the vacation house, Byron considered his options. Going directly to Jack's apartment to confront him with the photo might be a mistake. Chances are he had nothing to do with the girl's disappearance. But if he did, Byron didn't want to give him an excuse to more thoroughly cover his tracks. How could he lure Blaze away from his house and show him the picture without raising suspicions? As he turned the corner, he saw Chrissy running toward him. She slowed her pace to a walk and stopped in front of the vacation house, leaning on her knees. *Of course!* Byron thought. *A compromise with Chrissy. That's how. This could be tricky, but the pieces are falling into place.*

Chapter Nineteen

"Chrissy!" Byron hollered. He lifted the box of doughnuts. "I've brought a peace offering."

Chrissy straightened and wiped the sweat from her brow. "Peace on whose terms?" she asked.

Byron covered the last few steps and faced his daughter. "On both our terms. I think there's room for compromise on this issue." He could see the surprise in her eyes. Popping open the lid, he said, "Here. Take one."

She glanced at the doughnuts and waved her hand. "No thanks. I'm too thirsty. What kind of compromise are you talking about?"

"Perhaps I was hasty in demanding you cut this relationship off completely. I'm willing to discuss other options."

"What kind of options?"

"I really don't want you to be alone with Jack until we get to know him better. Considering his record, I don't think that is an unreasonable request." He could see her eyes clouding with indignation. "Now listen. Before you blow up, hear me out."

She crossed her arms, and her lips tightened, almost disappearing.

Byron continued. "I would like to have Jack over for dinner tonight."

"Really?" The clouds of resentment parted.

"Yes. I want a chance to get to know what he's really like. He and I could have a man-to-man talk. Then you two could spend the evening here, playing cards, watching a movie, whatever. All I ask is that you give me a chance to know him better."

Chrissy nodded. "I guess that's fair. Besides, I've already invited him over for dinner tonight."

Byron could not squelch the irritation in his voice. "You already invited him even after I asked you not to see him again?"

"Yes, Daddy, I just had to get you two together again. Jack is a great guy. You just don't understand him yet."

"Okay," Byron said. "I'll let this slide if we have come to an agreement. You see Jack only at this house with adults around until I get to know him better. Agreed?"

"Agreed," Chrissy said. "With time I know you'll like him."

"I'm curious," Byron said. "Where did you run into Jack?"

"On the beach. He was performing card tricks for the vacationers. He's always entertaining people."

Right, Byron thought. *Always fooling people.*

*   *   *

Byron found Elijah on the upper deck, eyes closed, stretched out on a redwood recliner. He tossed the paper, and it landed in Elijah's lap, startling him. Grabbing the paper, Elijah asked, "What's this?"

"Check out the front page," Byron said.

Elijah held it at almost arm's length to adjust his focus. "Kitty Hawk woman reported missing," he mumbled. He read through the article and examined the photograph. "Hmmph."

"That's it? Hmmph?"

"Laura Redinger? Who is she?"

"I don't know. Remember Dugan's description of the dead girl he found in the marsh?"

"Long brown hair, all tangled and muddy?"

"That's right. Look at the photo again."

Elijah glanced at the paper and shrugged. "So what? Dugan imagines things. He saw a dead deer and thought it was a dead body."

"Maybe," Byron said. "But what if the killer saw Dugan in the marsh that day. Remember, Dugan said he could hear someone following him in the weeds. After he took off, the killer could have removed the body and replaced it with the deer."

Elijah pointed at the image. "You think Dugan found this girl in the marsh four days ago?"

"No. I'm just speculating. Maybe we should show Dugan the picture."

"I don't think that's wise. Dugan's tends to make up stories. Stimulating his imagination with this picture won't help the kid."

Byron collapsed into the chair next to Elijah. Leaning forward on his knees, he closed his eyes and rubbed his forehead. "There's something about this girl. I have an odd feeling inside. Either she's dead or in a lot of trouble. For some reason I believe I"'ve been called here to do something about this."

"Are you talking about your dreams?"

"Yes. The dreams, the horse, and the strange feelings I had at the top of the lighthouse. I'm either going crazy or else God has brought me here for a purpose—maybe to rescue someone."

"If this girl is already dead, how can you rescue her?"

Byron lifted his head. Tension strained the muscles in his face. "I don't know. All of these things are churning inside me, but I have no answers."

"I guess we could show the picture to Dugan if you think it would help."

Byron waved his hand at the newspaper. "Let's just wait. I want to show the picture to someone else before Dugan sees it."

"Who's that?"

"Jack Blaze."

"You think Blaze has something to do with this?"

"I don't have any proof. Just a gut feeling. If he is involved, I'd like to find some evidence."

Elijah sat up. "How?"

"He's coming over for dinner tonight. I told Chrissy she's only allowed to see him at this house. I want to observe his reaction when I show him this headline and photo. If he reacts suspiciously, I'll move forward on my plan. Hopefully after dinner they'll pop in a movie or play some games. That will be my window of opportunity. I intend to break into his house and look for evidence."

"Are you kidding me? Who do you think you are, Sergeant Joe Friday?"

"I think I look more like Magnum P.I."

"You need a sidekick. I'll go with you."

Byron held up his hand. "No. One person snooping around someone's house is conspicuous enough. Besides, I need you here to keep an eye on Blaze just in case he leaves early. I'll keep a cell phone on me."

"Right," Elijah said. "I'll guard the home front and make sure he doesn't pull any tricks. I told you that guy has occult powers. "

"Just make sure you watch his every move and call me if he leaves."

"Don't worry. If he tries to leave, I'll sit on him."

"I don't think that would help."

Elijah's expression muddled. "Why not?"

"He'd probably levitate until you lost your balance and fell off."

"Very funny."

* * *

That afternoon Byron's anxiety mounted again. To relieve the stress, he decided to go for a six-mile run. Before he left, he thumbed through the phonebook and found the street map of Corolla. He located Barracuda Street on the south side of town near the ocean. Closing the directory, he determined his route for the day's run—the first half-mile would take him by Jack Blaze's house. He wanted to know the exact location so he wouldn't waste time trying to find it later that evening.

As he exited the house, the humidity engulfed him like stepping into a sauna. Although the air was oppressive, he moved determinedly across the deck and down the steps. Breaking into an easy gait, he hadn't run more than twenty steps before a large drop of sweat trickled down his forehead and into his eye. He wiped it away and blinked, countering the burning sensation. The sky was bluish gray with darker patches of clouds hunched and threatening near the horizon. Watching the street signs, he navigated through the maze of lanes until he reached Barracuda Street, which ran perpendicular to the sea.

Finding 212 was easy. Byron correctly guessed it would be on the second block back from the ocean on his right like the other even-numbered houses. As he ran by, something odd occurred to him—it looked just like the house he had rented in Pittsburgh during his first year of seminary: a one-story white cottage with plenty of windows. *Good*, Byron thought. *He's sure to leave at least one of those windows unlocked.*

With the house located, Byron sensed a weight lift from his shoulders. *Difficult tasks are completed one step at a time.* He watched his feet slapping the asphalt. *One step at a time.* As he neared the end of the street, he opened his stride, crossed a section of ground sparsely covered with sea grass, and charged up a sand hill. The soft surface hampered his progress, but he leaned into the slope and pumped his arms. By the time he reached the top, sweat poured down his face, stinging his eyes. His breathing accelerated, lungs struggling to process the thick air. As he crested the final dune, the sea breeze met him, a welcomed reprieve from the swelter. He coasted down the other side and across the beach, turning north onto the wet strip of sand left behind by the receding tide.

Running along the edge of the water proved much easier. The breeze seemed to lift him. With incredible volume, the surf roared, shutting out the voices of people and cries of gulls. Byron noted the dark cumulus clouds stacked ominously over the ocean and attributed the large waves to a storm at sea. As he advanced, the number of sunbathers and beachcombers diminished. He could see the cabled piers separating the public beach from the wildlife preserve just ahead.

The image of Blaze's white cottage infiltrated his mind, sparking memories of the little house in Pittsburgh. He recalled several of his classmates gathering one night around the kitchen table to cram for a test in Hebrew. One of them brought a couple of six-packs of Iron City Beer. During his undergraduate years, Byron had stumbled occasionally when it came to alcohol, overindulging at parties and even drinking at local bars. Although he seriously pursued a relationship with God during those college days, the temptation to tie one on with the boys occasionally overpowered his developing faith. As a young seminarian, he had hoped to overcome such indiscretions. However, the night they studied for the Hebrew exam began a series of Bible and beer sessions at the little white house for the rest of the year. The study group called themselves the *Brotherhood of the Black Sheep*.

Byron always tried to limit himself to two or three cans. He reasoned the Bible didn't instruct believers not to drink, but rather not to get drunk. Unfortunately, he did not always stop at three cans. He remembered many nights feeling woozy as he rose from the table to see his buddies to the door. With time and the added responsibility of ministry and family, he distanced himself from former activities he now judged inappropriate. Because he had an image to uphold in the community, drinking too much with friends or colleagues was out of the question.

No one in his immediate family knew about his beer bouts with the *Brotherhood of the Black Sheep*, not even Lila. Chrissy's words echoed in his mind: *If anyone should understand Jack Blaze, you should, Daddy.*

He reached the wildlife preserve and funneled through the narrow gap in the piers.

As he lifted his knees in transition from walking to running again, he puzzled over Blaze's confession. *Why didn't he try to hide his past from Chrissy? It's almost as if he doesn't care what people think of his background.* Byron couldn't decide if that was good or bad. He couldn't imagine exposing some of his past sins to his family or congregation. Blaze seemed so different from him, and yet there was a connection. The truth suddenly struck Byron like the slap of an unexpected wave: *I was like him when I was younger. Maybe my behavior was not that extreme, but to some degree we were similar. Growing up without a father made me suspicious of adult males. Authority figures probably thought I was insolent. I know I've changed, but am I that much better?*

When he glanced up, the black figure appeared like a phantom one hundred yards ahead. It stood in the middle of the firm sand, waiting, watching him approach. Seeing the stallion rattled him. He wondered if the horse remembered chasing him to the gap in the posts. As he neared he slowed and stopped thirty yards away. The horse snorted and stamped, its mane whipping shoreward in the breeze. Byron decided to cut across the beach and circumvent the animal. As he stepped through the dry sand, the horse followed like a defensive back shadowing a receiver before the snap. Angling back to the ocean, Byron watched the horse swing round, matching his movements.

"What do you want from me?" Byron said.

The stallion lifted its head and whinnied, shaking its mane.

The word 'lighthouse' popped into Byron's mind.

He turned cautiously and looked southward. From over a mile away, the Currituck beacon barely jutted above pines that rose from the other side of the dunes. The dark clouds had drifted into shore, climbing higher into the sky like a prophet mounting the pulpit to preach damnation. The dream flashed across his inner screen—the girl calling for help in the dark boathouse and the satanic presence.

I need to get to the top of the lighthouse. There's something I'm suppose to see there. He turned to face the horse. It raised its head and whinnied again. If he ran at a good pace, Byron knew he could reach the lighthouse in less than eight minutes. "I'm on my way," he said. "No need to chase me."

Although he was far from top shape, he pushed hard for the first half-mile, slowing only to weave through the posts at the cabled fence. He didn't run on the public beach for long. As soon as he could, he cut across the sand to the nearest beach access steps that climbed the dunes and led across a walkway to one of the resort neighborhoods. On asphalt Byron encountered less resistance. He headed to the main road and tried to pick up his pace, but the humidity smothered him. Despite the difficulty, every step drew the redbrick spire nearer.

By the time Byron turned the corner, ran the block to the base of the lighthouse, and stopped, his legs ached with fatigue, and he huffed harshly to catch his breath. He leaned over and sweat dripped off his face, dotting the sidewalk. Looking up, he saw a small crowd waiting in line. Then he remembered an important detail: *I don't have any money on me. Doggone it. How can I get to the top without money?* He slogged to the back of the line and scoured his mind for some possibility. In the distance a low murmur of thunder rumbled.

Standing in front of the entrance, the attendant, a man with black-framed glasses, raised his hands. "I'm sorry," He announced. "I just saw lighting. Looks like a big storm's on its way. We'll have to close until it passes."

A chorus of disappointment released from the crowd as the tourists who had just descended filtered out the door.

Byron felt a large raindrop splash the back of his head. As the people dispersed he watched the attendant enter the door and then reappear with an easel displaying a wooden sign with the words: CLOSED DUE TO INCLEMENT WEATHER. When the man looked up and noticed Byron watching him, Byron nodded, turned, and strolled in the opposite direction. He stopped and leaned against a tall pine tree.

The man walked past and said, "I'd find cover if I were you. Looks like were in for a heckuva storm."

"Yes, sir," Byron answered. "I certainly will."

Thunder rumbled again, this time much louder. A few raindrops filtered through the branches and pine needles and splattered randomly on the sidewalk. He watched the wet spots slowly blotch the redbrick surface. When he looked up, he saw the attendant enter the Keeper's house and shut the door behind him. Byron turned and walked to the lighthouse entrance. He glanced over his shoulder. Several people had gathered under a stand of oaks to his left, but they were laughing and talking, oblivious to Byron's presence. He slipped behind the sign and reached out to turn the doorknob. It was unlocked. Quickly he opened the door and slipped inside.

For a few seconds, the utter solitude of the interior spooked him. He glanced around the workhouse room, noting the objects obscured in the dimness—the table with the vase of day lilies, the old photographs and antiques. He hesitated as if he expected to see the ghost of the Keeper of the Light emerge from the shadows. With the buzz of gooseflesh tingling his arms and neck, he rushed into the base of the tower.

Looking up, he saw the steps spiraling above him. The long tapering tunnel created an incredible sense of depth that trifled with his vision, causing slight dizziness. He closed his eyes and shook his head, trying to shake off the reverse vertigo. When thunder crashed again, he headed to the steps, running full speed up the first flight. As he ascended, his legs became leaden, and the repetition of stairs and landings felt like a dream from which you cannot awaken. His breathing became harsh, and he slowed his pace, but then saw the final flight and struggled to the top. He lunged across the landing, crashed into the door, and fumbled for the knob.

When the door swung open, the wind rushed into the tower, a cold blast that pushed him back a step. He steadied himself and moved forward, leaning against the onrush of air. On the parapet, he sensed he had ascended into the midst of the angry sky. He circled to the west side of the spire and gazed upward, gripping the rail. The cloud prophet loomed over him, dark and intimidating. Lightning streaked from the midst of the blackness and struck near the Whalehead Club. Thunder roared vehemently, vibrating the ironwork on which Byron stood. The storm released a burst of rain, the droplets stinging Byron's face and arms. Looking below, he could see the people who had gathered under the trees, scattering in all directions. The torrents lashed down on them in waves.

Byron leaned over the rail and squinted through the downpour. From the direction of the Whalehead Club, a tall girl, wearing a white blazer and slacks, ran toward the lighthouse, her long blond hair whipped by the wind and rain. He couldn't tell for sure, but she looked like Adrienne Lawrence, their guide from yesterday's tour.

"Adrienne!" he yelled, but she couldn't hear him.

She stopped when she reached the road to allow a pickup truck to pass. Byron looked to his left. A jolt of panic rushed through him when he saw a black car—similar to the one Blaze drove—come to a stop and beep its horn. She turned to peer into the passenger window. Byron strained to see the driver through the windshield, but the windows were tinted. Adrienne approached the passenger-side window.

It occurred to Byron that the scene God had wanted him to witness from on high was unfolding before him. He shouted, "No! Don't get in!" But the wind and thunder muffled his words.

She held up her hand and shook her head, trying to politely refuse the driver's offer. The rain continued to drill against the pavement, and the driver persisted. The door popped open, and Adrienne stepped back. Byron saw a hand in the shadow of the interior, waving her on. Finally, she relented and stepped into the car. Byron's heart sank. He leaned over the railing and tried to see the license plate as the vehicle pulled away, but he couldn't make out the numbers. The red taillights glared at him like demonic eyes. He watched, hoping he could tell which direction the car would go, but it disappeared behind a thick stand of trees. Looking up, he saw the churning darkness of the thunderhead pass over, almost within reach.

In a rumble of thunder he heard the words: "Who are you?"

Incredulously he stared into chaos, unable to respond. The words came again, louder, clearer: "WHO ARE YOU?"

Byron whirled around to see a thin man, bald with a grizzly gray beard. The rain pelted his forehead and funneled down the deep wrinkles of his face.

"I'm . . . I'm Byron. Who are you?"

"Well Oi ain't Saint Peter, that's for sartain. Oi'm the keeper, but the only pearly gates Oi'll show you are at the county jail. Get the heck off this parapet before you get struck by lightning!"

Byron hurried around the irate man and descended the spiraling steps. The memory of his conversation with Adrienne Lawrence in the hallway of the Whalehead Club echoed in his mind—her hopes of becoming a doctor and missionary, his friendship with her father. *Dear Lord, is she in danger?* He did not stop at the bottom, but rushed out the door, knocking over the easel and sign. Sloshing through the grass, Byron focused on the road, but the black car had vanished. He ran down the lane for several hundred yards, glancing to the right and left at the few crossroads, but he saw no sign of the vehicle. Fatigue overwhelmed his leg muscles. He stopped in the middle of a large puddle and leaned on his knees. Raindrops rippled the surface of the water, distorting and segmenting his reflection. He turned and walked in the opposite direction. By the time he reached the vacation house, he felt physically and emotionally exhausted.

Chapter Twenty

Byron sat at the bottom of the front steps and watched two dragonflies circle and dart above a rhododendron bush in the front yard. The lowering sun broke through the clouds glinting the winged creatures with opalescent beauty. After his run, he'd taken a shower and dressed for dinner, brooding and aloof as he replayed the scene at the lighthouse over and over in his mind. Lila commented on his gruff mood, but he just grunted. To get away from everyone, he descended to the lowest level of the structure, the bottom tread of the front steps. There he waited for Jack Blaze to arrive. He wanted to see if Blaze's black car had tinted windows.

The fresh air after the storm and the play of the dragonflies helped to alleviate his morose disposition. The insects had always seemed otherworldly to Byron—like their namesake. They moved through the air with such peculiar lilting and shifting, as if unrestricted to the normal principles of flight. He loved their odd colors and iridescent wings. As he watched the aerial acrobatics in the glimmer of the dying sunlight, he guessed they were engaging in a mating ritual, enticing and chasing one another.

When their flight plunged recklessly to the base of the rhododendron bush, Byron noticed that only one dragonfly reappeared above the green leaves and pink flowers. He watched for more than a minute, but the insect remained alone, oddly shifting positions in the air. Curious, Byron walked to the bush and looked down. The mate had been caught in a large spider web that stretched from the plant to the grass to the house, the strands like thin spokes of a bicycle wheel with a large zigzagging stripe of silk down the center. He wanted to reach out and pull the doomed creature from the sticky threads, but he hesitated. A large black spider with splatters of bright yellow around the abdomen crawled quickly up the web and began spinning its silk around the insect. Byron leaned to get a closer look. The spider worked masterfully. Within a minute, the dragonfly looked like a mummy wrapped in a silken cocoon. Then the spider lowered its head as if to kiss its victim, but

Byron realized the true purpose of the act: it had bitten into the cocoon and now sucked the life juices from the dragonfly.

Repulsed, he stood and backed away. As he did, Blaze's black Sunfire pulled into the driveway. The last rays of the setting sun sent yellow streaks across the tinted windows. A chill flowed over him as if ice water had been dumped down his back. Byron composed himself to face the illusionist. The door popped open, and Jack emerged, wearing khaki shorts and a dark blue t-shirt.

He nodded and smiled—the half-sneer that always rubbed Byron the wrong way.

Byron studied the young man's face before asking, "How are you this evening, Jack?"

Blaze shrugged. "I'm hungry. Haven't eaten all day."

"You've been busy, I presume?"

"Yes, very busy. Sometimes I get . . . wrapped up in my work."

"Creating illusions or guiding tours?" Byron asked.

Blaze smiled. "Illusions, of course. Guiding tours is only a temporary means of support."

"Of course." Byron couldn't detect any suspicious modulation in the tone of Blaze's voice. He's good at what he does, Byron reminded himself. He pointed to Blaze's Sunfire. "I saw a car just like that when I was out running. Did you happen to drive by the lighthouse today, just about when the storm hit?"

Blaze hesitated, thinking. "No. I drove over to pick up my paycheck, but that was before the storm."

Byron motioned to the front door. "Let's head upstairs. I believe dinner is about ready."

"Sounds good," Blaze said as he trotted up the steps. "If I weren't a vegetarian, I could eat a horse."

Before ascending, Byron glanced at the web. "How about a dragonfly?" he mumbled, but Blaze didn't hear him.

* * *

Lila prepared spaghetti with marinara sauce spiced with onions and plenty of chili flakes in deference to their guest's dietary preferences. A huge bowl of iceberg lettuce topped with tomatoes, carrots, mozzarella cheese, black olives and mushrooms sat at the center of the table. Hot garlic bread, stacked in baskets at each end and still steaming from the oven, saturated the air with its delectable smell.

Everyone greeted Jack warmly except for Elijah. He kept his distance and watched Blaze with tentative eyes. When Byron had the chance, he elbowed Elijah and instructed him quietly to lighten up and not display such an air of suspicion. The big man acceded quickly, nodding to assure Byron that he grasped the strategy. His attitude flip-flopped, becoming overly friendly to Blaze, and Byron cringed, realizing Elijah lacked clandestine skills. The boys accosted Jack with requests for a card trick, and he obliged them while the women finished supper preparations. Byron noticed Chrissy continually fawning at Jack's side, overly attentive to his every move and word.

When Lila announced the spaghetti was ready to be served, they gathered around the table. Not wanting to hear some Buddhist nonsense about food being a gift of the universe and a sacrifice of life, Byron didn't offer Blaze the chance to pray. Instead he asked everyone to bow their heads and said his usual blessing, ending with great emphasis: " . . . in *Jesus' name* we pray. Amen."

Everyone seconded the Amen. Even Blaze.

Light-hearted conversation flowed during the meal—the women's shopping trip to the local plaza, the weather, the boys' miniature golf tournament earlier that afternoon, Elijah's collection of shells, Chrissy's workout at the sports center, the wonderful food—normal exchanges that brought a sense of connectedness to their lives. Garlic bread circulated the table, and almost everyone welcomed second helpings of spaghetti that Lila readily dished out. For the most part, Blaze added little to the banter, but always replied politely whenever asked a question or prodded for an opinion.

After they ate, Byron tried to draw Blaze out of his reserved state, hoping to relax him with conversation before thrusting the photograph in his face.

"So, Jack," Byron said. "Chrissy tells me you're one of the hardest working young men she knows. Do you have aspirations of being a famous magician one day? Another David Copperfield perhaps?"

"That's not my style," Blaze said.

"Jack wants to perform street magic," Chrissy added.

"Street magic? What do you mean by that?" Annie asked.

"I'm interested in the spontaneous reactions of everyday people. For example, I'll walk into one of the tough neighborhoods in New York and perform for three or four teenagers or a group of homeboys in front of the housing projects."

"Isn't that dangerous?" Lila asked. "Walking into some rundown neighborhood and performing for strangers? They could . . . they could . . . attack you."

Blaze shrugged. "It's where I'm from. I'm more comfortable around gang-bangers than I am around middle-class suburbanites. Besides, whether you're from the Bronx or the Hamptons, human nature is human nature. People enjoy my performances and react similarly despite their social class."

"How can you make a living walking the streets doing card tricks?" Elijah asked.

"I want to travel across the country with a small video crew in the near future. We would stop in towns and cities along the way and film what I do. It would be a documentary. Later we could sell it to cable networks. I'm not obsessed with making a lot of money. I've been working odd jobs and saving what I can to finance the trip. To me it will be like a safari, but my aim is to capture the candid moments of people reacting to my illusions."

"I still don't think it's very safe," Lila said, "—traveling across the country and stopping who knows where. There's so much evil in the world today."

"This world's not a safe place," Jack said, "but I fear no evil."

"Why not?" Byron asked. "Terrible things happen to innocent people all the time."

"People tend to fear what they don't understand," Jack responded. "After seeing my illusions, some people even fear me."

"Is that a desired objective?" Byron asked.

Blaze took a large gulp of lemonade and returned his glass to the table. "No. But it is a natural response. They fear me because they lack understanding. I don't try to create or avoid it. I just accept it."

"I see," Byron said. "But I must disagree with your stance on the subject. You say you fear no evil. Sometimes a healthy fear of evil can save your life."

Blaze rubbed his chin, his dark eyes intense. "I have discovered the opposite is true. Fear can have a paralyzing effect. Those who yield to it surrender the advantage to the one who is out to harm. I learned that lesson on the streets."

Byron leaned forward. "Did you see this morning's paper?"

"No," Blaze said. "I rarely pick up a paper."

Is he lying? Byron wondered. *If he kidnapped this girl, surely he would have been checking the papers.* Byron turned in his seat and lifted the newspaper from the top of the light stand behind him. As he handed the paper to Blaze, he said, "A good dose of fear may have helped this girl. My guess is that someone abducted her—someone she should have feared instead of trusted."

Blaze studied the image. His expression changed subtly, brows tensing. "You may be right, that is, if she *was* abducted. Then again, fear could have been her downfall. Your guess is as good as mine."

"She worked at one of the resort hotels not far from here, down in Kitty Hawk." Byron watched Jack's eyes carefully and noticed they widened slightly.

Blaze nodded. "She looks familiar. I performed a couple of feats at the Heritage Park a few days ago. She may have been in the crowd."

"Can I see the picture?" Dugan blurted. He stood, sliding his chair back.

"You don't need to see the picture," Elijah said.

"Please? I want to see what she looks like." He circled around the table to where Blaze sat.

"Here," Jack said and handed him the paper

Dugan's eyes widened. "That's her!" he exclaimed

"Who?" Elijah asked.

"That's the dead girl I found in the marsh. I swear, Uncle Elijah. I swear."

"Dugan, we've already discussed this. You found a dead deer in the marsh," Elijah said.

The color drained from Dugan's face as he glanced around the table. "It's her. I know it is . . . except . . . except . . ."

"Except what, Dugan?" Byron asked.

"Except she's missing the mark—the evil mark the killer carved into her forehead."

"Please, Dugan," Annie said. "Don't make up stories."

Dugan's eyes filled with frustration.

Byron looked at Blaze and noticed he was fully focused on the boy.

"What did the mark look like?" Matt asked.

"Please kids, don't encourage him," Annie said.

"Does anyone have a pencil?" Dugan asked.

"I do," Mark said, reaching into his pocket and pulling out a small green one. "I kept this from the miniature golf match today." He handed it to Dugan.

Annie glanced at Elijah and shook her head.

Dugan laid the paper on the table and carefully drew several lines on the image. He held it up and showed everyone. "That's what it looked like." On her forehead he had drawn a capital 'I' with a circle over top of it. Through the circle was a diagonal slash.

Byron glanced at Blaze, who was staring at the photo, and noticed a strange look in his eyes, as if he were replaying a scene in his mind.

Chrissy caught the peculiar expression too and rested her hand on his shoulder. "Jack?"

He turned and looked at her.

"What's the matter?" she asked.

He blinked several times, looked at the floor and swallowed. "I don't feel quite right," he said, placing his hand on his chest. "I think I better head home. I'm sorry. I hate to part with this good company."

Dugan dropped the paper on the table as if the mark had possessed the page and shocked his hand.

Byron looked at the image of the girl and then at Elijah. His friend's eyes seemed charged with apprehension.

"I hope it wasn't the spaghetti," Lila said.

"No," Jack responded. "The spaghetti was delicious. Sometimes I get these odd spells. Nothing to worry about, really. I'll be fine. I just need to go home and ride it out."

"If you're dizzy or sick, you shouldn't drive," Annie said.

Blaze stood and took a deep breath. "It's nothing like that." He glanced at the newspaper again and quickly looked away. "I'll be fine. Thank you so much for the wonderful dinner."

"I'll walk you to your car," Chrissy offered.

"That's not necessary," Jack said.

"I don't mind." Chrissy jumped up, slipped her hand around Jack's elbow and escorted him down the steps.

"I hope he's all right," Annie said.

"Does anyone else feel sick?" Lila asked. "Maybe it was the spaghetti."

"The mark scared him," Dugan said.

Everyone looked at Dugan and then at the newspaper.

Annie said, "Elijah, please throw that paper away. It's disturbing. And, Dugan, I don't want to hear any more about it. Oh, that imagination of yours."

"For someone who doesn't fear evil, he certainly seemed shook up," Elijah said, picking up the paper and rolling it into a tube.

An interval of uncomfortable silence ensued until Annie and Lila started lifting plates and bowls from the table to carry to the kitchen.

"Elijah, could I talk to you out on the deck?" Byron asked.

Elijah tapped the roll against his palm. "Sure thing."

Byron slid the glass door open, crossed the deck, and looked down. In the dying remnants of the day's light he saw Chrissy waving as Jack backed out of the driveway.

"Good," he said.

"What's good?" Elijah asked as he stepped to the railing.

"I wanted to make sure Chrissy didn't get into the car with him. I forbade her to be with him anywhere but at this house, and she agreed. I guess I should trust her."

"Trusting her is fine. Just don't trust him. That photograph shook him up quite a bit."

"I know. Especially the mark Dugan drew."

Elijah rubbed his beard. "Makes me wonder. Maybe Dugan did see a body."

"Maybe it was Laura Redinger."

Elijah nodded.

"Something happened today that I have to tell you about."

Elijah raised his head. "Go ahead."

"I climbed to the top of the lighthouse during the thunderstorm."

"You what?"

"You heard me."

"And what happened?"

"I saw Adrienne Lawrence, our tour guide from yesterday, crossing the street. A car with tinted windows that looked liked Blaze's vehicle pulled up, and the driver offered her a ride."

"Did she get in?"

Byron nodded. "She tried to refuse, but the driver persisted, and she finally climbed in. I know it doesn't prove anything, but I kept remembering my hospital dream—the blond girl crying for help. I'm convinced God has brought me to this place to stop something terrible from happening."

"What can we do?"

Byron pointed to the south. "Blaze lives about a half-mile that way. We have to act now. If there's evidence, we've got to find it. If Adrienne Lawrence is in trouble, we need to help her."

Elijah grabbed Byron by the shoulder. "What're we waiting for, good buddy? Let's go."

* * *

Elijah and Byron told their wives they were going for a walk. By the time they covered the half-mile to Blaze's house, night had fallen. Standing across the street, they observed the scene. The *Sunfire* was parked in the driveway, but no lights could be detected through the front windows.

"He must be in a back room," Byron said. "Let's cut through the side yard."

After looking in both directions to make sure no one was watching them, Byron led the way, crossing the street and slipping into the shadows between the houses. They progressed to the middle of the house where light filtered through the curtain of a small window and cut a swath of pale yellow into the darkness. Byron edged along the wall and stopped at the window. Through a crack in the curtain, he could see a sink and commode, but no sign of Blaze.

"It's the bathroom," he whispered and then ducked under the stream of light, crawling on all fours past the window.

At the next window they stopped and peered in. A bowl of fruit, a pitcher and an empty glass sat in the middle of a small table surrounded by four chairs; a weak light above the kitchen sink lit the edges of the objects like a baroque still life. On the other side, Byron noticed a doorway leading to an adjoining room.

Byron pointed and whispered, "He must be in the room straight across."

"That's on the other side of the house," Elijah said. "Let's circle the back."

Elijah led the way around the back porch to the other side. When they reached the window, Elijah gripped the trim and leaned slowly to take a quick peek. He jerked his head back and faced Byron with wide eyes. Leaning, he whispered, "He's sitting on the floor facing the window, but his eyes are closed."

Elijah stepped aside, and Byron looked. Five candles surrounded Blaze, bathing him in flickering light. He sat naked in a strange position—legs crossed with each foot wedged against the opposite thigh, the bottoms facing up. On the floor in front of him, a small ceramic dragon, head lifted upward, sent a steady stream of smoke through its mouth and nostrils. The contorted angle of Jack's legs made Byron wince. His hands were cupped in front of him, thumbs touching. Sitting perfectly still with eyes shut, Blaze looked like a bronze statue in the middle of a shrine room.

Byron backed away and tugged Elijah's elbow, leading him to the back porch. "What's he doing? Is that some kind of occult ritual?"

"I don't think so," Elijah responded. "I believe that's called the *lotus position*. He's meditating. I've researched many religions to better defend my own beliefs. That's the way Zen Buddhists seek enlightenment."

"Enlightenment?"

Elijah nodded.

"What'll we do?"

"Let's wait. He can't sit that way forever. His legs will go numb."

They retreated to the back porch and crouched near a large bush. With every minute that passed, Byron's suspicions of Blaze diminished. He reasoned that a killer or kidnapper would be hastily hiding evidence or torturing his victim, not seeking enlightenment. Still, enough doubt remained to patiently continue the investigation. After ten minutes they edged to the window again. Blaze had not budged, as if he were frozen in time.

Returning to the shrubbery near the back porch, Byron asked, "What's with this guy?"

"He's a weird one," Elijah said.

"Let's think about this. Why would he get so upset about that strange mark Dugan drew, abruptly leave the dinner, come back here, and meditate?"

Elijah rubbed his beard. "If he was the killer, knowing his mark had been identified would shake him up."

"Yes," Byron replied, "but wouldn't that motivate him even more to get rid of any evidence and cover his tracks?"

Elijah shrugged. "Maybe he already took care of that."

Every ten minutes for the next hour they crept to the window and peered in. Although the candles slowly burned down, Blaze remained unchanged. They circled the house several times, listening for any knocks or grunts or muffled screams a hostage might make but heard nothing. Frustrated, they walked back to the vacation house.

Chapter Twenty-one

By midnight, everyone had gone to bed, but Byron couldn't sleep. He lay, staring at the ceiling. Whenever he closed his eyes, his visions and the memory of Adrienne climbing into the car cycled through his mind. Trying not to awaken Lila, he slithered out of bed and slipped on his shorts. After mounting the steps to the kitchen, he placed the kettle on the stove for tea. Like a lion pacing his cage, he crisscrossed the great room, waiting for the water to boil. *What am I supposed to do, Lord? If I knew, I'd do it. Maybe I'm overreacting—everything blown out of proportion in my mind. Maybe Adrienne Lawrence is home right now sleeping soundly.* Byron wanted to believe that, but he couldn't.

He considered all his options. Returning to Blaze's house offered an outside possibility. He could at least circle the premises again and listen for suspicious noises. On the way he could weave through the resort neighborhoods just in case a call for help rang out. To Byron it was like trying to look for an obscure verse in the Old Testament without a concordance—so many pages to find so few words.

When the teakettle whistled, a new possibility popped into his mind—why not just call Adrienne? *Why didn't I think of this before? All this worry may be over nothing.* He pulled the pot off the burner and slid it to the middle of the stove, the hissing of the steam fading with the shrill noise. After he snatched the phonebook from the counter, he flopped it onto the table and thumbed to the L's. There were several Lawrence's, but no Adrienne's or even A's. *How could she be listed, you dummy? She's just here for the tourist season.* He slammed the book shut. For a few moments his thoughts stalled, but then he grabbed the phone and dialed 'O'.

When the operator answered, he said, "Yes, I need the number of an Adrienne Lawrence. I believe she resides in Corolla. She's only lived here for a month or two."

"One moment, please."

He snatched a pencil lying nearby and opened the phonebook. An automated voice announced the number, and Byron wrote it in big, unmistakable letters on the corner of the page. He took a deep breath, and as he exhaled, the tension in his shoulders eased. *What if she answers? What do I say? Who cares? That would be great if she answers. It doesn't matter what I say.* With great deliberation, he dialed the number. It rang, and he counted, "One . . . Two. Come on. Come on. Three . . ." After twenty-five rings, he gave up.

The weight on his shoulders returned with increased pressure. *Now what do I do? Do I call the police and tell them I'm concerned because a young girl got into a strange car during a rainstorm, and she's not answering her phone? That's sounds ridiculous. I barely know her. They'll ask me why I'm making midnight calls to some twenty-one-year old I just met.* With elbows on the table, Byron leaned his forehead against the heels of his palms. *What do I do, Lord? I've got to do something. What if the girl from Kitty Hawk skipped out of town with her boyfriend. Who knows where Adrienne might be? Fast asleep. Visiting a co-worker. Taking a midnight stroll along the beach.* He sat up and raked his hair with his fingers. *But if she is in trouble, I can't just sit here. I have to do something.*

He stood and headed for the steps. On the way down he prayed: *Lead me out of this state of confusion, Lord. If Adrienne Lawrence is in trouble, I'm willing to help. Give me some kind of direction.*

When he pulled open the front door, his heart leapt in his chest. Standing on the porch, wide-eyed, Jack Blaze glared at him.

"You!" Byron snarled. "What do you want?"

Jack raised his hand, and Byron stepped back. "Please," Jack said. "I had to come back. The mark."

"The mark?"

"The one Dugan drew. I can't get it out of my mind."

Blaze looked like a man possessed—eyes desperate, beads of sweat on his forehead.

Byron pointed at him. "You stay right there. I don't want you coming near my family."

"What? I would never harm anyone in your family."

"You can talk to the police about the mark."

"Mr. Butler, listen to me. I've seen that mark before. I think I could identify the killer if I could just remember where."

Byron stepped forward, drawn by words he never expected to hear. "The killer of the missing girl?"

"Yes. When Dugan drew that symbol on her photograph, I knew he was telling the truth. A good illusionist can read a person—analyze the slightest variations of facial expressions and tone of voice. Dugan saw that dead girl in the marsh. I have no doubt about it. And the mark on her forehead is the same mark stashed somewhere in my mind. For the last three hours I've been using every mental technique I know to make the connection."

"Why did you come back here?" Byron asked.

"Meditating at home didn't help. The memory was much stronger upstairs in the great room. I need something to jar my brain—the newspaper photograph, the girl's face, the mark—anything that will help trigger the memory. I need to be in that same spot where the feeling hit me so intensely."

A flurry of thoughts rushed through Byron's mind: *Is he sincere or is this another illusion? Did the picture disturb him or was it the mark Dugan drew? I've got to remember. It **was** the mark. That's what caused his strange reaction. Not the picture. When Elijah and I investigated, we saw him meditating just like he said. Maybe he's telling the truth.* Beneath the swirling doubts, Byron felt a calm assurance gain a foothold—like a prayer had been answered. As he looked into Jack's eyes, his anxiety faded and hope flickered.

"I have to tell you something," Byron said. He hesitated, wondering again if Blaze could be trusted. Sensing the concern in Jack's eyes, he went with his gut instinct. "There's more at stake than just finding this girl's killer. Today, during the storm, I saw a young woman climb into a black car. I thought it was your car."

Jack shook his head. "It wasn't my car, Mr. Butler. I picked up my check at the Whalehead Club, but I made it home before the storm hit." Jack looked down for a moment. When he looked up, his eyes widened. "Was the girl Adrienne Lawrence?"

Byron's heart pounded. *Did I trust him too soon?* "Yes. How did you know?"

"Adrienne and I have worked together for almost two months at the Whalehead Club. We've become good friends. When I was meditating this evening, a vision kept breaking my focus on the mark—the image of her against a wooden wall in the shadows of a dark room. It didn't make sense, but I couldn't keep the scene from interrupting my meditation."

Byron felt adrenaline surge through him. He remembered Chrissy saying that Jack felt he had a connection to him—*Was the connection Adrienne?* His words rushed out: "I've had several dreams about her—in that same room, crying for help . . . and then the presence of evil overwhelmed me."

"She's in trouble," Jack said, and those words confirmed the portent that had haunted Byron for the last month.

"Come on. Let's go upstairs. I'll try to find the newspaper."

* * *

In the great room, Jack sat at the table, struggling to remember as Byron sorted through the trashcan. The newspaper had disappeared, and Byron had no idea where it could be. He circled the room, lifting objects and looking behind furniture.

"I could wake up Elijah," Byron said. "He might know what happened to it."

Jack sat with his eyes closed, as if trying to break into another realm. His breathing accelerated and drops of sweat trickled down his forehead.

"Is there anything else I can do to help?" Byron asked.

The words broke Jack's concentration. He shook his head. "I must have seen the mark somewhere for just an instant—not long enough to establish its context. If only I could remember exactly where I saw it."

When Byron saw the dark figure at the top of the steps, he knees almost buckled. Steadying himself by leaning on the back of the couch, he gasped, "Dugan, you almost gave me a heart attack. What are you doing up?"

Dugan walked to the table and looked up at Byron. "I couldn't sleep. I kept thinking about that dead girl and the evil mark on her forehead." He turned to Blaze. "What are you doing here, Jack?"

"Listen, Dugan. I've seen that mark, too. Do you know what happened to the newspaper?"

"Aunt Annie told Uncle Elijah to get rid of it."

Jack put his hand on Dugan's shoulder. "I need some help. I'm trying to remember where I saw the mark. Could you draw it again for me on another piece of paper?"

"Sure," Dugan answered.

Byron went to the kitchen counter and grabbed the nearest available paper and pencil. It was the map of local tourist attractions Jack had used in his card trick on the night of the cookout. He spread it on the table and said, "Draw it here, Dugan. There's an empty space next to the picture of the Whalehead Club."

As Dugan carefully drew the symbol, Byron noticed Jack staring at the hole where the knife had pierced the map on the Whalehead Club's front door. Blaze's eyes intensified, as if he could see another world through that tiny aperture.

Dugan finished drawing the mark and stepped back. Jack studied the symbol and then lifted the map and looked from Dugan to Byron. His gaze returned to the mark as his hand slid under the map. Byron watched closely as Blaze's finger poked through the hole. His hand continued to rise, splitting the paper, bursting through the image of the mark and the Whalehead Club.

"Now I remember," Jack said. "I saw the mark on the handle of Kenny Queen's knife."

Dugan gasped, and Byron put his arm around him. "Are you all right?"

"The heart," Dugan said.

"What heart?" Jack asked.

"On the night I got lost in the marsh, I followed an owl to a pine tree next to the sound."

"Did you see something?" Byron asked.

"Yes. Someone had carved a heart into the tree. The top letters were K.Q."

"Kenny Queen," Jack said.

"Do you remember the bottom initials?" Byron asked.

"They had an X over them, but I could still read them—L.R."

Byron looked at Jack and said, "Laura Redinger."

Chapter Twenty-two

Byron glanced from Jack to Dugan and saw uneasiness mirrored in their faces. An odd thought occurred to him: *What an unusual trio of rescuers the Lord has assembled. God help us.* With little time and few options, Byron knew they needed all the help they could get.

"We can't go to the police," Byron said. "We have nothing on Queen."

"I know," Jack agreed. "An odd symbol and initials carved into a tree don't amount to much. I'm guessing he has a reputation as one of the good ol' boys at the station. They would laugh us right out of town."

"Besides, if Adrienne Lawrence is in trouble, we can't waste any more time. Do you know where Queen lives?"

"'Fraid not. He should be in the phonebook."

Byron grabbed the directory and flipped to the Q's. His finger slid down the page to Queen's name. "No house number. Just the street name: *Lost Lagoon Drive.*"

"I've seen that sign," Jack said. "It's about three hundred yards past the lighthouse along the gravel road."

"That's not far from here. I say we travel on foot. Less chance of being noticed. We can get there in four or five minutes if we walk fast."

"What about Dugan?" Jack asked.

Byron turned to the boy, tousled his red hair, and patted his shoulder. "You better stay here, Dugan. We appreciate all your help, but we can handle things from now on."

Dugan's shoulders slumped, and he hung his head. "But I want to go too," he protested.

Byron crouched to address him face to face. "We need you here in case anybody wakes up and wonders what happened to us."

Dugan raised his head, his expression becoming earnest. "I've studied books on crime scene investigation. Detective work is in my blood. I know how to find clues and evidence."

Byron reached out and touched his shoulder. "This is what I want you to do. Hang out here in the great room near the phone in case anything happens. Stretch out on the couch there. If the phone rings, answer it as quickly as you can. It'll probably be me on my cell phone. You can be our main man here at headquarters. Okay?"

Dugan considered Byron's offer and hesitantly nodded. "I guess so."

Jack extended his hand and Dugan shook it. "You're a good man, Dugan," Jack said, and Dugan shrugged.

Byron grabbed his cell phone from the charger on the kitchen counter and slipped it into his pocket. His mind and body felt electrified, as if he were a teenager about to toe the line for the mile run at the state track meet. He wondered if he should grab some kind of weapon and opened the nearest drawer. After he snagged a handful of utensils, he turned and faced Jack. "Should we take a weapon with us?"

Jack stifled a smile. "The spatula and whisk won't do much good, but maybe that nutcracker will come in handy."

Byron looked at the kitchen implements and tossed them back into the drawer. *Calm down, you Bozo.*

* * *

With the help of the full moon, Byron's night vision kicked in quickly. The steady breeze intensified the outbreak of goose bumps on his arms and legs, but the brisk pace helped to warm his muscles and dull the jitters. Within minutes they passed the Whalehead Club. The structure stood like a black fortress against the starlit sky, the five chimneys spaced like sentinels across the top of the roof. On the other side of the road, the Currituck Lighthouse towered above the silhouettes of pines and oaks. The beam flashed for several seconds, a bright swath of light sweeping above the beach houses, over the dunes, and out to sea.

Ahead, the gravel road disappeared into the shadows of overhanging trees. When they entered the tunnel of limbs and foliage, seeing became more difficult. With every step into the darkness, Byron's apprehension increased. Jack seemed unfazed, intent on finding Queen's house as soon as possible. Byron had to quicken his steps several times to keep up. The unusual man exuded confidence and determination. Byron realized he had greatly misjudged him. Although they hadn't said much since leaving the house, Byron wanted to communicate with Jack, to bond like athletes before the big game or soldiers on the verge of battle.

"I hope you've got a good plan," Byron said.

"Not yet," Jack answered. "It's too soon."

"Too soon?"

Through a break in the trees, the moon lit Jack's face as he nodded and smiled. "No sense in making a plan until we analyze the circumstances."

"Right," Byron said. "Like calling an audible at the line of scrimmage."

"Exactly. As soon as we understand what's happening and our opponent's intentions, we'll have to think fast."

"Fast thinking has never been my forte," Byron confessed. "I like to ponder things before acting. I'll research my sermon topic for six hours before I write the opening line."

"Where I come from, thinking fast is a matter of survival."

"Maybe that's why you're such a good illusionist. You've learned to read people quickly and respond before they catch on."

"Growing up in the 'hood does have its peculiar outcomes. I learned fast that a card trick or a stunt helped to keep the bad dudes on my side. When I was a young gang member, they liked keeping me around for entertainment. My skills saved my butt more than a few times. I'd keep my eye on the crack heads and killers. Whenever necessary, I'd pull out a deck of cards or a trick coin. I always figured if you can't whip 'em, bedazzle 'em. Worked every time."

Byron nodded. Considering Jack's skills, Byron wondered why he didn't break away from gang life before it entangled him. "I guess once you join a gang, it's hard to get out."

"Next to impossible, unless you move to Corncob, Iowa. Very few kids are that lucky. After several years, I became a leader. Jail time for stealing cars and banging was a routine part of the program. I would have died on the streets if it wasn't for my mother . . . and magic."

"Chrissy told me about your mom's illness and her hopes for your future. I had a good mom too," Byron said. "She never married. I was the only kid in my neighborhood without a dad. They called me *Bastard Butler*. Believe it or not, I got into my share of fistfights and trouble too. Mom stood by me through the worst of it."

Jack glanced at him. "And after all that you became a minister?"

"That's right," Byron replied. "The Lord makes some odd draft choices when he puts his team together."

Jack held out his hand, and Byron focused as best he could in the darkness. "Give me some skin," Jack said.

Byron felt dense for not catching on, and despite the quick pace, managed to reach out and slap Jack's hand.

"Look's like we're on the same team tonight," Jack said.

For several seconds Byron pondered the reversal that had occurred in his relationship with this former street punk. He was beginning to like Jack Blaze.

"Look," Jack said, stopping Byron short with his hand.

Byron looked up and saw the old wooden sign nailed to a willow tree. The white paint glowed phosphorescent in the moon's light: LOST LAGOON DRIVE.

The narrow dirt road cut through the marsh, tall trees, and tangled growth deepening the blackness except for a few spatters of moonlight that filtered through branches. The fetid smell of stagnation hung in the air, and squadrons of mosquitoes buzzed and attacked. Byron slapped his face, shoulders, and legs to repel the onslaught. The road snaked deeper into the marsh toward the sound. Byron strained to identify any form of architecture ahead. After progressing about 75 yards, a red glow caught his attention, chilling him to the core. *Those red eyes.* When they disappeared, he reached and grabbed Jack's elbow.

"Did you see that?" Byron asked.

"See what?"

"The two red spots up ahead."

"Spots? No I didn't see anything."

"Come back a little ways." As they backed a few steps up a slight incline, the red eyes reappeared, moving slightly every few seconds. "Something's watching us," Byron whispered.

"I don't think so," Jack said. "But the house is definitely in that direction."

"How do you know?"

"Those spots are electronically generated. Come on. We're almost there."

As they moved forward, the red eyes disappeared and reappeared several times before completely vanishing. As Byron strained to see into the shadows, several shapes took form—the gable of a bungalow angled against murky boughs, and two windows flanked a screen door. In the left window Byron noticed a red tint against the glass but didn't see the eyes. A few steps climbed to a deck that stretched across the front of the house. On the right side, the rear end of a car stuck out beyond the railing. Byron edged closer and saw the vehicle's hue was very dark, probably blue or black. He turned to Jack, who already had mounted the steps.

Jack's impulse to move quickly disconcerted him. In his younger years, Byron's devil-may-care attitude ruled his decisions and got him into trouble. After high school he developed more self-control. Preparation and patience were the basis of his occupation. Had he lost his spunk? Watching Jack, he marveled at the man's nerve. *Maybe I need to be more impulsive again.* He gathered his courage, tiptoed up the steps, and stood beside Jack near the screen door.

"What're we gonna do?" Byron whispered.

"Knock," Jack said. "If Queen answers, we'll tell him one of your boys is missing—maybe sleep walking or something like that. We'll ask him to help hunt. Then you can call home to check and say the kid's back safe and sound. In the meantime, I'll try to find as many clues as I can while we're in the house."

Byron nodded.

Jack knocked, rapping four times. After about thirty seconds, he knocked again. Nothing stirred.

"Let's go," Jack said. He opened the screen door and entered.

As soon as he stepped in the front room, Byron saw the red eyes. His muscles tensed as if a jolt of electricity charged through his body. They stared from a black computer screen atop a desk across from the window. Every few seconds, they jumped to a different part of the screen. "Some screensaver," Byron said.

Jack nodded. "Nothing like being greeted by Lucifer himself. Back in the woods we were on a slight incline, just the right angle to see them through the window."

Byron took a deep breath to relieve the tension in his chest.

"Brought this with me," Jack said, pulling out a small flashlight. "Thought it might come in handy. I'll check the back rooms. See what you can find out here."

Byron circled the room and inspected the couch, recliner and entertainment center. When he reached the desk, he stared at the screen. The diabolical eyes glowed, burning into his retinas. He closed his eyelids, but the red dots remained, re-inducing the horror of his dreams. Fighting the terror, he opened his eyes, moved closer and noticed a camera next to the keyboard. Reaching for it, he bumped the mouse, and the screen lit up with the smiling face of Adrienne Lawrence.

The dread that had started in his stomach rushed upward, filling his chest and throat with alarm. He stepped to the hall and called, "Jack! Come here!"

Jack hustled into the room and clicked off the flashlight. "Oh no," he said as he crossed the room. "Queen must be obsessed with her."

"Do they know each other?"

"He makes security checks at the Whalehead Club. I think they may have gone out to lunch once or twice."

"Is it possible she likes him?" Byron asked.

"I don't think so. Adrienne rarely says a bad word about anybody, but she told me Queen's too conceited for her tastes. Lately she's been avoiding him whenever he makes his rounds."

"That explains her hesitation to climb into his car."

Jack pointed to the screen. "See the pixelation. He probably took the photograph from a distance without her knowing and cropped it in an image editor." He reached and picked up the camera. "I wonder if he left the disc inside?" He turned it over, and by the light of the screen, found the latch. The back popped open revealing a small disc. Quickly he tapped the button on the computer unit to open the CD drive, placed the disc in the slot and nudged the drive closed. Grasping the mouse, he navigated to the proper drive folder. A series of image icons appeared in the window. Jack double-clicked the last file. An editing program opened, displaying the picture—Adrienne on the front lawn of the Whalehead Club addressing a tour group.

"That's the picture he cropped and used as his desktop wallpaper," Jack said. He moved the cursor to the bottom of the screen and clicked the photograph folder. When it popped up, he dragged a selection rectangle around the next five icons, highlighting them, and then hit the Enter key. One by one the images opened in the editing program. The next four displayed candid shots featuring Adrienne—crossing the street, entering a store, walking along the beach, eating a sandwich at the Wild Horse Café. The fifth shocked them: a close-up of Laura Redinger's face, eyes wide and dull. From the slices on her forehead, blood had dripped through her brows, around the creases of her eyelids and down the sides of her nose and cheeks.

Byron gasped and stepped back. Jack selected the remaining picture files and hit the Enter key. As the images opened, the sensation of evil overwhelmed Byron. He saw Laura Redinger from various angles, wearing only undergarments, handcuffed spread-eagled to a wooden-planked wall. Someone had beaten and bloodied her. One photo presented a compound fracture of her arm. Turning away, Byron struggled to control an overwhelming urge to vomit.

"These are trophies," Jack said.

"Trophies?" Byron could barely say the word.

Jack ejected the disc and put it in his back pocket. "Queen's a masochist. He gets some kind of sexual kick from doing this. He took the pictures to record his conquest, like an athlete collecting trophies to remember the victories."

"We've got to find Adrienne before it's too late. Did you see anything in the back rooms?"

"No," Jack said. "Nothing suspicious—no women's clothing or unusual smells. Couldn't find anything that would indicate foul play. Let's check outside."

Before passing through the front door, Byron glanced at the computer screen. The red eyes had reappeared, as if to taunt him. A sense of urgency increased with every second accompanied by an utter feeling of helplessness.

"Where could Queen be? He left his house wide open." Byron said as they crossed the porch. *Maybe he's watching us.* He imagined Queen jumping him from behind, sticking the knife to his throat, and slicing his windpipe. He wanted to flee from the darkness and find a safe place to regroup.

Jack stopped at the bottom of the steps and scanned the canopy of branches above them. A few stars blinked through the open spaces. "Maybe we should call the sheriff." He patted his back pocket. "There's enough evidence on this disc to make an arrest, even if it means jailing one of their own."

As Byron reached into his pocket for the phone, a muffled scream filtered through the woods.

"Did you hear that?" Jack asked.

Byron dropped the phone back into his pocket and pointed. "I think it came from that direction."

In the distance a woman's voice shrieked: "Please! Leave me alone! Don't hurt me again! Please!"

Jack bolted toward the woods.

Chapter Twenty-three

J ack's charge toward the woods ended abruptly as the snarled undergrowth and branches prevented his entry. He pulled out his flashlight and searched along the border of the thicket for an opening. Close behind, Byron stumbled and sloughed through the weeds, determined to keep pace. As they progressed, they encountered a trail that bore its way into the marsh. Trees laden with creepers and vines walled the path like a cave, and Jack's small light barely penetrated the opacity of the tangled shadows.

To Byron, advancing fifty yards seemed like a mile. He thought about Lila and the kids. They were oblivious to his circumstances. He remembered kissing his wife goodnight and telling her he loved her. They had repeated the same ritual for so many years without much thought of the depth of its meaning. A simple kiss and a few words were too easily taken for granted. He wondered if he would feel the soft brush of her lips and caress of her hand on his cheek again. His children's faces passed through his mind. A knot formed in his throat, almost choking him. He swallowed, trying to dispel the panic, but the tension returned, constricting like hands tightening around his neck. The woods finally thinned, and the sight of the Currictuck Sound, dappled with moonlight, helped to calm his nerves.

Reaching the bank, they stopped and inspected the scene. A loon wailed not far off shore, its drawn-out warble like a sad song. Jack grabbed Byron's arm and swung him to the left. "Over there," he whispered, pointing at a stand of cypress trees growing from a wedge of land that jutted into the cove. Between the trunks Byron could see the black shape of a small building suspended above the water. *The boathouse in his dream!* Chips of light glowed through chinks in the siding, giving the odd appearance of remnant embers on a charred log. They approached the structure, intently listening. Above the lapping of water against the piers, they heard a man's low voice and a woman's sobs.

Jack pitched his voice low. "It's an old boathouse. We should be able to see through those small holes and gaps in the planks."

The building looked like a one-room cabin on posts. A short walkway on the other side of the cove led to the entrance, but from their position, the quickest approach to the building was through the water. Before Byron could say anything, Jack slid down the bank, turned and offered him a hand. As Byron descended, the water soaked his shoes and socks, adding the shock of sudden cold to his already jittery state. They waded through the knee-deep water to the side of the boathouse. Jack quickly found a gap between the planks and peered in. Byron skirted around him, stood on his toes and looked through a knothole.

When Byron saw Adrienne stripped to her bra and panties and handcuffed spread-eagled to four U-bolts on the wall, he knew God had called him to save her. Wanting to move now, he turned to Jack and whispered, "Let's go."

Jack shook his head. "Not yet. I can see Queen. He's got a knife. His gun may be near. Gimme a minute to think."

Byron couldn't think. He looked through the knothole again and saw Adrienne's bruised cheek, and the corner of her mouth trickled blood. A red welt crossed the bicep of her right arm. Her blouse and trousers lay in a heap in front of her. Then Queen moved into view. Shirtless, wearing department-issued shorts, the knife slung from his hip, he stood slapping his nightstick into his left hand. He stepped forward and poked her in the belly with the end of the baton.

She heaved and pleaded, "Please . . . don't hit . . . me again," her breaths choppy and spastic.

"You don't admire me, do you?" Queen asked above the rhythmic slapping of the stick on his palm.

Adrienne nodded, eyes aghast. "Yes . . . yes . . . I do. You are . . . handsome."

"Really?"

Her head bobbed anxiously but unconvincingly. "Yes. Very handsome."

"You're not just saying that because . . . because I've . . . slapped you a few times?"

She shook her head. "No. No. I mean it."

A carnal smile crossed his face. "Do you like being slapped?"

Her head swiveled as she struggled to hold back tears.

Queen dropped the nightstick onto the floor. It thudded and rolled a few feet. Turning to his left, he faced a full-length mirror. He struck a classic pose, arms flexed above his head, abdominal muscles rippling in the harsh light. As if in a bodybuilding competition, he pivoted and faced Adrienne, bringing his arms down slowly, rigidly pausing with knees slightly bent.

"I don't think I believe you," he said, maintaining his position. "If you were really impressed, you would compliment me while I pose for you."

She quickly complied. "You. . . you are strong, good looking. Tall. Very strong."

"That's much better," Queen said, relaxing and shaking out his arms. He bent over and picked up a curling bar near the wall. Facing her, he pumped the weights repeatedly to his chest.

"You look like a champion weightlifter," she said.

Queen smiled. "You want me, don't you?"

She hesitated, but then nodded.

"Are you lying?" He dropped the barbell, and it clanged at her feet.

She tensed, blinking.

He stepped toward her, placing his hands on the wall above her shoulders. Leaning, he kissed her roughly on the lips. When he backed away, her face twitched.

"You're lying," he growled. "Your kiss betrays you."

She lost what little composure she had summoned. A few sobs escaped, and tears streamed down her face.

"I'm not stupid," Queen said. "I know when I'm being rejected. For the last two weeks you've avoided me like I'm some kind of freak. But you're going to discover something very irresistible about me." He dropped to the floor in front of her, catching himself with his hands. After executing a set of pushups, he rested on his hands and knees, reached out and grabbed his nightstick. He thumped it on the floorboards at her feet. When he stood, he neared to within inches of her face. Slowly and harshly he said, "*I will not be denied.*"

When Jack grabbed Byron's bicep, Byron almost jumped out of his shorts.

"Listen," Jack whispered. "Stay here. I'm going back to shore. I'll circle around to the walkway. When the timing is right, I'll barge in on them. I know how to make Queen chase me. He'll want to eliminate any witnesses. Once he takes off, get in there and set Adrienne free. Maybe I can outrun him. Don't know. I'll do what I can."

"What if he shoots you?"

"He's not wearing the holster, but he has the knife and nightstick. Do you have a better plan?"

Byron shook his head.

"Then let's do it."

Jack patted his shoulder and headed to shore. Byron watched him cut through the water, the moonlight glinting on the ripples of his wake.

When he turned back to the knothole, his heart pounded like a piston into his throat. His eyes scanned the room, looking for something to pry Adrienne from the wall. Refocusing on Queen, Byron saw him pull out his knife. Adrenaline jolted him again. He stifled an urge to yell, *Leave her alone!* Glancing across the cove, he saw Jack's silhouette advancing to the walkway. *Hurry Jack. Hurry.* He looked back into the hole to check on Queen. The cop held the knife by its blade so that Adrienne could see the design on the handle.

"I will not be denied," Queen repeated. He pointed to the mark on the knife handle. "That's what this symbol means. My father gave me this knife after I won the state wrestling title. All my life Dad told me I was the best around, a chip off the old block. Said I could get anything I wanted if I refused to give up."

He slid the knife back into its sheath. Spreading his legs, he held his hands out, as if preparing to wrestle. "In the last round of the championship match I was down ten to four. But I wouldn't be denied. With a minute to go, I broke loose from my opponent and reversed him. Somehow I knocked him off balance. When I took him down, my knee landed on his arm. The whole crowd heard the bone crack. Broke right in half. It was the sweetest sound of my life. Like a bulldog on a mailman, I attacked. His coach shouted to stop the match, but I didn't let up until the ref jumped in. It was all over but the screaming. I almost tore his arm off."

Queen flexed his muscles and expanded his chest. "What do you think?" he said.

This time Adrienne stared at him in horror, giving no false compliments.

"I can't hear you." He pulled his nightstick from its loop and slapped it into his hand. "You remind me of my mother."

"T-t-t-tell m-me about her," Adrienne said, regaining her wits.

"She never had much good to say about me. Always calling me stupid. Saying I was going to be a bum just like my old man. Dad knocked her up when she was in high school. They had to get married, and she hated me for it. I looked just like him. When I was ten, the bitch left us. I couldn't have been happier. Took off with some banker—some smart guy with a master's degree. Haven't heard from her since. You're just like her." He spat into Adrienne's face. "I hope she's dead."

Eyes closed, Adrienne trembled as the saliva dripped down her cheeks. She took a deep breath. "I'm not your mother, Kenny. I'm sorry she abandoned you, but I had nothing to do with it."

"The hell you didn't. You and Laura Redinger and all those other bitches who told me to get lost. But I won't be denied any more. Laura found that out the hard way and so will you."

"Who's Laura?" Adrienne asked.

"Why should you care?"

"I think I'm very different from her."

He shook his head. "You're all the same. I dated her in high school. Took her to the homecoming dance. She was the Queen of the ball and I was the King. I loved her, but she broke up with me two weeks later to date some faggot. Told everyone I was a conceited jock."

His eyes glared, and a sinister smile crept across his face. "Not long ago our paths crossed again. She had biked up from Kitty Hawk for exercise. It was at the end of my shift. I tried to talk to her, but she was too interested in your buddy Whodinny. Heading home from the station, I saw her walking the bike along the side of the road. She had a flat tire. Being the gentleman that I am, I offered her a ride. She wanted me to take her home, but I wanted to give her another chance. I brought her back here."

"Another chance?"

"That's right. But she blew it. I know when I'm being lied to. That's why I'm such a good deputy." Queen slapped the nightstick into his palm one more time then rested it on top of Adrienne's arm near the red welt.

"Please don't hit me again," she pleaded.

He tapped her bicep. "The crack of a bone—it's the sweetest sound I know."

Adrienne closed her eyes and squirmed against the planked wall.

"Any last words? Compliments? Flattery? Go ahead. Tell me how desirable I am. Tell me how smart I am. But I warn you: Don't lie. If you lie, you die."

What's Jack waiting for? Byron thought. He turned to head toward the entrance of the boathouse, but stopped when he heard the door crash open. Instantly, he pressed his eye back to the knothole.

"Jack!" Adrienne gasped.

Queen spun around.

Jack seethed, "You're a repulsive, disgusting sonovabitch. And that's no lie."

"Well, if it ain't Mr. Whodinnny. You must have used your extra sensory perception to find my little hideaway." Deliberately, Queen slapped the baton in his hand. "Welcome to my world, you half-breed bastard. And this is *my* magic wand. Can you read my mind now?"

"There's not much to reading your mind," Jack said. "If brains were electricity, you wouldn't have enough power to light a firefly's rear end."

Queen lunged and swung the stick, but Jack jumped back, dodging to the left. Before the deputy could regain his balance, Jack pivoted and shot out the door yelling, "Catch me if you can you can, Ape Brain!"

Queen charged through the door and thundered down the walkway after him. "You might be faster than me," he shouted, "but I can run forever. It's just a matter of time and distance."

From the shadows of the boathouse, Byron saw Jack sprint along the shore toward the cypress trees. Ten yards behind, Queen kept pace. When Jack cut in between the trunks, he tripped over a root and tumbled onto the ground. Byron watched in horror, muscles tensing for a possible charge through the water. Queen dove on top of Jack and whipped the nightstick. A loud thud sounded and Jack groaned. Stepping forward, Byron strained to see into the shadows. The silhouettes jostled on the ground between the trees. Indecision paralyzed Byron for several seconds, but then he saw one body break away and stagger toward the path through the marsh. *God, please let that be Jack.* With renewed hope, Byron retreated into the shadows of the boathouse. The other figure sprung to his feet and charged after the first, their footsteps fading into the blackness.

Byron high-stepped through the water and climbed onto the walkway. When he burst into the boathouse, Adrienne screamed, eyes wide with fear.

"It's me. I'm here to help."

"Reverend Butler. Thank God!" she exclaimed. Her body slumped, hanging from the cuffs like a rag doll, as if she had expended all reserves of strength.

Byron rushed to her and cupped his hands around her cheeks. "Hang in there, Adrienne."

"Please, get these things off me," she said.

His hands slid away, coated with the sticky wetness of saliva, sweat and blood. Reaching up, he grabbed the chain of one of the cuffs, yanking against the U-bolt. Her hand flapped with each pull. "I need to get you out of here before he comes back."

"He's got the keys on his belt."

"What can we use to pry off these U-bolts?" Byron pivoted and inspected the room. A few old fishing nets sloped from the rafters and several crab traps were stacked in the corner. A bench press and barbell sat near the mirror. A wide lifting belt hung from a nail on the wall, and weights were scattered on the floor along with the curling bar.

He scooped up one of the weights and tried to batter the heavy-duty U-bolt. Because of the nearness of her hand, he had to strike it with accuracy, diminishing the force of the blow. After a multitude of hits, he had barely budged it.

"Hurry!" she pleaded. "If he comes back he'll kill us."

He tried a slightly different angle and skinned his knuckles. "There's got to be a better way."

"The barbell!" Adrienne shouted. "Take the weights off of it."

Byron understood immediately. By threading the bar through the U-bolt, he could use it as a lever to rip the screws out of the board. He dropped the weight to the floor and charged to the bench. Gripping the spring collar that secured the weights, he wiggled it off the shaft. He grabbed the end plate to slide the other weights off the bar. They clanged one by one to the floor, barely missing his toes. When the last weight fell, the unbalanced bar flipped like a mousetrap and cracked against the wall. He hopped over the bench and grabbed the bar, pulling it down to remove the other collar. The weights slid off into a pile.

After dragging the bar back to Adrienne, he inserted the end through the U-bolt. With a great heave he yanked, and the wood creaked and splintered.

"He must have bolted the thing on the outside."

"Hurry, please," Adrienne begged. She kept looking at the door.

With all his might he jerked the bar repeatedly. After several minutes the bolt broke loose along with a huge chunk of wood. Adrienne's arm fell limply, the shackles dangling from her wrist.

"This is taking too long," Byron grumbled as he slid the bar into the U-bolt near her right foot.

"What happened to Jack?" Adrienne asked.

"He's trying to lead Queen away from here so I can set you free. God be with him." Byron pulled the bar with great force and the plank began to split. "If Queen comes back, we're in trouble." Byron yanked again, but the bolt held fast.

Adrienne closed her eyes and whispered a prayer.

Not far from the boathouse, a loon wailed, a plaintive cry that rose from the darkness and faded into silence.

Chapter Twenty-four

Dugan couldn't sit still any longer. He jumped off the couch, tore across the great room and pulled open the sliding glass door just enough to slip through onto the deck. Leaning against the rail, he gazed toward the lighthouse. The beam pierced the night, a shaft of light sweeping across the ocean. *I should be out there with them. Why wouldn't they let me go? They need me.* He tried to remember the name of the road on which Queen lived. *Lost . . . Lost . . . Lagoon Drive. That's it. Jack said it was about three hundred yards past the lighthouse along the gravel road.* He pictured the area in his mind. *That's where we played bike catchers. I could find them in no time.*

All the hours at the library he'd spent reading detective stories and studying crime books had filled his mind with valuable knowledge. Becoming an investigator was his dream. Everything happened so fast. This was his big chance to help, but with each passing minute the door of opportunity closed. He turned and peered through the glass at the telephone on the counter.

Someone else can answer that phone. I can't stay here. They need me at the scene of the crime. After squeezing past the sliding door, Dugan crossed the great room and hurried down the steps. As he left the house, one thought possessed him: *I'm gonna help rescue a lady and solve a murder!*

The lonely journey through the shadows chipped away at his courage. To think Deputy Queen had murdered someone sent shivers through him. *Three nights ago he found me in the marsh. Everyone thought he was a hero. Those same hands that killed Laura Redinger gripped my shoulders.* Remembering the dead woman and the agony she must have suffered increased his nervousness, tightening the muscles in his chest and burning his stomach.

He turned onto Lighthouse Drive and inspected the clumps of trees and shrubbery lining the road. *I've got to be careful. Keep my eyes open.* When he stopped to look at the beacon, he felt his knees shaking. He bent over and rubbed his legs, thinking maybe he should head back just in case Byron called.

Through the halls of memory, laughter echoed—mean laughter. The shapes of trees and shrubs became the forms of classmates taunting, and mocking him. He could hear Tyler Maxwell, Leonard Scales, and Mary Lou Preston calling him names: *Hey Red Top! Here comes Doogie Breath. You're not a lethal weapon. You're the Lethal Wimp.* He remembered walking home with Chucky Longbone, insisting he threw the fight with Mary Lou because of the Honor Code. With renewed determination he steadied himself, took a deep breath, focused on the beam, and marched toward the lighthouse.

As he neared a stand of trees at the base of the lighthouse, he heard footsteps in the distance but couldn't see anyone. He dashed to the largest trunk and pressed his back against the bark. The footsteps got louder along with the sound of hard breathing. Slowly, he peeked around the edge and saw one man chasing another. They cut across the lawn from the direction of the gravel road. Not more than ten yards away, the one in front stumbled and fell onto the grass, gasping for air. Moonlight outlined the larger man standing over the fallen one. Dugan clearly saw Kenny Queen lift his nightstick.

"Don't be stupid, Queen," the other man said between breaths. The voice belonged to Jack Blaze. "You kill me in front of the lighthouse and a hundred people will see my blood first thing tomorrow morning."

As if on cue, the beacon flashed, sweeping across the beach houses and dunes.

Queen glanced up at the beam of light and back to Blaze. "I'm not as dumb as you think, Whodinny."

"Adrienne's friends at the Whalehead Club know how she feels about you."

"So what?"

"Think about it. If they find me murdered and Adrienne missing, you'll become a suspect."

Queen glanced at the Whalehead Club. "Not if you swan dive off a tall building."

"What?"

"Oddballs like you do it all the time—snuff out the life of a pretty girl and then kill themselves. It's called murder-suicide. Everyone knows you're a strange bird. They'll think the mystic must have lost his marbles."

"I don't plan on committing suicide." Jack struggled to his feet.

Queen whipped the stick, striking Jack on top of the head with a loud thud. Jack slumped to the ground like a sack of laundry.

Seeing the violent act sent waves of terror through Dugan. He pulled back and pressed himself to the tree. *Please God, don't let Jack be dead. I could be next.* He felt his heart beating so hard he wondered if Queen could hear it.

"Don't worry, Whodinny," Queen said. "I'll take care of all the arrangements, even the suicide note. I'll stick it in your pocket before I toss you off the roof of the Whalehead Club."

Dugan heard rustling, grunting, and footsteps moving away. He glanced and caught the silhouette of Kenny Queen striding toward the Whalehead Club with Jack drooping from his arms. Quickly, Dugan scooted to the other side of the tree in case Queen turned to look behind him. *Why didn't I stay by the phone like Byron told me? What do I do? I could go back to the beach house and no one would know the difference.* Peering around the tree, he watched the dark form diminishing. He took a deep breath to calm his nerves. *If Jack is alive, someone has to help him.* Feeling terribly alone, he looked at the beacon of the lighthouse. It sent a brilliant ray slashing through the sky. When it darkened, Dugan sprang from the tree and sprinted to the corner of the keeper's house. He slipped into the shadows of a tall pine next to the porch and observed Queen crossing the road under a streetlight.

The cop moved quickly out of the light and onto the Whalehead lawn, blurring into a row of hedges and small trees. Hugging the perimeter of the woods from the house to the road, Dugan advanced. When he reached the road, he dashed across and headed for the cover of the hedges, diving into the their dark shadow. After catching his breath, he peered above the bushes and spied Queen crossing the small bridge about fifty yards away. Keeping low to the ground, Dugan zigzagged from tree to tree until he reached the bridge. There he waited until Queen appeared in the glow of the streetlight near the parking lot. With Jack bouncing in his arms, he mounted the few steps and melted into the blackness of the porch. Dugan listened. He heard the movements of a body being lowered to the ground and the jangling of keys.

Waiting for Queen to enter the Whalehead Club, he tried to come up with a plan. He figured the cop would carry Jack to the third floor and toss him out the window or somehow haul him onto the roof and drop him from the top. How could he stop him? *The suicide note! Queen would have to put Jack down to write the note. Maybe he'll need to find a pencil and paper.*

Or maybe I could make a noise downstairs. When Queen comes looking for me, I'll take the back stairs to the top floor and try to wake Jack up. With the half-baked plan thrown together, he hurried through the yard and across the front porch.

Dugan reached for the doorknob and turned it. When the door drifted open, the darkness of the inside faced him like a cave where a monster lived. He wanted to run in the opposite direction, but somehow he steadied his nerves and entered. Inside he could hear footsteps above him, going up to the second floor. His eyes got used to the darkness, and he noticed traces of faint moonlight through the windows of the next room. He remembered the location of the main staircase—in the rear, just inside the back entrance where the tour began. Watching his feet pass through the tilted rectangles of moonlight on the wooden floor, he hurried through the next room and another. From there, he found the hallway and the bottom of the wide staircase.

The steps, rising into the darkness, seemed like a scene from an old scary movie. Looking to the second floor, he heard Queen's creaking steps. As quietly as possible, he scurried to the second floor and paused. He looked down the long hallway but, as expected, saw no one. From above him came the sounds of someone going up the stairs to the third floor. Dugan took a deep breath and squeezed his hands into fists to steady the jumpiness inside. *Jack needs me.* He walked halfway down the hall and turned up the flight of stairs that led to the servant's quarters. At the top, he slowed his pace and peeked around the frame of the doorway. Barely visible in the darkness, standing near the middle of the hall, Queen held Jack, head and legs hanging down.

Queen cursed and said, "I forgot about the padlock." He pivoted, stomped to the end of the hallway and dropped Jack onto the floor with a loud thud.

Moonlight spilled through the window lining the edges of their bodies with a silver glow. Dugan saw Queen fumbling with something on his belt. The cop knelt and flipped Jack over. Although Queen blocked his view, Dugan heard the sound of metal clicking and clanking.

A few feet down the hall and to the right, he noticed a door—maybe one of the servant's bedrooms. He edged into the hallway, back pressed to the wall, sliding sideways. When he reached the door, he turned the knob and it opened. As Queen stood and faced him, Dugan slipped into the room. He held his breath and waited, closing the door to within a fraction of an inch. The sound of the deputy's strides grew louder.

Dugan's heart pounded. The black shape passed by. Then came the steady beats of feet going down stairs.

When he was sure Queen had left to another part of the house, Dugan slipped into the hallway and headed toward Jack. After only a few steps, he stopped to see what Queen had been mumbling about. There he saw a small door with a padlock on it. *That must lead to the roof. Deputy Queen needs the key. That's why he went downstairs. Now's my chance.* He rushed to Jack and dropped to his knees. Immediately his hopes sank. In the moonlight Jack's wrist had been handcuffed to a pipe that connected to a radiator against the wall below the window. Dugan yanked on the link, but the pipe held steady. Turning his attention to Jack, he noticed a large lump on the top of his forehead.

"Jack! Jack!" he whispered. "Wake up!" Dugan slapped his face several times but could see he was out cold. Leaning over, he pressed his ear to Jack's chest. *I can hear his heart. He's still alive.* A feeling of helplessness flooded over him. *What can I do?* He sat back on his haunches and looked down the hallway, fearing Queen's return. Seeing and hearing nothing, he closed his eyes and tried to think. *How can I get Jack to wake up? I got it. Water! I need to find water.*

He jumped to his feet, spun around and entered the nearest servant's bedroom. After he circled the bed, he pushed open a door on the opposite wall. Through a small window, the moon's glow licked the edges of a bathtub's white surface. He flipped on the light to find something to hold water. The instant brightness startled him, and he squinted. *Oh no. What am I doing? What if Deputy Queen's in the hallway?* He clawed at the switch and missed. In a panic, his fingers fumbled over it and the room went dark. When his eyes adjusted, he found a trashcan beneath the sink. He placed it in the tub and yanked on the faucet, water pouring full blast. The liquid roared into the container, and Dugan tried to adjust the pressure. *Could Queen hear it through the plumbing?* The can filled quickly, and he turned off the faucet.

After heaving the container from the tub, he staggered into the hall. Without hesitating, he dumped the whole contents on Jack's head. The man stirred, face muscles twitching as the water trickled off. He blinked and opened his eyes.

"Where am I?" Jack moaned.

"Shhhhhh. He might hear you."

"Who are you?"

"It's me, Dugan."

Jack tried to pull his arm over to prop himself up, but the cuff halted his attempt, the metal rattling against the pipe.

"How can we get you loose?" Dugan asked.

"Don't worry about me. Get out of here. Go for help."

"But he's gonna kill you."

Jack's jaw muscles tightened. "Get going!"

When he saw Jack's eyes grow wide, Dugan turned around. Queen's form appeared as he stepped into the hallway. Dugan gasped. Queen charged toward them.

"Run!" Jack shouted as he pointed with his free hand. "Down the servant's stairs!"

Dugan stepped over Jack's legs and fumbled with the knob. With a good shove, the door flew open, and he rushed down the narrow stairway. A few steps from reaching the second floor, he heard thundering stomps not far behind him.

*   *   *

Byron heaved with all his strength, yanking the bar and splintering the wood. The effort ripped the last U-bolt from the wall, and Adrienne's arm fell free. "Let's go!" he ordered as he tossed the bar. It clanged against the weights strewn on the floor. She rushed out of the door, her shackles flopping against the wooden planks. After he scooped up her shoes, Byron tore after her.

As they hurried across the footbridge, he called: "To the right!"

On shore, Adrienne hesitated, panic stricken.

"This way," he said, grabbing her hand and pulling her along the shoreline away from the trail that led to Queen's bungalow. Byron noticed the stony ground and led her a few feet into the woods, out of the moonlight.

He shoved her shoes toward her. "Put these on so we can move faster."

"I just want to get away from here," Adrienne said as she wiggled one foot, then another into the slip-ons.

For the next several hundred yards, they progressed without much difficulty. Whenever trees or undergrowth infringed on the narrow space between woods and water, they waded into the sound until they circumvented the obstruction. Several times the water came up to their waists, but the footing was solid. Once they could no longer see the boathouse, Byron led them into the fringe of the woods and stopped.

"We've got to keep going," Adrienne pleaded. "He might be out here somewhere."

"We're safe for now. He won't know where to find us," Byron said, unbuttoning his shirt. "Put this on." He held it open to assist her.

Adrienne awkwardly slipped her arms into the sleeve with the cuffs still attached to her wrists. Her hands trembled so much she had trouble fastening the buttons.

"Everything's going to be all right," he assured her.

"What about Jack? Do you think Queen . . . killed him?"

"I don't know." Byron reached into his pocket and pulled out the cell phone. "I've got to call the police." When he pressed the *On* button, he noticed it no longer glowed. "Oh no," he sighed. "It's all wet." He held it to his ear. "No dial tone."

"What're we going to do?" she asked, rubbing her arm, the cuff rustling against the shirt.

"Let's keep going. The shoreline will lead back to the Whalehead Club. We should be safe. Is your arm all right?"

"I think so. He cracked it with his nightstick when I didn't tell him how beautiful he looked. I didn't realize that's what he wanted . . . me to . . . say . . ." He voice faltered as she choked back tears.

"Don't think about it," Byron said.

She swallowed, halting her sniffling. Anger filled her eyes. "He's a monster. I couldn't fight him off. God help me if I ever face him again. God help me."

Byron took her by the hand. "Come on. We've got to keep moving." *God help all of us.*

They came upon a thick stand of trees and tangled vines that extended into the water. As they waded around the growth, Byron noticed the reflections of the stars and moon on the surface like tiny jewels with one large pearl wavering in the middle. The beauty of the scene broke through the curtain of fear that had shrouded his mind. An overwhelming calm spread over him.

"I hope Jack's all right." Adrienne said as they moved through the water.

"Me too. If anyone can outsmart Queen, Jack can. I've never seen a man so cool in the face of danger. He's the one who really saved your life."

"You both did."

"Guess it was a team effort," Byron said, remembering Dugan's contribution.

"I know Jack can outsmart him, but can he outrun him?" Adrienne asked.

Byron looked at the moon. "I don't know. Let's hope and pray he does." He recalled Queen leaping on top of Jack between the trees by the cove. Then oddly, words Jack had spoken to him at the vacation house on the night of the cookout echoed in his mind: Sometimes we have to battle sharks. *God grant Jack strength for the battle,* Byron prayed.

As they advanced along the shore, Adrienne also said a prayer—the Lord's Prayer. When she uttered the phrase, *Deliver us from evil,* she hesitated and added, *Please, God, please, deliver us from evil.* Then, like a scratched phonograph record, she repeated it several times. The pattern of words quickly formed on Byron's tongue: *Deliver us from evil. Please, God, please, deliver us from evil.* When they rounded the clump of greenery, their prayers halted as the Whalehead Club came into view. From a dormer window, a light flashed on for several seconds and off again.

"Did you see that?" Byron asked.

"Yes. That's odd. There shouldn't be anyone in the Whalehead Club this time of night."

Chapter Twenty-five

Dugan turned the corner and sprinted down the second floor hallway. When he reached the main staircase, he grabbed the post and swung himself down the steps, taking three or four at a time. Queen thundered behind, closing the gap. Dugan feared at any second the cop's baton would thump *him* on the head. At the bottom he slashed to the right through the entrance hall and into the great room. Like a ballplayer stealing second, he dove under the big piano and spun around to face his attacker. Queen skidded into the room.

"I'm tired of chasing you, boy," Queen huffed. He knelt and looked under the piano.

Dugan felt like a cornered animal.

"You can make this easy or difficult and painful."

Dugan watched the killer walk toward him. He scooted backward across the cork-tile floor. On the opposite wall he saw their dark reflections in the full-length mirror, as if he were watching a scary movie, but this one was real. Every part of his body shook.

"You do what I say, and I won't hurt you," Queen said. "Hear me? Come out now."

A long pause followed as Queen waited. In the silence Dugan's heart pounded as he stared at the cop's muscular calves. *What'll I do? Just can't give up.*

"Last chance. I'm going to count to three, then I'm coming after you. One . . . Two . . ."

As he counted, Dugan managed to back from under the instrument. On the count of three, he stood and faced Queen, piano between them.

"That's better," Queen said, leaning on the back of the instrument. "Now walk around here to me."

Dugan shook his head. "Y-you're the one who k-killed the girl."

"What girl?" Queen asked as he circled the piano.

Dugan kept pace, using the piano for a barrier between them. "The d-dead girl I found in the marsh—Laura Redinger."

"You're wrong, boy. This is all a big mistake."

"I saw your initials on the tree."

Queen stopped circling. "What're you talking about?"

"On the tree by the sound: K.Q. and L.R. But her initials had an X carved over them."

Queen's expression darkened. "So what? Just a few letters carved into a tree."

"You buried her near there. I know you did."

"How could you know that?"

"The owl led me there."

"Now you're talkin' crazy."

Dugan's head swiveled. "I'm not the one who's crazy."

"You think I'm crazy?" Queen snarled. He flew around the piano. Dugan sprinted for the door. Fear super-charged his legs and rocketed him down the hall. He shot up the first flight of steps with Queen stomping behind. He cut down the second floor hallway and flew up the servant's stairs. Halfway up, he felt the burning tiredness through his leg muscles. As he neared the top, it seemed like had he gained a hundred pounds, each step took full effort. Like in a slow-motion nightmare, he ran down the dark hallway. Queen's fingers scraped the back of his t-shirt. Dugan tried to lengthen his stride, but his foot back-kicked Queen's leg, and he tumbled to the floor. The cop managed to stop without stepping on him, hovering above like a lion about to kill its prey.

Dugan looked up, expecting the face of a madman. But Queen's angry expression faded as he shifted his gaze from Dugan to the radiator at the end of the hall. The deputy's mouth fell open. Dugan turned and looked. The handcuffs lay linked to the pipe on the floor. Jack Blaze had escaped.

Queen clamped his hand onto Dugan's arm and jerked him to his feet. The deputy's grip sent jolts of pain through the boy's muscles. Queen pivoted and glanced around as if the illusionist had disappeared into the very air they breathed. For a few moments there was silence, a total stillness as if Dugan had just gone deaf. But then a distant note sounded—one made by tapping a key on a piano. Queen's eyes bulged. He grabbed Dugan's shoulders, lifting him off the floor. Dugan felt the man's anger shaking through his thick arms, his hands clamping like vices. The piano sounded again, rambling through several notes.

"Help me, Jack! Help me!" Dugan shouted.

"Shut up!"

Queen's breath smelled like stale corn chips. The cop's breathing quickened, and Dugan almost choked. Queen's head swiveled, his eyes inspected the doors along the hallway. When he saw the servant's bedroom door half open, he backed through it, dragging Dugan with him. Inside the room, he located the clothes closet. Holding Dugan with one hand, he yanked open the closet door.

He snatched the boy by the collar of his t-shirt and pulled him to within an inch of his face. "If you try to get out of this closet, I'll kill you. Do you understand me?"

Dugan nodded frantically.

"I'll hunt you down and slice your throat." Queen shoved him into the blackness. Dugan stumbled backward three steps before hitting the wall as the cop slammed the door.

All light had been extinguished. He blinked his eyes, but the darkness covered him like a thick blanket. Then he heard a sliding noise, the sound of someone shoving a heavy piece of furniture across the floor. Something banged against the closet door several times. *I'm trapped. Like a cricket in a box. He jammed something against the door so I can't get out.* The racket outside the closet door stopped, and Queen's footsteps trailed away.

Dugan waited, listening. A minute passed with no sounds. He stepped forward and fumbled for the doorknob. Clasping it, he turned, but the door moved only a fraction of an inch before hitting something solid. Frustration and fear bubbled in the pit of his stomach. He imagined Queen's knife against his throat, and a large lump formed there. The muscles around his windpipe got tight. He wanted to cry. With his shoulder, he shoved against the door using all his strength, but it wouldn't budge. His eyes watered, and he felt a drop trickle down his cheek. The dam of determination he'd built against the flood of tears threatened to break. About to bawl, he stepped back from the door and felt something tickle his ear. Thinking it a spider, he clasped his hand against the side of his head. Between his fingers he felt a long thin string. He pulled it away, and a burst of light filled the closet.

* * *

In the great room, Jack had rocked and slid the base of the ten-foot mirror back and forth until he'd positioned it a few feet from the wall near the entrance. With little time and an aching head, he had desperately devised the plan to lure Queen away from Dugan. After playing the notes on the piano, he rushed to the back of the mirror and waited. Jack counted on the heavy wooden backing, thick ornate frame and plate glass to fall hard on the cop. He didn't think it would kill him but hoped it would cause bodily harm, enough to disarm and subdue him. As footsteps sounded in the hall, Jack pressed his hands against the back of the mirror. With the footsteps came rhythmic slapping of the nightstick against the palm. Jack peered around the edge of the frame, ready to tip the slab of wood and glass.

Queen stepped into the room, his club poised in front of him.

"I'm right here, Ape Brain," Jack said, tipping the mirror.

Queen pivoted and swung, glass shattering as the slab of wood crashed on top of him, knocking him to the floor. Jack mounted the back of the mirror and jumped in an effort to crush Queen's bones. The cop groaned, air rushing out of his lungs. When Jack jumped a second time, the slab tilted causing him to land off balance and tumble into the hallway. Looking up, he saw Queen's hand emerge from beneath and grasp the frame. A primeval growl bellowed from under the slab. Like a pro wrestler heaving a giant opponent off before the final count, Queen thrust the wooden panel into the air. It flipped over and landed with a loud clamor beside him, glass clinking and breaking. When he sat up, the moon's glow lit the killer's face. Blood ran from cuts on his forehead around his eyes and down his cheeks forming a macabre red mask. He grabbed his nightstick and rolled onto his hands and knees. Jack scrabbled to his feet and raced down the hallway.

Knowing the building intimately, Jack pounded up the steps, hoping to lead Queen through the complex of interconnecting guest rooms on the second floor. At the top he turned to see Queen rounding the post, legs and arms pumping furiously as he ascended. If Jack could confuse the cop by weaving in and out of the suites, he might be able slip away to the third floor to look for Dugan. His head pounded and vision blurred as oxygen debt increased, but he focused all inner reserves to keep going. Ten feet down the corridor, he cut into a guestroom and slammed the door behind him. By the time Jack reached the door to the adjoining suite, Queen plowed into the room. Jack slammed that door, scrambled over the bed and out of the entrance, crossed the hallway and entered the opposite room. As he jetted into the next suite, shutting the door behind him, he heard Queen enter the previous room. Now he had a lead. He blasted out of that room, crossed the hall and entered the nearest room. He wanted Queen to feel like a rat in a maze.

Forcing himself to breathe quietly, he listened with the door slightly ajar and tried to detect Queen's whereabouts. He heard the deputy enter the hall, walk in the opposite direction and open a door at the far end. *Yes!* Jack thought. *Ape Brain has no idea where I am. I've got to time this perfectly. If he sees me in the hallway, the chase begins again.*

*   *   *

Dugan squinted against the naked bulb. The string danced across his cheek, tingling the surface of his skin. As his eyes adjusted to the bright light, he noticed a rectangular panel on the ceiling trimmed with baseboard. It reminded him of the one in his bedroom closet that led to the attic. *Of course! That's my way out of here!* Hope supported the crumbling dam that withstood the flood of tears. He inspected the closet for a way to climb onto the shelf above the clothes rod. Seeing the doorknob, he figured he could use it as a foothold. He reached up and clamped his hands onto the shelf. To secure his foot on the knob, he had to twist slightly and lift his leg in an awkward position. With his foot lodged on top of the knob, he gripped the shelf and pulled himself up. At the same time, he pressed his foot against the knob until he reached the height where he could extend upward and lift his other leg onto the shelf. With tremendous exertion, he thrust from the knob, successfully lunging onto the solid board.

He glanced up and saw the access panel easily within reach. Sitting on the shelf, Dugan pressed his fingertips on the wooden rectangle. When he shoved, the panel brushed against the edge of the opening and broke free. Shifting onto his knees, he lifted and flipped it over a wooden beam. Dust drifted down as he peered into the attic. The light from the closet barely reached the steep rafters, the timbers like dark ribs of the inside of a whale. Dugan swallowed and gathered courage. Squatting, he extended his arms into the opening and slowly stood. Once his torso had cleared the frame, he braced his hands on the beams and lifted his legs from the closet.

Although the glow from below diminished quickly in the huge attic, Dugan could see many braces and studs, darkening with each repetition into the blackness. The heat and stale air raised beads of sweat on his forehead. Droplets trickled down and stung his eyes. Thick dust covered the beams, and filthy cobwebs hung in the openings.

From behind him came a clattering sound of many wings flapping. *Bats!* He covered his ears as the whoosh of wing beats brushed by his body and around his head. *The light! It's attracting them.* He dipped into the opening and groped for the string. He felt something land in his hair and shook his head furiously to dislodge it. With a swoop of his arm, he felt the string wrap around his fingers, and he pulled, putting out the light. In total darkness, the attic quieted as the bats settled.

Once again, Dugan felt like a blind man. Blinking failed to faze the blackness. As the slow seconds passed, he wondered when Queen would return to check on him. Turning the light out helped to prevent suspicion. With the closet door still blocked, Queen wouldn't feel the need to check inside. Then again, if he did check inside and turned on the light, he would notice the opening. Dugan decided to replace the panel just in case.

He fumbled in the darkness until his fingers brushed over the panel. To secure it over the opening, he reached out with one hand until he found the rectangular space. Carefully he lifted and lowered the cover, adjusting as the back of his hands found the ledge of the opening. Pulling his hands away, he heard the panel slide into place.

Now I've got to move as far away from this spot as I can, just in case he comes looking for me. Dugan stood, balancing on the wooden timber. Carefully, like a tightrope walker, he extended his foot and felt for the next timber. At the same time he held his hands out to maintain balance and check for any wooden braces blocking his path. As he progressed , he hoped his hand wouldn't accidentally land on a bat.

* * *

Peering through a half-inch crack in the door, Jack watched Queen pass and prayed the deputy wouldn't reach for the knob. He listened as the footsteps halted and another door creaked open. After waiting a few seconds for Queen to enter the room down the hall, Jack slipped into the corridor and hurried toward the servant's staircase. He tried to walk like a cat—softly, silently. Before turning onto the steps, he glanced to make sure Queen hadn't emerged from the room.

Up the stairs he padded, his feet barely making a sound. As he tiptoed down the third floor hallway, he whispered, "Dugan! Dugan!" He paused in the middle and glanced at the roof access door and padlock. Another possibility formulated in his mind. Nodding, he thought, *That might be the way to do it.*

He walked to the end of the hallway and noticed the servant's bedroom door half open, the one near the radiator. After pushing it wider, he saw the chiffonier butted against the closet door. The bed had also been slid over a few feet and positioned against the chest of drawers.

"You in there, Dugan? It's me, Jack," he said, barely audible. No reply. As quietly as possible, he angled the bed away and slid the chest back from the closet. He opened the door and whispered, "Dugan!" Stepping in, he examined the space with his small flashlight to make sure the boy hadn't huddled in the corner. *Where is he? Dugan must be stronger than he looks.* Jack figured adrenaline empowered his thin muscles to inch the door open till he could squeeze through. Pushing the furniture back wouldn't have been as difficult. *Dear God, I hope he has the sense to get out of here and go for help.*

Jack hustled out of the room and down the hall to the roof access door. Staring at the padlock, he reached into his pocket and pulled out a small leather case not much bigger than a pack of matches. He opened the flap and examined the selection of delicate picks *Can't use the same one I used on the handcuffs. Here's the one that'll work.* He extracted the right pick and wiggled it into the keyhole on the padlock. Within five seconds it popped open. After dropping the lock into his pocket, he swung back the access door. In the darkness, he could barely see the ladder. It rose into the attic and extended to a heavy hatch on the ceiling. *I'm going to lead that monster onto the roof, backtrack and then lock him out there. If he wants off, he'll have to jump.*

*   *   *

As Dugan progressed through the attic, his hands touched something hard with patterned grooves. It felt like a brick wall. *A chimney!* He remembered counting the five chimneys when Mark, Matt, and he saw the Whalehead Club for the first time. Trying to estimate the distance he had traveled from the servant's bedroom, he guessed he'd arrived at the second chimney. He worked his way around it, wanting to put as much space as possible between him and the closet opening. If Queen came after him, the cop would have to cross the entire attic and look in every corner.

After rounding the chimney, he heard the noise. It sounded like a door opening. His eyes, now well adjusted to the dark, focused on a faint glimmer directly in front of him. The glimmer became a ray of light outlining the rungs of a ladder that climbed to the ceiling. He heard someone below as the flashlight's ray flashed through the dust particles. *It's Queen!* He backed against the chimney. He wanted to circle to the other side but feared his movements might be detected. The figure quickly climbed the ladder to the top and focused the light on some kind of latch on the ceiling. With a grunt and a heave, the person flung open the large hatch, and a rectangle of violet sky dotted with stars appeared. As the man came down, Dugan noticed his shape seemed thinner than Queen. *Could it be Jack?* He disappeared into a hole in the floor.

Then he heard the man shout: "Hey, Ape Brain! I'm up here! Come and get me! You couldn't find your own butt with both hands tied behind your back!"—It was Jack's voice.

Dugan wanted to holler, *Jack! I'm up here!* But he suddenly realized Jack's plan—for some reason he wanted Queen to follow him onto the roof.

After several seconds, Dugan heard the pounding of footsteps in the hallway below.

Queen's growling words erupted: "You're a dead man, Blaze! I swear on my father's grave, I'll kill you!"

Jack scrambled up the ladder.

Dugan held his breath.

"I'm up here!" Jack yelled.

"What! How in the hell did you get this lock—"

"Magic," Jack said as he climbed through the hatch.

"I' give you magic," Queen said as he ascended. "You picked those locks like a common thief—a damn gangbanger."

"Meet me on the ridge," Jack yelled, his words trailing away. "We'll play King of the Hill."

As Queen progressed to the top, he blocked out the stars. When his black form leapt onto the roof, the violet rectangle reappeared on the ceiling like a TV screen with tiny dots of light blinking down. Dugan extended his foot to find the next beam. Step by step he advanced to the ladder, keeping his eye on the stars. He reached out and grasped the nearest rung. Swinging his leg around, he secured it on the step of the ladder and shifted his weight to pull the other leg over. *I gotta get outta here. Queen wants to kill me. I'll go for help. Call the police.* As he took a step down, he heard the rumble of footsteps on the roof above. Thinking about Jack, he hesitated and gazed up at the rectangle of stars.

* * *

The steep pitch of the roof, expanse of sky, and long drop to the ground intensified Jack's dizziness. His head pounded as he scaled to the ridge, struggling to keep his balance. He turned to see Queen spring from the hole less than fifteen feet behind him. The cop paused to pull out his nightstick.

"Come and get me, Queen," Jack said.

"You can count on it."

Jack's next step faltered, and he barely recovered by falling forward, straddling the ridge. The footing on the slick shingles was treacherous. Looking up, he spied the middle chimney protruding from the peak of the roof. *If I can just get there first, circle round and beat him back to the hatch.* He plodded forward, trying not to look down the precipitous copper slope. As he neared the wide chimney, he could hear Queen closing in. He picked up his pace but had to extend his hands to keep from pitching to the right or left. At the chimney he angled down. Immediately he realized the error of his strategy—the roof slanted too severely. His feet slid out from under him, but he managed to turn and grasp the ridge as he fell. With both hands he held tightly, belly flat against the slick copper.

Queen lunged, swinging the club. Jack let go as the nightstick whacked the spine of the roof. Sliding swiftly, he reached for the chimney. His fingers caught the grooves between the bricks, slowing his descent. Desperately he clawed and managed to stop by gripping the last brick. Peering up, he saw Queen hugging the chimney, inching toward him. His vision wavered with the pounding in his head. He scrabbled with his free hand and feet in an effort to stand. As his right foot scraped against the shingles, he detected a texture that had formed on that section of the roof. *Bird droppings! Grace's deposits from heaven!*

"How you going to disappear now, Whodinny?" Queen asked as he bowed and whipped the stick at his hand.

Jack let go of the brick and rolled onto his back to slide into the swath of the osprey's excrement. Pressing his hands and feet against the rougher surface, he slid to a stop. Like a crab, he backpedaled on all fours up the slope until he reached the ridge. He waited at the top to make sure Queen pursued him.

Clinging to the grooves between the bricks, Queen edged around the bottom of the chimney. Jack standing on the ridge, leaning on the bricks, met his gaze.

"Who the hell are you? Spiderman?" Queen plodded up the slope.

"Right now, I'm the King of the Hill, but I'm leaving my throne. It's all yours, Queen." Jack pivoted and scooted down the opposite side, hands gripping the grooves between the bricks. He knew he had to move quickly to maintain a lead, time enough to get around the chimney, cross the ridge, climb into the hole and close the hatch. Looking up, he watched Queen arrive at the peak. The throbbing pain in his skull accelerated. After slipping around the base, he advanced two steps up the other side. His vision blurred with the intensity of the aching in his brain. He blinked in an effort to clear his head, but blackness encroached as if he had entered a tunnel. Resting against the bricks, he waited a few seconds for full vision to return. Just below him, he heard Queen scuffing around the bottom of the chimney. The deputy reached for him. When Jack charged up the slope, he lost his balance, stumbled forward and dove for the ridge. Grasping the crown of the roof with one hand, he turned over. The stars swirled above him, and he closed his eyes to fight off the vertiginous state.

"I've got you now," Queen said as he methodically mounted the slope.

* * *

When Dugan reached the top of the ladder, he heard the scuffle. The moonlight coated everything in silver. Straddling the ridge, Queen hovered over Jack and lifted his club.

"NOOOOOOOOO!" Dugan screamed.

His cry startled Queen. The deputy looked up, backing half a step. The nightstick rattled against limbs piled atop the chimney. A loud screech sounded from above and a winged shadow passed over Dugan.

When the huge bird landed on Queen's face, the cop let out a terrible scream. He dropped his nightstick, and it clattered down the roof. The flapping of wings and ripping of claws jolted his head against the bricks. Queen bounced forward, swatting to release the bird's grip. His toe caught on Jack's arm. As the deputy fell, the bird sprung upward with rapid wing beats into the starry sky.

Fifty yards from the Whalehead Club, Byron and Adrienne halted when they heard someone scream, "Noooooooo!"

"That sounds like a kid," Adrienne said.

"Dugan!" Byron exclaimed.

As they sprinted to the building, the clangor of someone tumbling head over heels down the slope of the roof alarmed them. Then the body plunged from the edge and landed with a sickening thud on the grass.

Approaching the body and recognizing Queen, they slowed their steps to a cautious advance. He lay on his back with his head turned toward them. Deep gouges scored the right side of his face, and his left eye had been ripped out. A gelatinous mass dangled from the socket on his left cheek. Blood covered his face.

"Dugan, are you up there?" Byron shouted.

"Yeah! Jack's here too. We're all right!"

"Thank God," Byron said.

He glanced at Adrienne. She stared in horror at the nightstick that had landed by her feet and then shifted her gaze to Queen.

"Is h-he d-dead?" she asked.

"I think so."

She crossed her arms and gripped her shoulders, trembling. Byron heard the clinking of the handcuffs.

"The keys are on his belt," Byron said. "I'll get you out of those cuffs in a minute."

He dropped to his knees and gripped the key clasp on the cop's belt. They jangled as he maneuvered it around the loop. Pulling them free, he turned and said, "I got 'em."

The swift hand snatched Byron's collar and jerked him forward. Queen's voice gurgled, blood bubbling from his mouth: "If I'm going to die, I'm taking someone with me." His other hand jerked his knife from the sheath and his arm flew up.

A flash of moonlight crossed the blade. Byron's heart leapt into his throat. As the knife descended, a black club cracked against Queen's arm, snapping bone. The knife jolted free, spun and stuck in the ground. His arm slumped, grotesquely misshapen, onto his chest as short cries of agony spurted from his lungs.

Byron jumped back from Queen's body. Hovering over both of them, Adrienne stood, the nightstick quivering in her hand. She looked at the club, eyes aghast. Her hand sprang open as if the weapon were hot steel. It rattled on the ground next to Queen's head.

Byron rushed to Adrienne's side and placed his arm around her shoulders. Trembling, she kept watching Queen. His shrieks rose in pitch like the cries of a pathetic dog until they faded into unconsciousness.

Chapter Twenty-six

At nine o'clock the next morning a homicide unit from the Dare County Sheriff's Office arrived at the beach house. Everyone gathered in the driveway. A tall police officer, wearing a black ball cap with "Dare County" arced over a golden star on the front, put his hand on Dugan's shoulder and said, "Young man, I'd like you to meet Officer Holmes."

Dugan crouched and stroked the top of the bloodhound's head. He felt the silky softness of its big tan ears. "Good to meet ya, Officer Holmes."

"His friends call him Sherlock."

"Can I call him Sherlock?"

"Sure," the detective said, mussing Dugan's hair. "I can tell he likes you."

The dog leaned forward and licked Dugan's face.

"If you can lead us to where you found the body, good ol' Sherlock will take it from there," the detective said.

The boy nodded. "No problem. I remember every turn."

Elijah stood with his hands on his hips, his face beaming. "That's my nephew," he said to the other officer, a short man with receding brown hair and sunglasses. "He wants to become a crime scene investigator when he grows up."

"He's a fine boy," the officer said.

The kids—Mark, Matt, Janey, Jimmy, and Leroy—had formed a semi-circle around Dugan and the dog.

Matt said, "Dugan's one of the bravest kids I know. Just the other day he knocked a shark in the head with an oar."

The officer nodded. "The young fellow is quite a hero."

Janey squatted next to Dugan. She reached out and stroked the dog's neck. "Isn't he beautiful?"

"He's a fine lookin' dog," Dugan said.

"I've got a present for you, Dugan." She reached into her pocket and pulled something out, extending her closed fist to him.

Dugan glanced up at her. He couldn't remember ever seeing a prettier smile on a girl. When he opened his hand, she dropped a large amber-colored stone into it. The morning sun set its round surface aglow.

"Thanks," Dugan said. "I've never seen anything like it."

"It's the biggest piece of sea glass I've ever found. As soon as I picked it up, I thought of you."

Dugan drew it closer and tilted it to observe the way the sun sent a golden ray through the glass and across his palm. "This might be from a sunken ship. Maybe one that Blackbeard looted."

The bloodhound nuzzled his hand and sniffed the stone.

"It's time to go," the tall officer said. He opened the cruiser's back door and commanded the dog to jump in.

"Can I ride in the back with Sherlock?" Dugan asked.

"Sure thing."

Dugan turned to face the onlookers. He shrugged and said, "I guess I'll see y'all in a little bit."

"You do a good job, son. We're proud of you," Elijah said.

The boys echoed Elijah's words.

When he faced Janey, a strong desire to hug her came over him, but he knew the boys were watching so he just smiled and climbed in the car. As the vehicle pulled away, he watched them wave.

Dugan felt different inside. He wasn't the same boy who got kicked out of the Martins Ferry Library a week ago. Something had formed deep within. He couldn't explain it, but he knew it had to do with what he'd been through and how he had faced his fears. That need to try to impress people was gone. Something strong had taken its place—courage and determination. Dugan liked the way he felt inside. Before all this had happened, he'd dreamed about becoming somebody. Now he already was somebody.

He directed the driver to the gravel lane, and they drove a couple hundred yards past the lighthouse and parked on the side of the road. Dugan led the way through the paths. Sherlock Holmes walked beside him, the tall policeman a few steps back holding the leash. As they neared the location of the dead deer, the smell of rotten flesh filled the air.

Dugan pointed. "It's deep in the weeds."

The tall officer knelt beside the dog and held a pink t-shirt to its nose. As the dog and man entered the weeds, the bloodhound immediately caught the scent of the girl. Agitated, sighing and yelping, it circled the maggot-infested deer carcass.

"I think we've got a strike, John," the tall officer said.

"The body was here," the man with the brown hair said. "Can't fool Sherlock."

"But where's it now? Should we dig?"

The other officer shrugged. "We have to. Can't leave any stone unturned."

"You won't find her here," Dugan said.

"What?" the tall one asked.

"This is where he first dumped her, but after I found the body, he came back and took her away."

"We've got to dig here just in case, son," the one called John said.

"But I think I know where he buried her."

"How would you know that?" the tall officer asked.

"I found a tree near the sound with Kenny Queen's and Laura Redinger's initials carved into it. There was an owl in the tree." Dugan looked down, struggling to find the right words. No matter how he would try explain it, he knew the officers wouldn't understand, so he said, "I know she's there. I just know it."

The two men glanced at one another, eyebrows raising, shoulders shrugging. Finally, the tall one asked, "How far to the tree from here?"

"Not far. If we take the path to the sound, we'll find it along the shore."

"We can always come back here and dig later," Officer John said.

The tall one nodded. "Okay, Dugan, lead the way."

About four minutes later they arrived at the tree. Sherlock Holmes sniffed excitedly around the trunk. He tugged the tall policeman toward the edge of the woods where a thick patch of trees and vines overhung a section of ground covered with old leaves and dried weeds. The dog scratched at the debris and bayed. With the head of the shovel, Officer John cleared away the loose vegetation. The ground appeared to have been recently disturbed.

"This could be it," the tall one said.

Officer John laid down the shovel and approached Dugan. Placing his hand on the boy's shoulder, he turned him away from the loose dirt. "Dugan, we can't allow you to watch this. For now I want you to stand by the tree and look out at the water. If we find the body, we'll seal off the area, wait for forensics to get here, then take you home."

He walked Dugan to the shoreline and told him to stay there. Dugan tried to look at the peaceful water, but the sound of the shovel scooping the ground distracted him. Glancing over his shoulder, he saw the heart and initials carved into the tree. He imagined Kenny Queen gouging the X over the L.R. The thought of Queen forcing the knife blade into the bark sent a shudder through him. He turned and focused on the sound where a sailboat glided into view, the white triangle of the sail aglow in the sunlight.

From behind, he heard the tall officer say, "Careful now. Take your time."

After several minutes, Officer John said, "Found something. It's a human leg."

"Are you sure?"

"Positive."

"That's enough digging. We've got a murder case on our hands now," the tall officer said. "I'll take the dog and boy back to the vehicle and call for a forensic unit."

"I'll keep things secure here," Officer John said.

At the car Dugan played with Sherlock Holmes while the tall officer radioed headquarters. Twenty minutes later the forensic investigation team arrived.

After the officers drove Dugan back to the beach house, they asked Dugan and Byron many questions and took statements. Before leaving, they reported that Queen had slipped into a coma, a result of the head trauma from falling off the roof. The swelling in the cranial cavity caused severe brain damage before the doctors could relieve the pressure. The tall officer doubted they would ever get the chance to question him. "If he survives, he'll be a vegetable. Chances are, they'll have to pull the plug on him. He'd be better off dead, anyway," he said.

* * *

The last two days of vacation passed quickly. Byron spent most of the time reading and resting. During the late afternoon on Friday, he decided to go for a final run along the beach to the wildlife preserve. He kept looking for the black stallion, hoping to see him. When he neared the dead turtle, the smell sickened him, and he decided to turn back.

Above the tall grass at the top of the dunes he barely noticed the back of the horse. He stopped and whistled. The stallion raised its head, munching on sea oats. Byron waved. The horse glared at him, as if resentful of the interruption. "Any word from the Lord today?" Byron shouted. The horse snorted and resumed grazing. *Guess not.*

He looked out to sea and watched a line of five pelicans skimming over the water, gently rising and dipping in unison. At his feet a bisque-colored crab scrambled across the sand and disappeared into a hole. A large wave rolled and spilled, causing a sheet of water and foam to rush up the slope, tumbling shells in its wake. Byron glanced up the shoreline and noticed the rising tide obscuring his latent footprints. *Better head back.*

As he ran near the edge of the water, he remembered an illustration he once used in a sermon: A man went for a walk along the beach to ease his troubled mind. On an isolated strip of shoreline he found a large seashell. Wanting to hear the powerful roar of the ocean as it billowed and rolled, he turned his back to the waves and held the shell to his ear. Because of the commotion of the surf behind him, he couldn't hear the sea in the shell. Frustrated, he tossed the shell back into the ocean. Although the man was in the presence of the actuality, he failed to recognize it. *Sometimes I'm a lot like that man.*

* * *

On Saturday morning, with the vehicles packed, everyone congregated in the driveway to say goodbye to Jack. From the eastern sky the mid-morning sun blazed down, a yellow disc of fire against the brilliant cloudless blue. The slight ocean breeze offered a welcome relief from the increasing heat and humidity. While the boys drifted into the next yard to talk to the neighbor kids, the adults chatted.

"Beautiful day for the beach," Elijah said, adjusting his denim fisherman's hat. "Too bad we'll be spending it crossing the mountains."

"The mountains hold much beauty too," Jack said. "It's all good."

"God saw all that he had made, and it was very good," Byron said. "That can be found somewhere in Genesis chapter one, I believe."

"I'll say Amen to that," Elijah said.

"I'll say Amen too, once we make it home safely," Lila said. "I hate that long drive."

"You'll have to come to eastern Ohio some time, Jack, and dazzle our town folk with your magic tricks," Annie said.

"Remember, Annie. They aren't tricks."

"I forgot. They're feats. Right?"

"Right. Tell you what. I'll make sure we stop in the Ohio Valley when my film crew and I travel across the country," he said.

"Jack, I have to say my first impression of you was downright dismal," Byron confessed.

Jack nodded. "They say you never get a second chance to make a first impression. If that's true, I'm in trouble."

"No need to try again," Byron said. "First impressions never last anyway. Sometimes I get focused on my own ideas of what's true and miss the reality. I might not like your tattoo or agree with your unusual spiritual views, but I don't doubt your compassion and courage." Byron held out his hand. "Please forgive me for misjudging you."

With both hands Jack gripped Byron's hand and shook vigorously. "No need to apologize. You didn't realize we were on the same team. Besides, trust is something you earn. We just needed some quality time together tracking a murderer."

Byron smiled. "That's right. Sometimes the best lessons in life are learned battling sharks. I'm glad the Lord brought us together."

"Just remember one thing," Jack said as he reached into his pocket.

"What's that?"

He pulled out a wristwatch and looked at the time.

"Hey, that's my watch!" Byron blurted.

Elijah and the women laughed uproariously, the big man doubling over.

Jack smiled and handed the watch to Byron. "You still have to keep your eye on me."

When Elijah straightened and regained his composure, Jack slapped him on the back.

"I wouldn't laugh too much if I were you," Byron said.

"Why not, Byron?" Elijah giggled, pointing to his wrist. "My watch is still here."

"Have you checked your wallet lately?" Jack asked.

As Elijah reached around and patted the back of his pants, his eyes widened.

Laugher erupted again.

"All right. Hand it over, Mr. Magic," he said.

Jack pulled the wallet from his other pocket and dropped it into Elijah's palm.

When everyone quieted, Lila said, "On a more serious note, Jack, have you heard from Adrienne?"

"Adrienne's a tough girl. She decided to head home and spend a week with her family. Before she left yesterday, she stopped by the Whalehead Club and told us not to worry about her. Promised she'd be back to finish out the summer."

"Adrienne wants to be a medical missionary," Chrissy said. "You've got to be tough if you want to last in the African bush country."

The boys, who had been tossing a Frisbee back and forth across the yard with the neighbor kids, approached the adults.

"Can we take one more walk along the beach with our friends?" Mark and Matt pleaded.

"Yeah, can we?" Dugan seconded.

"No. It's time to go. Everybody in the car," Elijah said.

Complaints bellowed from the children, but Byron reinforced Elijah's order.

"I get a window seat!" Matt said.

"Me too!" Mark hollered, charging to the blue Suburban.

* * *

As the adults offered their final goodbyes to Jack, Dugan drifted over to Janey, who waited in the yard.

"Thanks again for the sea glass," Dugan said. Her golden-brown eyes melted his insides. "I've got something for you too." He reached deep into the pocket of his baggy shorts, pulled out the gift and handed it to her.

"A sand dollar! Oh it's perfect," she said as she examined it.

"My aunt Annie told me if you break the shell open, you'll set five white doves free."

"I don't want to break it. I'll keep it forever." She rubbed her fingers gently over its delicate surface.

"Well . . . I guess I gotta be going." As their eyes met, that strong urge to hug her came over him again. He glanced at the Suburban and saw Matt and Mark leaning out the window, talking to Leroy and Jimmy. Turning back to Janey, he couldn't help himself. He stepped forward, and they embraced.

When they parted, Janey gasped. "Oh, Dugan, I broke the shell." She held out her hand. The sand dollar had cracked perfectly down the center.

"Look," Dugan said. Between the two halves he counted five miniature doves. "It's true. You set them free."

"You keep half and I'll keep half," Janey said, handing him a section of the sand dollar.

He held it up and she raised her half to unite with his.

"One day we'll meet again," she said and then turned and threw the five small doves into the wind.

"Dugan! Time to go!" Elijah called.

"Goodbye," Dugan said. As he walked to the Suburban, he inspected his half of the sand dollar. He had to take a deep breath to get rid of the odd feeling in his chest, but the breath didn't take it away.

* * *

Byron took one last walk through the house to make sure nothing had been left behind. After he went out the front door and walked onto the deck, he looked down to see Chrissy and Jack standing close to one another near the bottom of the steps. Everyone else had climbed into the vehicles.

Chrissy glanced up and gave her father an irritated look.

"What?" Byron asked. "I'm just keeping my eye on Jack like he told me to do."

"Please, Daddy. Just give us two minutes alone."

Byron walked down the steps and pointed to Jack. "No tricks now."

Jack raised his hands and smiled. "Remember. You can trust me."

After climbing into the driver's seat of the van and closing the door, Byron stared out the windshield. Chrissy and Jack held hands and talked for several minutes.

"Hurry up," Byron muttered. "We've got a long drive ahead of us."

"Shush," Lila said. "Give your daughter a chance to say goodbye. She may never see the guy again."

Finally Jack kissed her, a tender kiss lasting a few seconds.

Lila reached over and touched Byron's arm. "That's the first time I've seen our daughter kiss a man besides you."

Byron grunted. Inside he sensed a melancholy aching. But as his daughter approached the vehicle, a flock of birds flew above her. Byron leaned against the steering wheel so he could watch them ascend—white wings flapping, bodies lifting on the breeze, soaring into the blue expanse.

Printed in the United States
81852LV00003B/1-63